CURLEY

I0576317

James A. Bryant, Jr.

Hamilton Books
an imprint of
University Press of America,® Inc.
Dallas · Lanham · Boulder · New York · Oxford

Copyright © 2004 by
Hamilton Books
4501 Forbes Boulevard
Suite 200
Lanham, Maryland 20706
UPA Acquisitions Department (301) 459-3366

PO Box 317
Oxford
OX2 9RU, UK

Library of Congress Control Number: 2003117116
ISBN 0-7618-2806-0 (paperback : alk. ppr.)
ISBN 978-0-7618-2806-8

For my parents, who taught me the meaning of vocation and the value of dreams.

AUTHOR'S NOTE

This novel is based on the life of my grandfather, Russell Norris. Some of the names have been changed for privacy purposes, and other characters are composites of several people who entered his life. I have, however, made every effort to remain faithful to the spirit of his life and times.

One of the themes running through this book is that of education. There are many American Indian students today who, like my grandfather, are forced to abandon dreams of a college education because of family or financial circumstances. With this in mind, I would like to urge anyone who reads this book and is in some way touched by it to consider contributing to the American Indian College Fund. For more information on this organization, please visit their web site at **www.collegefund.org** or call **1-303-426-8900.** Thank you.

James A. Bryant, Jr.
August 2003
New Orleans, LA

ACKNOWLEDGEMENTS

I would first like to thank my wonderful grandparents, Russell and Minnie Norris, and Donald and Garnell Bryant. No one has been more blessed than I have by your love and the example you have set for integrity and moral character.

Thanks to Holly Bryant, who carefully read the early drafts of the manuscript and made important suggestions and improvements. I also would like to thank Dr. Ronny Russell for his incomparable friendship.

A very special thanks to Dr. Bonnie Gourneau and Dr. Nadine Tepper for believing in the project even before its completion. Thank you both from the bottom of my heart. Also, thank you to Dr. Mary Ruth Laycock for carefully and thoughtfully reading the manuscript and making important suggestions.

Thank you to Joe Kollar and Chip Rose for believing in art and reminding me constantly of its importance. And to Kevin Bryant, who was always willing to listen to me complain or dream! You three are my brothers, and I love you dearly.

I would like to thank my parents for their years of support and for the many, *many* sacrifices they have made for me and my family.

Finally, and most importantly, my deepest gratitude goes to my beautiful and supportive wife, Ginger. You are the light and love of my life, and none of this could have happened without you. Writing is a solitary and often lonely job, and you never once complained about the long hours I spent on the road or in front of the computer; and you were always there to lift my spirits. I love you more than I can say or show, u'sti'i.

PART ONE

THE PHOENIX RISES

CHAPTER ONE

The March winds ripped through the storehouse, searching hungrily for skin to beat upon. They whipped against the mountains and howled in the night, making it impossible for the people to sense the difference between animal and spirit. Molly Runningwolf sat in the chair by the fire, staring out the window expectantly. Donald Tyson took little notice of her as he stocked the shelves behind the counter. She rocked at a restless pace, only occasionally looking away at the white man.

Other than the occasional straggler business had died off around four that afternoon. By that time all the people had bought or scrounged for whatever items they felt were necessary for surviving the coming storm. Some white folks had come through the reservation a couple of days earlier with news that the radio was predicting a blizzard. Of course, this was no news to any of the older folks like Molly, who had felt it in their bones for days. Still, many had waited until the last minute to stock up on supplies like lantern fuel and canned goods. But that was only for the wealthy, anyway. The other folks, the majority, had put aside wood and the dried or drying hides and meat of animals months before. It had been an unusually mild winter, so most of the Cherokee people felt their supplies were ample.

Molly started as the wind carried the plaintive howl of a train through the cracks of the storehouse wall. Even Tyson stopped and looked out the window. The train would roll through Whittier and stop in Bryson City. Lately, that sound carried with it the voices of the dead young Indians and whites who had given their lives in Europe. The Indians and mountain folk stopped and listened now to a sound that they had taken for granted only months before. It could mean a loved one was coming home to be laid to rest forever.

"Eunice in today?" she asked Tyson finally, breaking the silence.

"Nope," was the only answer she received. She stopped rocking.

Tyson felt her gaze upon his back, penetrating right through him and hot enough, he thought, to fry the beans right there on the shelf.

"She ain't been in, she ain't had that baby, and she ain't dead. What else can I tell you?"

"Husband home yet?"

"Now Molly you know that boy ain't gonna be home for weeks yet. He can't just up and come home. That wife, and that *baby,* got to have something to eat."

"They ain't gonna go without," she remarked with distaste. Tyson turned to face the old woman. She was still staring out the window, as if the conversation had never been going on.

"You know that for a fact?" he asked.

Molly turned her gaze on the storekeeper again.

"Yep." Tyson let out a growl and turned back to his work.

"She comes from good people," Molly continued. "We take care of our own--always have. She comes from good people."

"Totally?"

Molly stood up, too quick to reveal her age. She straightened out the front of her flowered dress and walked towards the door.

"Now just where are you going?" asked Tyson.

"Done talking to you," she said as she wrapped her shawl around her head and opened the door with one effortless motion.

"Now, Mrs. Runningwolf....." but the door was closing. Tyson shook his head. The old woman was protective of her young friend. Always had been. Mostly out of love, partly out of necessity. Eunice Swayney was the daughter that Molly had never had, and the young woman that inspired some of the most admiring glances and the cruelest asides on the Qualla Boundary reservation. She was beautiful, intelligent, and, arguably, from good stock -- some of the finest among the Eastern Band of Cherokee Indians. But that heritage was also where the controversy lay. Eunice's origin had many versions, and not all of them were even remotely charitable.

Molly Runningwolf was not the historian of the Cherokee and she had not achieved the status of Beloved Woman, but she was well liked and respected by nearly everyone on the reservation. Like most of the Indians, she tried to keep her distance from the surrounding whites. It wasn't a matter of prejudice, but the Cherokee had learned that the less contact they had with the whites the better their own fortunes were served. There had been a few notable exceptions, of course. Like Mr. Thomas. That man was a hero among the people. He had lead a group of Cherokees during the Civil War and, after the war, had seen to it that the people were able to hold on -- by the white man's rules -- to their lands. Most of the whites, though, still saw their Indian neighbors as a nuisance, a relic from a period they found convenient to forget. But, while Molly played by the unwritten rules of not doing anything that could raise the ire of her white neighbors, she was more willing than most to stand up to the whites if she felt backed into a corner. The story of her battle with the men who had come to take the census a few years earlier was legendary around the reservation.

The whites had decided that they needed to know exactly how many Cherokee were left in their little corner of North Carolina. They claimed it was for a population study, but many Cherokee joked that they just wanted to know exactly what it would take to finish the job they had started. As usual, when these whites arrived with their pen and paper, they began making demands and changes. The first order of business was to change these silly Indian names into something more practical -- like Smith, Jones, Washington or Jefferson. But Molly had stood in front of those white men and steadfastly refused to give up Runningwolf. Many whispered to her to let the whites put whatever they wanted on their paper---they would know she was a Runningwolf. But that was not enough for this proud woman. After tense negotiations, the white men finally decided to be done with the woman and let her keep her savage name. Still unsatisfied, Molly demanded that one of her Cherokee friends who could speak and read English verify that the white men had gotten it correct on their paper. They had.

Maybe it was in this episode that Molly taught Eunice the importance of identity, but Donald Tyson doubted it. In his years among the Indians he had become convinced that they were born with an understanding of who they were and what they were all about. And Molly Runningwolf would probably have fought anyone who tried to take that away. But she always seemed particularly burdened when it was Indian doing it to Indian. Especially Eunice Swayney. There was a soft spot in her soul for that beautiful young woman. And that was why Eunice had announced as soon as she learned that she was with child that Molly would be that child's godmother.

CHAPTER TWO

There is a spirituality to the mountains that cannot be explained to one who has not personally stood in their shadow or felt their teasing, reassuring breath upon his face. There is a force that, inexplicably and undeniably, draws a man both closer to the face of God and reminds him of his own insignificance, often within the same moment. Keats had his coastline, the people of the Carolinas and Tennessee have their Smokeys. Within the holy walls of these mountains one can hear the thunderous echo of the powwow drum and the plaintive, pleading wail of the local church organ vying for His busy ear. Red and white men alike have tried to tame their majesty, to carve a niche for friend and family to prosper away from the watchful eyes of neighbors. It was within these mountains that the Swayneys had made their home. Long before the whites brought their "civilized" last names there were men and women with Cherokee blood criss-crossing the trails and admiring the view. It was here that Eunice Swayney called home.

The Swayneys were not the typical Indian family. They did not exhibit many of the characteristics denigrated by the white locals. They were not uneducated, shiftless or lazy. The fact that they were Cherokee, however, was not lost upon them or their neighbors. Eunice's father, Lorenzo Dow Swayney, was one of the most educated men in all western North Carolina. He had advised council members and been the confidant of chiefs. He could read, write, and speak circles around most of the surrounding whites, but he could not command their respect. Not that this was something Lorenzo worried about or wished for: he commanded respect where it mattered to him most, among his people. Among the *Tsalagi*.

His only concern in the winter of 1918 was for his daughter Eunice. Eunice had been born as the black sheep of the family and was living up to the expectation. She had followed in her father's footsteps and gotten an education; after receiving her nursing degree in the summer of 1915, she returned to the reservation to practice what she had been taught. In fact, Eunice and her younger sister Dora constituted the only

Indian-administered health care the locals could get. The future had seemed bright for the young Indian woman. Lorenzo couldn't help but notice the way the young men glanced at his daughter. There was no denying that she was beautiful. She had her mother's sultry eyes; eyes that could inspire a man to greatness or reduce him to ashes, depending solely on the intent behind the gaze. Lorenzo also couldn't help the occasional daydream about the road that surely lay ahead for his daughter. She would undoubtedly be the wife of a great man someday--maybe even chief herself!

Then came the family disaster. Love is the great equalizer, and Eunice fell deeply in love with a man who had the approval of no one close to her. His name was Rodney Ray Norris. He had rarely set foot in a schoolhouse, and when he had it was only after considerable detective work and diligence on the part of the missionaries. He spoke only in broken English and was known to partake in the occasional bout with the bottle that had become such a plague among the Cherokee people. Lorenzo was adamant that his daughter *not* marry this man who was so clearly below the Swayneys.

But Rodney Ray Norris had plenty going for him in the young eyes of the up-and- coming Cherokee princess. Unlike almost everyone else within the Qualla Boundary, his jet-black hair had beautiful, thick waves running through it. Early on this had been a point of considerable embarrassment for Rodney. The other Indian children teased that those curls signified that he must have either a little white or a little black mixed in somewhere. These jokes led to more than a few lips cracked wide open and noses to burst into a flood of blood. Rodney found nothing amusing about the theories surrounding his heritage.

In addition to his wavy hair, Rodney had a smile that seemed to transmit a raw energy to the people lucky enough to fall within its sphere. His walk was buoyant and his demeanor a friendly, if cautious, jaunt through life. He had a gorgeous singing voice that he let loose after a few beers. There was an air of danger about the way he presented himself to strangers and acquaintances; a sense of serenity and devotion in the way he acted around those he loved. And he came to love Eunice very deeply.

They had known each other in school. She was the teacher's pet, he was the bane of every missionary's existence. His questions ranged from whether or not the Holy Ghost was the same as the Great Spirit to, "If Jesus thought he was needed by the Indians *and* was all powerful, why didn't he deliver his message to the Cherokee himself?" or "Why would such a kind and loving Son of God wait until many native generations had died and gone to the white man's Hell to have His story told?" Of course, these explosive questions were asked in Cherokee, which only further infuriated the Christians. Rodney liked to joke with his friends that, for this, he had tasted more soap than fry bread when he was young -- all for speaking his own language. Eunice had looked out for her young friend as much as she could. As the favorite of the white teachers, she was frequently called upon to translate what he had said. She cleaned it up as best she could, as often as she could. Rodney might ask the white teacher, "Why, since Jesus had long hair should I cut my own?" Eunice quickly translated it into, "Why was Jesus killed?" These questions gave the do-gooder a chance to pontificate on the unselfish nature of Jesus without causing Rodney a beating or a mouth washing. Eunice never thought she was doing Rodney any harm. As her own father often said, the Cherokee didn't need any goddamn white from Rhode Island telling *them* about sacrifice.

Eunice took care of Rodney in the classroom and he took care of her outside of it. When the other kids began wagging their vicious tongues about her mother he was always there, quick as lightning. Boy or girl could expect a patented Norris ass-stomping if they tread too heavily on Eunice's or her mother's honor. Although neither of them noticed it at the time, their friendship had all the makings of love from the very beginning.

When she was old enough, Eunice went away to become a nurse. She came home as often as she could, and occasionally she and Rodney would see each other. More often than not, though, she spent her time at home teaching her father everything she herself had been taught. Meanwhile, Rodney wandered from job to job and bottle to bottle. Eunice worried about him a great deal. He made most of his money sneaking booze onto the reservation, a job that could easily get a young Indian thrown in jail or killed. When she finally returned home for good, Rodney was beginning to feel restless with his station. He had plenty of money to throw around the reservation, but his ill-gotten gains made him the envy of no one save the totally destitute or the completely dense. He had no taste for being a poor Indian's hero. When he learned that the Railroad in Bryson City was looking for workers, he decided to apply. When the only thing that kept him from getting the position was the language barrier, he sought out his old school friend to teach him the intricacies of the English language.

As their summer afternoons turned into late evenings conversing awkwardly by the stream that rolled through Big Cove, Rodney and Eunice began to rediscover each other. They began to hold hands as they walked through the fields. She began to share her dreams of getting off of the reservation someday; he began to talk about wanting to support a family without being embarrassed by the way he made his money. Eventually they were kissing each other good night, only to lie down and dream about their future. Each new sunrise brought the promise of new revelations, declarations and confessions, each sunset the unbearable requirement to fall asleep apart from one another.

One night, after an intense session of translation and grammar, Eunice and Rodney walked towards her family's house. Rodney always stopped several paces away from the door so that Mr. Swayney wouldn't know exactly whom Eunice was helping. This night, as the autumn leaves danced around their heads, Rodney took his friend's hand. They stared at each other for a while, unsure of what to say. Finally he let her hand drop, gave her his special wink, and turned away. As he began to disappear into the evening, Eunice called to him in Cherokee.

"I love you," she said.

In the distance, in English, floated an answer.

"I--lo-love--you--also."

Eunice smiled and turned toward home.

CHAPTER THREE

Lorenzo Swayney had built a considerable network of both friends and enemies around Qualla Boundary. There were those who knew him as the man who, at Christmas, slyly dropped presents off at the orphanage. Oh, he had never admitted to it, that would not have been his way. But they knew it just the same and admired him for it. There were others who knew him as the man who lived in that ostentatious ranch house in Big Cove, away from the traditionals and closer to the heart of the surrounding white community. There were still others who saw him as a hybrid, a man capable of great charity and humility as well as fits of pride and rage. His youthful bouts with the bottle were legendary, even among a people known for having their difficulties with firewater. And, although he had slowed down considerably in his middle age, it was still common knowledge that he was, despite his usual good humor, not a man you wanted angry with you, drunk or sober. Lorenzo undoubtedly would have agreed with them all. He was a pragmatic man who delivered whatever the moment called for. He had learned long ago that a man did not have to boast or strut in order to be resented. Therefore, he did not believe in undo humility. He knew what he had accomplished, and to hell with anyone who expected him to apologize for it. He paid no attention to the gossip of the community--it did not worry him. He knew, of course, that as a powerful member of the reservation he was bound to be the subject of much of it.

"You don't have to be smart to get educated," they would sneer, "you just need some Irish in you." Or "Tell the guvment you're a breed and they'll give you what you need. Let them know you're real and they'll make you beg and steal." That rhyme did crack him up. Maybe white blood, however little or much, had made his life a little easier. But Lorenzo, like the others, knew the taste of soap and the feel of hickory as a result of the Indian blood in his veins. And the fact remained that he had returned to Qualla with his education to try and help his people. And help them he had. He had intervened many times to help the Cherokee hold on to what was left of their nation and their culture. He always made an appearance, as close to the front as possible, at church on Sundays. But he also was there, in the middle of the night, when traditionals snuck into the woods to chant and pray for the health of a loved one or the good of the nation. He lived in both worlds because, as he often insisted, an Indian had no choice. There would come a day, he counseled, when the dances and the drums could be brought back into the daylight where they belonged. But that time had not arrived. Lorenzo knew well the story of the Ghost Dancers and their fate. He would not allow the same to happen to his people. If they would just bide their time, there would come a day when the white man would have to allow them to practice their religion again. After all, the whites that Lorenzo knew were all so busy grabbing souls and acres that they had forgotten the true nature of their own religion. They acted as if God had created them in His image and given them authority to mold Mother Earth into *their* image. Yes, someday the white man would not only allow the Indian ways to return, he would seek them out. There would then be no choice for the survival of the world. This he believed, and he defended these beliefs against any and all comers. So, if some people wanted to make him the object of their contempt and their treacherous talk, let them.

He 'was not, however, as generous or forgiving when the talk surrounded one of his children. Lorenzo was no fool. Friends had been telling him for weeks about the budding "romance" between his daughter and that trash from across the river. Others of a less charitable persuasion had taken perverse delight in asking about Eunice's new boyfriend. Lorenzo heard the ecstasy in their voices when they asked. There was joy for them in their knowing that one of the mighty Swayneys was being seen all over the reservation with a boy who not only didn't have a college education, but could barely read or write. Of course, he had known for some time that she had been tutoring Norris, but he had no idea that she had started some kind of relationship with him. However, that was exactly what he was hearing wherever he went.

Lorenzo was confused and a little troubled at the attitude of his peers. He had never, he thought, acted as though he were somehow better than any of them. He had gone out of his way to help them, one and all, whenever they had asked for his assistance. Still, he had to admit to himself that they were at least partially right. Maybe he didn't think he was better than the others, but he hadn't worked as hard as he had only to have his daughter start her life in the same place he had begun, as if she had no other opportunities. That was ridiculous and totally unnecessary.

Lorenzo was left with the difficult question of how to put an end to this silly affair, if it was indeed that. He couldn't talk to Eunice himself -- she was too hardheaded. No, it would have to be someone else in the family. The most obvious answer was to have his wife Cora talk to her. Lorenzo, knew, though, that would threaten to open a wound he had hoped long-healed; a wound he had sworn never to reopen. Besides, Cora would simply never do it. Her nature wasn't shaped for such confrontation. She was quiet, very reserved -- almost timid. She had a temper Lorenzo had the misfortune to experience many times, but it took a great deal to bring that side of her out. Lorenzo was never quite sure what was going on behind those dark, black eyes of hers, but he knew she would have nothing to do with this business.

That left one of Eunice's siblings. That, too, would be a move requiring considerable attention to family politics. Anything that Eunice perceived as pressure or as having his fingerprints on it would backfire. He would never ask one of his children to lie to another one, but whoever took the task would have to practice the art of selective revelation.

The child closest in age to Eunice was Grace. The two had been close since they were very young; it was a relationship forged in the fires of alienation. Lorenzo thought long about the prospect of sending Grace to talk some sense into Eunice. But there were too many things that could go wrong with sending her. She was too much *like* Eunice. Grace spent too many evenings on the back porch staring into the stars to see anything wrong with Eunice's newfound love. No, his second child was a dreamer, and this job called for someone with their feet planted firmly on the ground. If Grace got herself caught up in the romance of the situation, as he felt certain she would, she would not make a persuasive ambassador for the family name. The last thing he needed was someone encouraging Eunice's bullshit Romeo and Juliet fantasy. Grace was out of the question.

Then there was Lorenzo and Cora's son, Chiltoskey. Chiltos, as the family called him, was clearly not the kind of young man used to winning arguments based on the strength of his logic. Lorenzo would never admit that his only son was a troublemaker, but he did have to admit that trouble seemed to follow the young Cherokee around. Chiltos, at only fifteen, had grown into a strange mix of mother and father. He was short, just a hair taller than Cora and considerably shorter than Lorenzo, but with his father's build. The combination made him, even for his age, an imposing figure. He had a penchant for missing class and, his father felt certain, was already discovering the power of alcohol. Chiltos was also too much like his mother in temperament. He was a man of few words. He also seemed to be nurturing a quiet resentment against Lorenzo, while this task called for someone who would question neither method nor motive. Chiltos could not be relied upon to have any meaningful dialogue with Eunice, but perhaps he could have a long talk with Norris and convince that young man it was in his best interest to leave the Swayney family be. Unfortunately, from the information Lorenzo had garnered about Norris, he sounded as though he could hold his own with Chiltos, and that simply wouldn't do. Making a martyr of the boy would make him irresistible to the starry-eyed Eunice. Besides, Lorenzo preferred to try diplomatic channels first. If those failed, perhaps then he would talk to Chiltos.

There remained only one option: Lorenzo's youngest daughter Dora. She was even- tempered, bright, and, most importantly, utterly devoted to her father. Of course this plan was not without its own problems. There had always been an underlying tension between the two girls, a sort of unspoken but ever-present competition. It was a contest that Eunice almost always refused to take part in, which only further infuriated Dora. In some ways, Lorenzo guessed that his youngest girl was enjoying Eunice's sudden infamy and fall from grace. But she would swallow her own self-interest if he asked. And he would make certain that she understood that on Qualla, no individual was seen as apart from his or her family. Eunice's disgrace would reflect on them all ... even Dora. Whether or not Eunice would listen to her was anybody's guess.

So that was it. The old man made the decision as he had made every one for the last thirty years: with only his heart and impressive mind as counsel.   Tomorrow he would send Dora to talk with his wayward child.

So much was riding on it.

CHAPTER FOUR

Dora had not wanted to do her father's dirty work. As far as she was concerned, if Eunice wanted to spend her time helping that Norris boy that was her own decision. She understood her father's concerns, but she had personally believed that Eunice was too damn cold to care about anybody--especially someone like Rodney Norris.

The relationship between the two sisters had always been adversarial. Eunice, because of age, had always had the opportunity to be the trailblazer, and conversely, Dora had been confined to the role of also-ran. When she herself had left Qualla to study nursing, the local Indians had told her they hoped she'd do as well as her sister. She had arrived at the Hampton Insitute in Virginia, her father and sister's alma mater, with the firm determination, some might even have called it a conviction, that she would not do as well....she would do better. And she had, for awhile. Her grades and her self-esteem had soared. She was finally out of Eunice's shadow. No one told her how lucky she was to have a sister as wonderful as the lovely Eunice. No one here compared her to that same lovely girl. Instead, they remarked what an incredibly hard worker SHE was, how lovely she was, what a great personality she had. And, for the first time in her life she knew that the attention was truly for her, it was not the mock-sincerity of some fool trying to get close enough to ask her if the rumors were true....

Ah, yes. The rumors. They had always made her even more resentful. She could not believe the ignorance of people, the naivete. Did they actually think that Swayney's would ever tell something like that to someone outside of the family? More importantly, did they actually believe that something like that was typical dinner conversation for her family? But there had been more than a few who had asked her. She remembered the old lady at church, taking her to the side with a smile and saying, "I hope I'm not prying, but I just must ask you something. Now, I don't want to upset you, I'm trying to help your family out by putting this awful rumor to rest. But, well, is IT true?" The IT was always spoken in a reverent whisper, as if that made it alright. Dora had been only nine when this concerned citizen asked her, and she had not had any idea what the lady was talking about. That afternoon she came home from church and, at the dinner table told her father what had happened. She remembered his face had flushed, and he had glared at her mother in a way Dora had never seen before. His eyes had an almost menacing look to them. Her mother had stood up, gracefully chasing the wrinkles out of her Sunday dress with her brown hands and walked out of the kitchen. Dora didn't see her the rest of the day, but she remembered hearing, or at least thinking she could hear her mother crying in her bedroom.

"Dotie," her father had said (he always called her Dotie), "that is nothing that you should worry about. It's just women being women, that's all."

"And eventually," Eunice interrupted with a sardonic smile, "the men will start being women."

Dora had looked from her sister to her father and back again.

"So," she thought, "they could tell Eunice but not me?" Now knowing became imperative.

"What is it Daddy?" she asked with the same enthusiasm as a child wanting to open a present. Thinking back now, she realized that the more apropriate tone would have been that of a child that hears a menacing noise outside her window.

"Nothing, my child," Lorenzo had replied in Cherokee. Dora searched her father's face. He only spoke in Cherokee during moments of absolute seriousness or when he had been dipping in the local moonshine. But her father had apparently forgotten that she was at the table, or even in the room. He was staring intently at Eunice, with a look of such sadness that she wanted to scream at him to stop...to laugh or smile...just stop looking that way. Eunice had risen now and was walking towards the door. She stared out the screen, a dreamy look across her face.

"You will have to tell her someday," she said, still looking outside. Lorenzo was now peering at his folded hands on the table top, as if he was enthralled with the shape, as if the webbing told a story only he could enjoy, only he could hear. Eunice walked out onto the porch and then appeared to jog off towards the creek. Dora waited for her father to say something, anything. But he only continued to stare at his fumbling hands. Dora had started to return to her meal, but she had no appetite now.

"May I be excused?" he asked. Still nothing from Lorenzo. She decided to risk the beating, anything seemed better than the suffocating silence of that kitchen. She ran out to find Eunice.

Ꮗ

"You know what Mrs. Davies was talking about, don't you?"

Dora found Eunice sitting on the grass, dangling her feet in the still-cold April water of Big Cove. She was going to mention that Eunice was sure to get whalloped herself for getting grass-stains on her Sunday best but thought that was pretty much irrelevant at the time.

"Um-huh," Eunice mumbled. Dora had to grudgingly admit to herself that, in the spring sunshine, her sister was truly beautiful. She had raven-black hair that shown brilliantly in the sun. Her slender figure cut a striking silhouette against the gentle flow of the river. She looked, thought Dora, like a feminine reed...a part of the landscape that was only discernible by her own sensuous presence. Eunice stared hypnotically at the water that swirled and giggled around her feet. But there were many beautiful women here in Qualla, especially in Big Cove. The bloodlines of Cherokee, Catawba, Irish and countless other wayfaring pilgrims mingled thoughtfully in the smiles of the men and women here. Still, there was little doubt that Eunice stood apart.

"It's her eyes," thought Dora. Something about her big sister's eyes made her an imposing and alluring character. Now, as she stood watching Eunice watch the river, she realized the eyes were simply magic. It was in Eunice's eyes that one could, if his heart were right, hear the footsteps of the Cherokee as they trekked across a continent into foreign land. In those eyes you could see the struggle for survival. The battle to do more than just get by...the battle to be, above all else, TSALAGI. She sat there gazing, seeming to dare the river to blink first. Her figure was reflected in the river, and the river itself was in turn brilliantly mirrored in her stormy eyes. Somewhere in between lay infinity. Somewhere between the eye of the river and the eye of the budding young Cherokee woman, even eternity swam upstream. Dora felt the jealous rage welling up within her.

"Well?" she finally asked, "what is it? What was she talking about? Why did Daddy tell you and not me?"

"Because it doesn't concern you."

Dora felt she was finally getting somewhere. "Well," she asked again, "does it concern you?" She almost spat the question. Of course it didn't concern Eunice. What had she ever done? She smiled smugly. She had trapped the great Eunice.

"Yes," Eunice said. She still had not looked away from the river. Dora's smile faded.

"How?" she asked.

"In everyway."

"Aw, come on, Eunice. Tell me what this is all about. Is Daddy drinking too much again? Wait, it's Grace isn't it? Oooh, did Daddy and Mom find about her and that boy holding hands? That's it, isn't it?"

Eunice laughed. It was a humorless laugh that made Dora furious. Was Eunice mocking her?

"It has nothing to do with holding hands, Dotie, nothing at all."

"Then what?" implored Dora.

"You're whining, Dotie." Eunice turned from the river and smiled at her.

"Please, Eunice, tell me what she meant. It ain't right keeping a secret. It just ain't."

"Isn't," corrected Eunice, tossing a stone into the water.

Dora ran up beside Eunice and stomped her foot. This had gone far enough. If Eunice didn't tell her she would....well, she'd push her in that river that she seemed to find so interesting...Sunday best and all. It would be worth the whipping.

"I want to know what this is all about and I want to know right now."

Eunice stood up, straightening her dress just as her mother had only a few minutes before. They were too much alike, thought Dora.

"This," said Eunice cryptically," is about history. And don't worry, you'll hear it all soon enough. A body can't run from history."

With that, she peeled her Sunday dress off, folded it neatly, and sat it on the bank. She kicked her shoes off and removed her underwear, tossing it on top of her dress.

"Well don't just stand there looking like a lost puppy, let's swim."

Dora started to protest but Eunice was already in the water, cutting across the current. Dora shook her head contemptuously. She would never understand her sister. She turned around, pouting all the way home.

It had not been until four years later that she learned the truth of the matter; learned the truth in the painful way that people often do when it comes to family secrets—from the uncharitable glee of a classmate intent on reducing her to ashes. Looking back, she could not even remember the name of the hateful child who had told her, only the venom cascading from her mouth as she did so. She didn't even remember the point of the argument, only how it had ended.

"You're a bastard," the girl had said, "just like that sister of yours."

Dora had not known what the word meant, only that it was bad. She had whipped her enemy and been sent home. Lorenzo was about to punish her when she asked him.

"Daddy," she had asked, "I'm sorry we were fighting. But she called Eunice a name and I was just defending her is all."

"It's good to stand up for family," he had said, "but not in this way. You're going to have to be punished, and I think you know that."

"Yes, Daddy," she had whispered. And then, "Daddy, what *is* a bastard anyway?"

She would never again feel such pity for her father. And that was when she had learned. He had not told her, he had simply walked away in mourning. But Eunice had come in, heard the story, and finally filled in the blanks.

"There was no need in defending me over that," she said, "'cause it's the truth. I am a bastard."

"What? What does that mean?"

And Eunice had explained as best she could. Lorenzo and Cora had not married at first, they had lived together (shacking up, as the locals called it). Eunice had been conceived during this period, and Lorenzo had refused to get married. He loved Cora and was intent on staying with her, but he would not allow those goddamn missionaries the satisfaction of pronouncing his love "valid" in the eyes of God. He believed it was already and needed no help from them. He had never even suspected that his decision would reverberate so painfully across the placid pages of history. But jealous minds never forget; a lesson he had learned too late to shield his daughter from the hate.

Dora sighed. Now that daughter was again antagonizing the wrath of the people around them. And she was being dispatched to save the Swayney name from more humiliation. It was a big job, and a job she found she had little taste for.

CHAPTER FIVE

Eunice had said goodnight to Rodney some ways away from her father's house. Neither of them really had any doubt that Lorenzo was on to their romance, they knew only that so far he had had the good taste not to mention it or try to intervene. Eunice had warned Rodney that it was only a matter of time before that happened. He had smiled at her and told her not to worry about it, he was not afraid of her father. Eunice, however, knew better than Rodney how formidable her father could be. She had seen him enter the lives of his children on many different occasions. He had not yet lost a battle over his children's future, and this fight was probably his toughest. Still, Rodney was a man that would stand up for what he believed in. He had no status in the community to worry about. In fact, taking on someone like Lorenzo would only increase his devoted follower's admiration. Rodney had become a sort of symbol for the "lowers" at Qualla--those Indians who did not have a college education, who struggled to keep food on the table for themselves and their families. His devotion to what remained of Cherokee culture in a time when militancy was not the fashion caused many of these men (and women, thought Eunice with a twinge of jealousy) to see him as a hero.

"Years ago," one young boy had said to Eunice, "he would have been a warrior."

Years ago. But now he was just a "bad seed," an Indian to be watched and kept in his place at all costs. And Eunice knew that her father was intent upon keeping him in this place.

Eunice crept through the house as quietly as she could. She could hear her father piddling about in his study, the small room off the kitchen where he retired to read his Bible and occasionally sneak a little moonshine. Her parent's bedroom door was closed, which meant that her mother, as usual, had already gone to bed. Dotie and Grace were in their room, with the door also closed. Eunice paused outside of it, daring herself to go in. She desperately wanted someone to talk to, someone to share her good feelings with. She was closest to Grace, she knew, but for some reason she wanted to talk to Dotie. The two of them had always been rivals, but it was no sense of victory that made her want to see her youngest sister. She thought, she believed, that Dotie could understand how she felt.

But knocking raised the possibility of alerting her father to her presence, and she was determined to avoid that confrontation as long as possible. She moved past the door.

Chiltos' door was open but the room was dark. He was still out. Eunice let out a nervous sigh. She knew that Chiltos was drinking pretty heavily and hanging around with people that were trouble. But it wasn't her place to speak to him. Father would do that. She crept into her own room and carefully closed the door. She undressed in the darkness and pulled the covers back on her bed. As she laid her head on her pillow she felt the uncomfortable crinkle of paper under her head. She rubbed her hand across the pillow and found a small note. Carefully, she reached into her nightstand and pulled out a book of kitchen matches that she kept there. The room filled with the crack of the match and the gentle, hot yellow light of the flame.

I'm going to town tomorrow for some things. How about going with me? We could talk? See you in the morning.
                                        Dotie

Eunice shook the match out. She got out of bed and walked over to her window. Outside, one of the many homeless dogs that roamed the reservation was yelping at the mountain wind. So this was how it would work. Dotie wanted to talk. Or had Lorenzo sent her? It was hard for Eunice to imagine Dotie making the first move. She went back to bed and tried to sleep. Tomorrow she would have to begin it. Tomorrow she would have to start battling her father. She felt herself beginning to cry but quickly fought that away. There would be no tears, she told herself. Nobody was going to take this feeling she had and turn it into anything but joy. Maybe she could make Dotie see, and maybe Dotie could get to their father. Outside her door, she heard the singsong cadence of her father's boots on the wooden floor. He was whistling some old song. It wasn't Cherokee...maybe Irish? Eunice tried to clear her mind. She adored her father. Everything she had done in her life had been to ease the family burden he carried with such a quiet strength. Sometimes she caught him staring at her with a look of such profound pain that it had broken her heart a thousand different times in a thousand different places. Whenever she caught him he quickly looked away and returned with a smiling glance. But the smile was always too late. She had seen the torment. Her every move since she was eight years old had been to erase that conflict, to remove the stain of betrayal that colored his soul. But now that might all go by the wayside. She had fallen in love with the wrong man. She wanted to spend the rest of her life with the wrong man. And Lorenzo couldn't allow that.

Eunice understood that his protest was for her own good more than any self-preservation. She was no fool, either. Despite what her father might think she understood completely the storm that would accompany her relationship. She knew what would be said, what WAS being said about her love with the Norris boy. People would snicker that Eunice had turned out just like they knew she would. You can pretty up trash all day long but it'll still be trash. Lorenzo was trying, had always been trying, to keep that prophecy from coming true. He was a practical man who had seen poverty and risen above it. He had lived hard so that his children would never have to. Lorenzo had believed that he had used up the family's share of mistakes when he was a young man and therefore his children should make none. He had no time for ethereal notions like love. He had gone that route so that his children didn't have to. He had placed Eunice in the position of marrying well. She could have (as he had always reminded her) the son of a chief if she wanted. Or one of the young men whose family owned one of the stores in town. There was no need for her to live and die in obscurity among the poverty that was an Indian reservation. Lorenzo Dow Swayney had nearly worked himself to death so that his daughter could marry whomever she wanted. He had just never imagined that she would want an illiterate Cherokee boy that roamed from job to job, paycheck to paycheck.

Eunice felt the tears welling up inside of her again. Each time she closed her eyes she saw the competing visions of Rodney's rugged, smiling face and her father's sad, disapproving glare. She fell into a troubled sleep as her father stood outside her door, listening to her toss and turn.

ಬ

"So, you wanna go with me?"

Well, that was blunt, thought Eunice. She was amused by the lack of pretense on Dotie's part. That could only mean that she wasn't quite feeling up to the task, whatever that task might be.

"Sure," Eunice said, "what are you going in for?"

"I wanted to pick up some material for a dress that mamma's making me."

"Are you going into town-town or are you just going into Cherokee?"

"I thought we'd just go into Cherokee."

Eunice nodded and said that she would need a few minutes to get ready. She was supposed to meet Rodney later that afternoon, but she realized that if the purpose of Dotie's trip was what she expected she may have to miss their date. There was no way to get word to him; she hoped that he wouldn't get angry. Dotie said that maybe they should just walk down. It was a long walk, sure, but it was an awfully nice day.

"Why don't you just say that you need to talk to me about 'that boy' that I'm seeing," Eunice thought. But if the excuse made things easier for Dotie she guessed she might as well play along.

As she dressed, she felt her heart begin to pick up speed every time she thought about what was coming. At least this would be the last morning that the family had to pretend like nothing was happening. The act was wearing thin for everyone, and it added a tension in the house that Eunice did not like. She wrapped her long, black hair into a tight ponytail and headed out into the yard. Her father and mother had both been conveniently absent when she awoke this morning. The mantle had been clearly passed to Dotie. In some ways Eunice felt sorry for her sister. She had no doubt that Dotie saw this as a way to further ingratiate herself with Lorenzo. Eunice had never understood her sister's belief that she was somehow lacking in their father's eyes. Still, with that motivation Eunice understood that Dotie might be prepared to go a long way to ending this relationship.

"Ready?"

Eunice took a deep breath. This was it, then.

"I'm ready."

The two young women strolled out towards the river without a word. Big Cove was bright and already very much alive by this point in the day. They passed neighbors harnessing up teams of horses, preparing for the week's final day of labor. The occasional farm hand stopped what he was doing momentarily to get a look at the Swayney sisters. Neither Dora nor Eunice seemed to notice. Having spent their lives under suspicious and accusatory glares the barely noticed looks of affection or longing. Soon, they were out of ear and eyeshot of their fellow Cherokees. There was an uncomfortable silence between them, the kind of quiet that only arises when there is something that must be said. Once in awhile, Dora would glance over at Eunice. Eunice was watching her feet glide across the gravel road. She could feel Dora looking at her, but decided not to return the glance. Somehow that seemed the proper thing. Finally Dora spoke.

"We haven't been seeing you as much around the house lately," she said, almost as if picking up a conversation. Eunice sighed.

"He's good to me," she said.

"What?!" Dora seemed stunned that her sister would have bypassed the opportunity to put off this confrontation.

"He is good to me and he makes me feel special and I never feel like I'm having to pretend around him and.....and I love him. And he loves me."

The two sisters had stopped walking now. Sparrows were circling about them and chirping happily, oblivious to the conflict.

"Are you sure?" That was all Dora could think of to ask. "I mean, how do you know?"

Eunice smiled.

"How do I know what?" she asked. "That I love him or that he loves me?"

Dora shook her head. "Well, either," she responded.

Eunice looked straight at Dora. This was the tough part. How did you explain to someone why you loved someone or how you knew that what you felt was actually love? It was like trying to explain why the wind against your face sometimes made you homesick for a time and place that you had never actually known.

"Jeez, Dora," she protested, "I don't know if I can explain that."

"Well, try."

Eunice looked around her. There was nowhere to run. It was make or break time.

"Well," she began cautiously, "let's see. When I close my eyes at night, I see his face. I replay everything we said and did before I fall asleep. Sometimes, lying there in my bed, I actually laugh out loud at something he said or did that day. Or even the day before. When I'm with him there is no restlessness, there is no wondering what might be happening somewhere else. In fact, there IS no somewhere else. The whole world seems to be right there with us. It's not that the world revolves around us, that's not right. It's that we ARE the whole world, y'know? Everything I see I see in terms of us. I see something in a store window and think, 'Rodney would like that.' Or 'Rodney would hate that.' It doesn't matter, the point is he's always the reference. Something happens to me that is a little out of the ordinary, anything, and I can't wait to tell him about it. I can't wait to see his face and hear what he says about whatever it was. I love falling asleep because I know as soon as dreams start he'll be there beside me, and yet, at the same time, I hate needing to sleep at all because that's just time I could be spending with him. I love that we finish each other's sentences; that he never looks at me like I'm crazy when I tell him I think I have something to offer my people. I love the way he can take one look at me and, without me having to say anything, know that I need to be held. Or listened to. Or talked to. I love the fact that he understands a sunset doesn't need to be talked about because it can't be captured with words. He just sits there and looks...and dreams. And I LOVE that. I love that it takes me an hour to say goodbye, even if I know I'm going to see him the first thing the next day. His arms feel like home, I mean the way home should feel, with no secrets and no veils. I feel safe and happy. Oh, God, happy is such a stupid word. It doesn't fit the feeling. Nothing does, that's the point. Don't you see, Dotie? I didn't mean to fall in love with him, I don't even think I wanted to. But I did. Like it or not he and have become kind of a club, and the rest of the world is just outsiders. I love him Dotie. I love him. And that's that."

Dora looked at her sister. She had never seen her like this. This strong, this vulnerable. You couldn't help but notice the way her whole face changed when she spoke of him. The way she positively glowed.

"I don't know what to say," she finally said. "I guess I thought maybe you were, I don't know, trying to show off or something. I thought you were trying to show Daddy that you were on your own or, I don't know."

Eunice laughed.

"I don't think either one of us would intentionally take Daddy on." Now it was Dora's turn to laugh. Both of them knew that was the truth. But the good humor passed quickly.

"You know that he sent me to make you end it, don't you?"

"Yes."

Both of them turned away and stared at the trees. They had gone completely still, as if waiting for the verdict. Dora walked away a few paces and picked up a branch that had fallen by the road. She knelt and began drawing in the dirt. Eunice watched her sister closely.

"I've always been jealous of you and him, you know?" she said. Eunice made no reply. There was nothing to say. "I guess I always felt that he liked you better. He worked harder to protect you. But I felt the sting too, y'know."

"I know," said Eunice, "and I'm sorry." Dora was crying now. Not much, she was too proud for that, but there were tears nonetheless.

"It's not your fault. People can just be cruel. But when they hurt you it hurt me too. I hope you know that."

"It hurt us all, Dotie."

Dora stood up and wiped her eyes. The steel was back in her mannerism now.

"You've earned this happiness, Eunice. I wouldn't want any part of denying you that. And, well, if you love him then, well, dammit I guess I'll love him too."

Eunice smiled. "Daddy's not going to be pleased with this."

"No," Dora agreed, "I suppose not. But I think together we can handle him."

"Together," Eunice repeated.

Grinning wickedly, the two of them decided to go into town after all and have a soda.

CHAPTER SIX

Rodney had been waiting on Eunice for nearly two hours. She had been late before, so he wasn't terribly worried. Their meetings were still being kept a secret, and that meant she couldn't pull herself away from someone without risking suspicion. He couldn't help but wonder what the hold-up was, though. Both of them had been aware that, in a place like Qualla, such a secret would not be their own for very long. The thought that her father was keeping her away flashed through his mind. Rodney had told Eunice that he was not afraid of Lorenzo, but that wasn't exactly true. He knew just enough about the politics of the reservation to understand that the same people who were enjoying his love with Eunice would also keep him from gaining any employment if the pressure from the right source was applied. And Lorenzo could be that source. He also understood that there was probably not one person in the area who was genuinely pleased about him and Eunice. They all had some secret motive for their smiles.

His thoughts turned to Eunice. So kind, so incredibly beautiful. He was not the best she could do and he knew that. There were men who wanted to gaze into her eyes who would someday carry influence and prestige, men who could guarantee her a life without want. He was not like them. The only thing he felt reasonably sure of offering her was a life of struggle. There were times, late at night, drifting between consciousness and dream, when he thought of never speaking to her again. Maybe that was the best thing he could do for her. She deserved better than he could give. And no man whose love is genuine can ever easily and knowingly wrench the woman he loves from her family; and that was the risk they ran.

Dreams. That was all Rodney Norris had. The most impractical commodity in nature was his only asset. Dreams were the fire that gave light to the soul, but they had never once in the sordid history of

Man quieted hunger or quenched thirst. He was not the man the locals thought him.   He was not the Robin Hood that the Cherokee so desperately wanted; neither was he the rogue Indian thug the breeds and the whites claimed. Experience had taught him that the actions of a man born with status were called ambition, while the same actions of a poor man were known as moral corruption.   Rodney was all too aware that he could not tame the tongues until he himself had become one of them. And God only knew how long that might take.

Rodney started at the sound of something approaching.

"Eunice?" he called expectantly.   But it was just a rabbit.   The animal stopped and gave him a wary stare and then darted away again. Rodney reached into his shirt pocket and pulled out a cigarette. What was keeping Eunice?   He took the first drag and inhaled deeply, watching the smoke swirl around his fingertips and dance away, forming tiny little clouds around his head. He turned again to his dreams.

Someday in the not too distant future, he believed, he and Eunice would leave Qualla.   They would go to a place where they were not within earshot of the Smokey Mountains, to escape the unfavorable echoes that might make their way to their new neighbors.   He would own his own shop -- maybe a couple of them -- and Eunice would be the head nurse of a team that all worked for her.   Mill and factory owners from all over North Carolina would call on him to repair their machines and to keep their plants running. He would be indispensable. Then he would take the money he made and buy Eunice the nicest house in the state. It would be a white two-story house with a big front porch and a swing for the two of them, just like she had said she'd always wanted.   They would have a large backyard with a clearing in the middle of it, they could lie under the stars and take stock of what they had -- just the way they did now without having to sneak around anymore.   They would be the toast of the town. And Lorenzo -- well, he would have to admit that Rodney had turned out all right after all. He would see that Rodney had made a fine husband. All that was a long way off, though. Until then, he had to hope that Lorenzo's wrath would be somewhat subdued.

"Rodney? Rodney, are you there?"

He dropped the cigarette and pushed it gently into the soil with his boot heel.

"Over here," he whispered.

Eunice stepped from the woods. She was wearing her blue dress, the one that Rodney liked best. The sun had already begun to descend below the horizon. With her hair tied back she looked even younger than she was. The beauty of this woman who loved him for reasons he thought he'd never understand again struck Rodney. Once she had seen him, she rushed into his arms. He held her tightly against him. Her hair always smelled so good. They didn't speak for several minutes. He locked his fingers around the small of her back, as if to hold off some unseen force trying to pull her away.

"What's happened?" he asked. Eunice stepped back and looked at him carefully. Her face was a mask of confusion. She seemed both happy and distraught.

"Daddy sent Dora to talk to me today." Rodney stepped away and pulled out another cigarette. He had known it would happen eventually; he had just hoped it would take longer for Lorenzo to swing into action. He was furious that the old man had sent someone else -- especially his daughter -- to do his own dirty work.

"And?"

"And she understands. She's going to stand beside me. We're not alone."

"We're alone," Rodney stated flatly.

"Honey, don't you understand? If he can't play Dora and me against each other, then he doesn't have any way to get to me -- not that he could have, anyway. Mamma won't try to keep us apart and neither will Grace. Dotie was his only shot, and she believes in us. We have nothing to worry about now."

"Eunice I think you're forgetting what your father's like. Your sister being on our side only means that whatever he does he has to do by himself. I don't think that'll stop him, do you?"

"Well, maybe not at first," she agreed, "but he won't wanna make everybody in the house mad at him. He's not crazy."

Rodney stared at her. She seemed to believe what she was saying. Maybe she hadn't heard all the stories about Lorenzo he had heard. Whatever the reason, Rodney believed she was getting her hopes up for something that was never going to happen.

"Eunice, I hope you don't honestly think that this means Lorenzo's now gonna ask me over for dinner."

"Well, no, but..."

Rodney put his arms back around her and kissed her.

"We're alone, Eunice. That won't change until I've shown 'em all who I really am. If Lorenzo has to go outside of the family to break us apart, that's just what he'll do. Don't you see? He tried the easiest way first. But he won't stop until you bring home one of those Big Cove Indians. Period."

Eunice turned away from him. She knew he was right. The tears were welling up inside again. Her throat was burning with the swallowed disappointment. She spoke without turning to look at Rodney.

"He just doesn't know you, that's all." Rodney placed a hand across her shoulder. The contrast of his cracked and calloused hand against the soft material of her dress reminded him again that they were from different worlds.

"And he doesn't want to know me. You can't change that."

"Well why do I have to choose, goddammit?" Rodney jumped as if slapped. He had never heard Eunice curse before. In fact, he always tried very hard to watch his own language in her presence. He felt her shoulder trembling beneath his hand. They were now surrounded by darkness, but he knew that she was crying. That was why she wouldn't turn to look at him. Rodney felt his heart breaking within his chest.

"Eunice, please don't cry; we'll be o.k. -- I promise you that. I'm sorry if I sound so,... -- I don't know enough words. But I'll make it alright, I swear."

She was shaking her head. Somewhere an owl screeched at the rising moon. The Swayneys weren't traditionals, but Eunice knew what that meant. Chills ran down her spine. The owl meant trouble. The owl meant death. The tears were flowing freely now.

"How?" she asked.

"I thought you weren't traditional," Rodney quipped. Both of them laughed at the joke. Eunice wiped her eyes and turned back to him. She buried her face in his shirt. He gently stroked her long hair.

"I love you, Rodney. But I could be a lot of trouble for you. Are you sure it's worth it?" Rodney laughed. It was a genuine laugh.

"Worth it? C'mon, Eunice. That's just crazy talk. I want to tell you something. Since I was just a little boy, maybe ten or eleven, I've had talks."

"Talks?" she asked.

"Yeah, talks. Well, a combination of talk, wish, and prayer. When I went to bed, I would talk to the wall, only, it wasn't the wall at all. It was a friend that wasn't really there."

"Imaginary." Rodney gave her a confused glance. "Make-believe," she said.

"Yeah," he agreed. "The point is we talked. I would lie there and tell this person everything I wanted to do. And then I'd answer like I was him."

"And what would he say?" Eunice asked.

"Oh, simple stuff. He'd say that I could do that if I wanted to. Or he'd tell me what a great idea something was. I'd tell him that I was scared of something or somebody and he'd say that I shouldn't be 'cause there wasn't nothing to be scared of. I'd tell him that someday we wouldn't go to bed hungry anymore 'cause I was gonna make enough money for both of us. I told him someday we'd be sleeping in a big bed with a real cushiony mattress instead of on that floor. And he'd tell me that he believed in me. And I felt better just knowing that he did. I told him someday we wouldn't hang our heads 'cause we were Indians. We'd walk proud; we'd strut all over these mountains like we were kings. And he agreed we would some day. I'd fall asleep talking to this friend. See, that was the talking part. The wishing and the prayer came from hoping that, y'know, someday it wouldn't be a wall talking back to me. That someday there'd be another set of eyes looking at me, telling me those things, listening to me talk 'til I fell asleep. And I finally found it. It was always out there. I guess," he said with a smile, "I just had the 'him' part wrong. It's *you*, Eunice. And I'm not gonna let it go for your father or anybody else. I'm yours until you come to your senses -- hell, maybe even longer. And yeah, it is worth it."

"I don't know what to say."

"Then just kiss me," said Rodney.

And the owl went quiet.

ഇ

Molly Runningwolf was sitting on her front porch, rocking gently back and forth. The shotgun in her hands was barely noticeable in the moonlight. Her eyes shifted across the expanse of her yard, waiting and watching. She was only a little over forty, but she carried her years and all they had meant with the dignity and forbearance of one twice her age. She had lived day by day, for that was the only was she knew how to survive. She was not a pretty woman; handsome was a more accurate description. Each wrinkle she saw her face was like a familiar lyric. Each trip to the mirror reflected a story...some which ended happily, others just resolved.

She was nearly as famous around Qualla for her constantly smoldering old pipe as for her acid tongue. Molly was the mid-wife of a nation. She knew each family's history, good and bad. She knew who was old money and who was no money and which field harbored what illicit encounter. Her eyes and ears missed nothing, but her conscience allowed no divulgences. She was the most qualified source of gossip and yet the last Cherokee to engage in such talk. Her business was knowing, not telling. She could be a maddening presence. Even so, she was sought out by the community on issues great and small. It was well known that if you wanted the traditionals to go along with something, you had better have Molly in your corner. She was the bridge.

Tonight she was rocking. She was trying to forget the ache in her gut and the nagging lump in her cheek. The smell of whiskey still lingered in the air. She had promised him: she knew, and so did he. "One more time," she had said. One more sorry time...

There was a slight rustle in the trees to her right. Molly stopped dead still. Her finger caressed the gun's trigger. She shifted slightly so that she was facing the noise. Her movements were nearly fluid. The rustling came again.

Somebody definitely in them trees, she thought. The moon was drawing shadows now across the grass, an old artist reaching for inspiration. To Molly's eyes there looked to be two of them, maybe more. He's come back, she thought. Her finger tightened around the trigger.

"Lord," she prayed silently, "I hope you ain't gonna be too mad about this. But I ain't got a cheek left." Something flitted to the left of the trees. Molly paused -- better make sure.

"Back for more?" she called in Cherokee. Silence. "Vernon? You better answer me while you still can."

"Ma Runningwolf?" Molly lowered the gun. It wasn't Vernon, that was for sure, but she wasn't sure just who it was.

"Who's there?" she called, again in Cherokee. If whoever it was answered, she could breath a sigh of relief. If not...

"It's me, Ma Runningwolf -- Rodney." Molly placed the gun beside her and stood to get a closer look. Rodney emerged from the woods holding hands with a girl.

"Well, you almost got yourself shot," she called with mock irritation. "Sneaking around like some kind of injun." She laughed at her own joke. It was a raspy but pleasant sound. Rodney walked up to the porch steps with Eunice in tow. He was going to ask how she was doing, but before he could, he saw the deep purple on her cheek. Her bottom lip was swelling. Rodney jumped the last two steps and moved toward her. Molly was already seated again. Rodney knelt beside her. Eunice stood back respectfully, in the yard.

"What happened?" Rodney asked.

Molly laughed again.

"Well you know as well as if you'd been here y'self." She looked at Eunice. "Come here, darling, let me get a look at you. Don't worry, you can't catch a bruise." Eunice smiled nervously. The bruise was very deep.

"Eunice," Rodney said, "you're a nurse. Look at this. She o.k?"

Molly pulled away.

"Course I'm alright. It ain't the first time. I just need a little ice on it. Problem is I ain't got none. Oh," she said to Eunice, "it looks worse than it is." Rodney walked over and picked up the shotgun. He held it in front of Molly with a disapproving smirk.

"Goin' rabbit hunting, Ma Runningwolf?" he asked.

Molly didn't even blink.

"No," she answered, "I was gonna shoot the son of a bitch." Eunice blinked nervously. Molly was clearly not joking. "And I still might if I get the chance."

"Ma, you can't just..."

"Now, I'm tired of talking about this. It's an old story. But this," she said, waving her hand at Rodney and Eunice, "is a new one. Still got a few things to be written, I expect? Sit down and tell me all about it."

Rodney knew better than to argue with Molly. The discussion was closed and that was that. He sat down beside her and crossed his ankles. Eunice sat on the top step, resting her hands on her knees. A mountain breeze had kicked up, sending a shiver through her. Before either could protest -- before, in fact, either of them realized she had moved Molly was returning from the darkened house with an old blanket. She gently draped it across Eunice's shoulders.

"Thank you, ma'am," Eunice said.

"Now, honey, " Molly replied, "I ain't got enough money to be rightly called that. But you are a polite thing, aren't you?" Eunice blushed.

"Ma Runningwolf, this is Eunice." Molly slowly nodded her head as if to remind Rodney that she had known that before he did.

"Well, Eunice, it's a pleasure to meet you. I must say I've already heard quite a bit about you." Even in the pale moonlight, Eunice could see the wink that passed between Rodney and Mrs. Runningwolf. To know that Rodney had talked about her made her feel special.

"Rodney has spoken very highly of you, as well," Eunice answered. Molly looked from one to the other. She was sizing them up with her eyes and, more importantly, with her heart. Eunice and Rodney both shifted under the gaze.

"Yep," Molly said finally, "you both got it bad. It's good to see. Where you coming from?"

"We were down by the saw mill. Talking." Molly cackled again. Her laugh seemed to reverberate across the mountains. Eunice found herself thanking God that it was dark out, because she was blushing again. They *had* only talked, but even to her knowing ears, the truth sounded terribly implausible. Rodney said nothing.

"How's your father?" Molly asked Eunice.

"H-he's fine. Do you know my father?"

"Ma Runningwolf knows everyone on Qualla," Rodney corrected proudly.

"Well, almost," said Molly. "Yes, honey, I know your father. He's a fine man. A might proud, but a good man."

"Too proud," whispered Eunice.

"Lorenzo isn't too pleased about Eunice and me going together," Rodney offered. Molly leaned forward and placed her hand on his shoulder. Her voice dropped an octave.

"Then you just give him a reason to be pleased."

No one spoke for some time after Molly's invocation. Her advice sounded so final, so romantically perfect. But, thought Eunice, Molly didn't understand Lorenzo's resolve.

"Your father is a stubborn man," Molly said finally, as if she had been reading the young woman's mind.

"Yes; yes, he is. It's not so much that he doesn't like Rodney -- he doesn't even know him. He just wants what he feels is best for me, whether I agree or not."

Molly sighed. "You can't really hold that against him, either of you. A child is your creation, the only thing that you leave of any value in the world. We've all watched Lorenzo work hard all these years so you kids could have the best of everything. And now look what you've done," she said with a smile, "You've gone and fallen in love with a boy who doesn't appear to be heading anywhere. Rodney's trouble is that he's always felt the need to find his own way. He's suspicious of any trail that has tracks on it already. Tsalagi. Your father is no different."

Eunice leaned closer to Molly.

"Mrs. Runningwolf, do you think my father will leave me and Rodney alone?"

"Never," answered Molly, shaking her head vigorously. "But you have to turn his interference to something good. No parent will ever leave a child alone. We just can't. This world's too damn nasty to leave them to their own instincts. But you have come to *tsu du go ta nv*, and even your father cannot stand in the way of this. No man can." Eunice looked at Rodney. Molly had lost her.

"It is the place in life when you have to decide who will be with you...always." Eunice saw that Molly was smiling broadly and rocking again. Suddenly, there was a commotion from the woods. She heard the sound of singing: raucous tones drenched in alcohol. Eunice shuddered. Rodney stood up and moved into the yard.

"Well, here comes trouble," said Molly, reaching across her lap and picking up the shotgun. Eunice instinctively moved behind Molly. "You go on in the house, baby. Nothing for you here." Eunice quietly obeyed. She cracked her shin on a table that was sitting ridiculously close to the front door. Grimacing, she made her way to the window and gently drew back the curtain. She watched Rodney. Her heart pounded in her chest so violently that she thought it might shatter the glass.

Rodney stood in the yard facing the noise that drew ever closer. After a few minutes, Eunice could see two approaching figures. An older man, looking to be about fifty, staggered through the yard with a half-empty bottle in his drunken grip. Behind him, also staggering, came a familiar: Chiltos.

"Hey, fellas," mumbled Rodney. The older man looked at him inquisitively. Eunice noticed that Chiltos was glaring at Rodney with what appeared to be hatred.

"Norris, what the hell are you doing out here this time of night?" asked the old man.

"I was out for a walk. It's a nice night for one. I saw Molly sitting on the porch and stopped by to talk. Mr. Runningwolf, someone hit your wife tonight."

Mister, thought Eunice. Not Pa Runningwolf. There was clearly a different relationship between these two. The old man burst into laughter. A grin spread across Chiltos' face as well.

"Someone?! Weren't someone, kid. It was me! And if she keeps mouthing off, I'll do it again." Molly walked out into the yard and stood at Rodney's shoulder. She held the shotgun at her waist. She appeared itching to pull that trigger. The expressions on both drunks' faces changed from light-hearted fun to sheer terror. Mr. Runningwolf obviously had no trouble believing that his little wife would blow his brains out right there on the spot. Eunice held her breath.

"Norris, this here ain't none of your business. You just go on home and let me handle this."

"Handle what?" asked Molly loudly. The old man started to move closer to her, but she raised the gun and leveled it right at his breast.

"Mr. Runningwolf, I think maybe you should sleep it off somewhere else tonight. Don't you?"

The old man looked from his wife to Rodney and back again. The gun was still pointing at his heart.

"Look, baby, all I want right now in this world is my own bed. C'mon. You know it was just a misunderstanding. Don't you?"

"I know that 'misunderstanding' is still swelling on the side of my face, that's all I know. And I know your drunk ass ain't settin' foot in my house tonight."

Old Man Runningwolf moved towards his wife. The drink had encouraged him that he was nimble and quick enough to give his wife another wallop before she could pull the trigger. Molly was under no such illusion, and she no doubt would have dropped him on the spot had it not been for Rodney quickly stepping in between the two of them. The old man stopped and looked into his young challenger's eyes.

"This ain't none of your business, boy."

"This woman is my business, Mr. Runningwolf. Now, why don't you go sleep this off."

Eunice stared at Chiltos. He had reached his hand into his pocket. Eunice was ready to scream out a warning to Rodney. She knew that Chiltos had taken to carrying a hunting knife everywhere he went. As Mr. Runningwolf backed down, Chiltos' hand slowly emerged from the pocket without the blade. The old man turned to Chiltos.

"C'mon, Chil, let's get out of here. The bitch ain't worth it." Molly threw a curse at him, but he didn't turn. He was already heading back into the woods. Chiltos had not moved. He closed in on Rodney. The smell of liquor rolled off him like a fog.

"Me and you have business still," he said. "If my sister ain't home safe in bed when I get there, I'm coming back to cut your guts out." He turned and followed his friend into the darkness.

Rodney and Mrs. Runningwolf headed slowly back to the porch. Molly was shaking her head in utter contempt.

Eunice had heard the ominous parting shot that her brother had taken at Rodney. She felt cold all over; she understood that her brother, when tanked up, was more than capable of trying to kill Rodney. And it was all her fault. Rodney met her at the door of the house.

"Easy, Eunice, it's over," he said, taking her into his arms.

"It is *not* alright, Rodney. Didn't you hear what he said? I've got to get home right now."

"Well, I'm going with you. You are not walking in those woods alone. Not tonight."

"No, Rodney. You should stay here with Mrs. Runningwolf. That man may come back here tonight."

"I can handle that sack of taters," Molly remarked. Rodney's face took on a pained expression. Eunice could see that he knew she was right. He couldn't leave Molly tonight; he did not want Eunice taking to those woods without him, not after what had just happened. Eunice took his hand.

"Honey, I've shot through those trees many times. I could get home with my eyes closed. Please, stay here with her."

"You stay," he said. Eunice shook her head.

"You know I can't do that," she said.

"I didn't mean *that*." Rodney protested, "You could stay with Ma Runningwolf. I'll sleep here on the porch. Wouldn't be the first time." He smiled at her,

and she thought he had never looked so perfect before. So valiant. Eunice wanted desperately to stay, to fall asleep in his protecting arms. They could shield each other from all this madness, all this sadness.

"I can't. That would destroy everything. You know it."

"Please be careful." He hugged her close to him. Leaving that embrace seemed the hardest thing Eunice had ever done. She leapt down from the porch and headed to the path that would lead her home. She heard Molly's voice float out to her:

"Come back and see me, honey."

"I will," she called back over her shoulder.

"I love you, Eunice."

She stopped for just a second and looked over her shoulder. Rodney stood with his hand raised in the air. Molly had her hand on his shoulder. Eunice walked back to the edge of the yard.

"I love you, too," she called. Then she turned and darted into the trees. She had to beat Chiltos home.

Molly walked into the house and felt around for the matches. She lit a lantern and placed it above the fireplace. It glowed eerily throughout the room. Rodney was still standing on the porch, staring after Eunice.

"Staring ain't gonna put wings on them feet," she said. Rodney sulked into the house and sank into a wooden chair setting by the door. He slowly leaned over and removed his boots. He propped his feet onto the table that had cracked Eunice's shin.

"Ma Runningwolf, I hope I'm doing the right thing."

"She'll get home fine, son," she said.

"That's not what I mean. I hope...I just want to make her happy. But I seem to be making nothing but trouble for her. That's not what I want. Do you think...."

"No I don't. Rodney, could you be happy without her?" Rodney thought for a minute. Finally he looked up at her, directly into her eyes.

"Ma, I can't breathe without her."

"*A ne lv to di,*" she said as the lantern light flickered and danced behind her head. "Make a way, child, make a way." She closed her eyes and began to rock again.

CHAPTER SEVEN

The weeks had passed with a speed that was brand new to Eunice. Since that night at Mrs. Runningwolf's she and Rodney had begun to see each other every free minute that they had. Their circle had come to now include Ma Runningwolf, who had begun to give them shelter from the searching eyes that seemed to lurk in every corner of the reservation. When the spring rains came charging over the mountains they would quickly head to her home. The three of them would sit around the kitchen, munching on dumplings and fry bread and saving the world's blackened soul. Molly would spend hours lecturing them about their people's proud traditions. She would light her pipe and pass it around the room, demanding that the young lovers each take deep draws of the smoke. Eunice was not particularly fond of the burning it caused in her throat, but she was not about to offend the venerable Mrs. Runningwolf. Molly laughed at the way her young friend's eyes would tear up each time the pipe passed by her nose.

"You'll get used to it," she counseled. She claimed that the pipe could cure any ailment that an Indian had. It didn't work for the white folks, she postulated, simply because they didn't believe.

After these dinner/religious times, Molly would always excuse herself into the backroom. She claimed at various times that she needed a nap (which was always a suspect reason since she never appeared to tire or give out) or that she wanted to read her bible. Eunice had thought this also a poor ruse since Mrs. Runningwolf couldn't read a word of English. It wasn't until Molly proudly showed her the bible, written entirely in Cherokee, that Eunice knew it was more than just an excuse.

When Molly retired, Eunice and Rodney would walk around the yard, sit on the porch, or just linger in the sweet smelling kitchen and talk about their future. That misty time that they could only dream of when they would be sitting in their own kitchen by their own fireplace.

The couple no longer felt the need to couch their discussions in vague notions of "someday" of "if." They no longer pretended that they could live even a moment without each other. They had comfortably moved from the realm of spinning dreams to the world of making plans. Only occasionally did they even worry about obstacles. Molly had assured them that the Great Spirit walked with them always, and they believed her.

The word "marriage" had begun to crop up in their conversations. At first, it was spoken almost in jest, each trying to feel the other out. But it was soon apparent that they both wanted to be with each other for the rest of their lives, and soon the word was spoken with a quiet solemnity. It began to take on a religious flavor, a soulful taste in their mouths. They began to discuss the ceremony itself. Rodney wanted it to be a traditional Cherokee wedding. He was insistent that they not began their lives together cramped in the four walls of a local church. He reminded Eunice that he had no love for the Christians of the reservation. They were the same people who had washed his mouth out with soap and blistered his backside because he refused to be ashamed of his history. He would not allow them to lord over his newfound happiness. Eunice, on the other hand, had always dreamed of a fine church wedding. She had grown up in church. Like so many other local Indians, she had managed to incorporate Christianity into her own Cherokee outlook. Her father had always taught her that that was the only way for an Indian to survive these days. But with Rodney there was no compromise. He believed in Christ, he told her many times, but he *did not* believe in his followers. And he felt that allowing those people to perform their marriage ceremony was a concession that, if only in its own symbolic value, would cast a shadow over their entire life together. No, they were Indians and must be married as such. Rather than fight about it, Eunice tended to avoid the topic as much as she could. If Rodney wanted to be married outside of the church, she would allow that. But he would have to allow her God to be included. Period.

For his part, Rodney had begun to do everything he could to make their dreams a reality. He had started work with the railroad and, although it was labor that any half-wit could
have accomplished, he threw himself into it with everything he had. His temper was as volatile as ever, but he managed to control it. He didn't deck the foreman when he called out, "Hey, chief, let's step it up a little, huh?" He quietly ate his lunch as the good folks from Whittier called out clever names at him. He tried to ignore the gender-bending

jokes about his hair. Any other time, he knew, he would have already lost his job and probably ended up in a jail cell for his troubles, but the money was good for the area, and that was helping get him ever closer to making Eunice Mrs. Rodney Norris. It was the first time in his life that he had felt so purposeful, so immune to the painful jabs of the whites. "Call me what you want," he thought to himself, "I'm in love." And the object of his desire was a woman that all these white-trash men would have died for, and that none could now have. It was, he thought, the only time in his life that he had obtained something the white man could not have and could not take. It was a feeling of power he had never before experienced.

In Whittier he had found the ring that he was going to give Eunice to make their engagement official. It cost well over a hundred dollars, a figure that made it seem totally safe from brown hands. The owner of the store had ran Rodney off at gunpoint when he tried to get a closer look, accusing him of surveying the store for a future robbery. Rodney resigned himself to staring at the shiny stone from across the street, thinking how good it would feel to walk into the store with a fist full of new money and buy that ring away from the white man. Just thought of the shocked look that would undoubtedly envelope the man's face caused Rodney to laugh out loud. Ma Runningwolf cautioned him to be careful. Those folks across the tracks were not to be toyed with, she said. But Rodney understood the way the outside world worked, if he had the money there was nothing the white man would say to him. Bringing that look to the man's face became a dream inside a dream for him.

Of course, working on the railroad would not bring him enough cash in a year to buy that ring. He decided to supplement his income the way he had since he was thirteen--he ran moonshine onto the reservation. This had to be done with the utmost caution. It was illegal in North Carolina to sell alcohol to an Indian. Even the breeds couldn't legally obtain it. But they were willing to pay good money to get their hands on it, and Rodney had learned the art of supply and demand a long time ago. Each Thursday night Mike Howell, a quarter-blood who now lived in Whittier, picked up several cases of good corn liquor from a friend in town. He would stash the goods in a tool shack at the depot. Around midnight Rodney and his cousin Lynn would cross the Qualla Boundary and place the booze in old hunting sacks. If they were ever stopped they would tell the officer that they were bringing back game. They always stuffed a newly killed squirrel in the top of the sack.

Rodney understood that this would not stand up to close inspection, but many of the police were themselves making a killing off of the trade, so he hoped they would only face perfunctory questioning. After filling the sacks they stealthily crept back onto the reservation, stashing the liquor in the woods near the Runningwolf cabin. Then, from one in the morning until three or four, Rodney and Lynn made house calls to their customers. It was safer this way, keeping the number of people who knew their hideouts and bases of operation to an absolute minimum. In those few hours, the smugglers could make more than in two weeks of railroad work. It may not be honest work, thought Rodney, but it was necessary.

Rodney did not concern himself much with the law. Everyone on Qualla understood that they were usually supplementing their meager income with liquor trade as well. He was, however, very concerned and careful that Eunice not find out what he was up to. She had made no secret of her bitter hatred for alcohol and what she saw it doing to their people. Since their relationship began, Rodney himself had been reduced to only occasionally sneaking a swig while delivering the goods to a customer. She was a tee-totaler, and had she known what her boyfriend was doing Rodney believed there was a good chance she would never have spoken to him again. It would make no difference to her that he was doing it for her. That ring would mean nothing to her if it had been obtained through what she often called "blood money." Truth be told, the extravagance of the Whittier diamond meant more to Rodney than it would to Eunice. He saw it as a chance to show her father and the rest of the reservation that he could and would provide the best for her. He knew that Eunice was not interested in such things. But he believed those beautiful hands should only have the best their little world had to offer, and if this was the only way he could provide it then so be it.

Ma Runningwolf, again with her ear firmly placed to the moccasin telegraph had asked him recently if the rumors were true, that he had become a main source of "trouble" on Qualla. Rodney had told her that, yes, he was bringing in liquor once in a while, but what the Indians did with themselves after he left their property was not his fault.

"Do you think Eunice will see it that way?" she had asked. Before he could attempt further excuses she was out in the yard, pulling weeds. Conversation over, Rodney thought. But Ma Runningwolf had not said anything to Eunice. Instead, she applied a steady pressure to his own conscience every time she saw the chance.

"You can't serve two masters, Rodney," she had told him. "You can not be Tsalagi and at the same time destroy all that that means."

Rodney had promised her that as soon as he had enough money to support Eunice he would turn the trade over to his cousin for good. As soon as the ring was on Eunice's hand he would give up the smuggling forever. Molly made him smoke on it, and she never said another word.

With every Thursday that passed Rodney came closer to the dream of the ring. He stuffed every denomination of bill imaginable into his tattered mattress, keeping a careful count of each one. He slept on the cash, dreaming of the life that it would make possible. Soon, there was enough. He would stay out of work that day and ride proudly into Whittier with his pockets full of money. He borrowed Ma Runningwolf's old mare and drove his heels into the side, his heart racing with excitement.

Whittier meant diamonds, and diamonds are forever.

CHAPTER EIGHT

There was no moon. The sky was filled with clouds that raced across the sky as if to make a previous engagement. The wind blew crisply across the valley; it was a lukewarm wind that made Molly Runningwolf's bones ache. She sat out on her front porch, alone as usual. Her husband was on another one of his binges. He would stagger home once in a while to sleep off the pain of his stomach ulcer and beg his wife's forgiveness and care. She never turned him away, and she hadn't yet shot him. He had seen that look in her eyes and knew she meant business. He had managed to keep his hands to himself and his verbal jabs became more and more pathetic as the days wore on. She rolled herself a cigarette and lit up. The tip stood out against the still darkness. Tonight she was not thinking of her husband. Her thoughts on this night were drifting out into the wooded darkness around her. Somewhere out there the young man that she had practically raised was taking the most important step of his young life. He was about to choose the woman that would be his partner, the woman that would give him a family and a future. The thought made Molly smile. She could not have been happier with Rodney's choice, even it was a controversial one. But controversy did not concern her. The Great Spirit had told her that the young couple would be together and she never questioned the wisdom of her Heavenly father. That was for fools, and Molly Runningwolf, as anybody could tell you, was no fool.

Molly thought of Lorenzo. She had known him for a long time, longer than Rodney or Eunice could imagine. She had seen him as a young man, hurrying along somewhere, trying to make a name for himself. He had been known for his temper and his indulgences, which was why the decision he himself had made was so surprising. No one had believed him possible of being a man of forgiveness. But he had, probably completely against his nature, sacrificed much for love. And he had paid for it over the course of twenty odd years. And now, even as he tried to hide it daily, everyone knew that there was a tender side to the man. He could deny it in words, but he confirmed it in deed with every passing year. Down deep, maybe way down, Lorenzo was a good man with a deep weakness--his family.

When Lorenzo looked at Rodney Norris, Molly surmised, he saw himself. A younger but no more vital version of the man he had been. Rodney had developed a taste for alcohol at a young age, as had Lorenzo. Rodney had an almost mythical temper that could explode at the drop of a hat, as had Lorenzo. Most importantly, both men were outsiders who were consumed with a desire to serve notice on their fellow men that they were important, even indispensable, to the world around them. Both men probably surprised themselves with their devotion to the Cherokee Nation. Lorenzo Dow had money, but not nearly as much as he would have had if didn't constantly give it away to needy Indians around him. Rodney, although with considerably less resources, was also a charitable influence on Qualla. But their similarities only drove a generational wedge between them that both men, in their stubbornness, saw as intractable. Lorenzo did not want his daughter with a man like he had been, he wanted her with a man like he had become. That was, after all, why he had worked so hard.

Still, Molly was enough of a romantic, even after all that she had seen, to believe that Lorenzo would come around. She believed that once the love was brought out from under the bushel he would have no choice. The air was filled with love when Rodney and Eunice came around. There was a sweet spirit that seemed to follow them around. It was in her eyes, in his smile. Words and thoughts were passed between them that no one else would ever know, they only felt fortunate to be included in the secretive process.

Molly stubbed out the cigarette and closed her eyes in silent prayer.

ಝ

Rodney and Eunice were sitting on the bank of the river talking about their day. Eunice had noticed that something was different with Rodney tonight. He had seemed preoccupied since she had first seen him. He was fidgety, more restless than usual. When she asked him what was troubling him, he had evaded her. Her mind told her that her father had done something, had somehow gotten to him. Or maybe there was a problem at work. It was a side of Rodney that she had never seen before and did not particularly like. With each moment that passed without his confiding in her she became more and more convinced that she had done something to hurt him somehow. On any other night like this they would have been talking as though it was their last moments on earth together, but tonight Rodney just stared absently into the black water. Finally, her patience gave way to her pressing fear.

"Rodney," she asked, "what's wrong with you tonight? Why aren't you talking?"

Rodney cleared his throat. Eunice noticed that his hands were trembling and his voice seemed to come from far off somewhere.

"Well, Eunice," he answered, "there is something I was wanting to talk to you about. It's pretty important." Eunice felt all the water drain from her mouth and run straight to her hands. She wiped them off on the hem of her dress and tried to speak.

"He's breaking up with me," she thought. "The pressure's just too much and he's decided that I'm not worth it." A red fury raged through her. Her insides were suddenly on fire against her father. She wondered what he had said to shake Rodney so.

"W-what is it, Rodney?" she asked. Her voice sounded weak and pathetic in her ears.

Rodney heard the trepidation in her voice as well. His heart seemed to skip a beat in his chest. His lungs tightened up, causing his breath to become labored. It felt worse than the first time he had taken a drag on a cigarette. In her wavering voice he heard a deadly skepticism. She knew what he was going to ask, Rodney thought. What else could she be thinking? They had been talking marriage for weeks now. When he said that he had something important to talk with her about, she must know what was coming. And her voice sounded like someone who was filled to the brim with dread. Oh, God, this is going to be so terribly embarrassing, he thought. There were plenty of people on the reservation who could tell her some story about when he had stumbled drunk onto their lawn or just evaded their buckshot as he nabbed a chicken or hog for his dinner. What girl would want to be married to someone with a reputation like that? But Eunice--prim, proper, religious Eunice--would not want to marry that kind of person. Great, Rodney told himself, she had waited to come to her senses after he had battled to get this damn ring. He decided that after she said no he would give the ring to Ma Runningwolf.

Eunice was wiping her hands on her dress. She looked positively miserable. Rodney was reminded what a tremendous young woman she was that she would dread saying no to a loser like him. She was too kind, he thought. He determined to make this as painless as possible for her.

"Well," he started, "I don't much think you're gonna like what I wanna say."

Eunice felt the tears. There was no controlling them. She made no sound at all, but they were visibly rolling down her cheeks. She realized that, even in a life marked by separation, she had never felt more lonely. Not ever. Rodney's hand was on hers now. He looked like he was dying. Well, she thought, at least it wasn't easy for him.

"Aw, Eunice, please don't cry. You know I hate it when you cry, and I'm just ...well, you know I'm just not worth it."

Easy for him to say, she thought.

"Rodney, please just say what it is that you brought me here to say."

Rodney pulled his hand away and reached into his pocket. He fumbled for a minute, trying to decide if the ring would make it harder for her to say no. He really did want to spare her pain. Finally he pulled the box out and cupped it in his hands. In the moonless night Eunice could not see what he was holding.

"Well, Eunice," he said, drawing in sharp, painful breaths, "we've spent a lot of time together lately. And I've enjoyed it, I really have. Fact is it's been the best time of my life. You and me, we've known each other practically forever, only we didn't really know each other 'til just lately. You bring out the best in me, see, and I feel really good when we're together and, well, ah, shit I don't know what I'm saying. I'm not good at this."

Eunice had stopped crying. She was going to be brave so that he didn't feel too bad about it all.

"It's o.k., Rodney," she assured him, "you're doing fine."

"You see?" he said, his voice rising. "That's just what I mean. I'm not doing fine at all only you're telling me that I am. It's like you know that I wanna say something great only I can't. So I fumble around like a chicken with it's head cut off, jabbering about and you hear, you hear..."

"Poetry," Eunice said. Rodney looked at her carefully. He stood up and took her hand, pulling her up as well. Eunice stared at her feet.

"If I look at him," she thought, "I'll just die."

"Eunice?" She looked up, into his eyes. She could be wrong, but she could've sworn they were misty. "You answer this however you want. You do what's best for you. But I'm bound to ask. Alright?"

"Alright, Rodney," she said with confusion. He was suddenly down on his knees. Eunice's heart began to pound within her. Could he be?

"Eunice I know that you come from good people. And I know that I ain't always been so good myself. But you've always seemed to see past that. You see the man I wanna be, not who I was. And I love you for that, Eunice. Now, you say that that bible of yours teaches that love ain't selfish, so maybe what I'm doing ain't love afterall. 'Cause I'm doing this because I don't ever wanna be without you. 'Cause I don't know what I'd do without you. The part that ain't selfish is that, well, even though it's gonna take some time, I promise that I am gonna be that man you think I can be. I WILL. And I promise to be true to you. I ain't never even gonna look at nobody else. Why would I? Anyway, that's what I'm promising. That's what I wanted to say."

"Well," said Eunice, "I believe in everything you said. I know you're gonna be something big because you're already somebody special. I hope I'm there with you when it happens."

Rodney suddenly realized that he had not asked her to marry him. He was still on his knees and Eunice seemed awfully confused. Rodney shook his head and laughed.

"Honey, I ain't quite finished."

"Oh?"

Rodney opened his clenched fist to reveal the box he was holding. With hands shaking he opened it up. In the darkness Eunice couldn't see exactly what it was, but she had recognized the motions, she thought.

"Eunice Swayney, I love you. Will you marry me?"

With no thought of propriety Eunice was on her knees in front of him, her arms flung around his neck. Now she was crying and making plenty of noise to boot. In the rush she had knocked the box from his hand. She was kissing his neck and face as though she had just discovered that they could be kissed.

"Well," Rodney asked, laughing, "is that a 'yes.'"

"OH God, yes!" she said. And then, jumping back to her feet and yelling, "YES, YES, YES, YES!!!!!!! I AM GOING TO BE MRS. RODNEY NORRIS! YES, YES!!!" She was twirling herself around, weightless in the mountain air. When she stopped, she saw that Rodney was still on his knees, pawing at the grass in front of him.

"What on earth are you doing?" she asked, slightly offended that he had not rejoiced with her.

"Well, Mrs. Norris," he said, cocking his head towards her, "I'm looking for the ring that you knocked out of my hand."

Giggling, Eunice quickly joined in the search.

ೞ

Eunice got her first real look at her engagement ring in Molly Runningwolf's parlor. The lantern light flickered off the diamond, sending dancing streams of light reflecting across the wooden floor. It was breathtaking, she thought. And it was certainly more than she had ever expected. It must have cost Rodney a fortune.

Molly had whistled through clenched teeth at the rock. It was beautiful, she agreed, just like the woman that was going to wear it for the rest of her life. Molly had then patted Rodney on the head as if he were no more than five or six years old and excused herself from the room. In the short time that Eunice had known her, she had never seen her look so proud. Rodney walked over to the rocker and virtually collapsed into it. The strain of the evening had been too much for him. Eunice walked over and sat by his feet, resting her chin on his knee. He gently stroked her dark hair. He still couldn't believe that she had said yes to him. He kept waiting to wake from the dream.

"Rodney," Eunice said, after some quiet, "this must have cost you so much, are you sure you, I mean WE can afford it?" The correction sounded so good in her mind that she almost fogot what the actual question had been.

"I'm sure, honey. It's paid for." Eunice turned to look at him.

"But how? Where did you get the money for a ring this beautiful?" Rodney rubbed his chin, thinking. Eunice cocked her head, waiting for his answer.

"Now Eunice I promised that I would never lie to you, and I ain't about to start just now. So how about not asking me that question, huh? I know that you wouldn't approve of how I came to that money, and I don't want no clouds darkening that ring tonight. You could say that I kinda took a short-cut this time so that I could get you that ring. Someday I won't have to do that to get you the best, but that's just the way things are right now. But I don't want that to change the way you feel about the ring. It still stands just as much for how much I love you as it would have if I'd worked two years for it. And this way," he said, smiling slyly, "we ain't got to wait two years."

Eunice attempted a look of mock displeasure but just couldn't keep from smiling.

"Nothing could change the way I feel about this ring, Rodney. And I'm never going to take it off."

Rodney laughed. "Well, I reckon you'll have to, at least for a little bit."

"Why?"

"'Cause we can't have Lorenzo seeing it. Right?"

"Wrong." Eunice stared into the lantern. "My father has to know. I will not cheapen this moment by lying, I'm telling him just as soon as I get home. Even if I have to get him and Mama out of bed." Rodney leaned up and kissed her on the cheek.

"Then I should be there with you," he said.

Eunice shook her head. "No, I have to do this by myself, honey. That's the best way. I don't want daddy feeling ambushed."

"I guess you're right. But are you sure you don't wanna wait?"

"The longer he doesn't know the longer before we can get married. And I don't want to wait any more for that, do you?"

"No."

Eunice stood and gave Rodney a tender kiss on his cheek. She looked back at the ring.

"I love you, kid," Rodney said.

"I love you. Now walk me home, please."

Rodney sighed.

"Here we go," he said.

As soon as she heard the screen door slam Molly Runningwolf began praying harder than she had ever prayed before.

"Lord," she called, "only you can open old eyes to young love. Lorenzo's heart ain't as hard as some say, God, you just make sure he knows that. I'll sure appreciate it."

Quietly, she opened her Bible and began to read.

CHAPTER NINE

It had not been a restful night for Eunice. When she had kissed Rodney goodnight her resolve had been rock-solid and unwavering. But as she tip-toed into the house and heard her father's pacing footsteps in the study she lost all her nerve. She decided to get a good night's sleep first, then she would tell her father about the engagement. After all, she would need to be as sharp as possible for the impending battle. Her goal was not rebellion, it was acceptance. She was going to marry Rodney Norris no matter what, but she knew that it would mean so much more to her if her father gave her away. She wanted the whole family there. She wanted to be presented as the new Mr. and Mrs. Rodney Norris to all the Swayneys. She wanted to look down from the altar and see her proud parents holding hands, smiling approvingly. She knew the depth of her love and of her conviction, and she believed that her father would have to see them in her eyes. Dora had.

She lay in bed, gently stroking the band of the ring with her thumb. She tossed and turned, wrapped in a blanket woven with the greatest happiness and the most torturous fear she had ever known. To Eunice it seemed like the whites who asked God for rain and then cursed the thunder. One could not usually have it both ways, she thought. Life was too often about choices. Freedom or slavery. Independence or chains. Heart or mind. Loyalty or devotion. Spirit or religion.

If she failed to win over her father, would that mean that she lost her mother's blessing as well? Would her mother dare stand against Lorenzo on this issue? She prayed softly. The beginning of one family should not be the end of another, she thought. And it didn't have to be.

She thought about the things she had been taught in church. "Honor thy Father and Mother," they said. But what if honoring one's parents meant turning your back on all you knew to be right and honorable? That couldn't be God's will, could it? And didn't they also say that a man should forsake his parents for his wife? Well, what about the wife? Was she allowed to forsake as well, or was this, like so many other things in the white's religion, the sole domain of the man? And how could a loving God ask someone to choose between the two? Eunice's love for Rodney had not usurped any of her love for her father and mother. It couldn't, because it was a totally different kind of love.

Or maybe Rodney was right. Maybe, when you got right down to it, love was an essentially selfish act. After all, you didn't love a person that you pitied, at least not in a romantic way. And you couldn't fall in love with someone just because that person was lonely and needed to be loved. No, love came when you met someone that complimented you, someone who completed the circle for you and with you. Love could not blossom in the dirt of responsibility. It was about passion, desire, and those were both selfish traits that had one's own needs in mind. Eunice couldn't love someone because she should. She was selfish enough to actually want happiness, and Rodney delivered in spades.

She called on God again, but apparently He wasn't home just then. No feeling of peace or assurance came over her. She remembered the time, many years back, that she had asked her mother how she had known that Lorenzo was the one. Her mother, in her way, had tried to brush the question away but Eunice had persisted.

"First we were friends," Cora had answered. "Then we weren't. That's how I knew."

"Mama, that makes no sense. What do you mean, then you weren't? Did you have a fight?"

"Oh, no, child. We just weren't friends anymore. With a friend, its a nice surprise if they show up unexpected. When people aren't friends, they way me and Lorenzo weren't, its a disaster if they don't. That's when you know."

That was all her mother would say about it. Only recently had Eunice known what her mother had meant. She and Rodney were no longer friends, either. It went much deeper than that now. Eunice found herself clinging to the hope that, since Lorenzo had known this feeling, he would not try to crush it in his child. When she finally fell asleep the sun was starting to peek over the horizon, winking at the world as if he already knew the punch line.

"Eunice, you gonna get up today?" It was her mother.
"Child you have got to stop staying out so late all by yourself. That river ain't no place for a girl to be alone. 'Sides, you know how people do love to talk."

Eunice blinked away the sleep. As she removed her hand from under her pillow she felt a snag and remembered. She was engaged! Cora was looking intently at her daughter.

"Are you feeling poorly, Eunice?"

"No, Mama, I feel fine. Just overly tired I guess."

Cora looked at her daughter in the morning light, struck by how much she resembled a younger version of herself. She stood to walk out of the room and allow Eunice some privacy while she dressed.

"Mama?"

Cora turned and saw that Eunice was holding out her hand, limp wristed. At first she didn't understand, then the sparkle hit her eye like a flash of heat lightening. She moved closer to confirm the apparition.

"Oh, Eunice," was all that she could say. Eunice sat up straight in the bed.

"Isn't it beautiful, Mama?"

"Yes it is, Eunice. Where'd you get it?" Cora was hoping there was a logical explanation.

"Rodney gave it to me last night. He asked me to marry him."

"And?"

"And I said 'yes.'"

"Oh, Eunice." Cora sat back down on the bed, shaking her head. Lorenzo was going to be furious.

"Mama, can't you be happy for me? Please? I love him and he loves me. Isn't that what marriage is all about?"

"Yeah, for the first three weeks. Then its about compromise and damn hard work."

Eunice laughed at her mother. "Well, you and Daddy have had four kids so I guess it isn't all bad." Cora blushed.

"Eunice, you watch that talk."

Eunice reached out and took her mother's hand.

"Mama, I am so happy. Please let me be. I have never felt like this before, not ever. And you'll like him mama, I just know that you will. He's nothing like those old men make him out to be. He's kind and gentle and just a wonderful all around person."

"Eunice, are you sure? This is a very, very big step."

"I'm sure, mama. More sure than I've ever been about anything."

Cora smiled. Eunice had seen that smile many times, in fact she saw it every time she looked in the mirror. Even in the happiest of times it was a smile without mirth, a sad turning up of the edges of the mouth that lit up a room and melted the heart of the hardest cynic. She took Eunice's hand.

"Then I'm happy for you, Eunice. Very happy."

"Will you help me with Daddy?"

Cora's face darkened. Her smile vanished and was replaced by a look of profound fatigue.

"It's gonna take a force more powerful than me to help you there, child. Lorenzo is dead set against this and I think you know that."

"Has he said something to you, Mama?"

"No, he wouldn't talk to me about it. But I have spoken to Dotie and I know that he has talked some with her about it. He has his mind already made up and that's gonna be hard to change. You know how he is."

"Yes, I do," Eunice agreed. "Mama, I don't want to have to choose between my father and my husband, but if I have to I will choose Rodney. You have to know that."

Cora said nothing.

"You don't think Daddy will make me choose, do you?"

"Eunice, I think you better be ready for anything. Lorenzo is not used to losing in a battle of wills."

"Will you help me, Mama? Will you talk to him for me?"

Cora rose from the bed and walked to the window, glancing across the yard.

"I'm afraid I would do your cause more harm than good, Eunice. Lorenzo blames me for all of this. Like everybody else on this reservation he thinks this is just the chickens coming home to roost."

Eunice walked over to her mother and put her arms around her.

"I don't want to hurt you any more Mama. I hope you know that."

"Of course I do, Eunice. You've always been a perfect daughter. I couldn't have been more blessed. But you don't worry about me now. I been living with this for a long time and I know good and well how to handle it. You have other things to concern yourself with."

As if on cue, they heard the front door close and Lorenzo's footsteps in the kitchen. They both laughed nervously.

"I will do any and everything I can for you, dear," Cora said. "But if it don't work out they way you want, just remember I love you. And so does he. It might just be awhile before he can show you that. Now I think we better go in the kitchen."

Eunice nodded her assent. They walked out of the bedroom together.

ෲ

Lorenzo was pouring himself a cup of coffee. He sat down at the table and lit a cigarette. The house was had that Saturday morning stillness that comes with older children. The coming of the sun meant an opportunity for them to primp and play with friends in town. Chiltos would be deciding what kind of trouble to get into when the sun went back down. Grace and Dotie would be comparing notes on the cutest eligible boys on the reservation, fighting over who should rightfully marry whom. And Eunice was almost certainly up at Mrs. Runningwolf's waiting for that Norris boy to show up. Lorenzo liked Molly, he always had. But he didn't want his daughter up there and he was bound to tell her that soon. First of all, everyone on Qualla understood that Mr. Runningwolf was too volatile and dangerous- - sober or dead drunk. And the same could be said for her so- called boyfriend.

Lorenzo had come to love these mid-morning times. It gave him and Cora a chance to be together alone, something they hadn't experienced in years. Cora usually protested that she had washing or some essential chore to do, but Lorenzo could still charm his wife. There was no lock on the door of their cabin, so they enjoyed the added sensation of feeling as though they were doing something dangerous. Teenagers added a sense of adventure to their parents lives in more ways than they probably knew! Lorenzo began to gulp his coffee now. He heard rustling in one of the back bedrooms. Cora was still a beautiful woman. All her enemies that had hoped four children would diminish her sweetheart figure had been terribly disappointed. She could hold her own with any of the young women around, Lorenzo thought. He stubbed out his cigarette and decided to go see what she was doing. He straightened himself up. She could still make him as nervous as a schoolboy. He smiled. As he entered the hall, he was surprised to see both Cora and Eunice walking towards him. He cursed his luck under his breath.

"Morning, honey," Cora said.

"Morning, Daddy."

"Well, what are my two favorite girls up to this morning?" he asked as he kissed Cora. He noticed the way the two of them looked at each other when he asked the question. "Well? What is it?"

"Lorenzo, Eunice has something she would like to tell you. Let's go in the kitchen and I'll make us all some coffee."

"I already had some," he said testily. Lorenzo was beginning to smell trouble.

"Well, let's go in the kitchen anyway."

As they walked into the kitchen the door swung open again.

Grace and Chiltos walked in, giggling about some mischief they had just gotten into. Eunice shot her mother a beggar's glance- -she did not want to have to do this in front of the whole family. Cora took both of her children by the elbow and gently led them back onto the porch. They were about to have an adult's conversation and she would appreciate it if they could stay outside for a few more minutes. Chiltos claimed he was an adult and should be allowed to take part, but his mother shooed him into the yard. She walked back into the house while Grace and her brother began debating what was going on.

Cora walked into a kitchen filled with the silence that precedes a family spat. Lorenzo was staring at his daughter with a look that seemed destined to burn a hole right through the young woman's soul. Eunice was staring at the cup rings that stood like ancient messages on the table top. Her hands were folded neatly under the table. Cora took a seat between the two of them. There was no need for any more pretense; she asked no one of they wanted any coffee.

"Well, what is it Eunice?" asked Lorenzo. Eunice couldn't look up from the table, her neck felt frozen in place. She was filled with a fear that just looking at her father would undo everything that had happened to her in the past few months.

"Eunice?" She heard her mother's voice, but it seemed to be coming from behind an oak door. All she could feel was her father's stare, piercing her, daring her to say what she had to say.

"Well, I ain't got all day, Eunice," Lorenzo said. "If you have something to say to me then I suggest that you say it."

Knowing full well that her voice was not going to work, Eunice simply forced her hand up from underneath the table and placed it directly in front of her father. Finally, she looked up and at her mother for support. Cora nodded.

"It's all right," her look seemed to say, "you can do this."

Lorenzo pulled out another cigarette and calmly lit it.

"What the hell is that?" he asked.

"Daddy, Rodney asked me to marry him last night and I said yes. This is my engagement ring."

Lorenzo carefully stubbed out the cigarette. "Well, Eunice, you can just as easily give it back. And that's just what you're going to do."

Eunice took a deep breath. "No, Daddy, I'm not. When I said yes, that's just what I meant. We're in love and we're..."

"What do you know about love?" he asked.

"I know enough to know that I'm in it, and..."

"Eunice I am not going to have this discussion with you. You are going to give that ring back to that hoodlum and that's all there is to it."

"Don't you dare call him that. He is no more a hoodlum than your own son."

Lorenzo's eyes seemed to ice over. His brow became a storm front as his jaw tightened. He rubbed his hand over his chin, as if in thought.

"Look, Daddy," Eunice continued, "I didn't mean that. It's just that..."

"You never talked to me like that before you met Norris." He looked directly into Eunice's eyes now: "I thought love was supposed to bring out the best in people. It appears to have you acting like a spoiled tramp."

"Lorenzo!" Cora was protesting. This was getting out of hand entirely too fast. Eunice stood from the table and walked to the kitchen counter, her back to her parents. Lorenzo was refusing to look at either of the women.

"I am sorry that you feel that way, Daddy. I have done nothing to shame you or my mother or myself. If Rodney and I have been sneaking around to see each other it is because you never gave him a chance. You sent Dotie to break us up before you even took the time to meet him. And apparently you would take the word over the little-minded fools around here over your own daughter."

"Eunice I know his kind. I know what they're like. He may talk of wonderful things to you, but he's nothing but trouble. And how in the world did that boy afford that ring? You know he stole it, the police are probably looking for him right now."

Eunice whirled to face her father. "He did not steal this ring, Daddy."

"Now that's quite enough you two," said Cora, trying to calm things down. "We need to all just sit down and talk about this thing like decent folk." But Lorenzo was hearing nothing. He walked up to Eunice.

"I am only going to say this to you once. I am not going to allow you to make this mistake. I know all about this Rodney Norris. He's a drunk, he's a thief. He's uneducated and he has no future. He will not be allowed into my family. Do you understand?"

Eunice had found her resolve again. She looked into her father's eyes. I love you, too, she thought. But if you make me choose....

"I am not asking for your permission Daddy. I am telling you that I am going to marry Rodney and I am hoping that you will be a part of our lives. But the choice is yours."

"There will be no choice. You will not marry that trash..."

"Stop calling him names!" Eunice yelled.

Lorenzo raised his voice over hers. "You will not marry that dirty little bastard as long as..."

"Stop calling him names I said!"

"Do you hear me, Eunice?" Lorenzo yelled back. Cora rose from the table. "That boy is nothing! Nothing! He's trash, just like..."

"Stop it! Do you hear me? I said stop it? Stop calling him those things. What right do you have..."

"Right?! I have every right to keep you away from that dirty skunk because I am your father."

"YEAH?! THEN WHY THE HELL WEREN'T YOU SO WORRIED ABOUT APPREARANCES WHEN YOU GOT MOM PREGNANT WITH ME?!!!!!"

Before Eunice could even regret the outburst the room was filled a thunderous crack. Her head rocked against the kitchen cabinet and she fell to the floor. She felt a warm trickle of blood flowing from her lip. Somewhere...it seemed like miles away, her mother was screaming. Her whole world was going dark. She heard Lorenzo's voice but couldn't make out what he was saying. Was he apologizing? She finally regained some of her senses and looked up. Her heart seemed to have been sewn to her face, the pulse pounding out against her teeth. Lorenzo's face was ashen. His body seemed consumed with the shakes. Her mother's arms were suddenly around her, lifting her up.

"I'm okay, mama," she managed. Lorenzo was now standing closer, trying to touch her.

"Don't come near me," she said through clenched teeth. She rubbed her shirt sleeve across her mouth. It drew back a dark crimson.

"Eunice please," he said, "please don't do this."

"Go away, Lorenzo," Cora said, helping Eunice towards the table. "Calm down."

"Eunice I only want what's best for you."

"You have no idea what is best for me," she answered.

She took a deep breath and drew away from her mother. She walked to the door and settled herself against the frame. She noticed that, incredibly, she wasn't crying.

"If you marry that boy," Lorenzo continued, "you are no longer welcome in my house. Do you understand?" Lorenzo's voice was thin now. Eunice realized that she had given him a shot that he was not likely to recover from.

"I understand. If that's the way you want it, then that's the way it shall be."

"Oh, Eunice, Lorenzo, both of you stop this nonsense." Cora was pleading with them. Eunice stumbled out the door and into the yard. Chiltos came towards her, hoping to get the dirt. When he saw the blood he stopped. He could only watch as his sister walked away. He looked at his house and saw his mother standing in the doorway weeping.

Inside, Lorenzo walked out o the kitchen and into his study. He collapsed in his chair, burying his head in his hands. Eunice had never, ever said that to him before.

He had lost her.

The family had lost her.

Lorenzo had told her to choose.

And she had.

PART TWO

INTO THE WORLD

CHAPTER TEN

The house was leaning against the weight of the winter wind, threatening with every new gust to give way. She listened to the piercing cries of the wind as it snuck through every possible crook in the foundation. She thought about some of the poems and stories she had read over the years. All of them had described the sound of the wind as "plaintive" or "mournful." As she listened in the waning hours of the day, she thought these words were all wrong. They made the wind sound as if it were a beggar, sweeping through the valleys seeking forgiveness and charity. Those writers missed the fury, she thought. They couldn't or wouldn't recognize the intrinsic power. Maybe that was why the Cherokee people felt a kinship with the wind. After all, they had a great deal in common.

The house lurched again around her head. She sat down in the chair beside her quiet fireplace. She had tried to light it several times already, quitting with a quiet curse and much frustration. It was too hard to bend down there, what with the considerable baggage she was carrying now around her waist. She also began to feel dizzy every time she leaned towards the dry wood she had somehow managed to arrange in their proper place. Finally she had draped her shawl around her shoulders and resigned herself to another night without heat. If it got to be too cold she would try and make it over to Ma Runningwolf's place. She hoped it didn't come to that, though. She felt certain she would never be able to make the walk.

She missed Rodney. He had left town three weeks ago to help draw the railroad line further into the state. He had very nearly turned the job down, saying that he shouldn't leave her this far into the pregnancy. But she had put on her best brave face and insisted that he go. There was no other way to make that kind of money in the area, and he was lucky to have been asked to go in the first place. In truth she had wanted him to stay with her. She was afraid that he would be gone when the baby arrived. Still, she drew up all her resolve and made him think that she would prefer that he leave. She had enough on her mind without having to worry about money, she had told him. So he had left. And now there was no fire.

They were married on April 19, 1916. It had been a beautiful, if slightly chilly, day. The good reverend Timothy Drysdale had presided over the service. Eunice and Rodney compromised by having a Christian minister perform the ceremony outdoors. Grace had sung Amazing Grace and Molly Runningwolf had ended the ceremony by proudly reciting the Lord's Prayer in their native language. The preacher had seemed extremely pleased by that. When they were pronounced man and wife, Chiltos had given a yell that seemed to frighten the preacher nearly straight into Heaven. Later, Rodney had laughed that Drysdale must have mistaken it for a war whoop--no doubt fearing for his scalp. That thought was most humorous, since the white man was renowned around Qualla for the truly awful wig he wore to cover his vast bald spot. His lily-white sideburns combined with his jet black (almost blue) wig led many of the Cherokee to mercilessly dub him "Reverend Skunk." It was rumored that Dyrsdale had sent away to Siler City for the wig, which all the Indians thought quite unnecessary. He could have acquired the same effect by killing any number of animals that roamed the mountains.

The ceremony had been almost perfect. Even with the weather and all their friends around, though, there was a quiet sadness that hung over the proceedings. Lorenzo had stayed far away from the service, as he had sworn he would. Cora, probably for the first time in their married life, had risked his enmity to be there. Grace and Dora were both there, looking beautiful as bridesmaids. Chiltos, who had decided it would be more fun to anger his father than cause trouble for his sister, had given Eunice away. No one had cried during the wedding. Eunice supposed that was more out of fear as to how the tears would be interpreted than any lack of emotion at her finally leaving home.

The young couple had spent their honeymoon curled up in an old canvass tent on the edge of Grandfather Mountain. It was all they could afford, that was true, but it was also their choice. Rodney loved the outdoors and loved sharing them with Eunice. Eunice enjoyed being anywhere he was. They spent three days hiking old trails and fishing. At night they would sit and tell each other stories. Eunice told Rodney stories he had managed to miss in school. She told him about

Lincoln and Washington, John Ross and Jefferson, Tecumseh and Lafayette. Rodney expressed mild incredulity that any white had written the words she ascribed to Thomas Jefferson, but was convinced after some good-natured pleading. While she excelled at recalling events from the past, Rodney enjoyed trying his hand at prophesying their future. He told her of the house they would someday own, of the cars that would replace their need for a good horse, and the massive garden that they would tend with their children. They gave voice to their passions, and each night fell into a satisfied and uncompromised slumber. As Eunice had told Rodney before dropping off on their last night on the mountain, they no longer felt the need to dream.

They returned from the honeymoon to a small cabin that Rodney had rented shortly before the marriage. Rodney chose for two reasons: first, it was near the Runningwolf place, which allowed Eunice to be near Molly and afforded Rodney the chance to keep an eye on Mr. Runningwolf. Second, it was only a short distance away from the river that Eunice loved so much. An additional benefit was its closeness to the general store that had just opened in Big Cove. This would allow the two of them to get the things they needed without making the journey into town. It also gave Rodney a greater buffer against accidental intercourse with Lorenzo. It was, to be sure, a far cry from the Swayney homestead, a fact not lost on the gossipy crowd. But behind the wooden walls with the gaping cracks, Eunice and Rodney set up a home.

Their first marital difficulty had come in the summer months. It was more a matter of humor than discord, though. Rodney had decided that no wife of his was going to have to walk very far to reach the outdoor toilet they used, so he set about crafting one that would adjoin the kitchen of their home. He built a small room that held the two chamber pots (piss pots, Rodney called them). It had a back door that swung out and allowed either of them to remove the waste and dump it far away from the house. Unfortunately, when the humid summer set in, there was an appalling stench that hung over the entire cabin. Despite their best efforts at keeping the "bathroom" cleaned, the smell would linger for days. Molly Runningwolf had admonished Rodney that there was a reason the good Lord made it so people took their shits outdoors, and he was finding that out for himself. Finally, a slightly dejected Rodney admitted defeat and went back to using the old outhouse. After a couple of weeks allowing the place to air out, Eunice turned the new room into a spacious closet. It was a smelly lesson, but one that had to be learned, she guessed.

It was also in July that Eunice realized she was pregnant. Rodney had danced through the house and nearly squeezed the baby right out of her when she told him the news. Molly Runnignwolf had immediately set out on knitting and sewing clothes for the youngster. In a rare moment of sobriety Mr. Runningwolf had even made a tiny pair of moccasins for the new Norris. When Cora and Grace stopped by to see her later that same week, they too had danced in joy. Eunice never heard what her father's reaction had been, and she had never asked. Dora and Molly Runningwolf had taken care of Eunice during most of the term, since Rodney was frequently away with the railroad. Their advice and counsel was always helpful, but they almost never agreed with one another. Dora prescribed medicine and remedies that came from the doctor's office or, at the least, from textbooks. Molly was always bringing by herbal teas and imploring Eunice to not neglect a good pipe smoke at least once a day. Eunice decided that, in order to insure she took the right advice, she would take both. Her own background as a nurse told her that Dora's advice was typically the best. But her own experiences had taught her that Molly's advice was not to be quickly discarded.

Eunice shuddered as a brisk shard of wind made its way under her shawl. She decided to try and light the fire again. As she stood, she felt a sharp pain stab her gut. She propped herself up on a hand against the mantle. Her breath was slower in coming, too. She finally steadied herself and bent towards the fireplace. The pain returned, this time with a bitter vengeance. For the first time in a long time, Eunice felt scared. Something was wrong in there, she thought. She decided to try and walk it off. As she moved across the floor the pain hit again, nearly dropping her to her knees. The silence of the little cabin was split by her scream. She had been hurting for most of day--the usual back and leg aches. But this pain was new. She suddenly realized that she had sweat pouring down her face, stinging her eyes. She felt her heart pounding away inside of her.

"Please, God," she thought, "not now. Just a few more days, God, and my husband'll be here."

Suddenly another bolt of pain raced through her. Eunice walked to the door. She had to get to Ma Runningwolf's place quickly. Something was happening, and she thought she knew just what it was. The new Norris, like its father, was not patient.

ຽ

Molly was padding up the old trail towards her house when she heard the yell. It came from Eunice and Rodney's place. She quickly back-peddled towards their cabin. She had no sooner turned and began the trek, though, when she saw Eunice coming towards her. She was walking funny, Molly noticed. Her first thought was that the young girl was carrying something heavy on her back. When she couldn't see anything there, she realized something was wrong.

"Eunice?" she called out. Eunice was crying.

"Ma Runningwolf, I think I'm having this baby." Molly broke into a sudden sprint that, in other circumstances, would have caused Eunice to break out in laughter. Molly threw her arms around her to hold her up.

"Were you headin' to the river?" she asked with a smile. "You know, we DO have young 'uns indoors these days." Eunice smiled back.

"What do we do now, Molly?"

"We get you to the store," she replied, "quick." She heard Eunice let out a slow moan. The front of her dress had suddenly gone damp.

"Good Lord in Heaven, girl, how long you been hurting?"

"Most of the day," replied Eunice. "But Molly I can't have this baby now. I want Rodney there."

Molly let out a chuckle. "Eunice, even your strong will ain't gonna hold this baby in no more. Now come on."

They moved as quickly as they could to the store. Molly pounded on the locked door with all her might. Mr. Tyson had apparently decided that business was done for the day. There was no light on in the place. If he had gone into town they were in real trouble. Molly began pounding even harder on the door. Finally she heard someone cursing at her from the other side of the wood. A light started moving towards them. Molly heard the latch swing open.

"What the he----Mrs. Runningwolf, what're you..." Before Donald Tyson had the chance to finish Molly was by him with Eunice in tow.

"Don, we're having a bay here, tonight."

"What? Well, uh, I ..."

Eunice let out a little yelp as the next pain fired off. Don backed away from her.

"It ain't catching, Don," Molly teased. Now is there somewhere we can lay her down?"

"Oh, yeah, yeah sure."

Donald led them back into the storeroom, where he usually spent his nights. He brushed away candy wrappers and soda pop bottles nervously. Molly took Eunice's shawl and laid it at the foot of the bed. Donald had the old woodstove fired up, so at least heat wouldn't be a problem. Eunice lay back, tensely waiting for the next pain to hit. Molly reached over and felt her forehead. She took Tyson's hand and pulled him out into the store, closing the door behind her.

"Don, I need you to ride out to the Swayney's. Tell'em you need to see Chiltos. Tell him to get out to Bryson City and fetch Doc Devereoux. Bring him back here just as quick as he can. I'm afraid this one's gonna be tough."

"She ain't gona die is she?"

"Not if you get outta here and tell Chiltos to ride like the devil's on his heels," she snapped. Tyson could see the worry in her face. He threw on his coat and grabbed a hat from the shelf. He rushed out of the store with the price tag still whipping around his face. Molly said a quiet prayer and went back in with Eunice.

ဆ

Nearly two and a half hours later Chiltos came bursting into the little store with Doctor William Devereoux at his side. Both men seemed ragged from the rushed trip in the rapidly falling temperatures. It was almost dark outside, and the white doctor looked as though he had stood, trying to face down an angry wind. His lips were chapped and cracking and his cheeks were blood red. Molly saw that her first order of business was to get some hot coffee in the doctor before he fell over. Chiltos, meanwhile, was nursing a small silver flask that seemed to be doing a fine job of insulating him from the cold.

"How's my sister?" he asked Molly.

"Not good enough for you to be getting drunk just yet," she replied coldly. Chiltos capped the flask and sat down in a corner of the store. Devereoux took a small black bag into the back room, where he stayed for nearly twenty minutes. Molly paced the floor, deciding it would be better to give the doctor a few minutes alone with the patient before going in. When the doctor finally emerged from the room, he looked as concerned as Molly felt.

"Mrs. Runningwolf," he said, "she's feeling a lot of pain right now. She really should be in a hospital."

"There ain't enough time to get her there doctor," Molly said. "Besides, we ain't got no way of getting her there that wouldn't kill her first." Devereoux sighed.

"The baby hasn't turned. I just don't know if I can help her here in this store. She really should be in a hospital."

Chiltos stood. "Doc, is there anything I can do? Please don't let my sister die."

"Dammit," Molly scolded, "keep your voice down."

Eunice cried out from the other room.

"Please, doctor," Molly implored. The doctor shook his head, but quickly began barking orders to Chiltos and Tyson. When he had finished with them, he began explaining Molly's role to her. In other circumstances, Molly would have taken great exception to the condescension in his tone, but this was no time for pride. The two of them entered the lantern-lit room. The light cast monstrous shadows against the walls. Eunice was squirming on the bed, clutching the sheets of the bed hard enough to turn her knuckles purple. Her eyes searched Molly's face for some reassurance.

"My baby," she asked.

Molly took her hand. "Everything's gonna be alright, honey," she said smiling. "You just take a hold of my hand and don't let go. Squeeze as hard as you want, you hear?"

"I want Rodney," she whispered.

"I know, child," Molly comforted. "But right now you just think about bringing his baby into this world safe and sound. O.k.?" Eunice yelped again as if she'd been hit. Devereoux took his place between her legs. Chiltos came in with a basin of water and rags.

"Give her that flask," Devereoux ordered. Chiltos quickly obliged. Molly stared at the doctor.

"Just a small swig," he answered.

Molly gave Eunice a tiny shot of the alcohol. Eunice grimaced.

"That's the stuff we kill each other for?" she asked. Molly's laugh filled the room. The doctor was working furiously now.

"Turn down that damned heater," he ordered as the sweat began to drip down his pointy nose. "I can't keep my glasses up." Molly chuckled quietly. Don Tyson came in with a pack of cigarettes for the doctor and Molly. He walked out of the room as quickly as he could. He wasn't family, and it didn't seem appropriate for him to see Eunice all spread out like that.

Soon, Eunice began to cry out louder. The doctor was cursing and mumbling under his breath. His hands were moving feverishly. His curses grew louder as Eunice's cries grew. Chiltos, unable to wait outside and listen, came in and stood in the corner. Molly noticed that he seemed to have been crying. The doctor sat back from Eunice, drawing his handkerchief across his face. He lifted his glasses to the top of his head.

"Mrs. Runningwolf," he said, "her husband should be here now. It doesn't look good." Eunice cried out and nearly tore Molly's hand off.

"That can't be doctor. Husband is off working for the railroad."

The doctor stood and turned towards the door. "I'll be right back." He walked by Chiltos and closed the door behind him. Molly wiped Eunice's face.

"Ma Runningwolf," she asked, "we're dying. My baby's dying?"

"No child," Molly said, "it just ain't easy." Eunice sat up.

"Ma," she said, "I want my Daddy." She fell back against the pillows.

"But Eunice...."

"I want my Daddy," she said, through clenched teeth and tears. Another pain launched through her worn out frame. She passed out. Molly looked at Chiltos. He looked as if he had just seen the Holy Ghost itself.

"Go see," she said.

"I'll do what I can," he answered.

CHAPTER ELEVEN

The little storehouse had developed a schizophrenic character. There were periods of anguished noise followed by intolerable and oppressive silences. Eunice was in and out of consciousness. Molly and the doctor were at each other's throats as she accused him of nonchalance in the face of a great tragedy. Devereoux took the charge as a great personal affront, momentarily forgetting the obvious closeness between the two women. But he supposed he had become, at least a little, desensitized to the death that surrounded child birth here in the mountains. Still, he was doing everything in his power to help the young woman.

Eunice drifted between dream and pain, screaming for her husband and begging the doctor to save her family. Molly left the backroom only occasionally to peer out the window, searching for any sign of Chiltos. Don Tyson would bring in snacks for the doctor and Molly whenever the room went quiet. Molly would stand by the window, smoking and complaining about the poor quality of the cigarettes provided by the storekeeper.

"I hope you ain't puttin' this on my bill," she told Tyson.

"If that girl and baby live," Tyson responded, "you can consider the whole thing on the house."

"They'll live," Molly said, stubbing out her smoke. She walked quietly back into the room. Tyson watched her go, thinking that, if things didn't go the way he hoped, she just might not recover from the blow. He had almost nodded off to sleep when the yelling started again. He couldn't help but think about the stories he had heard about Indian women not making a sound during child birth. If that was really true, then the Indian girl in the back of his store was surely dying. He was startled at the sound of the front door swinging open.

Lorenzo strode into the general store looking like misplaced royalty.

His head held high, his consciously confident stride made Don Tyson
more than a little nervous. Lorenzo walked right passed him, without a
nod or even a glance. Chiltos entered the store behind him, shook off
the cold and stood, intently watching his father. Tyson was struck by
the look of angered respect that the old man managed to draw from his
son.

Molly heard the door swing open and expected Tyson to enter
bearing more coffee or cigarettes, Her heart nearly stopped when she
saw the old man. She didn't think for one minute that he would come
here. She remembered something Eunice had told her about Lorenzo
many months ago. When she and Dora had been young, Lorenzo had
made them repeat the sentence, "There can be no compassion without
contrition when there has been complicity." Eunice, after explaining to
Molly what the sentence meant, said that her father had drilled that into
them to improve their vocabulary. Now Molly wondered if maybe
there hadn't been more to it than that.

Lorenzo strolled past the doctor without a word.

"Hello, Molly," he said.

"Lorenzo," was all she could manage. She stood and allowed him to
sit by his ailing daughter's side. He took his place without bothering
with a 'thank you' and reached over to feel Eunice's forehead. He
gently brushed her hair away from her eyes. Reaching into his coat
pocket, he pulled out his handkerchief and wiped the sweat from her
face. Molly couldn't help but see the way his face pulled tight in pain
at the sight of his strong-willed daughter laying wilted there in the
storeroom. He sighed quietly, almost totally to himself.

"What's happening here, Doctor?" he asked. The point of the
question was clear: he wanted to be briefed as quickly as possible so
that he could take command. Unlike Molly, Lorenzo saw no reason
why this situation meant he should take any orders from a white man.
The doctor apparently understood the implication, as well, for his tone
with Lorenzo was very different from the way he had spoken to Molly.

"She's in terrible pain and has been for some time. The baby has not
turned. When she is conscious I tell her to push with all her strength,
which she does. But every time I think we're getting somewhere she
passes out again. Pain and exhaustion, you see? As you can see there
has also been considerable bleeding. To be blunt, sir, we have to get
that child out of there, dead or alive, if this girl has any chance herself
at all." Lorenzo nodded.

"Go outside," he told the doctor. "Get yourself a smoke or a drink or whatever you think you need. Then get back in here for the duration. We're gonna have this baby."

The doctor sat there in stunned silence. He was used to working with poor mountain folk, all of whom were easily intimidated by the diplomas on his wall and his position in the community. He was not used to taking orders---especially from an Indian.

"Is there a problem doctor?" Lorenzo asked when the man failed to move.

"No," the doctor stumbled, slowly getting to his feet, "no problem." He walked from the room, shaking his head in disbelief.

"Damn, Lorenzo," Molly said, chuckling. But he was paying her no attention. He moved another string of hair from his daughter's face.

"Little Reed," he said, "Little Reed can you hear me?" Eunice moaned.

"Rodney?" she asked.

"Little Reed it's Lor---it's Daddy." Eunice's eyes slowly blinked back to life. Molly saw the tears welling up in their corners.

"Daddy, oh, daddy I'm so sorry. Please..."

"That's done, now. For the moment we have other troubles," he said with a smile.

"Daddy, don't let my baby die."

Lorenzo laughed softly. "That's in God's hands, Little Reed." He took her hand in his. "But you know how nobody around here wants me mad." Eunice smiled. "I'm here now," he continued. "The doctor will be back in here in just a minute. You have to be strong, Little Reed. When the pain hits, you have to fight it. I'll fight it with you. But everything depends on you keeping your head and keeping awake. You can do that, now, I know you can. And if I have to, I'm gonna tell you to just quit trying and give up, 'cause you haven't done anything I've told you to in quite sometime." Lorenzo smiled down on his daughter.

"I love you, Daddy."

"And I you, sweetheart. Now," he said, turning to Molly, "let's get that doctor in here and have us a baby." Molly went into the store to find Dr. Devereoux.

"Are we gonna make it, Daddy?" asked Eunice.

"Yes," he said softly, "we are."

The doctor entered the room, looking refreshed but a little peeved at the treatment he had received.

"Ready?" he asked Eunice. She looked up ate her father. He

nodded to her reassuringly.

"Ready," she stated flatly. Devereoux took his place at the foot of the bed and began ordering Eunice to push with all her might. Eunice began, through clenched teeth. Molly stood in the corner and watched. Lorenzo was holding her hand, as she had been doing, but something in the room had changed. There was a determination in the air that had been missing before. The element of tragedy had been replaced with one of hope. Lorenzo urged his daughter forward, mostly gently, but sternly when it was needed. 'Come on Eunice' he would say. Or if she seemed to be wavering, he would tell her 'Push Little Reed, push harder.' He wiped the sweat away before it got anywhere near stinging her eyes, all the time paying no heed to the beads that strolled down his own face. Molly wasn't sure how long it had been going on when she heard the doctor say that he had it. The baby!

"We're almost there, Little Reed," Lorenzo said, "just a little more."

"My baby," she cried, "is it alright?"

"Go get me some clean rags," Devereoux barked to Molly, ignoring Eunice for the moment. Molly rushed from the room.

"Clean rags," she called to Don, who was trying to nod off behind the counter. "Get me some clean rags." Tyson leapt into the air and grabbed a handful of brand-new towels from the shelf behind his head. He tossed them across the floor to Molly. She ripped them from the air and darted back into the storeroom.

"Here, doctor," she said. Eunice was grunting and pushing harder than she had all night. Lorenzo was still coaching his heart out.

Suddenly, like the first blast of sunshine on a summer morning, the room filled with a new cry. Eunice's painful moans and her father's strong voice were replaced with the delightful wailings of a newborn. The doctor frantically cut and pulled, tied and arranged. The rags seemed to float around the child's body, removing blood and afterbirth. The doctor peered at the creation and, suddenly, smiled.

"Ma'am," he said, "you have a son." Molly's head fell against her chest with relief and fatigue. Lorenzo fell back into the chair and wiped his own face. Eunice was laughing and crying all in one helpless motion. Doctor Devereoux stood and walked the baby over to his mother. They had waited long enough to meet each other, he thought. Molly got her first glimpse of the baby and cried out with joyous amusement.

"Good Lord, would you look at the head of hair on that young'un?" Lorenzo looked up and a smile enveloped his features. It was the first time he had smiled like that in a long time.

"Curley," he said.

"Yes," Eunice agreed, giggling. "Curley." Devereoux placed the child in Eunice's arms. He looked so beautiful, so healthy. Eunice was seized with the thought that she had almost lost him. She looked over at her father. She had never seen him looking so tired or, she thought, so happy. She held out her arms and handed her son to him.

"I'd like you to meet your grandson," she said. Lorenzo reached out and took the child in his arms. To everyone's amazement, he began cooing and aahing at the baby. He took his voice up about three octaves and began talking as though he himself were just barely older than the child in his arms. No one in the room (or the reservation for that matter) could remember a time when Lorenzo Dow Swayney had been certifiably silly. He looked up and saw the shocked stares of the people around him.

"Don't tell anybody," he said with a smile. He looked back down at the baby. "Curley," he repeated, "my grandson."

ह०

Eunice fell asleep almost as soon as Doctor Devereoux left. Her new son, whom she officially named Russell Devereuox Norris, nodded off quietly beside of her. Molly and Lorenzo tip-toed out of the store into the cold, early morning air. Chiltos and Don Tyson were both knocked out in seperate corners of the building. The stars were just beginning to give way to the pale light of a mountain's winter morning. The chill felt good to both Lorenzo and Molly. They stood, smoking quietly, for a long time.

"I didn't think you'd come," Molly said finally. Lorenzo stared away, his mind clearly somewhere else.

"There was no way I wasn't coming. Absolutely no way." He said it matter-of-factly.

"Hmmph," was all Molly could manage for a response.

"Molly," he said, "do you ever watch the sunset?"

"As often as I can," she answered.

"Last week, Thursday, I think, I went out and watched the sun set over the river. It was a beautiful sunset. It looked like the Great Spirit had just thrown hundreds of colors across the horizon, seeing how they'd look together."

"I've seen those," she said, "they sure are pretty, alright."

"Do you know there is not a more heartbreaking thought on God's earth than to look at one of those and think, 'There's no one out there looking at this and thinking of me.'"

Molly looked away, suddenly very uncomfortable.

"Now, Lorenzo, I don't think for one minute that you believe Eunice ever stopped thinking about you these months."

"No, no I don't. But it was a sad thought. And that's not how it should be."

"So what now?" Molly asked, wondering if Lorenzo remembered that Rodney would be coming home soon to claim his family. Lorenzo looked at her thoughtfully.

"Everybody knows that's not the son-in-law I wanted," he said. "But it ain't worth losing Little Reed to prove a point. Nothing would be worth that."

"Why do you call her Little Reed?' Molly asked. She had been wondering that for sometime. Eunice had never mentioned the name to her before.

"When she was about seven, I guess," Lorenzo said, "we went swimming in the river. It was getting ready to storm, and the water was rougher than usual. Eunice kept getting pulled down. Her and Dora both. Well sir, Dora got out of that water. She was sick to death of skinning her knees an getting her nose filled up with water. But, even after I called her to come on out, Eunice wouldn't. With God as my witness that girl stood there, daring the river to knock her down again. Finally I had to threaten to whip her for her to come out." Lorenzo smiled at the memory. "After that I called her Little Reed. Then when she came back from schooling I guess I figured it was too child-like for her. She sure was a stubborn child."

"I wonder where in the world she got that from?" Molly asked. Lorenzo said nothing, just nodded.

"Well," he said, flicking his cigarette into the yard, "I suppose I should go on home and call my wife grandmother."

"Yep," Molly said, "I reckon you should." Lorenzo pulled his coat a little tighter and began walking towards home.

"Thank you, Molly," he said before turning away. "Thank you for being here tonight."

It was Molly's turn to just nod. She turned back into the store to go check on the new mother.

CHAPTER TWELVE

There is something about looking into the eyes of a child that, in the same instant, reminds you both of your mortality and your legacy. Rodney returned from the road to find a brand new family waiting for him. His son, now already known to almost everyone on the reservation as Curley, was nearly two months old when he finally saw him. Eunice met him proudly at their door with the child squalling in her arms. Rodney grabbed his son and danced around the yard with him, screaming for anyone within ear shot of him to come and see. Of course, his wife informed him that the neighbors had *ALREADY* seen the child, but that didn't make any difference to the proud pop. Molly was soon on thee doorstep smiling at the scene. That night Rodney killed a deer and the young couple feasted with Molly and the child.

It didn't take long, however, for Rodney's euphoria over the birth of his son to be replaced with an almost suffocating sense of pressure. The railroad job was over, and the money he had made wouldn't last forever. He found himself in the position he had been in most of his life--scrounging again for that next job, that next paycheck. The difference this time was that there were two people at home depending on him. Most of the good paying jobs available to him were off the reservation, most of them requiring him to travel somewhere and do something to improve a community other than his own. And although he desperately wanted to provide, he also wanted to be there to watch his child grow up. He wanted to make sure that Curley got the male attention he needed. It was true that Molly could teach him how to hunt and fish, but that was the job of the father, not the godmother.

The obvious answer was to take his family away from the Qualla Boundary and find work somewhere else. Somewhere where Rodney could earn a good living *and* remain with his family. But he and Eunice didn't really know how to exist anywhere else. Nothing would change the fact that they were Indians and that Indians weren't welcome in communities other than their own. Besides, he wanted Curley to grow up Tsalagi--he wanted his son to grow up in the shadow of the same mountains that he had always gazed upon. Only in these mountains, Rodney thought, surrounded by these people, could the child receive his spiritual birthright.

Still, if the choice was between providing and remaining, well, that was really no choice at all. Nurturing the soul was all well and good, but it couldn't be done on an empty stomach. Sometimes Rodney dreamed of leaving Qualla, making a fortune and returning to live in comfort. But he understood that the likelihood of that happening was very slim. He tried to hide his fear and frustrations from his wife, hoping that the answer would appear as it had so many times in the past. He spent hours walking familiar trails hoping to hear some voice with an answer. He cursed the silence of the trees and stomped the very ground that was causing him such doubt.

Rodney tried as best he knew how to shield his wife from his worries. There were times when he wanted to tell her, to just scream out everything that was weighing on his mind, but that wasn't really his way. Her near-reconciliation with Lorenzo didn't make matters any better. Rodney found himself consumed with a fear that, if he told Eunice of his concerns about their financial state of affairs, she would turn to her father for help. And while Lorenzo might now be more willing to slip them some cash for the moment, Rodney felt certain it would come with the obligatory "I told you so." After all, Lorenzo *had* told her so. But the silence in the cabin spoke volumes to Eunice, who knew her husband well enough to know that something was troubling him.

Her first thought was to assume that Rodney was having trouble dealing with his new family. Her husband had always had a solitary nature, a need to spend time weaving dreams and conjuring images for the future. Neither of those things was easily acquired with the presence of a new-born around the house. Eunice tried to compensate by taking Curley with her whenever she left the house, leaving Rodney with time to himself. But soon he was complaining that he didn't see his wife and child enough.

Molly was of no help to the young mother. Her response to any trouble was to meet it head on, to tackle it with both hands and ring the trouble right out. Eunice felt that she should respect her husband's privacy and allow him to come to her whenever he felt ready.

"Child," Molly scolded, "the surest way to hurt someone you love is to try and protect 'em too much. This is cramping your heart and you better face it before your imagination turns it into something that you can't get round."

Face it was exactly what Eunice finally decided to do. The long walks in the woods and the terrible quiet that hung over their dinners soon became more than she could handle. She just had to wait for the right time to bring the subject up. She wanted to wait until her husband seemed to be in a good mood to hit him with all her questions, but the fact that he never seemed to be in a good mood was, of course, the largest part of the problem to begin with. Again, Molly was no help.

"Love him real hard and then ask him," she advised. "A man can't tell a lie after having relations, takes too much damn energy. 'Course the danger there is that he's done asleep before you can ask him anything."

The moment finally came one night after putting Curley to bed. Rodney was sitting on the steps of their home, smoking and staring absently at the night sky. The green was starting to dress down the trees again as spring snuck onto the reservation from across the mountains. Eunice sat beside her husband and took his hand. He gave her a quick smile that, as far as she could tell, was about as genuine as a white man's promise. The obvious lack of sincerity tore through Eunice, who had already begun to play with the thought that maybe Rodney just realized that he didn't really love her enough to want to grow old with her. It was that possibility more than anything else that had motivated her to get on with the conversation she didn't really want to have.

"Honey," she started, "I think me and you should talk."

"Can I go first?" he asked. Eunice was surprised at his eagerness.

"Well, sure you can, Rodney."

He stood from the steps and paced in the yard. He dropped his cigarette and continued to grind it long after it had ceased to glow in the night air----one of his dead giveaways that something was on his mind.

"I've gotta leave tomorrow, Eunice," he said. "There's a highway project down in Asheville and a buddy of mine from the rails managed to get me a spot on the crew. I'll probably be gone a few weeks, maybe a month. Is that alright?"

Eunice stared at her feet----one of her dead giveaways that something was wrong.

"Well, no, Rodney, that's not alright. I mean, I'll, we'll miss you. Curley's awfully attached to you, you know? But I guess you gotta do it. We're running sort of low right now, aren't we?"

Rodney sighed. "Yeah, yeah we are. That's the only reason I'm even willing to consider leaving y'all. I don't see as we've got much choice right now." He searched his wife's face for any sign of understanding.

"Well, I understand that you've got to do what you've got to do. Is there anything I could do to help?" Rodney understood that Eunice was working her way towards offering to earn money herself, something that he simply did not want to happen.

"No," he answered, " I think you should stay home with the baby. We've already talked about that."

"Yes, I know we have. But Rodney, I could take Curley with me. There are enough people right here in Big Cove that could use my help. I wouldn't have to go very far from the house. And if I ever did Molly would be more than willing to...."

"Eunice, I am still capable of making our money." The harshness in his tone surprised Eunice. He seemed to be scolding her and defending himself in the same breath.

"Rodney, I wasn't saying...."

"Well don't," he interrupted. He turned from her as he spoke. He had lost all control of his voice, giving away more than he had intended. He felt her eyes burning right through his back.

"I'm sorry," he said, still not facing her.

"It's alright," she said, moving up behind him and wrapping her arms around his waist. Rodney placed a hand over hers and sighed. They stood there silently for a time, listening to the trees.

"Rodney," Eunice said, "you know that I believe in you. Don't you?"

"I don't know if I believe in myself," he said. Eunice felt a shudder move through her husband's body. He moved her arms from around his waist and turned to face her.

"I do not want to go," he said flatly. "But we need the money and I don't see any other way, well, any other *legal* way to get it." He smiled.

"No bootlegging, Rodney," Eunice said coldly. That would not be an option. "I'll start working before I will allow that brought into my house. If supporting this family means tearing others up...I'd as soon starve." Rodney laughed.

"Well," he said, "I'm glad we could discuss it like adults." Eunice didn't return his good humor.

"I mean it, honey. No liquor."

Rodney moved away from her and began pacing again.

"Well there are two choices around here," he said, taking on the air of a lecturing professor, "bootlegging or farming, and I can't say as I know a damn thing about farming."

"And you might as well forget what you know about the other," Eunice said. "We will find a way."

"How?" he asked. "I can't just wave my arms and make up jobs around here. And I don't want to spend the rest of my life missing my son growing up. You and Molly would have that young 'un so spoiled there ain't nobody gonna wanna be around him."

"Now wait just a minute," Eunice interrupted.

"No, I won't wait. I should be here with you and Curley. Hell, I want to be here. But I can't be with you and keep you up at the same time. That just ain't possible."

"What about my father?" Eunice asked. "He could help you out learning about farming until...."

"No," Rodney spat. "I will not accept Lorenzo's charity."

"Rodney, it ain't charity when its family."

"I ain't family to him and I never will be and you know it."

"Then let me start my nursing again."

"Eunice I done said no," he said.

"Well, Rodney, if you ain't gonna let anybody help you then I guess your just in a world of hurt, huh?" Eunice turned and stomped towards the cabin door. She stopped suddenly at the foot of the stairs. "But I'll tell you this, Rodney Norris," she fired across the yard, "I ain't had a meal yet paid for by pride." And with that she bounded into the house, slamming the door behind her.

Rodney lit another cigarette and sat down in the middle of the yard. This was the last night he would spend with his wife for weeks. And this was not, he thought sadly, the way he had wanted to spend it.

PART THREE

DIFFERENT

CHAPTER THIRTEEN

The years had flown by as only time can, with no warning and only deeper and harder creases on the face to show proof of existence at all. There had been no time for introspection or doubt. Life had become reduced, as it too often does for the poor, a blur of bills and temporary jobs. There were, of course the good times as well. Curley began talking a mile a minute, walking, and asking piercing questions of his parents about the world that surrounded him. Birthdays came and went and milestones were passed. Molly Runningwolf and the entire Swayney clan reveled in each new story that Eunice and Rodney told, and the parents themselves were only too happy to share each moment in their child's life with anyone that would listen.

But even the good times were marred by the nagging doubts that every day seemed to bring. The concern about money ate away at the edges of the young couple's minds like an acid. Eunice tried not to allow herself to think about what dire straits they were so often in. There were weeks at a time when the money was excellent, at least for the area. Rodney would pull down a great construction job and be away for weeks at a time, sending the money as often as he could. But then there were the other weeks when either the weather or the economy seemed to conspire against them. Eunice felt the intense pressure during these weeks, She was asked (although never explicitly) during these times to be there for her son, balance the family's budget, and prop up her husband's failing self esteem. The silence in the cabin brought down a pressure on Eunice that left her feeling like someone was sitting on her chest. Rodney moped around the rooms, staring at walls and looking for something, anything to occupy his time. He answered Eunice's questions with only monosyllabic grunts and ignored her obvious attempts at conversation. He managed to be out of the house whenever there was company, mistakenly believing that he could fool his neighbors into thinking he might be out working.

It was a silly thought. No one on the reservation was working. The farmers were still getting their crops out to market and were also feeding their families with the surpluses. But any man who made a living with his hands in anything but dirt was at home, driving their wives and friends near crazy. Many who seemed unable to scratch together enough cash to keep their children in shoes somehow managed to always have enough to buy that jug of whiskey and drown themselves in violence and self-pity. The women who loved these men either looked the other way or risked the bruises that plagued so many of these homes during the lean times.

Rodney avoided these men with every ounce of energy that he had, At first he topped the list of everyone on Qualla for a drinking buddy based solely on his reputation as a young man. But word quickly got around that Rodney had been "whupped" by that wife of his and would not tip a glass with anyone. There were some, the more jealous and malicious around Qualla, who claimed that since Rodney had married into money he thought he was simply too good to hang around a bunch of poor and drunken Indians. A rumor even made the rounds that Rodney needn't work at all because Lorenzo was footing the bill for the young couple's life. Luckily Eunice was able to quash this story before it reached her husband's proud ears.

Then came the mysterious trip East. Rodney had given Eunice only a few cryptic clues as to why or even where he was going. It had been six weeks since Rodney had left the house with any purpose other than killing time. She was also aware of how incredibly sensitive Rodney had become about any suggestion that he spent too much time away from his family. If he felt that Eunice was trying to drop any hints about the subject he crouched in an immediate defensive stance and came out fighting. Eunice decided that whatever the purpose was, if it gave her husband purpose and lightened his cloudy mood she would ask no questions.

Of course, that did not mean that she could not put her ear firmly to the ground and listen for any hints that others in the community might have about work. After all, Rodney was not the only Indian who made his living by working on the rails and road projects. She knew of at least four or five other wives who had husbands frequently working on the same jobs as her husband.

The concern began to show itself when she realized that these other men were still slinking around the reservation. Wherever Rodney had gone, he had gone alone. It bothered her more and more each night as she had to answer Curley's questions about where his father had gone and when was he coming back. She tried to answer her son as reassuringly as possible but her mind began to scream out all the questions that she didn't want to think about.

She tried to remind herself that she and Rodney loved each other and had a relationship that most people only dreamed of and few could truly understand.

"We like the same things," she reminded herself, "we finish each other's sentences."

But even in the confines of her own head these things sounded like desperate rationalizations. Lying alone in their bed at night, she would think about all the stories she had heard as a child and as a young woman. The Indian men, married men, who had gone away to work on some job and had been seduced and romanced away from their wives by white women. White city women. These women, she had heard, were intent on getting themselves an Indian man. White men bored these women, she had been told. And they were out to prove something, something they could only prove by bringing home a man who was not white. These unsuspecting and utterly foolish Indians were nothing more than the manifestation of some childish rebellion. But that didn't save their marriages. Of course the women were ultimately disappointed. They wanted a warrior, a Geronimo, in bed. What they usually got was a hard drinking Indian who hated himself and eventually her for having turned his back on his people. But, again, that did not save their marriages. Their Indian wives were left behind, shattered by thoughts that they were inferior or that they had failed in their attempts to make a family.

"I'll kill the bitch," Eunice whispered to the ceiling. Blushing she realized that she was probably planning on killing a non-existent rival. Probably. Then, thankfully, Rodney came home.

There was a look on his face that told her, without doubt, that something very big had happened. His face wore both great excitement and trepidation. His answers were all vague and calculated. He seemed to dodge all the questions she posed about his journey. When she asked what he had been doing, his only answer was that they would talk after Curley went to bed. His gleeful romps around the cabin, yelling at the top of his lungs as he chased his growing son around it told her that he was not to be disturbed. Eunice couldn't help but reflect on the thought that it had been a long time since she was so anxious for the child to fall asleep.

That night she and Rodney gathered by Curley's bed as he said his prayers. As he began rattling off the seemingly endless list of people and things he was thankful for (Molly, Lorenzo, Cora, Dotie, trees, birds, etc.) Eunice felt Rodney's hand creep against the line of her thigh. As quietly as possible she tossed it away. Curley continued to list nearly everything in the universe and Rodney kept probing. Through the half-slit of one eye she peered at her husband. That devilish grin was enveloping his face. Eunice tried her best not to smile when he met her eye and began waving his hand as if to hurry the child along. She gave him the most disapproving look that she could muster, but it clearly didn't work. Finally, mercifully, Curley said "Amen." Rodney leaned in and planted a kiss on his forehead.

"'Night, son," he said quietly.

"G'night, daddy."

Eunice went through the same routine, adding as she always did that if there was anything he needed during the night, he could just call out to her. Then they were holding hands and walking towards the bedroom.

Rodney dropped to the bed and pulled a fresh pack of cigarettes from his shirt pocket. It was, at least, the third pack that he had gone through since being home.

"You're smoking too much, honey," she said.

"Uh-huh," was his only reply. That told her something. Rodney hated to be mothered. Eunice sat beside him on the bed and placed her hand on his outstretched leg.

"O.k., Rodney, let's have it."

"There are going to be some major changes around here soon," he said. Eunice felt her heart leap into her throat. She felt the sudden urge to scream at him that she knew what he had been up to and that she thought she had a right to know who the woman was. But she held her tongue.

"You wanna explain?" she asked.

"C'mere," he said and tried to pull her closer to him. Eunice moved away.

"Just tell me Rodney. I am not in the mood for any games. You went God knows where for God knows what and I am tired of thinking about it. Just tell me what's going on." Rodney sighed. He moved closer to his wife and stubbed out his smoke.

"I got a job." Eunice waited. There had to be more, she knew, but her husband seemed to be done talking. He appeared worn out by having had to say that much.

"And?" she asked. Her patience was running out. "You've found jobs before that took you away from Qualla. What is about this one that's so special?"

"This one isn't going to take me away from Qualla," he said, "its going to take all of us away." Eunice caught her breath. Studying her husband's face she saw that he was not joking.

"Leave Qualla?" she asked bewildered. "Why?" Rodney laughed.

"Because," he said, "I have missed enough of our marriage and my son's life. I do not want to miss any more."

Eunice was completely caught by surprise. This was nothing like what she had expected.

"What is the job?" she asked.

"I'm going to be the foreman at a textile mill," he said smiling. He was obviously pleased with himself to be able to call himself a foreman. She had to admit that it did sound much better than just a plain construction worker.

"And where is the job?" she asked. She suddenly realized that that was probably the first question that she should have asked. Rodney took a deep breath.

"Cramerton," he said. Eunice felt the tears gathering like rain in her eyes. She thought about the amazing turn of events that this conversation symbolized. Only a few short months before she had been the one suggesting that maybe they should leave the reservation so that Rodney could find a steady source of income that would not constantly take him away from his family. He had steadfastly refused to even consider the idea. And now they were each feeling the exact opposite.

"Oh, honey," she said, "that is so far away."

"I know. If I thought that I could provide the life I had promised you and stay here I would do it. You know that. But the fact remains that I can't and I never will be. There just ain't any jobs here that can keep a man with a family up. So, like you said, maybe I have to go to where the jobs are."

Eunice didn't know what to say. He was right; that was what she had told him. And for once, she thought, he had actually listened to her.

"It's just so far away," she repeated. "So far away from Ma Runningwolf, and Mom and Dad and Dora and, well, and everybody and everything that you and I have ever known.

"It's good money, Eunice," he said.

"Money isn't everything."

"It is when you don't have any," he corrected. "You should know that. How long do you reckon we could keep going like this? I'm tired, Eunice. Tired of the struggle to make ends meet and tired as Hell of missing you. I'd rather be with you than any of them other Indians you mentioned." He smiled at her. "I love this place, too. I never much thought that I would really leave here. But the time has come to make this move, and I think that down deep somewhere you know that. I want to give you that life we used to talk about, before the hard times took it all away. Damn it, Eunice, I miss laying beside you on the river bank and dreaming."

"We can still do that, Rodney."

"Maybe you can," he said, "but I can't. Laying there now and talking about the great things we were going to do. Wondering all the time how we were going to eat. That would make me feel like a goddamned fool."

"Rodney, don't talk like that in front of me."

He pulled her close to him.

"I'm sorry. But there is a big difference between dreaming and running away. And to lay out there under them stars and talk about things that we weren't doing everything in our power to bring true ain't nothing but running. Nothing." He pulled away from her and shrugged with frustration. "I can't talk like you, Eunice. I reckon I ain't making no sense right now."

"Well," she said, "keep trying." She was suddenly reminded of their early days, when they sat alone for hours and she had tried to help him talk "smart," as he had called it.

"Qualla is a great place for dreaming, " he said, "but an impossible place to make those dreams come true. There," he said proudly, "that's what I'm trying to say to you."

Eunice studied Rodney's face. She noticed for the first time how old he was beginning to look. The flesh around his jaws was now hanging loose, and his clothes seemed to be draped carelessly around him. There were dark circles under his eyes and his hands weren't as steady as they had been when they had first met. She began to cry.

"Oh, baby," he said taking her in his arms, "please, honey, don't do that to me." The tighter he held her, the harder the tears fell.

"I'm sorry," she cried.

"Sshhhh," he whispered.

"It just isn't fair. Why do I have to choose between being able to make it and staying here with my people? I just don't understand." Rodney said nothing. "They'll never accept us," she continued. "You've said that yourself. No amount of money will ever change what we are. Never."

"But we'll have each other," he said. "And that's always been enough, ain't it?"

"Yes, but we've never faced anything like this. This is not like anything that's come before."

"Eunice, I need you to have faith. I need you to have enough faith for both of us. I'm scared too, you know? But the way I see it, Qualla will always be here. If we go out there and we fail, then we'll come back. I ain't too proud for that." She gave him a skeptical look. "O.k.," he admitted, "maybe I am. But I'd do it for you and Curley. But I need to try. I don't want to die not knowing whether or not I could've made it. Whether or not we could've made it. I can handle not making it. But," and he hit these words with a power that almost made her shudder, "I MUST KNOW." Eunice looked deep into her husband's eyes. His step may have become a little slower, but those eyes still sparkled with the fire of the brightest stars of heaven. And, somehow, they still made her melt. Searching her heart, she knew only one thing---this was the man she loved. The only man. And she did, in fact, believe in him and his dreams.

"I want to learn how to drive," she said.

"What?!" The question had clearly stumped Rodney.

"If this job means such good money, then I want us to get one of those new cars and I want to learn how to drive it myself." Rodney's laughter echoed throughout the house.

"It's a deal," he said, wiping the tears from his own eyes. "I love you."

Eunice nodded.

"We have some packing to do," she said, in her most business-like voice.

"Uh-uh," he said shaking his head. "First things first." Luckily, Curley slept through the night.

CHAPTER FOURTEEN

They had both been surprised by his answer. Lorenzo had simply insisted to them that, no matter what arguments they presented against it, Curley would stay with him and Cora until they had settled themselves into their new home. Rodney and Eunice suppressed the urge to tell the old man that was exactly the thing they had come to ask him for in the first place. It was going to be difficult enough for them to find housing and get everything moved and in place by themselves. Dragging a six year old around would only complicate matters.

"I think he will stay here," Lorenzo had stated. "It will allow the two of you to put your house in order and it won't disrupt his world any more than necessary."

"Mother, is that alright with you?" Eunice had asked. Cora had smiled and nodded. She was struggling to keep her emotions under control. She was and really always had been terrified of the outside world, and the thought of her eldest daughter alone in the middle of it didn't sit so well with her. Of course, she wouldn't be alone. Rodney would be there, and Cora had always liked Rodney. Besides, Eunice trusted him completely, and she had always been an excellent judge of character.

"I....we appreciate that a lot Mr. Swayney," Rodney had said. "And thank you, too, Mrs. Swayney." Again Cora simply nodded. Lorenzo did not acknowledge the gratitude.

The next hour or so was a barrage of questions about where they were going to be living, exactly what was Rodney's job, what the people he had met in the area were like, were the streets paved, and others. Eunice tried not to seem as overwhelmed as she was feeling. After most of the curiosity had been satisfied, Lorenzo invited the couple to stay and have dinner with them. It was only the two of them now. Chiltos stayed different places and sort of wandered around the reservation, a perpetual embarrassment to his proud father, Dora was living in a small home that she was trying to pay for with her work as a nurse, and Grace was off to school. It was the first time Rodney had ever been asked to eat with the Swayneys. Eunice quickly pounced on the invitation before her husband could think better of it.

"Rodney," Lorenzo said, raising his tall frame from the table, "would you help me kill one of those chickens, please? My aim ain't what it used to be." Lorenzo smiled and walked towards the door before Rodney could even answer. The answer to Lorenzo's request was assumed. Rodney glanced at his wife, who then glanced at her mother. Cora simply shrugged as if to say that she had no idea what was going on in her husband's mind.

"Oh, for God's sake," Lorenzo said without turning, "I think the boy can handle himself." He turned and flashed a wicked smile at the two women. "I promise to bring him back in one piece." He walked out the door, allowing the screen door to slam behind him for exclamation. Rodney stood and walked out behind him. Even after all this time, just the sight of the old man's slightly drooping back was still a little intimidating.

Lorenzo had killed the chicken as only he would or could. He set it loose in the yard and then chased after it with his slingshot. He missed once, but on the second shot he had beaned the bird across the head, stopping it cold.

"Is it dead?" a bewildered Rodney had asked.

"Well, if it ain't it will be," Lorenzo answered with a smile. "I know what a lot of folks around this town are saying about me, now," he continued, as if that was exactly what they had already been talking about. "But I ain't out here chasing chickens around my yard because I'm eccentric or just plain crazy; I do it because it's the best target practice in the world. You never know, Rodney, when you might be called upon to be a good shot." Rodney nodded uncomfortably. He hoped that wasn't a veiled threat. Lorenzo plopped the chicken's limp body over a tree stump that he had left in the yard for just such an occasion.

"'Course, if I was walking by somebody's house and I saw them running around the yard with a slingshot trying to kill a chicken that they owned I guess I'd draw the same conclusions. But I ain't crazy." He winked at Rodney. "But don't tell anybody. Keeps 'em off my property." Rodney laughed as Lorenzo handed him an axe. "Now whack away, boy so we can have us some supper."

Rodney drew the axe back, wondering if that was all Lorenzo had wanted to tell him. If it was, he was going to have his own doubts about his father-in-laws professed sanity. The axe sliced through the neck of the chicken and embedded itself in the wood underneath. Lorenzo was lighting a cigarette.

"You want one?" he asked. There was one thing about smokers that Rodney had known for years. It was a rule that also held true for drinkers. If someone offered you one of whatever their chosen addiction was, it usually foreshadowed a conversation of varying seriousness. The look that had crossed Lorenzo's face said all that needed to be said about the degree in his own mind.

"You know," he began, "it's no secret to anybody I guess that I didn't care for you very much." Rodney tried to take some consolation from the fact that Lorenzo had spoken in the past tense.

"No, sir, I reckon you made that pretty plain for all of us." Lorenzo laughed as smoke drifted around his white hair.

"Well, I have never been much for hiding my feelings."

"Neither is your daughter," thought Rodney.

"And besides that," Lorenzo continued, "my instincts for people have served me very well. It's kept me out of that hornet's nest at tribal government and kept my head above water financially. But I have, from time to time, been wrong." Rodney's heart nearly stopped. It would have been easier for the surrounding mountains to jump up and walk towards the ocean as it was for this man to say those words. When Lorenzo had asked him to follow him outside he had hoped for, at best, a mild scolding for the fact that he was taking Eunice into the white man's world. This was far more than that.

"And this time?" Rodney asked, deciding to press his luck.

"You gonna actually make me say it?" Lorenzo was smiling, but it was clear that he was looking for a reprieve from this oppressive sentence.

"Yes, sir, I am," Rodney answered. "I kinda think I've earned it." Lorenzo tossed away the cigarette.

"Yes. Yes, you have." He took a deep breath. "Alright, I was wrong. You make her happy. And you've given me a beautiful grandson. You're good to both of them, and these days that appears to be quite an accomplishment. No, that *is* quite an accomplishment."

Rodney hardly knew what to say.

"Thank you, sir."

"You wanna know why I didn't like you before?" asked Lorenzo.

"Because I was poor," Rodney stated matter-of-factly. Lorenzo cackled and nearly doubled over with the force of his laughter.

"Hell, no," he said. "Is that what you thought?"

"Well, sir, with all due respect, I can't see as I ever done anything to wrong you or your family besides just being me and being poor. There's nothing else that I ever did that I can think of." Lorenzo raised himself up to his full height. His eyebrows darkened his countenance as they contorted themselves to show utter displeasure. Rodney hoped that he hadn't pushed the issue too hard. He thought that it would be a shame to screw up an opportunity like the one that had shown itself.

"It didn't have a thing to do with your being poor, boy," Lorenzo said. His tone was still warm, giving Rodney some hope. "It was," continued Lorenzo, "the fact that I didn't think that you *minded* being poor."

Lorenzo pulled another cigarette from his pocket and then motioned for Rodney to help himself to another one. Rodney obliged. The fading sun was setting behind Lorenzo's head, giving him an other-worldly aura. Rodney was struck for the first time by how much he grudgingly admired this man. There were plenty of Indians in Cherokee with a few dollars to their name who somehow soothed their wounded souls by bossing around other, less fortunate Indians as if they were feudal lords barking out instructions to their serfs. But at the first sight of a white man, even a down-and-out one, they turned into mushy lapdogs, prideless paupers who extended their hand and lowered their gaze in obvious and infuriating deference to their "betters." Lorenzo was not and never had been one of these Indians. The charge that he held most of his own kind in contempt was certainly true. But Lorenzo held the entire world in contempt. Everyone seemed to lack his vision and he was angry at God and the world for that fact. Skin color didn't matter, nor did money in the bank. Lorenzo was just as cold (and admittedly condescending) to a white man as to any Indian that ever crossed his path. In fact, he liked to tell people that he preferred Indians, because at least they knew who they were and what they were all about. Nearly every white person he had ever met was under the impression that not being born black or Indian was the equivalent of being born royalty. Lorenzo was capable of and likely to end that illusion quickly. Damn the consequences, he would tell his astonished audience, what is there left for them to take?

Rodney suddenly realized that Lorenzo was still speaking. He had tuned out whatever it was he had been saying. All he had caught was something about minds changing. Deciding that this was not the time to fake his way through a conversation, he asked the old man to repeat himself. Lorenzo cleared his throat and began again.

"What I mean is that I thought you had no ambition. No drive and no vision. Let's face it, there is very little of that left around here. Rodney, when Cora and I started we had nothing. We ate because I could kill practically anything with my blowgun and she could make anything taste good." He winked. "Good combination, yeah?"

Rodney laughed. "Yes, sir, a very good combination."

"Anyway, it wasn't easy. But the point is that I was never satisfied with that life. I know what some of the others around here say about 'Swayney wants to be a white man' and all. Well, that's bullshit. Why would anybody trade our heritage for one of thieves and rapists and murderers who are only our neighbors because they screwed up their first home? But I'll tell you something else: I may not want to be a white man, but I *DO* want a little of what he's got. Hell, I figure most of it is my birthright anyway."

Rodney nodded his absolute agreement.

"Do you know who we are, Rodney? Really?"

"Yes, sir, I think so."

"Think? That won't be good enough where you're going, boy." Rodney felt the color rising in his cheeks. "I'll tell you who we are. We're what's left of the pig-headed, stubborn sons of bitches who just refused to go on the Trail. That's who we are. Our ancestors told them soldiers 'If you find us you can kill us, but we ain't leaving on our own.' Then in desperation those chicken shit whites killed a man and his family and called it even. Even for what? You ever ask yourself that? Now they teach our own children that the government let us stay here. Let us stay? On our own land? In our own nation? BULLSHIT!!" Lorenzo spat the word. "If they had chased our ancestors, Rodney, it would have taken them too damn long to round 'em all up. If they ever could have. And we'd have damn sure taken some of them with us. And don't think they didn't know it."

Lorenzo pulled a handkerchief from his back pocket and wiped off his face. It was clear that he was beginning to tire. But the fire in his eyes was still glowing hot. The old man had worked himself into quite a mood.

"Anyway, we refused to go. And, against the odds, we're still here.

We still ain't safe, but we're here." Lorenzo sighed. It was a heart-breaking breath that seemed to groan with the weight of the years and tears. "I've buried too many, Rodney. Too goddamn many. And not one of them died a warrior's death or anything noble. They starved. They froze to death. They took their own life. You name it, I've seen it. And I'm tired of it. I'm tired of being proud of the past, sick of the present, and scared about the future. Don't get me wrong, now, I ain't nowhere near ready to give up on my people. But I don't think I'll live to see the day when every Cherokee holds his head high. I hope you will."

"Me, too," Rodney said. His voice sounded like a pitiful squeak in his own ears.

"So that's why I want to see ambition in the nation's young men. That's the first step--believing we can do better and then going after it. Every time I had a little surplus from planting I would put it away. Then when I had enough I would pick me up another piece of land. Used to drive Cora crazy. She thought we should build a house right away and settle in. But before long, I was planting more, buying more, and eventually making more. 'Course when I started making it pretty good, the council refused to approve any more of my land purchases." He chuckled. "But the bastards acted too late. By the time they got around to telling me I couldn't buy any more land the fact was that I didn't really need any more. Before too long the same Indians that were against me on the council were calling me in to help them out of trouble. And I helped.

Now I guess its your turn, boy. I don't want to see Eunice or Curley go away, but I know why you're doing it and I can understand. You want more than this, and I hope you find it."

"Me, too," said Rodney, "my wife deserves it."

"Yeah, and I might've spoiled her just a little bit, too."

"Just a little," Rodney agreed. Both men laughed and then unconsciously looked around to make sure Eunice hadn't heard that one.

"We'll take real good care of Curley while you get settled," Lorenzo assured Rodney.

"Oh, I have no doubt of that."

The two stood there in silence for a little while longer.

"Well, let's get this bird inside and eat. And Rodney...."

"I won't say a word." Lorenzo smiled.

"Thank you."

"Thank you."
The dinner was one of the best Rodney could remember.
And Lorenzo felt the same.

CHAPTER FIFTEEN

The change in Lorenzo was not lost on the people of Qualla. He seemed somehow softer, kinder, less angry at the world. There was no doubt that he was still capable of unleashing his considerable wrath on someone who crossed him, but he seemed less on edge. Anyone meeting the man for the first time would have a very difficult time believing the stories that circulated around Cherokee about his white-hot anger. It was also easy for any one to see why Lorenzo had changed: the grandson tagging along everywhere he went.

Grandparents are perfect; they can commit no wrong and they never fail. Nature has decreed it to be thus. Folks around Qualla marveled that Russell Deveruox Norris did not have a permanently damaged neck from his constant attention to every move that his Grandpa made. His little arm stretched out expectantly, waiting for the little hand at the end to be enveloped by Lorenzo's oversized and calloused one. His eyes were full of awe and respect when he looked at the old man, and a smile seemed perpetually glued across his face. The normally gregarious and outgoing child grew solemnly quiet whenever Lorenzo spoke. It was as though he was doing more than merely listening; Curley was *studying* his Grandpa.

If imitation truly is the sincerest form of flattery, then no man ever received more accolades from his own flesh and blood than Lorenzo Dow Swayney. Curley was a wonderful mimic, but the impeccable impersonation of his Grandpa was not satire. It was pure adulation, as everyone who witnessed it well knew. Merchants and people passing the couple on the street would stop to ask Curley a question, any question, just to watch the act.

"Well, you sure are a cute one!" they would exclaim. "How old are you?" That would set Curley going. He would stroke his chin gently with his thumb and index finger, frown slightly, and furrow his dark eyebrows. After a few seconds of this he would narrow his eyes to slits and say, "Six years old, ma'am. Six years old." Lorenzo and the questioner would be sent into gales of laughter. Curley would smile self-consciously and stare up at his Grandpa as if to ask, "Did I do it right?" This was repeated several times a day, every day.

The times spent alone were no less satisfying for Lorenzo's ego. Curley hung on every word that the old man said. There is a charm and a fascination for the old to the very young. This is especially true in the Indian community.   Age is not a sign of worthlessness and inconvenience among them; it is a testament of perseverance and accrued wisdom. The knee of an elder serves as both school-house and sanctuary for an Indian child. It is here that they learn the stories of family achievement and their people's collective greatness. They are instilled with a passionate pride that does not leave them. That is why, even in the face of abject poverty and near desolation, an Indian may seem to an outside observer to be the most arrogant of species. It is difficult for these people to understand that they are not defined by material wealth and earthly goods but by the words driven into them by their parents and grandparents.

Curley marveled at the stories shared by Lorenzo. He learned about his great-great grandfather, Screaming Bear Nick, who had terrified the good white folks in the mountains with his drunken taunts and threats of the coming "Indian Uprising."   He had heard about his great grandmother, Laura Swayney, who had fled from the murderous hands of whites to these mountains. She was a Catawba, Lorenzo told him, and ran from the death that surrounded her to make her home in the Cherokee nation. There she had met John Wesley Swayney and been married. John Wesley was what Lorenzo called an "American mutt," mostly Cherokee, some Catawba, and some Irish. He had been a hard drinker, a vicious fighter and a difficult husband. Lorenzo did not comment on what kind of father he had been. His devotion to his late mother was, however, clear even to a five year old. Lorenzo related to Curley, even at this age, that there would always be people on and around Qualla who would not accept them as "real" Cherokees. They pointed to the Irish blood in J.W. Swayney and the fact that Laura had actually been Catawba. But, Lorenzo said in the same tone he would have used to scold Curley, "you are Cherokee, and don't you ever forget it."

Lorenzo liked to tell the story of his grandfather and great-grandfather. In 1864, at Loudon, Tennessee, the two of them had enlisted in the Union Army. The son, John J. Swayney, had by some poor decision by the corps commander (at least in terms of family politics) been given a higher rank than his father, James Swayney. The elder Swayney apparently quickly tired of taking orders from his impertinent son, at which point he promptly cracked the young man's head with an axe. John survived and, luckily for the Swayneys, the war between the states was soon over. Lorenzo would double over with laughter as he told the story, although Curley couldn't help but think that was a terrible thing for a son to do to his father.

Lorenzo also told many stories about his sister Arizona. He was clearly proud of her and what she had done, but it was also clear that talking about her pained him. Like Lorenzo, she had enrolled and graduated from the Hampton Institute in Virginia. Arizona had gone on to be a school teacher. She had returned to the reservation to teach, and she was almost single handedly responsible for teaching and, therefore saving, an old, traditional mode of Cherokee basket weaving. Many had complained that she had no business teaching that stuff--it wasn't a part of the three Rs that they wanted their children to learn. It was time, they argued, to let go of the "old ways" and move on.

"That is something you should also know," he told Curley quietly. "There are plenty of people in this world, Indians included, who are not proud of who they are and where they came from. In fact, sometimes I think we Indians are the worst."

"Why?" asked Curley innocently. Lorenzo smiled and gave his grandson an gentle pat on the head.

"When you've been told you're no good long enough, son, you might start to believe it. That's what happens."

"Who told your sister that she won't no good?"

"The same people who told me the same thing," Lorenzo responded. Curley shot up from the grass.

"Who said that?!" he demanded. "You are the best, Grandpa. The best ever!"

"Well now that might be overstating it....a little, anyway." Lorenzo smiled. "Curley the world is full of people who will try to tear your past from you. They'll offer you shiny toys and all manner of nice things if you just promise to be and think and act just like them. And if you don't, why sir they'll yank those things away just as quick as you saw them. That's why you must never, *ever*, turn your back on your family or your people. You understand me, don't you?"

"I think so, Grandpa." Curley looked awfully confused.

"Well, don't you worry about it, now. Someday you will understand what I mean. And when that day comes, don't you forget what your old Grandpa told you, hear?"

"Never, Grandpa. I promise."

₠

"Peace on earth, goodwill towards men," Lorenzo said with disgust. He was telling Curley the story of Wounded Knee.

"It happened out west somewhere," he said. "An Indian man had claimed that he had been given a dance for all the Indian people to do. He called it the Ghost Dance."

"Ghosts?" Curley asked, frightened.

"They were *Indian* ghosts, son," Lorenzo said soothingly. "Ancestors really. This dance would supposedly, if done right, bring back all the Indians who had died and help get our land back. All of us. But some white folks caught wind of it and got scared."

"Why?" asked Curley. It was becoming his favorite question.

"Huh, because they ain't as secure about their beliefs as they might have you think." Curley nodded in agreement. "That's something else you should know, son," Lorenzo continued, "you don't change a man's heart with a loaded gun. You change it through the strength of your argument or you don't change it at all." Lorenzo saw that his grandson didn't exactly understand that creed, but decided to let it slide until a later date.

"Anyway, these white folks got all worried and told those Indians that they had to stop doing that dance. Well, as Indians often do, didn't nobody listen to them whites. They kept on dancing and singing and praying. I've heard stories that their chants could be heard all across those plains, carrying their haunted and powerful message right into the heart of those white people's towns." Curley's deep, dark brown eyes had grown as big as saucers at just the thought.

"So those whites asked the government for help. And the government sent in the army to put a stop once and for all to the Ghost Dance." Lorenzo paused for dramatic effect and to make sure that Curley was still listening. That, as usual, was not a problem.

"What happened to them Indians, Grandpa?"

Lorenzo hesitated for just a moment. The thought darted through his mind that perhaps this story was too heavy a burden for a person of only six years of age. But there was a louder voice, a stronger one, that insisted the truth be told.

"They were killed," he said, "for holding fast to their beliefs." Curley swallowed hard. He didn't know what he should say or think.

"Does that still happen, Grandpa?"

"Not in that way, Curley. The choice is still the same, though. You can stay a part of what you are and risk death or try and be something that you're not. Join the white man or lose it all. That's the choice nowadays."

"What if you don't wanna be one of those white men?" asked Curley, thrusting out his chest as if he were ready to take on anyone or anything. "Does that mean you have to get killed?"

"No, son, it just means you must work twice as hard for everything. But if you are willing to do that, you can make something out of yourself that will make your Mama and Daddy....*and me* proud."

"Then *that's* what I'm gonna do," Curley nearly shouted. Lorenzo pulled the boy close against his chest, their hearts pounding together like drums.

"I'm sure you will, Curley, I am absolutely sure you will."

Cora poked her head out of the screen and called the two to supper. Curley jumped and ran ahead of his grandfather to the house. Lorenzo sat still for a minute, thinking about the times they were spending together and the fast approaching time when he would have to say goodbye to the little man that was growing so fast. He reflected on the fact that he had once had much the same conversation with his own children in this very yard. They had ended up doing him proud, he thought. Eunice and Dora were both making their way in the world, doing the best they knew how. Chiltos had lost his way, but he was not that much different from Lorenzo at his age.

Eunice was especially pleasing. She had faced so much in her young life that it would have been very easy for her to have decided that it wasn't worth the struggle. But every arrow that had come her way had only made her stronger and more resolute. The height of her chin and the strength in her step was directly proportionate to the number of snickers she faced. Lorenzo was very proud of the daughter he had brought up. No matter what others knew or thought they knew, they could not take that away from him ever.

"C'mon, Grandpa! Let's eat!"

Lorenzo found his strength and stood. He gave a quick glance around his yard, much the same way an English noble might have scanned his country estate. Lorenzo had resigned himself long ago to the fact that he would never find complete peace of mind. The world and his own desires would not allow it. But he thought that, perhaps, he could have some measure of the peace that "passeth all understanding" through the smiles and successes of his grandson. After all, grandchildren are perfect.

Nature had decreed it to be thus.

CHAPTER SIXTEEN

Lorenzo was carefully trimming the edges and bark away from the y-shaped piece of dogwood that he had removed from the tree. His hands were moving slowly, more methodically than usual so that Curley could pick up on every move that was made. As far as Curley was concerned, this was just further evidence of the genius of his Grandpa.

"Now, there we go," said Lorenzo as he peeled away the last unwanted piece of bark.

"There we go," echoed Curley.

Lorenzo stood and carefully laid the wood in the stove, twisting and turning it with an old iron fork.

"Now we'll bake it so that it can handle the force of being pulled over and over. We'll get any moisture left in there out so you'll have a better slingshot."

"Yeah," said Curley excitedly. Cora came into the room, looking considerably younger than her years in her Sunday dress.

"Um-um," Lorenzo said, "don't Grandma look good?"

"Pretty as a picture," agreed Curley, employing another phrase that he had heard Lorenzo use.

"You boys just give it up," Cora teased. "And while you're giving it up you can *hurry* up. Both of you shake a stick and get moving before you make me late for church." Lorenzo took the slingshot out of the oven and began blowing it to cool it off.

"You can't rush an artist, honeypot."

"You can," she answered, "when that artist has promised to accompany you to church and is still piddling about the house when he ought to be done dressed. Now get!" Lorenzo smiled.

"C'mon, boy, we better not make Grandma mad."

"No, sir, wouldn't wanna do that." They both went to their rooms and began quickly putting on their Sunday best.

As usual, Curley had found it exceedingly difficult to keep his eyes open during the preacher's sermon. The stories that the white man told just never seemed to be a match for the ones he heard during the week from Lorenzo. But he had kept his eyes open because his Grandpa had told him how much it meant to his Grandma. In the back of his mind, however, he couldn't help but think more about finishing that slingshot than getting into Heaven.

Lorenzo and Cora always walked to and from church. Even in the dead of winter when the winds off the mountain were cold enough to freeze your eyelids shut, they would trudge to the church on foot. The journey took a little longer with Curley, but it was also more interesting. Lorenzo and Cora had been making the trip for decades now, and they had long ceased to notice the almost overwhelming beauty that they passed each week, in any season. Curley never failed to point out these things. Leaves falling, clouds rolling, wind blowing, all of them were amazing feats to his young eyes.

"Grandpa, Grandma, look at that!" he would exclaim, pointing at whatever had caught his eye. The charm for the old couple was in the child's assumption that everything was still young and new to them as well. They would both feign amazement and wonder, and the boy would cackle with delight and gallop off to investigate. It was worth the extra time, Cora told Lorenzo, just to be reminded they were still alive.

When they arrived home they all ritualistically tore off their church clothes and jumped into the most comfortable outfit they had. These clothes were faithfully washed and hung out to dry on Saturday afternoon by Cora. After changing, Lorenzo would walk purposefully into the living room and draw his blow-gun down from above the mantle. He would inspect it as carefully each week as he had the last. Then he would walk into the kitchen and pull several darts from the pantry, again giving them a careful once over to make sure that they would serve his purpose. And each Sunday, just like clockwork, Curley would beg Lorenzo to go along. Lorenzo had always steadfastly refused. It wasn't a concern that the boy would get hurt. He felt confident he could keep a watchful enough eye on him to make sure that didn't happen. The problem was that Curley had no conception of what it meant to sneak. His bounding steps and constant questions would scare off any would-be dinner in a second. And

Lorenzo looked forward to Cora working her culinary magic with squirrel or rabbit.

"Grandpa, can I come?" Curley asked as he raced out of the back bedroom that had once been his mother's.

"Now Curley, we go through this every single Sunday," Lorenzo answered, trying to muster a tone of annoyance. Cora stepped out from the kitchen , wiping flour off of her hands onto her old checkered apron. Curley looked down at his feet.

"I know," he said, answering Lorenzo's attempt at being annoyed with his own attempt at sounding and looking pitiful. "I just thought maybe I could help." Cora smiled. Both of these men were actors of the highest quality, she thought.

"Let him go with you, Ranz," she said, pulling out her own pet name for him.

"Please," Curley moaned.

"Can you be quiet?" asked Lorenzo. "I mean really, really quiet?"

"Yeah!" Curley nearly screamed his answer. Cora laughed out loud.

"I mean it," Lorenzo said sternly, "if you go running around and whooping there won't be an animal on this reservation that don't go the other way."

"I'll be quiet as a mouse," Curley whispered. Lorenzo sighed. He had been outgunned this time.

"Alright," he said. "You can go with me." Curley let out a yell that, a hundred years before, would have terrified white folks for miles. The glance from Lorenzo quieted him.

"Sssshhhhh," Curley agreed smiling. Lorenzo turned for the door so the boy would not see his grin.

ᏀᎧ

There were storm clouds coming up over the mountains. Lorenzo thought they seemed to be predicting snow. It was getting that time of year again. It would be harder to find something good to eat today. Curley had walked over behind some trees and was relieving himself. Lorenzo glanced over to make sure he hadn't wandered off too far and then turned back, lighting a cigarette. He pulled his old coat a little tighter around him. He heard Curley coming up behind him.

"Can I have one?" he asked.

"One what?" asked Lorenzo, confused.

"A cigarette," Curley said matter-of-factly. Lorenzo laughed.

"No you cannot."

"Why not?"

"Because you have to have worries to be allowed a smoke. And a five year old doesn't have any worries."

"Six," Curley corrected.

"A six year old don't either."

"I *have* worries," Curley stated emphatically. That brought a deep belly laugh from Lorenzo.

"What in the world do you have to worry about?" he asked through his chuckles. Curley began nudging the leaves around his feet with the toe of his boot.

"Stuff."

"What stuff?"

"Mama and Daddy," the boy said. He looked up at Lorenzo. His eyes were glistening with small tears. "They're coming back, aren't they?" Lorenzo dropped the blow-gun to the ground and pulled Curley close to him. He could feel the tension racing through the boy like a fever. Curley was struggling not to let his Grandpa see him cry. That would be unbearable to the boy.

"Curley," Lorenzo said, "you listen to me and you listen to me good. Your Mama and Daddy love you to death, and they are coming back here to get you just as quick as they can. I promise you that. You know Grandpa wouldn't tell you a lie, don't you?"

"Uh-huh," Curley mumbled.

"Well then you quit worrying. They'll be back soon to get you. Honest." Lorenzo pulled Curley away and winked at him.

"Can you and Grandma go with us?"

"No, son, we can't. Me and your Grandma need to stay here."

"Why?"

"Well, Curley, me and your Grandma are old. For us to up and leave Qualla and try to start all over again...well, it just wouldn't work, that's all." The answer sounded terribly feeble even to Lorenzo.

"I don't understand," Curley said.

"This is our home, son, and we just can't leave."

"But it's my home, too," Curley stated. "And Grandma always says that home is wherever kinfolks are."

"Ah, hell, Curley," Lorenzo said in frustration, "don't go listening to half the stuff women'll tell you."

Curley didn't say anything; there was nothing to say. He knew his

Grandpa knew the answer to everything, but that didn't help him comprehend what he was being told. The wind kicked up suddenly, spinning a mini-tornado with the dust and leaves around Curley's feet. Lorenzo sat silently staring at his own feet. Those feet, he thought, wouldn't begin to know how to tread the roads that lay ahead for his grandson. For the first time he felt a real sense of terror at the thought of this young boy being thrown to the wolves that lurked in the outside world. He made himself push the thought to the far edges of his mind, that corner that stored whatever he didn't want to think about just yet. The mind, Lorenzo thought, was like an attic. When too many things got stored in that or any corner, it would have to be sorted through and dealt with. But not now, not today.

"We'll always have each other, Curley," he said, not looking up for fear of being betrayed by his emotions. "Distance and time can't change that." Curley didn't respond. For the first time, Lorenzo was struck with the thought that his grandson might not completely believe him.

"Dammit," Lorenzo said flatly. Curley looked up. "Here," Lorenzo continued, extending the cigarette to the boy, "but for God's sake and mine don't tell anybody." Curley took the smoke and jutted out his chin as Lorenzo lit the tip. He took a deep drag and then coughed violently.

"Thanks," he said as the tears poured down his face. Lorenzo laughed and peered back into the woods--looking for dinner.

As they walked back into their yard Lorenzo saw Cora standing on the front porch waving something in her hands like it was burning her.

"A letter from Eunice," she yelled. Curley took off from his grandpa's side and flew up the steps. Lorenzo felt a pang of dread rush through him. As he walked slowly up the steps he handed a rabbit to Cora and took possession of the letter.

"What does she say?" he asked, not bothering to expect the envelope.

"Well, I don't know," Cora answered, "I was waiting on you before I opened it. Don Tyson brought it by not more than an hour ago. It came through yesterday."

"Oh," Lorenzo said, walking into the house and feeling through his pants pocket for his knife. Cora studied her husband's face.

"What's wrong, Ranz?"

"Nothing," he said, forcing a smile. Cora just grunted. She knew not to push, but she was not fooled by the smile. She had seen more sincerity in the face of a missionary. Lorenzo pulled the letter from the envelope. Curley was practically bouncing off the walls.

"What does she say?" he asked. "What does Mama say?" Lorenzo lowered himself in his rocker while Cora lit the lantern over his head to give him better light. She handed him his reading glasses. Lorenzo cleared his throat as Curley dropped to the floor and waited as if he were about to hear a bed time story.

"Dear Russell, Mama and Daddy,

Rodney and I are doing fine. I hope that everything is well there in Qualla. I also hope that Russell is behaving himself and being a good boy. I'm sure he is."

Russell (his Mama thought he was getting too big for a name like "Curley") blushed and smiled broadly at the mention of his name.

"We are almost settled here in Cramerton. I must admit that I miss you all a lot. There is nothing to look at here---no mountains and no creek. No Big Cove! Please tell Mrs. Runningwolf that we send her our love. Rodney has started his job and he is liking it just fine. He says for me to be sure and tell Daddy that it is fun having white folks working under him for a change. There are a few men here who have given him some trouble, being Indian and all, but I want you all to know that most of the people here have been really very nice to us. I hope that makes everyone feel better. It has certainly put my mind to rest.

I have two very important pieces of news for you. The first is that we have started renting ourselves a very nice frame house. It sits on First Street (imagine street names!) and I think it is very pretty. It costs a lot, I think, but Rodney says that is just the way it goes here. Right now we only have a bed and a couch, but we are very comfortable. There will be plenty of room for all of us, I think. I will be coming to get Russell around Christmas time. I can't wait to see how my boy has grown!

That brings me to my next piece of news. I am going to have another baby."

Cora gasped and Lorenzo smiled. Curley looked at them both carefully, not sure what this all meant.

*"Rodney says that should not surprise you, since we don't know anyone
here to go and visit at night. He is very excited about it and I am too. I
hope it will be a little girl, but I think Rodney wants another son. I told
him he was selfish!*

*Well, I should be going. I can't wait to see you all. Please tell
Russell how much his Daddy and I love him and can't wait to have him
down here with us. We love you all very much.*

Love always,
Eunice Norris

Lorenzo carefully refolded the letter and slid it back into the
envelope. He looked at Cora and smiled. This one, she thought, was
real.

"Well, son," he said, "what do you want? A brother or a sister?"
Curley wrinkled his nose. Why had his mama and daddy gone and got
a new baby with him away? Didn't they know that he was going to be
with them soon?

"Neither," he said, and Lorenzo and Cora both laughed. They had
been through this themselves with their own children. "Mama's coming
soon?" he asked.

"Yes, dear," Cora said to him.

"But don't think you can talk her out of having this baby," Lorenzo
said, still laughing, "even *your* charm can't change these facts." Curley
laughed too, even though he wasn't really sure what his Grandpa meant.
Cora quickly chastised her husband.

"Sorry," he said with a wicked grin. "Well, boy, let's go sit on the
porch while Grandma makes dinner. I reckon I better speed up all
these stories I've got left to tell you." Curley jumped up and beat his
Grandpa out onto the porch. As he was leaving, Lorenzo felt Cora's
arms wrap around his waist. He stopped.

"You know this news makes us really old, don't you?"

"Speak for yourself," he said, turning to face her. He gave his wife
a passionate, best-friend kiss. "That seem old?" he asked.

"That," she said, blushing, "could never seem old." Curley called
out to his Grandpa from the porch.

"Coming," Lorenzo called. "You," he said to Cora, "I'll deal with
later." Turning on his heel, he regally walked out to his anxious
grandson. Cora walked shyly back into the kitchen.

As Lorenzo lectured on the proper way to use a blow-gun, Curley couldn't keep his mind from wandering. His world seemed a lot more chaotic than it had when he had crawled out of bed this morning. He would be seeing his mama again soon, and that was good. But everything else seemed to have spiraled out of his control. He would have to part with his grandma and grandpa soon, and that was a prospect that his young heart could not process. And to top that off, he was now about to get a little brother or sister. Although he couldn't formulate exactly what he thought about all the things going on around him, Curley was experiencing for the first time a time-tested truism:

Sometimes, life just isn't fair.

CHAPTER SEVENTEEN

Lorenzo and Cora had decided to put off trimming the tree until their eldest child reached Qualla. The decision did not sit particularly well with Dora, who wanted the tree done on the Saturday after Thanksgiving as it had always been done, but she knew better than to try and talk her parents out of the delay. The sibling rivalry had not diminished with Eunice's move away from Cherokee. In fact, the move had only served to increase the level of competition that Dora felt with her sister. She privately promised herself that, as soon as it was possible, she would head out into the world like Eunice was doing. Like most of her peers, Dora had come to believe that any thing white must be better. By contrast, any thing Indian was backwards and out of touch with the fast paced modern world. Her time at the Hampton Institute had only confirmed these beliefs. In school she was, like the other Indian and black students, urged to embrace the white man's mores and priorities.

She heard the nasty remarks that floated around Qualla in the days after Eunice and Rodney had departed. They were "uppity," they were "trying to be white," they were "forgetting who they are." But she couldn't have cared less if they said the same things of her when she left. In fact, more power to the narrow minds and bitter tongues that launched such poison arrows at her sister. They were the ones who would still be stuck in poverty long after the Swayney sisters had made a fortune in the white man's world. Making ends meet as a nurse on Qualla was a near impossibility. But out there, in the world, she had heard stories of women making perfectly good livings as a nurse. That was what she had wanted, and Eunice's leaving had only strengthened her resolve to make it happen.

Don Tyson brought Eunice into Qualla on December 21, 1924. Eunice was struck by the fact that so little had changed in the months that she had been away, yet nothing felt the same. Every store front, every shack and house, every brown and white face was tainted with the feeling of something past, something belonging to another part of her life that was now far more distant than the miles or the months between where she had been and where she had gone. Qualla remained static but she had somehow changed profoundly. This place was still and always would be an integral part of her and who she was, but she no longer felt part of it. Despite what the others said as she passed, it was not that she thought herself somehow better than them. But she had now committed the one act in life from which there is no return and no forgiveness---she had dared to look for and find more. She understood something that they never could, that a person can dearly love something and yet still not find contentment with it. Qualla had shaped her. She would define herself.

It was unclear to Eunice where the bitterness came from that she felt when she saw old faces around the reservation. It was too simplistic, she believed, to chalk all of it up to envy. Of course that was part of it. Envy, however, was usually a quiet emotion. It showed its face in snide little remarks and biting asides. But this was different. There was a vitriol in the attacks that stunned her. Anger always seemed to be lurking just below the surface of the people that spoke to her.

"It's nothing more complicated," Lorenzo told her when she mentioned what she had felt to him, "than simple fear. These people are terrified of you now because you know something they don't. They're afraid you might end up happy, and that you might tell them about it. They've all built walls around themselves so that they feel safer. They convince themselves that there's nothing worthwhile out there that they don't have right on their doorstep. If you come in here and tell them that you've found something of value outside their sheltered lives, why, you might as well tell them that their God just died. It couldn't shake them any worse."

So Eunice spent most of her time playing down her happiness and acting as though she wasn't too proud of what she and her husband had dared to do. The pretense revolted her but it seemed the most expedient way to keep the peace for the time she would be there. As long as she didn't challenge their petty security with her own happiness things would be fine. The entire sham made her feel ill. It was unlike her, unlike her family, to act any way other than the way they felt around others. But she wanted to enjoy her time in Qualla as much as they would allow her. She was just glad that Rodney had been forced because of work to stay behind. More than being angry, the accusations that he had turned his back on his people because he wanted to provide more for his wife and family would have cut him to the bone.

There were others, more numerous but as usual less vocal, who flocked to the Swayney household to hear all about life in the city. They kept Eunice up until late in the mountain night asking questions. Did everyone there have cars? What kind of clothes did they wear? Were they friendly? How did they talk? Did they make fun of the young Cherokee couple? Eunice answered each one as fully as she knew how, with as much patience as she could muster. They seemed so fascinated. They were like wide-eyed children opening a shiny new package. They made Eunice as sick as those who were afraid to hear what lay beyond the reservation's border, because they were only a nicer flip side of the same rusty coin. These sycophants in many ways made Eunice angrier than the nasty locals who avoided her. The ones consumed with their provincial terror were merely afraid that the white man *might* be better than they; these friendly types were utterly convinced it was true. The whole thing became *a li so qui lv di* on the young woman's shoulders, leaving her feeling like a stranger to everyone except her family and, of course, Ma Runningwolf.

Molly was circumspect about the whole situation. She admitted that she, too, had been a little worried that maybe Eunice wouldn't want to spend time with an old woman after the lights and glamour of the big city. But the two had hit their stride as if Eunice had never gone away. Eunice was soon pouring her heart out to her friend just like before. Molly asked many of the same questions that the others had, but more out of an unspoken suspicion than a deep-seated awe. They laughed about how lost Eunice had felt when they first arrived, and at how she had marveled at all the things so readily available in the stores down there.

"I'm telling you Ma Runningwolf," she said, "there are women down there who I'd swear have never worn anything in their life except store-bought clothes." This truly impressed Molly, who had only had two dresses in her entire life not made by her mother's or her own hand. And although Eunice had owned plenty of store dresses in her life, she also knew how to make her own.

They also talked about the whites. Molly asked if it the city whites smelled funny when they got wet, they way these mountain ones did. Eunice laughed and said that yes, that seemed to be true no matter where the whites lived. Molly asked if they had any trouble with the

white folks, since they weren't one of them. Eunice answered that, so
far at least, there had been no trouble. Molly shook her head as if to
acknowledge what they both knew: sooner or later there would be
some from someone. Eunice also told Ma Runningwolf the big news
that, since they had another baby on the way, Rodney had reluctantly
agreed to let her find some part-time nursing work. She laughed at the
incredulous way that the old woman looked at her.

"Oh," she said smiling, "he can't resist me. Bless his stubborn heart
he tries, but he just can't." At that both of the women cackled.

The major discussion was of the new child. Ma Runningwolf
informed Eunice that she had seen the baby in a dream and that it
would be a healthy baby boy. Eunice grimaced and said that she was
really hoping to finally have another girl around the house.

"I'm tired of being the only one around there that pees sitting down,"
she said. Molly shrugged. Maybe later, she said, but she felt pretty
certain that this wouldn't be the time. She had complete confidence in
her dream. Eunice sighed.

"But you should be very happy," Molly continued. "This child will
have a very special bond with your first-born. They will compliment
each other very well. And you will need them." Molly said the last
sentence with a grim nod. Eunice pressed her for more information,
but her friend waved her away; she was through talking. Through the
blue smoke that drifted and danced around Molly's head Eunice thought
she detected a note of sadness and it scared her.

"Don't worry so much, child," Molly intoned, "can't you just be
happy that your child will be healthy and will get along with Curley?"
Eunice decided not to ruin her holiday by pressing the issue. But it
wouldn't leave her mind throughout the rest of her visit.

꙰

Lorenzo sat in front of the fireplace, a bible opened on each knee.
On the right knee was an English translation of the King James Bible,
bound in rich leather that still cracked when it was opened and smelled
fresh. On his left knee was his Cherokee version of the good book. It
was tattered and its pages methodically marked and bent. As he had
opened it, several pages from the book of Psalms, his personal favorite,
had floated down around his muddy boots like autumn leaves. He
thumbed through each until he found the story of the nativity. A
Swayney family tradition was about to continue, now with three
generations taking part. Lorenzo surveyed his brood with an easy

satisfaction.

Cora sat to his right, as she always did, smiling approvingly at Curley's every utterance. She had been the one to lean down and retrieve the Psalms that had fallen on the floor. Her hand gently rubbed the side of Lorenzo's leg, making circles, tracing life.

Dora sat next to her father, a place she had made a beeline for as soon as dinner had been eaten. She looked soft and young in the orange glow of the fire. Her hair and clothes were put together with an immaculate precision normally reserved for those heading out on the town in a big city. She sat straight as an arrow, looking more and more like her father with each passing day.

Chiltos was standing in a corner diagonally behind Lorenzo. It was his way to avoid his father's steely glance, especially whenever the Bible was brought out. He shuffled his feet to and fro, nervously biting at the inside of his lip. It seemed that he would rather be somewhere else, but that this was a tradition even his rebellious nature dare not flaunt. Occasionally, his eyes would meet with Eunice's and a grin would spread across his face. He loved Curley and thought the young boy was able to inject a certain air of irreverence that he would've never been able to get away with.

The only non-family member, Molly Runningwolf, sat beside Eunice and directly across from Cora. Molly's pipe was again lit and billowing nearly as much smoke as the logs in the fireplace. She, too, would now and again glance at the wiggling child beside her. He would smile at her and she would return the favor, thinking of her dream and all that this young man could become. She violently pushed away any thoughts that, soon, this young boy would go away and return only as a visitor to the land of their people. She consoled herself with the knowledge of who his parents were---two proud young Cherokee lovers who would not let Curley forget.

Eunice sat directly across from her father, beside Molly, with Curley on her lap. He was fingering the outline of the slingshot that his grandfather had given him after dinner as an early Christmas gift. She surveyed the family, her mind racing across and through the winds of time to all the previous years that they had gathered here like this, to hear this story, to celebrate their survival as a people and a family. She remembered when she and Dora had mischievously told Chiltos that their father liked it when he was interrupted during the reading because it showed him that they were still awake. She remembered the wonderful suspense and exultation that accompanied Christmas Eve and the bright mornings that followed with gifts under the tree. Mostly, she remembered how, every year, their father had excused himself after Christmas breakfast and left the house with a burlap sack, staying gone until it was nearly dinner time. It wasn't until many years later that she had learned Lorenzo was out taking small gifts to the children of families who otherwise would've gotten nothing. As a teen, she and Dora had gone with him, helping him distribute the goods faster.

As those memories ran out of her head she stared solemnly and disapprovingly at the outline of the stone chimney rising up above Lorenzo's head. Her eyes then went to the floor as she thought about what had once lived down there, down in their basement. Her father liked to talk about how he had made his money by hard work---farming and acquiring pieces of land whenever he could. She knew, as they all did, that that was only part of the story. For years there had been a still brewing almost continuously under their feet, with the smoke ingeniously being routed out the chimney with the same smoke that emanated from the family's hearth. The trick had kept the revenuers and missionaries at bay for years, until Lorenzo had made enough money to buy their acquiescence or, at the very least silence. He had truly made most of his money distilling and selling the very liquid that he now spent so much time damning; the same liquid that had, like a mighty river, flowed between him and his only son. Lorenzo Dow Swayney, Qualla's self-appointed guardian and local temperance leader, had at one time been the biggest and most successful moonshiner the Cherokee had ever known.

Eunice also thought about those two texts on her father's knees. He would read to them the story of the Christ child and, usually, shed a sincere tear at the end. But his battles with the missionaries was legendary and, while he could not himself be considered a "traditional," he had always been one of their most vocal supporters. This, Eunice thought, was the true essence of being an American Indian. If, at the end of the day, you made sense to yourself, let alone anyone else, you had truly accomplished something. It was an existence steeped in irony and contradiction. But those were not the kinds of things that she wanted to think about. Not this year, not now.

She also found her mind and her heart sailing away, as she had known it would, on a sad current towards her husband. He was sitting all alone down there in Cramerton. She wondered how he would spend this Christmas Eve, with his pregnant wife and six year old son away from him. Knowing him, he would probably eat some cold sandwich, drink a lot of iced-tea, smoke, and sit by their fireplace staring at nothing. It made her sad to think of him there, all alone on this special night. He had promised her that they would exchange gifts when she returned from Qualla. But right at this moment it was his presence, not his presents, for which she yearned the most. Eunice sighed as Lorenzo began reading. He would begin by reading three or four verses from his worn Cherokee bible and then read the same verses again in English. This took a little longer, but no one, not even the six year old, missed the significance. In this house, Cherokee was always given precedence and it would always be this way. Lorenzo's clear and steady voice rang throughout the house, giving an urgency to the story. Even Chiltos stopped his nervous swaying at the sound of the man's voice. Curley became still and listened with rapt attention to his grandfather's words.

When Lorenzo had completed the story, he inserted thin, silk bookmarks into each book and turned to place them on opposite ends of the mantle. Sitting again, he motioned for Chiltos to move in closer. Then he stretched out each of his arms and unfolded his palms, Cora and Dora each taking hold of one. They both then reached out in turn until the entire group was sitting in a circle, holding each other's hand. Lorenzo bowed his head silently and Cora said quietly, "Let us pray." Almost in unison, the group bowed their heads. Lorenzo began to pray.

"Our Father, we ask for Your forgiveness and mercy, as evidenced in the gift you sent us in your son, Jesus Christ. We ask that you walk with us all our days and help us to be the people that you would want us to be. If we fail, Lord, let it always be because we reached too far, never because we didn't try. We thank you for this family and all that you have given us. Two of them will soon be leaving us, and we ask especially that you watch over and protect them. Let them walk as their ancestors walked---their path straight and honest, their heads held high with the dignity earned by those who went before them. No matter what new things they see and amazing things they witness out there, may they never bow their head or bend their knee to anyone but You. Amen."

When they all raised their heads, only the men weren't crying, and that seemed to be more from a concerted effort than any lack of feeling. Eunice noticed they were all looking at her expectantly, as if silently asking "Can't you stay a little while longer?" Chiltos dropped his hands to his side and went back into the kitchen. Cora followed, dutifully ready to make him something more to eat. Curley rushed to his grandfather and began talking hurriedly about the game that they would catch together with this slingshot. Lorenzo stared lovingly at Eunice, his eyes seeming to tell her that, although it was tearing his heart out, he understood and was proud. Soon, mercifully, the silence was broken with Christmas carols being belted out by Dora and Chiltos. Lorenzo dragged his fiddle out of the closet and began throwing out an odd mix of carols and hymns and popular music. Molly smoked happily, Curley danced around with everyone, and Eunice sat in the corner watching it all with a deep sense of melancholy. Qualla tugged at her heart one last, desperate time, just to make sure she knew what she was doing.

ℂ

New Years Day had dawned bright but bitterly cold. Don Tyson would once again be her companion and chauffeur on the trip back to Cramerton. In addition to making some profitable business contacts in the area, the bachelor storekeeper had apparently met a young woman there who had stolen his heart. He was more than happy to have an excuse to make the arduous journey again.

The family had all gathered at the house to say goodbye to Eunice and Curley. There was an uncustomary sense of sentimentality in the air, one that every person gathered there tried to beat back with as much self-discipline as they could muster. Even Chiltos seemed to be moved by the experience, hoisting Eunice's trunks onto the back of Tyson's cart and slipping her some money for the trip.

"I got that money honest," he instructed her, "so don't argue with me about taking it." Eunice had smiled and kissed him on his strong, square jaw.

"I love you, Chiltosky," she said, "and I pray for you. Please be careful. O.k.?"

Her brother smiled and nodded his assent. Eunice turned and found Dora had crept up behind her.

"I want you to know that you haven't won just yet," she said smiling. "I'll be right behind you before you know it."

"You'll always be welcome in our home," Eunice said. "Always."

"Well," Dora shot back, "maybe just until I get that mansion of my own." Both of the women laughed.

"And what about Eddie?" Eunice gave her sister a sly, knowing glance. Dora had been seen lately in the company of Eddie Swimmer, a young Cherokee that seemed to drive all the local girls crazy with his stories of the war and all he had seen. Swimmer also was the proud owner of a fast, if slightly used automobile. There were those, older women, who laughed at Swimmer's insistence on still wearing his Army uniform to the local dances and corn-shuckings that were held. But it seemed to have its desired effect on the young girls. Including, apparently, Dora Swayney.

"Ah, don't you worry about Eddie," she said dismissively, "I know what that one's all about. I just like being seen with him because it drives those other hens so crazy. But don't tell Daddy. I'm kinda enjoying watching him squirm." Both of them laughed loudly at their secret joke and then embraced. When they separated, Dora was wiping a tear from her eye.

"I love you, Eunice. And that young'un of yours, too."

"We love you, Dotie," Eunice said, also crying now.

"Please girls, don't start *that* whatever you do." Cora had now joined the circle. They all embraced, a messy mix of laughter and tears. Eunice couldn't help but notice the difference between leaving now and the way it had felt before. Now there was nothing to come back and retrieve. She was leaving nothing behind that needed to come with her. It was a painful realization.

"Oh, good God." Lorenzo was bounding down the cabin steps with Curley in tow and Don Tyson at his side. "I was hoping to avoid all this mess."

"Me, too," yelled Curley, trying in vain to match his grandfather's intensity. That seemed to break the tension and ease the burden they were all feeling.

"I was able to break Tyson here and get a reasonable price for transporting this brood down south," Lorenzo said with obvious satisfaction. Tyson shook his head like a defeated prizefighter trying to clear the cobwebs from his head.

"Daddy, the deal was that Rodney would pay Mr. Tyson when we arrived. You really didn't have to do that."

"I *wanted* to do that," Lorenzo corrected, pulling his daughter into his arms. "Call it a last effort at being your father." He smiled down at her.

"I'm going to miss you, brown eyes," he said quietly. "But I'm proud of you. And, well, I think you know how much I love you." He walked her over to the buggy. With one effortless motion he had placed her in the seat. Tyson crawled up into the driver's side and grabbed the reins. He was already thinking of his lady friend and becoming anxious. Lorenzo looked down and saw that Curley was still clinging to his pant's leg. The sight made his heart sink. He had managed to adjust earlier to the absence of his daughter. This was new. And it hurt.

"Well, boy," he said, steadying himself, "are you ready to see your Daddy and your new house?"

"No." Curley had a very surley tone.

"No?" Lorenzo asked. "Well, I know your Daddy sure is ready to see you. And your Mamma can't wait to show you off to all them new friends they've made down there."

"Can you come with us?" asked Curley, searching his grandfather's face for any sign of weakness.

"No, son, I think I better stay right here. This is my place."

"Mine, too, Grandpa," Curley said. Lorenzo looked up at Eunice. She seemed genuinely worried for the first time that maybe Curley wouldn't go with her. Lorenzo bent down so that he could look directly into the boy's face.

"No, Curley. This ain't your place. Your place is with your Mamma and Daddy, wherever they might be. Can you understand that?" Curley looked down at the ground, avoiding his grandfather's eyes. It was becoming obvious to him that he was going to lose this argument. "Son, I need you to do something for me. It's real important. Will you do something for your old grandpa?"

"Yessir," Curley said suspiciously.

"I need you to go with your Mamma and watch out for her. Her and your Daddy need somebody around to keep them straight and I think you are just the man for the job. It would make me feel a lot better to know that you were down there taking care of them for me. Alright?" Curley looked back at Lorenzo. Tears were welling in his eyes, making them seem both darker and brighter than Lorenzo had ever seen them.

"I'll do it, Grandpa. I'll watch 'em for you." Then he hugged Lorenzo with enough force to take his breath away. Lorenzo lifted the young man in his arms and into the cart.

"I love you, Curley Norris."

"I love you, Grandpa. And grandpa?"

"Yes, son?"

"I won't forget where I come from."

Lorenzo smiled.

"I know, son," he said, nodding towards a strange place, "they won't let you."

CHAPTER EIGHTEEN

Curley was staring at the ceiling again. There were no dancing shadows, no lights darting back and forth against the backdrop of his bedroom walls. There was only an oppressive stillness and an opaque silence that muffled even the clearest of thoughts, the most daring of dreams. Curley inhaled deeply, but there was no smell of life. He could find no confirmation that there were any spirits around him, watching over him, conversing with his anxious mind and lonely heart. The room felt like a crypt to him.

Where had the leaves gone, he wondered. Those beautiful leaves that this time last year would have been weaving a complex and sophisticated shadow ballet all across his vision. Where were the crickets and tree-frogs that had provided the melody, the orchestration for those dancing leaves? And what of the midnight howl of the reservation dogs? Where had they gone? He thought of the songs that flew from the jaws of those dogs, as they called to one another as if they were sharing the day's news. Once in a while he could hear the neighboring dogs bark here, too, but it was so different. They sounded angry, as if they were itching for a fight. Not like the dog songs of home. Nothing here was like home. He wondered where all those wonders had gone. But, of course, they had gone nowhere. It was he who had left them behind. They still sang and danced and cried. He could just no longer hear them. He closed his eyes tight, trying to call up a vision or a smell or a sound--anything--that would feel familiar. It was no use. He rolled over onto his side and slipped his hand searchingly under his pillow.

There it was. That brought a smile to his drawn features. The feel of the rubber straps of the slingshot eased some of the loneliness. But it did nothing to fill the hole that seemed to be expanding in his soul. He recognized that something within was missing, he just couldn't put his finger on exactly what it was. He had heard the word "homesick" tossed freely around by his parents, but he didn't think that was it. Surely homesickness couldn't be this consuming. He stroked the slingshot more forcefully. The hole began to ache now with a violence that surprised him. Normally, it was a dull ache. This pain actually made him grimace. Curley thought of all the bumps and bruises he had acquired over his seven years. Yeah, he thought, he preferred physical pain to this stuff. He wasn't sure this pain would ever scab over and heal.

He tried to make himself think of tomorrow's planned activities. His Dad had told him over and over that it was going to be lots of fun. It was the first "day off" that Rodney had had since Curley and Eunice had arrived from the mountains weeks ago. Dad had promised to spend all of it with Curley. They were going to go to the park. Curley thought about that word with a contempt bordering on absolute disgust.

The Park. What a joke. Who needed a park? What exactly was a park? From his father's descriptions it sounded like a place where people went to look at animals, plants, flowers and the like. Had white people gone so far as to place nature on a reservation the way they had the Cherokee? That sure was how it sounded to Curley's young ears. Back home, if he had wanted to commune with nature all he had to do was step out into the yard. Here, apparently, they had to make a special trip for the same experience. Who had the power to fence in nature in such a. way? And why would someone with that kind of power want to do that anyway? Was this really the work of the "white man" that he had heard his grandpa speak of so often? Curley only knew one thing for sure: if this was the work of this white man he would never come to understand him. Not ever.

∞

The morning had opened the new day with a powerful spring shower, then given way to a bright and unseasonably warm day. Eunice was the first up, and she began making breakfast for her husband and son. She was graceful in the kitchen, softly singing old songs and swaying her hips to the rhythm and music in her head. Her stomach was now protruding quite a bit. She would be bigger this time it seemed. She was not very happy about that thought, but it seemed to be out of her hands. Rodney kept telling her not to worry about it, that he loved the way a pregnant woman looked.

"They glow," he told her smiling. Of course that was a time-honored line that had probably originated with Adam. They weren't glowing, Eunice thought, they were sweating. And no man liked to see his wife get to be as big as a house. But to complain meant to risk getting on the wrong side of a pregnant woman's raging hormones. And no man was that stupid, so they had come up with the line about how they loved the "glow" and they stuck to it no matter what. Just as well, since Eunice felt she would probably personally remove a vital part of Rodney's person if he commented on her ballooning weight. Adam had known exactly what he was doing.

"Morning, honey pot," Rodney said as he emerged from the bedroom. "You been up long?"

"Nope."

Rodney sat down at the kitchen table. Eunice placed a hot cup of coffee in front of him.

"This'll open that other eye," she said with a grin.

"Hmmph," was all Rodney could manage. He was not a morning person.

Eunice enjoyed watching her husband in the morning. His hair stood nearly straight up on his head and he seemed to wear a frown that could never be removed. He squinted at the barest light and didn't get his mouth and mind working together until he had been up at least half an hour. It had been most fun when Curley was three and would rise early with a million questions for his father, all of which took the greatest effort to answer. Finally Eunice had been forced to step in and let her brain-dead husband off the hook. It had been great fun to watch.

"Still going to the park?"

"Uh-huh."

"Good. I think Curley will enjoy that. And it'll be good for the two of you to spend some time together before the baby arrives."

Rodney nodded. He watched his wife glide across the floor, from cabinet to stove and back again. It was difficult to see because of the bright light in the room. Eunice had insisted on hanging yellow curtains in the window, magnifying the morning sunlight that already burst into the kitchen. He was sure she had done that on purpose, knowing the way he did that she thought his morning squint "cute." Still, he could make out enough to see that she was beautiful. Her black hair hung down between her shoulder blades and moved with her hips. He noticed that she was beginning to look a little disproportionate now, her thin legs and arms and then that bulging stomach. Rodney smiled. That stomach was bulging with another son. Molly had told Eunice so.

"What are you thinking?" she asked.

"Oh, I was just thinking about those damned yellow curtains. We should've got black." He smiled.

"The sunlight keeps us healthy, Rodney. You haven't been away from Qualla long enough to have forgotten that." She smiled back. Rodney thrust his hands to his heart as if he had just taken a dagger. Eunice laughed. The door to Curley's room opened and her son walked out, looking more like her, she noted, than he had when he had gone to bed. He was as bright in the morning as any yellow curtains.

"Good morning, honey," she said. "Are you ready for breakfast?"

"Nah, I'm not really so hungry right now."

Eunice gave Rodney a worried glance. She had been told of Curley's legendary eating habits by her parents and sister, but since they had arrived in Cramerton he had barely eaten at all. She had remarked to Rodney that she thought he may be losing weight, but he had told her that she was just worrying too much.

"Son, you need to eat. Me and you have a big day ahead of us." Rodney smiled and Curley forced a smile back.

"O.k., maybe some toast?"

"Coming right up," Eunice said, trying to sound cheerful. Lorenzo had told her that her son regularly ate two eggs and some bacon when he stayed with them. She tried to push the worry from her mind.

"So," Rodney asked, "are you ready to go to the park with me?"

"Um-huh," Curley said, trying to look pleased and excited. Rodney noticed the effort that his son was forced to exert just to try and smile. He could feel the frustration building within himself. He took several deep breaths, reminded himself to be patient, there had been many changes in Curley's world, and stood from the table. He walked slowly to the pantry and reached under some old blankets lying in there. He pulled out a kite that he had made for their excursion. Old newsprint, sticks from the mill, and twine. He was pleased with himself as he looked it over. He walked back over to the table and laid it in front of Curley.

"What's that?" asked Curley.

"That," Rodney answered, "is a kite. It flies in the wind."

"Like a bird?" Curley's eyes had gotten bigger, and Rodney thought this time it was without very much effort at all.

"Almost. Except unlike a bird a kite needs our help to get off the ground. You see, you'll run and then the wind will catch it, and it'll take off up into the sky. And then you can control where it goes."

"Wow!" was all Curley could manage.

"So you wanna go to the park or what?"

"Yessir!"

Rodney smiled at Eunice and she smiled back at him. They were both pleased. It was the first genuine excitement they had seen from their son in quite some time.

ৰ১

Curley thought the park looked like someone's backyard. Someone with lots of money for toys and gadgets. He couldn't help but think as he looked at the wide open space what great farmland this would've made. But he guessed there was enough farms around to justify placing this tract aside. Still, try as hard as he might to get his mind around the idea, it seemed strange. Somebody should tell Grandpa about this place, he thought. He could buy it up and give it some useful purpose.

There were other, strange people populating the park on this day. There were chunky women walking around with their chunky children, smiling and pointing out things that Curley and Rodney had both taken for granted.

"Look at the ducks!" one large, pink woman had told her pink son. He had clapped his hands together and squealed with delight.

"Ducks!!" he agreed.

There were other women walking around, dressed as though they were going to church. Curley watched as their jewels gleamed in the early-Spring sun and dangled back and forth like the hands of a grandfather clock. These women all seemed to know each other, but Curley noted that they must not really care for each other. They would speak like dead people, taking an obligatory notice of each other but not really warming to the occasion. Curley wondered if they belonged to some kind of club, because they were all wearing hats that shaded their faces from the sun. Many of them wore some kind of strange paint on their faces. There was one fat white woman that really scared Curley. He looked away quickly, trying to avoid his brain taking too close notice of her. She would show up in nightmares, he felt pretty sure. She was wearing more of the paint than any of the others. Her lips were a bright and artificial red. At first Curley thought that she might be bleeding. The warm air was causing her to sweat profusely, and the paint was driving down her face in greasy streaks that looked like a thin brown version of the Occonoluftee. She was wearing a shiny blouse that had large, circular, dark rings under each arm. When she raised her hand to greet friends and neighbors it looked like she was carrying a small lake under her arm. Curley tried not to think about her any more than necessary.

He also couldn't help but notice the way these people looked at him and his father. Rodney seemed oblivious to it all, walking purposefully towards the big field where they were going to launch this kite. But Curley saw it. Some seemed to turn their nose up as if they smelled something rotten. Others flashed a smile that looked to Curley a lot like the one on the face of the kid who was apparently seeing ducks for the first time. It was a mix of curiosity, pity and delight. It made him very uncomfortable. There were others who seemed to stare longer than they should---much longer than was polite. There were even some who would stop and point at them. Curley began to wonder if there was something wrong with him, or if he and his Dad had something on their clothes.

"What are those people looking at?" he asked Rodney.

"A couple of really damn good looking Indian men," Rodney said, smiling. Curley wasn't sure how that accounted for the people who seemed to be smelling something as they passed, but decided against pressing the issue.

The sun was shining bright and warming the ground, but there was no wind. Curley had not been interested in the so-called "monkey bars" or the shiny, silver sliding board. He had wanted to see this contraption of Rodney's get off of the ground and soar like a mighty eagle. Rodney handed him the string and told him to run with all his might. Curley obliged, and the kite bounced and dragged along the ground behind him. Once in a while it would jet up around his shoulders, but then it would crash back to the ground, lifeless. It was all a very big disappointment. Curley ran as hard and as long as he could, but finally there was just no denying that the kite was nothing like a bird at all. The Great Spirit's design had been much better.

"There's no use, Dad," he said finally, "this thing just ain't going nowhere." Curley noticed that his father seemed even more disappointed than he felt. "But it was a good idea," he comforted, "just not enough wind today I guess."

"Yeah," Rodney agreed, "not enough wind. I sure did want you to see that thing fly, though." He walked over and placed his hand on

Curley's shoulder. "I wanted you to have some fun today, boy. Your Mamma and me are both kinda worried about you."

Curley looked at the kite.

"I'm sorry," he said. Rodney knelt down beside his son.

"There's nothing for you to be sorry about, Curley. We just want you to give this new place a chance. I know everything seems strange to you. That's going to be so for a while. But if you'll just give it a chance I really think you'll enjoy being here. I really do. If I didn't think you could be happy I would've never brought you and your Mamma here. You know that, don't you?"

"Yessir, I do. It's just that....that...."

"That what?"

"Well, I love you and Mamma. But sometimes I really do miss Grandpa and Grandma. A lot."

"That's o.k.," Rodney told him, "we all do. But this is our home for now. And if you come to love this place, that won't mean that you love Lorenzo and Cora any less. You know that don't you?"

"I guess so." Curley supposed that he had thought that liking this place would be a lot like betraying his grandparents.

"Son, I just want you to promise me one thing. I want you to promise me that you will give this place a chance. Will you do that for me?"

Curley nodded. "I'll do that for you," he said. Rodney smiled. His son was more like a man than many men he knew.

"Thank you."

They decided that it just wasn't worth the effort to try the kite again. They agreed that they would go ahead and start the three-mile walk home. The sun had passed its zenith, so the day was beginning to cool down some. Rodney noticed that Curley's step seemed to be a little lighter than it had been on the trip to the park. He hoped that their conversation had done some good.

As they neared the edge of the park, Curley noticed a thin white woman heading towards them. She appeared to be having a great deal of trouble with her young daughter. The child, around three years old, was screaming bloody murder about something. The poor mother appeared nearly at her wit's end, alternately coaxing and shouting at the child to behave and stop the yelling. Curley couldn't help but feel sorry for the woman as he also wondered if he had ever acted like that. Then he saw a light go off in the woman's eyes as she saw them nearing her. He thought maybe this was a woman that worked with his Dad at the mill.

The woman stopped walking and knelt beside her daughter. She grasped her daughter's shoulders with her hands, so tightly that Curley saw her knuckles turn a milky white.

"Do you see them?" she asked the child fiercely. The child, whose face was beet red and streaked with dirt and tears, turned her head slowly towards Rodney and Curley. She nodded.

"If you don't straighten your ass up," the mother scolded, "those two are gonna get you and scalp you. Do you understand?"

Curley watched as the little girl's eyes glazed over in terror. The screaming stopped and the tears dried up. The child pulled her mother closer and began to noticeably quake in her tight leather shoes.

"That's better," the mother said, standing and taking her daughter's hand. Curley looked up at Rodney to see if he could get some clarification on what had just happened. What exactly was getting "scalped" anyway? He knew what getting spanked meant, but he had never heard of a child or anyone else getting scalped. And what did that have to do with him and his Dad? Why did the little girl look at them with such potent fear? When his eyes found his Dad's face, he was shocked at the expression. There was an anger and a hurt sketched across Rodney's face that Curley had never before seen. His jaw was clenched so tight that Curley thought he would have been able to crush stone. He seemed to be shaking from somewhere down deep. It was not the tremble of a man afraid, though, it was the tremble of a man barely controlling his rage. Curley was suddenly afraid that he had accidentally done something that had infuriated his Dad this way. The mother and daughter were now passing them. Curley watched as the child nearly tripped up the mother, clinging desperately to the hem of her dress. The mother looked right past them. Rodney's hands clenched in fists, relaxed, then clenched again. They walked silently out of the park.

"What is 'scalping,'" Curley asked Rodney when he was sure that they were out of earshot of anyone. Rodney didn't say anything.

"Dad," Curley pressed, "what did that woman mean?"

"Nothing," Rodney said tersely.

"But why was that little girl so scared of me and you? Huh? What is scalping?" Rodney nearly whirled to face his son. His eyes were blazing like two forest fires. There was pure hatred in his stance. His voice dripped sparks across his chin.

"Goddamnit, Curley let it go." Curley recoiled from Rodney's anger. He took several steps away from his father, afraid that the fists dangling by his side were about to flash out and strike him down. "I'm sorry, son. I'm so sorry." Curley was confused. He had never seen his Dad like this. If he believed it possible, he would've sworn that his father was on the edge of tears. Still, he had to know.

"Why was she scared of us, Daddy? I want to know." Rodney looked away. After several moments of silence, he collapsed onto the ground and crossed his legs. He pulled a cigarette from his pocket and lit it, inhaling deeper than ever before in his life. The sun was beginning to edge its way over the trees now, casting long orange shadows over the world. How in hell was he supposed to tell his son that the little girl was afraid of him because of the color of his skin and what that stood for in her world? He could lie, of course. Why burden him with this knowledge at such a young age? Just as the thought crossed his mind Rodney felt the breeze kick up around his head. Suddenly, he could swear that he smelled Qualla. Then, as sure as he was sitting there, he heard Molly whispering in his ear.

"He should hear that from you, Rodney Norris. You can't keep him from knowing the truth. And he may never forgive you if he has to learn it from somewhere or someone else."

Rodney turned quickly, half expecting Molly to be standing behind him. She was nowhere around.

"That little girl was scared of you because you are an Indian." Rodney said it as quickly as he could. Curley's brow creased and he frowned. He did not understand what his father was saying.

"Well, that doesn't make any sense," he stated matter-of-factly.

"No," Rodney agreed, "it doesn't. But it is something you must learn to live with, son. There will be more like her. You must learn to ignore it, as much as you can."

"Why didn't you smack her?" Curley asked. "I could tell that you wanted to."

Rodney laughed. "Yeah, yeah I reckon I did want to. But we don't hit women. You know that." Curley nodded. It had been a childish remark.

"And if she was a man?" Rodney had to tread carefully here. His honest answer would've been that if she had been a man he *would've* killed the son of a bitch just to teach him a lesson. But that was not the answer Eunice wanted Curley to hear.

"You still ignore it, son. It's not worth troubling about." When he was older, Rodney promised himself, he would give him a very different answer. Curley appeared no more at ease than he had been when he was full of questions. In fact, the answers seemed to have confused him even more.

"I don't think I understand," he said.

"I know you don't," Rodney said. "After all these years I'm still not sure that I understand. Just let it go for now, son. We'll talk about this a lot more when you're older. O.k.?" Curley nodded his head.

"O.k.," he said with grim resignation. The two of them walked on towards home. Rodney felt the urge to hold his son's hand but knew that the boy was too old for that now. So he just walked as close to him as he could, wishing to God he could protect him a little longer from the world. As they neared home, Curley broke the silence.

"White people sure are strange, aren't they Dad?" Rodney chuckled.

"Yep," he agreed, "they sure are."

CHAPTER NINETEEN

The normal, day-to-day activities around the Norris household were radically altered by the presence of the new baby. Ray Norris seemed intent on proving to the world that his lungs were as strong as anyone's, maybe just a little stronger. Curley longed for the days when he had been able to sleep through the night without the ear-piercing screams of the baby tearing through the house. Curley was finding himself in constant trouble now as he tried to make up for lost sleep during the school day. For the first time since his arrival in Cramerton Curley had found himself in the office of the school's principal, Mr. Abernathy. Sensing that the boy was just suffering from fatigue and not contempt for the learning process, Abernathy had let the matter slide with just a stern rebuke. Curley couldn't help but notice that it seemed this new addition to the family was only capable of eating, sleeping, crying and messing himself. Curley had already, only a few months after the birth, made a vow to himself not to ever have children. The only remotely clever thing that the kid did was pee in their Dad's face while being changed. That, Curley had to admit, had been very funny indeed.

His parents seemed to be aging thanks to their new schedule as well. Rodney usually fell asleep in front of the fireplace immediately following dinner instead of making time for Curley the way he had in the past. Curley didn't hold this against his father, though, since he understood how tired everybody was first hand. Eunice seemed to be coping better than the rest of them, although she, too, showed some occasional signs of the strain. Curley heard the padded sounds of her slippers on the wooden floor four or five times a night---every night. During at least half of these trips he had heard Rodney's heavy trod following closely behind, the smell of a lit cigarette trailing behind him into Curley's bedroom. At first Curley had worried that they might move the wailing child into his room to shorten their nocturnal journeys; but so far the baby remained in the den near the smoldering ashes of the night's fire. Curley thanked God every night in his silent prayers that it was important for a newborn to stay warm.

Curley was glad to find that he eventually built up an immunity to the screeches. As the weeks turned into months he was able to sleep through all but the most insistent of wailings. He listened intently as his Mom and Dad argued over the nighttime duties. Eunice had insisted that, since Rodney had to be up for work early every morning, he should stay in bed and let her handle the child. Rodney, for reasons that his son just could not understand, insisted that he be near his wife at night when she had to get up from the bed and trek across the house. It was the first time that Curley had really had reason to question his Dad's judgment, maybe even his sanity.

Mrs. Hatley, the black woman who had served as Eunice's midwife during the delivery, still stopped by once or twice a week, on her way to or from work. She admitted that there was a soft spot in her heart for this Cherokee family. Curley had heard his Mom apologize to the woman for "not being quite as quiet as you'd been led to believe," a remark which, for reasons that Curley didn't understand, had sent the woman into gales of laughter. Curley always stayed a little ways away from Mrs. Hatley. Although it was clear that his parents liked and respected her, she was still the first black woman he had ever seen. And an imposing one at that. Curley had wanted to ask several times if she was just a really dark Indian, but had been afraid that the question wasn't appropriate for a boy to ask an elder. For her part, the woman seemed to notice the boy's reticence around her, but she seemed unphased by it. This was, after all, little Cramerton. She had become used to the stares and even the jibes that went along with being who and what she was in a small Southern town.

Saturdays quickly became the day that Curley's world revolved around. That was the day that Rodney, who typically worked Sunday through Friday at the mill, was around the house all day. Actually, the truth was he was usually anything but around the house all day; and wherever he wandered he took Curley with him. It was on these days that Curley came to know the bustling main street life of Cramerton. After breakfast he and his Dad would head out to scan the shops and maybe try some of the local eating spots. Every Saturday seemed like a carnival to Curley. The people were dressed in strange fashions and seemed to be in a perpetual hurry. The streets themselves hummed with the sounds of automobiles---a monster that truly fascinated the

young man. Every trip down to Main Street would leave Rodney
swearing to buy himself a car as soon as it was possible. The idea
thrilled Curley. His dreams were filled with images of him and his
family skipping through Cramerton in a brand new car. He wondered
why his Dad didn't just go ahead and buy one and stop talking about it.

This Saturday in April 1926 was no different at the start than any of
the others had been. Curley and Rodney spent most of the afternoon
peering into store windows and pricing things that Rodney swore he
would come back to buy for Eunice. Curley had begun to get restless
as they headed back down Main Street and towards home. He was now
hoping that Rodney wouldn't want to look into any more stores,
because his stomach was beginning to growl and he was looking
forward to the pork chops Eunice had promised would be waiting on
them when they got back. But, as usual, there was one more store.
Curley wanted to protest but knew better than to whine around his
father. He shrugged his shoulders silently and followed Rodney into
the store.

Curley couldn't help but think to himself that this store needed to
make up its mind as to what exactly it wanted to be. There were
dresses and there was furniture. There was jewelry. There were
perfume bottles and vases and plastic flowers. Essentially, this store
seemed to be trying to sell everything all at once. Rodney moved off
into a corner to take a long, hard look at some rings sitting in a large
glass case. Curley stepped away to investigate the back of the store a
little further and see if he could get a gage on what this place was
about. That's when his eye fell on the treasure sitting all alone near an
old red velvet couch. The way the light fell upon the item made Curley
feel sure that some higher power had placed him here in this store to
find this very thing.

From the other side of the store Rodney saw his son gazing in awe at
the battered old musical instrument in a far corner. Curley seemed to
be frozen in time, no part of his body was moving. He looked like a
statue. Rodney moved over and placed his hand on Curley's shoulder,
causing the boy to nearly jump out of his skin.

"Look at that, Dad," he said in a tone reverent enough to be spoken
in a church. Rodney nodded. "Ain't it a beauty?"

"Yeah, I reckon it is," he agreed.

"What is it?" Rodney laughed loudly. He felt sure that his son
wanted this thing, even though he didn't know what in the hell it was.

"Can I help ya'll?" A balding white man had come up behind them and was smiling the salesman smile. It was toothy and phony.

"What's that?" Curley asked, pointing to the instrument.

"That thing? Why that's a banjer-uke," the man responded. "It's sort of like a guitar and a mandolin and a banjer all rolled into one. Wanna try it out?"

"Yeah!!" Curley very nearly shouted his response. Rodney was wary of putting the instrument in his son's hands. He knew the policy of any pawn shop was "you break it you buy it," and he didn't imagine that he had the money to buy this instrument. But, being the good salesman that this man obviously was, the instrument was in Curley's hands before he could form his hesitation into words. The salesman folded his arms and watched as Curley began to strum the old and tinty strings on the banjo-uke, hesitantly at first, then with more and more feeling.

"The boy's a natural," the man said, flashing that toothy grin at Rodney.

"Um-huh," Rodney grunted without commitment. Curley looked up at his Dad and smiled. His hand was flying now against the strings, pounding at some inner rhythm that only he could hear.

"This is great," he said. Rodney smiled at his son's poor attempt to sound casual about the whole thing.

"Well, what do ya think, Mr., uh, Mr...."

"Norris," Rodney said, extending his hand, "Rodney Norris."

"Well, Rodney, what do ya think? The boy obviously has talent."

Rodney resented the fact that this little white man called him by his first name so easily. A white customer would have probably received more deferential treatment.

"I know my son has talent," he snapped.

"Can I help you let him take this banjer-uke home?" the man asked, oblivious to Rodney's tone. "We do accept trades."

"How much do you want for it outright?" Rodney asked. Curley stopped pounding on the instrument and listened. Was he going to actually get to have this magnificent thing?

"Outright I can't let it go for less than twenty-five dollars." Rodney laughed.

"That things wasn't worth twenty-five dollars when it was brand, spanking new. And I believe even the boy can see that it ain't exactly brand, spanking new."

Curley recognized his Dad's tone of voice. It looked like he wouldn't be taking the "banjer-uke" home after all.

"Well," the man said, "I suppose I could let you have it for twenty." The toothy grin flashed again. "We got us a deal?" Curley felt his heart pounding in his chest. The feel of the instrument was so right, so natural. Surely his Dad wouldn't let a deal like this one slip through his fingers. After all, the man had just dropped *five whole dollars* off the price.

"No, sir, I don't believe we do. But we thank you for your time. C'mon Curley." Curley's glance went back and forth between the men. Was that it, then? No banjer-uke? Rodney had already turned from the man and was heading for the door. The white man's hand reached down and took the instrument away from Curley, sitting it back in the hallowed corner.

"Sorry, boy," he said as he walked back to his counter. Curley sulked out of the door several steps behind Rodney. Rodney stopped after a few feet to let his son catch up to him. He put an arm around the boy and couldn't help but notice how much taller his son seemed. They walked for a while without speaking.

"I'm sorry you couldn't have it, son," Rodney said. Suddenly he was painfully aware of being poor again. They were better off financially than they would've been back on Qualla, but they were still not where Rodney wanted to be.

"Did you think I had talent, Dad," Curley asked, "or was that man just saying that to get us to buy that thing?"

"No," Rodney said emphatically, "I did think, and do think, that you have talent. Truth is I just don't have the money to get that banjo right now. I'm sorry."

"That's alright," answered Curley, "maybe we can come back and get it when we get the car."

Rodney chuckled.

"That's exactly what we'll do," he said, "I promise."

CHAPTER TWENTY

Curley was trying his best to delay his arrival home. Making his way back from school had become more and more of an adventure. He darted back and forth between trees and bushes. One moment he was a daring secret agent, outmaneuvering his would be captors and making a brilliant getaway. The next second he was transformed with the miraculous power of a child's imagination into a soldier, bravely dodging the bullets of the Axis Powers to rescue his friends trapped in No Man's Land. Whenever he saw a passerby coming towards him he straightened himself up and walked past as a respectable young man. There were the close calls, of course, but he had managed to elude the eyes of the world's too many grown-ups pretty well. It was a game that he played for the sheer amusement and because he did not really want to get home. Things there had changed.

First there were the chores. He didn't mind doing some work around the house. He had always done that. But with the arrival of this new person in the house he seemed to be carrying more and more of the weight. When his Dad came home from the plant he seemed determined to spend countless hours playing with the baby. For Curley it seemed an obvious excuse to just not do anything. After all, the child couldn't actually *do* anything yet. You *couldn't* play with him. All he did was smile occasionally and drool constantly. But the kid was clearly more interesting than taking out the garbage. So that left the job for Curley.

Then there was the child itself. Ray was not a bad child, per say, but he wasn't exactly quiet most of the time either. The problem was he didn't say anything. Only annoying noises came out of the child's mouth. And to top it all off these strange sounds that flew easily from the child were always taken as a sign of genius by his parents. Curley couldn't help but think that it would be fitting if the child grew up and could only make the same goo-goo noises that his Mom and Dad made to him. If the poor kid grew up thinking that was really the way human beings talked, well, it would be a very difficult road for this one indeed.

Going home would not have been so bad if Curley could somehow have made known his feelings. That was essentially the biggest problem--he had been backed into a corner of devotion and near adulation of Ray. He heard his mother telling friends and neighbors about how well he was "coping" with the change in their home. He heard his father brag about what a great "big brother" he was already becoming. Curley's devotion to and respect for his parents had not diminished one bit, and the thought of disappointing them by letting them know that he was being driven nuts by the way things were going was more than he could handle. He had no interest in making his own parents out to be liars. That left him playing the role of doting brother and obedient son.

A truck came barreling down the dirt road and snapped Curley out of his day dream. As the dust settled he knelt down in the dirt and carefully traced out his name with his index finger.

Russell Deveroux Norris.

He stepped back and took a good look at the words. If you looked at them too long, they inevitably began to look wrong. But he knew that they were right. And they looked good. He smiled at his artistry. Just this afternoon his teacher had told him that his handwriting was improving quickly and would soon be as good as his classmates. Curley had thought about what his Grandpa always said to him in the letters he sent. "Work hard at your studies," he implored at the end of every letter, "They'll help you get ahead." Curley, as always, took Lorenzo's words to heart. He applied himself the best he could in everything, especially working with numbers and words. The power of both fascinated the young man. When he had started school, his teacher had told him that he was woefully behind the white kids in the class. Curley had watched and picked up on her disbelief when his parents assured the teacher that their child would catch up. Curley stored that look in a special place in the back of his mind. Whenever he was tempted (and it was often) to give up in frustration and just go outside and play like the others he called that look up. Then he went back to work with a determination that would have amazed his reluctant teacher and even his supportive parents. Eunice would, once in a while, catch a glimpse of her son, hunched over his books with his mind seemingly on fire, and smile. Between her and Rodney there was enough stubbornness to fill twenty children with a more than average resolve. But when she saw Curley in those moods she thought that he had already inherited the lion's share of it. She would bring him a glass of cool water and tell him not to ruin his eyes. He would look up at her and smile but say nothing. With his books he retreated into his own world.

Curley looked up and saw that he was almost home. The outline of the frame dwelling was clear against the sky. He sighed and tried to find his happy face. He wondered if he would find the time or the opportunity to tell either of his parents about his teacher's compliment. He shrugged it off. Ray couldn't stay cute or interesting forever. He obviously hadn't.

Curley stepped quietly up on the front porch. He hoped that Ray was awake. He hated having to tiptoe through the house like a burglar on the prowl. He walked in to find his mother sitting at the kitchen table....alone. That meant Ray was sleeping. He quietly placed his school books in the corner of the kitchen.

"How was your day, baby?"

"It was o.k.," he answered. He noticed that his Mom was barely concealing a grin.

"Just 'o.k.'?" she asked. Curley could feel himself being set up for something. But the grin meant that, at least in his Mom's eyes, it was something good.

"It was really kinda good," he said.

"Oh, why's that?"

Curley pulled himself up a chair beside Eunice.

"Well, my teacher said that my writing was gettin' better and that she thought it wouldn't be long before I could write as good as all the other kids in the class." Eunice straightened up.

"Oh, Russell, that is wonderful news! I knew you could and I knew you would. You are smarter than most of those kids in your class, I think. You just started late. You'll have to tell your Dad as soon as he gets home. Alright?"

"Yes, Mom," Curley said. He was pleased that the news was going to get its proper due.

"Well, I *am* proud of you. And I have some news of my own for you." The slight grin broke out into an all out smile now. Curley was nervous. The last piece of "good news" she had for him was Ray, and that hadn't lived up to all it was cracked up to be.

"Oh, what news do you have for me?" he asked with more than a little trepidation.

Eunice stood from the table.

"I think it might be more fun if I showed you instead of telling you. Follow me."

Curley was very nervous now. He followed Eunice down the short hallway that lead from the living room to their bedrooms. He tip-toed gently past Ray's crib. Eunice stopped in the doorway of his room and turned to him with a broad grin on her face.

"This is your surprise," Eunice said. Curley moved beside her and peeked into his room. He scanned the floor and the walls. He didn't see anything different in the place. Then his eyes rested on his bed. It was made up for him, that was a surprise. But there was something else. Curley felt his breath catch in his lungs. Sitting there on top of the neatly arranged covers and pillows was the instrument that he and his Dad had seen at the pawn shop. It looked more beautiful sitting in his room that it had in the corner of the shop. He looked at his Mom in disbelief. For once, Curley was at a total loss for words.

"Mom," he asked, "is that for me? Is that really what it looks like?" Eunice giggled happily.

"That's right," she said, "your Daddy bought that for you last night. He knew how much you loved it and he worked very hard to get it for you."

Curley moved about half the distance to the banjo-uke and then stopped. He stood and stared for what seemed like an eternity.

"Well for heaven's sake, Russell," Eunice said, "go get it."

That was all the encouragement Curley needed. He covered the last half of the room in what felt like one gigantic step and bounded on the bed. He grabbed the instrument and began fumbling around with it, self-consciously at first. Then, picking up steam, he began to really get a feel for the strings and the frets and their relationship to his hands. As Eunice stood in the doorway watching her son she was struck by the fact that Rodney had been right, he *did* seem like a natural when he held the banjo-uke. As Curley continued to strum away, faster and louder with each passing second, they both heard Ray wake up with a scream. Curley looked at Eunice with an embarrassed and apologetic glance.

"Now don't you worry about that," Eunice assured him, "it was time for your brother to wake up anyway."

Curley nodded and dutifully put the instrument down.

"Uh-uh," Eunice chided, "you keep playing. Maybe the sound of you making music will calm Ray down." She nodded as if to make sure that Curley got the message-----keep playing. He was surprised at his Mom's reaction, but decided not to question her wisdom. He picked the banjo-uke back up and went at it again with the dedication of a man whose very existence depended on the sounds his hands could make.

ꝏ

Eunice met Rodney at the door with a warm hug and a very happy smile. There was also the unmistakable look of contrition on her face.

"My husband," she said, "you were right and I was wrong." Rodney pulled away from her and stared into her face. Eunice had to laugh at the shock that was written across his features.

"Before I even ask what you're talking about," he said, "I'm gonna have to ask that you say that again. Just so's I'm sure that I heard you right."

Eunice had been against spending such a considerable sum on a play thing that she felt Curley would be done with in less than a month. She was sure that this was a passing fancy, and that the spent money would come back to haunt them as the vaunted "banjer-uke" sat collecting dust in a corner of their mill house.

"You were right and I was wrong," she said. "Just listen." Rodney cocked his ear and heard the unmistakable sound of semi-music coming from the back of the house. He smiled and listened carefully. It wasn't exactly the most beautiful thing that he had ever heard to be sure, but it also did not sound like the ramblings of yet another untalented musician wannabe.

"That Curley?" he asked.

"Yep," Eunice answered, "and he's been doing that all afternoon. Rodney you were right, he is absolutely in love with that thing."

"I told you he did," he said. "And he's not at all bad at playing that thing either, huh?"

"Not bad at all," Eunice agreed. "He told me earlier that he was going to get really good at playing it and then go play music with his Grandpa. Can you imagine that? Him on that thing and Daddy on his fiddle? They'd keep everybody in Qualla up all night!"

Rodney laughed out loud at the picture taking shape in his mind of that little scene.

"He in his room?"

"Yes," said Eunice, "and he has an audience." Rodney was going to ask her what she meant, but she had already moved into the hall. He followed behind her. When he looked in, it was on of those scenes that parents live for. There sat Curley on his bed, strumming for all he was worth, with Ray standing in his crib on wobbly legs, smiling to beat the devil. Curley looked up and saw Rodney. He dropped the instrument and ran across the room embracing his father.

"Thank you, Dad," he said. Rodney squeezed back.

"You're welcome. Now go back over there and play me a tune." Curley walked back to his bed and took the instrument in hand.

"O.k.," he said, "but I ain't too good. Yet."

Rodney smiled at his son's confidence. Curley obviously also believed that he was born to make music. As he began to pound out notes and send them flying through the night, Rodney doubted anyone who could see him would doubt it.

CHAPTER TWENTY-ONE

Everybody called him Mr. Abernathy. That was expected from the children, but the parents followed suit as well, deferring to the man that had presided over local education for twenty-odd years. He was not a physically imposing man, but he commanded respect with his quiet confidence and his unyielding devotion to the children of the community. He treated everyone he met with respect, but he did not shy away from calling a child or parent to task if he felt it was needed. The piece of paper hanging on his office wall, from the University of North Carolina at Chapel Hill, distinguished him from practically everyone that came in. But the fact that he never flaunted or even really mentioned his education made him all the more effective in this small town. In fact his secretary, who also doubled as his wife, had practically had to force him to hang that paper up in the first place.

"Some of the dumbest people I have ever met," he said, "have had pieces of paper just like this one. And most of the wisest did not."

Still, for all his bombast and his demurring manner, Mr. Abernathy was a very vocal proponent of education and the benefits that it could bring.

"An education," he was fond of saying, "can open doors for you. What you do once you get in is up to you."

Born and raised in Gastonia, he had returned after college to try and inspire the local population, to elevate the children. It was not always easy. In this part of the country children were still expected to put their chores ahead of any "book learning;" often because the successful completion of those chores could mean the difference between eating and starving. Abernathy knew he had to strike a balance, and the fact that he respected the occupation of farmer and mill worker endeared him to an initially skeptical county.

He had his eye on Russell Norris from the very beginning. It was concern, not benevolence, that had motivated this early interest. Russell was too dark to be going to this school, and Mr. Abernathy knew it, although Russell's parents apparently did not. This was Jim Crow country, and although Russell was Indian and not black, that was not a distinction that was going to mean a thing to many people in Gastonia. The fact was that he was dark and was therefore different, and difference did not sit well with many of the good Christian people around this town. The idea of a dark skinned boy sitting in the same class with their sons, and especially their daughters, would be enough to get Curley killed. And Abernathy too for allowing it to happen. But Rodney and Eunice Norris had not even asked for permission. They had allowed their son to come to the school with no fanfare and no prior warning. Abernathy had decided to simply wait it out and hope to God for the best.

It was possible that either he had overestimated the hatred of his community or he had underestimated the Norris family. As he soon found out, the fact that Russell was a student at West Gastonia was not exactly a well kept secret. And to top it off, the locals seemed to be fine with the idea. As it was, Rodney Norris was well known in the area as a hard-working and fair foreman in the mill. He had managed to command the respect of the whites early, and they were willing to accord the same respect to his wife and child. Through sheer hard work and determination the Norrises had won a place in the community. Mr. Abernathy couldn't decide whether that said more about the town or the family, but either way it gave him a glimmer of hope.

Still, Mr. Abernathy understood that the arrangement was tenuous. There were many who were waiting patiently for the Indians to fail and show their "true colors." Abernathy looked in on Curley when he could and spoke with the young man and his teachers often, marking progress and making sure things were still sailing smoothly. That was how he happened by for "show and tell" that day.

৪৩

Curley had been telling his friends and classmates to expect "something big" for that Friday. The show and tell sessions that the teacher gave them had finally, mercifully rolled around to the N's for that day. He promised them a show that would put the rock samples and everything else they had seen to that point to absolute shame. Soon the entire school was buzzing with rumors about what Curley would bring in. Some said he was going to bring in a bow and arrow. Others said he would be bringing in a scalp. Curley put those rumors to rest as quickly as they reached his ears, knowing that if he let the rumors get too exotic his real exhibition would be anticlimactic. As it was, everyone in the school was already anxious, including Mr. Abernathy. He felt confident that no scalps were going to be displayed in his school, but he did still have his worries. He had also heard that Russell was bringing in a so-called "peace pipe." That might sound romantic to some Northerner, but it would not play here in the fundamentalist atmosphere of Gastonia. It could well start a riot. He stood at the back of the class with Mrs. Johnson and waited nervously. The Cherokee student had arrived on campus with something wrapped lovingly in a burlap cloth and had guarded the identity if the package with vigor. Mr. Abernathy tensed as Curley headed to the front of the small class with his sack in tow. He rocked on the balls of his feet, ready to put an end to this show and tell as soon as things got out of hand.

There was a gasp as Curley brought the banjo-uke out of it's makeshift case. Curley smiled. Then the gasp was quickly followed by a collective groan, a groan that sounded like disappointment.

"Now, just wait a minute," Curley instructed them knowingly. After all, they hadn't heard anything yet.

But they had heard something. Mr. Abernathy and the teacher both quietly groaned and then smiled at each other, both ashamed that they had been heard. Curley was not the first child to discover a latent talent for the fine arts. No, they had heard more off-key warbling in their years in education than anyone should, by right, really have to have heard. The banjo-uke was a new touch, that was true. Normally they had to wait until the poorly named annual "talent" show where the young vocalists would sing and dance, or one of their classmates would butcher a classical piece on the school's aging and battered piano. The yellowing keys were stroked and banged for what seemed like an eternity until, mercifully, the slaughter ended. Both Mr. Abernathy and the teacher had become masters at the art of the fake smile and the warm, generous applause. They prepared themselves mentally for the same challenge here.

"Ma'am," Curley asked the teacher, "mind if I sit on your chair?"

"No, Russell, that will be fine," she answered.

Curley sat down and made himself comfortable. He cleared his throat and cracked two of his knuckles (the others didn't cooperate, angering him slightly). He gently and knowingly formed a G chord on the frets. He strummed down in one polite and easy stroke. Mr. Abernathy's face contorted before he had the time to control himself. The instrument was badly out of tune.

Then something different happened.

"Oops," Curley said with a shy grin. Then he began to carefully tune the instrument. The class began to squirm.

"Trust me," Curley said, "it'll be better this way." He winked at a young girl in the front row. Mr. Abernathy tried to remember a time when a student had actually tuned anything in his presence. Maybe this wouldn't be too awful.

Curley strummed again. Better. In fact, good enough to pass. But not good enough for Curley Norris's debut. A few more careful twists. Then another strum. One more slight twist. One more strum.

"That's it," Mr. Abernathy whispered under his breath.

"That's it," Curley said confidently. Mr. Abernathy looked at the teacher and shrugged.

"Ahem," Curley said, to end the little conversations that were still floating across the room. Silence.

"This one here is my Mom's favorite." He struggled for a minute with his F chord. He took a deep breath, let it out slowly, and found it perfectly. He strummed to get the key right in his head. Then, with little warning, he began singing "The Old Rugged Cross."

ON A HILL FAR AWAY
STOOD AN OLD, RUGGED CROSS
THE EMBLEM OF SUFFERING AND SHAME

It was not only on key, it was beautiful. Mr. Abernathy pulled his handkerchief from his pocket and stealthily wiped a tear from his eye. Curley's eyes were tightly closed, his head would sway back on forth on certain words.

AND I LOVE THAT OLD CROSS
WHERE MY DEAR SAVIOR DIED

There was pain in his voice, pain and redemption. No child moved. Curley had cast a spell that would have put the best shaman to shame.

SO I'LL CHERISH THE OLD RUGGED CROSS

Curley's voice was climbing steadily higher, preparing the way for a powerful finish. Once in a while he would open his eyes and take a quick peek at his audience, making sure they were still with him. Yep, his grin seemed to say, still there.

I WILL CLING TO THAT OLD RUGGED CROSS

The teacher was glancing at her students. They were enraptured. She wished to herself that she could have that impact on them.

AND EXCHANGE IT SOMEDAY FOR A CROWN

Mr. Abernathy watched as the students tensed up, ready to explode with their applause and adulation. The Indian student he had so worried about was not only now one of them, he appeared to be leading them. Whether they knew it or not.

YES, I'LL EXCHANGE IT ONE DAY FOR---A---CROWN.

The classroom erupted into claps and shouts. Even Mr. Abernathy, who had seen much, was caught up in it. He clapped so loud and so hard that his hands became purple and would later ache. The children were crying "more, more" at the top of their lungs. Curley smiled and shrugged his shoulders. He was teasing the crowd.

"Ma'am?" He looked at the teacher. It almost looked like he was daring her to stop him and his momentum.

"Certainly, Russell," she said, "I would love to hear another one, too."

Curley nodded. That was it for the formal education that day. It turned into an impromptu concert. The Curley Norris Show. Mr. Abernathy excused himself after the fourth song, telling Curley what a wonderful talent he had as he walked out of the classroom door. The teacher took a seat at the back of the class and occasionally caught herself nodding along to the rhythm of Curley's strumming hands. Curley watched as the girl's eyes began to glaze over. It was a look he would not forget and would even come to cultivate.

Even when it was time to go home, many of the students lingered around, asking Curley how many songs he knew, how long he had been playing, did he ever make any money at music? When the crowd thinned it was just Curley and the teacher. She simply shook her head in amazement and told him to keep up the good work. Curley placed the banjo-uke back in its case. He stared for a minute at the empty classroom. He smiled. It was quite possibly the biggest smile any young man had ever worn, anywhere. He couldn't wait to get home to dispatch a letter to his Grandfather.

Curley Norris had arrived.

CHAPTER TWENTY-TWO

"So this is what stage fright feels like," Curley thought.

The ballroom of the Arlington Hotel in downtown Gastonia was teeming with the affluent and influential of the county. Curley moved closer to his host, Mr. Abernathy, when the large wooden doors to the room opened and revealed the mass of people. The principal smiled and laid his hand on Curley's shoulder.

"Don't worry," he assured him, "you're going to knock 'em dead."

Curley's sweaty hand clutched the bag that held his instrument even tighter. This banjo-uke was the only thing that felt familiar to him in these surroundings. His young eyes scanned the room, taking in every detail of this early brush with greatness. He didn't think he had ever seen this many people in one place before. They moved easily among each other, smiles plastered across their faces, hands outstretched in a perpetual greeting. Heads bobbed as familiar jokes passed from one person to the next. Names were dropped. Politics, mostly local with a smattering of the pressing national concerns of the day, was debated and tossed back and forth. Mostly, though, the room was filled the innocuous din of polite small talk. These people were here to be seen, not heard. Curley watched with a sense of awe as his principal, a man he had never imagined outside of the dusty confines of the schoolhouse, mingled freely and seemed to know just what to say to everyone he encountered.

Curley answered each introduction with a courteous "How do you do?" He had to admit that the people seemed to be very open. He quickly felt his anxiousness dissipate. He was beginning to feel at home here. He quietly mocked himself for having been so timid earlier. After all, was he not the grandson of Lorenzo Dow Swayney, the man whose council had been sought by chiefs? He could handle these people, he decided. No problem.

He sat at a table with Mr. Abernathy and a man named "Edwards." Curley couldn't decide if that was the man's first or last name, but that was all anyone that passed by called him. Curley decided to stick with "sir" and whatever other pronoun was appropriate rather than risk the possible humiliation of inserting or deleting a necessary "Mr."

Curley was also struck by the seeming invisibility of the men who served this crowd. They were all black men, the most Curley thought he had ever seen. They weaved their way between the tables, taking orders and fetching drinks and entrees for the powerful men. But they were almost never acknowledged except when they were being told what to do next.

The man waiting on Curley's table was a withered old black man with white hair and most of his teeth missing. That fact, however, did not stop the man from smiling profusely as he jotted orders down in his small yellow pad. He started with Edwards, who seemed somehow annoyed that the man didn't instinctively know what he wanted to eat. He then moved to Mr. Abernathy, whose tone was lighter but still quite formal and perfunctory. Then the man asked Curley what it was he wanted. Curley decided to play it safe and ask for the exact same thing Mr. Abernathy had ordered. After all, he thought, you can't go wrong with steak. As he was turning towards the kitchen, the waiter noticed the sack lying by Curley's feet.

"That a guitar you got there?" he asked, smiling broadly.

"No sir," Curley proudly corrected, "this here is a banjo-uke."

"Oh, I see," the waiter said. "My nephew...."

"That'll be all," snapped Edwards. The waiter looked as if he had been slapped. He apologized and bowed so low Curley thought it might have been a clue as to how he lost those teeth. The waiter quickly scuttled away to the kitchen. Edwards simply smiled at Mr. Abernathy and shook his head in resignation.

"Hard to find decent help, I guess," he said. Mr. Abernathy laughed nervously. Curley suddenly felt the tension and fear returning. Maybe this was going to be a tougher crowd than he had thought.

৪০

The meal was eaten, the minor business and silly speeches given, and all eyes were focusing on the evening's entertainment: Curley Norris. He felt his hands beginning to water down again when Mr. Abernathy moved to the front of the room to introduce him. His heart was pounding within his chest and he felt the saliva in his mouth running for cover, leaving him as parched as the desert.

"Gentlemen," Mr. Abernathy began, "it is my belief that I have produced a real treat for you this evening. The young man that you are about to hear is one of our best students and a fine young man in his own right. He comes from a good and decent local family."

Curley couldn't help but wonder what his Grandpa would have thought about that last remark. He could hear Lorenzo in his ears saying, "No, you're from Qualla. Remember?"

"Now I know what you are all probably thinking," Abernathy plowed on, "you're thinking 'Oh, no, not a *student*. I believe I can safely count myself as the foremost expert in the room on talent shows and recitals that leave one and all seeking the safety of silence."

The men in the room guffawed with laughter and punched each other's shoulders. Mr. Abernathy, Curley thought, got off a good one.

"But you will find, as I did, that this young man is an exception to the rule. He is a young man with tremendous talent, and I hope you will all join me in encouraging this gift of his. So," Mr. Abernathy now tucked his notes back into his suit jacket, "without any more buildup and so that I can put this boy out of his misery, please won't you welcome Mr. Russell Norris."

Curley felt a wave of uncertainty wash over him as the crowd burst forth with applause. He forced a smile and sat on the small stool provided by one of the omnipresent waiters. He carefully removed his banjo-uke from its "case" and gave it a quick tuning. He was getting to the point now where the process of making sure all the strings sounded off in tune with each other was little more than an afterthought. He looked over the sea of faces and carefully noted their expressions. He didn't know a word for it, but he could tell that, although fully prepared to be charitable, these powerful men were not expecting much from him. As usual, he found his inspiration in his desire to prove them wrong.

"Thank you," he said, "I'm not used to playing in front of this many people. And I sure ain't used to playing in front of this many grownups."

There was chuckling from the crowd.

"Anyway, I am gonna play for ya'll tonight, and I hope that you get some enjoyment out of it. And I thank you all for the chance."

And with that Curley began to play and sing. He started with hymns, then threw in a few popular selections, and then closed with another hymn. At the end of each song there was enthusiastic applause, a sound that intoxicated Curley. He couldn't help but feel that, if they'd just let him, he could sit here and play all night. But Mr. Abernathy had stressed that these were important men who could not have their time wasted, so Curley had timed himself methodically and made sure that his set would run no longer than half an hour. But when he tried to get and up and let the men go home something strange happened. They wouldn't let him. They called on him to do one more, and then one more. He had to politely tell a few of them that, no, he was sorry, but he didn't think he knew that song.

"You need to learn that one, son," one man commented, "I think you could really do it nice."

Curley thanked the man and said he would sure try to learn as soon as he could.

"Well, when you do," the man said, "I want you back here to play it for us." The other men in the room applauded and shouted their seconding of the motion. Curley Norris was a hit.

ॐ

As they sat in Mr. Abernathy's car outside of the Norris home, Curley was still thinking about the reception he had received. All the way home Mr. Abernathy had said how proud he was of Curley and how much the men had enjoyed his performance.

"Why, Russell," he said with a huge grin, "you may have just grabbed the school enough funding for the next *two* years."

"Well, sir," Curley said, "I sure do hope they liked it. 'Cause I sure did like doing it."

Mr. Abernathy placed his hand again on Curley's shoulder.

"Russell, I tell you they absolutely loved it. They were already asking me when I thought I could get you back for another meeting. Honestly, son, you knocked 'em out there tonight. Oh, that reminds me...."

Mr. Abernathy lifted himself up slightly and reached into his pants pocket.

"This would be yours."

He reached his hand out and offered Curley a neatly folded bill. Curley took it and opened it up hungrily.

"*Two Dollars*?!" he asked in amazement, "for just playing and singing. Oh, Mr. Abernathy there must be a mistake here. Two whole dollars?"

Abernathy laughed.

"No mistake young man," he answered, "that is the fee that you now command for a personal appearance. Russell, you are now a professional musician."

Curley's hands were shaking with excitement. What would he do with all this money?

"Thank you for coming tonight, Russell. And please thank your mother and father for allowing you to come. Hear?"

"Yes, sir," Curley said, "I sure will. And thank you for asking me. And please thank all those nice men for clapping and giving me two whole dollars."

With that and a handshake, Curley exited the vehicle and watched Mr. Abernathy put-put away into the dark night. He sat down on the front step looking at his banjo-uke and then again at the money in his hand. He was much too excited to sleep, he wanted to run in and tell his parents about the incredible night he had had and then show them the money he had made.

"Professional musician." The words sounded like brilliant poetry in his mind. He could not imagine a more melodious phrase in the English language. Smiling, he walked into his house. He was somehow very different than the boy who had left.

PART FOUR

A MAN

CHAPTER TWENTY-THREE

It was 1934 and the whole world had turned upside down. Five years earlier, Black Tuesday had rocked Wall Street to its very foundations, leaving stunned brokers to dive to their death on the cold city pavement below. Most of the people in Cramerton and the surrounding areas watched with apathy as the news rolled in from the nation's financial center. These people were not stock holders or speculators. They were working folk, and as far as they could tell the crash that had terrified the movers and shakers in New York barely affected them and their lives. Many even read with a certain level of enjoyment the trials and tribulations of the wealthy. They had, after all, been struggling all their lives to put a roof over the heads of their family and insure that there was always food on the table. Now maybe some of those people in suits would know what it was like to have dirt under your nails. It would serve them right to have the starch in their shirts replaced by sweat.

"Greed," Rodney Norris proclaimed at the kitchen table one night in early 1930, "will bring this nation down."

But the complacency and the smirks were soon replaced with looks of terror and a gripping sense of panic. Although most of these people would never really understand why, they soon saw the tragedy of Wall Street playing itself out on a smaller scale on Main Street. The first inkling they had that something was wrong came in a front page obituary. A man named Edwards had shot his wife and two children and then turned the gun under his own chin, splattering his brains on their fine new wall paper. The crash had tapped out his funds and left him no more than a pauper. Edwards was not a man willing to start from the bottom all over again. So he stepped out on a Saturday night and took his family with him.

Curley was visibly upset at the tragic turn of events. What was

happening in the world to make a man so obviously sure of himself and
his place take his own life? The Great Depression was coming home to
Cramerton.

And, of course, it didn't stop with the death of Edwards. That was
just the opening salvo of a war that no one seemed to know how to
fight. The politicians, the president included, continued to promise that
prosperity was "just around the corner." But the only thing people
could see around the corner was yet another farm on the auction block
and the lines at the local church growing ever longer with proud men
and women seeking assistance. Mills closed their doors or sent most of
their workforce home. With each paycheck came the fear that a notice
would be included instructing the receiving party not to return to work
on Monday. As a respected foreman in his own plant, Rodney
promised his family that his job was safe as long as things didn't get
any worse. But they did get worse, and he held his breath along with
everyone else, trying to keep up his brave face for the family. But
Eunice understood well how precarious their situation was. The ground
had already collapsed under too many people that they knew for her to
think for one minute that they were free from danger.

All the while, their little family continued to grow. By the summer
of 1933 Curley was not just an older brother, he was the established
elder statesman of a virtual army of young Norris men. Lorenzo Dow
Norris followed Ray. Houston Clay followed him. Francis Wilbur
followed him. And then in August of 1933 James Roosevelt Norris
was born, signifying the family's new found devotion to the Democratic
Party as well as a filling of the ranks. Rodney had insisted that their
new son be named after President Franklin Delano Roosevelt, whose
election the previous November had left the country with a glimpse of
hope for change and a "New Deal."

"That son of a bitch Hoover doesn't do anything but go fishing,"
Rodney had once complained to his wife. The Republicans had worn
out their welcome with the country and the Norrises.

But the sweeping change and the sudden turn of fortune that many
had hoped for seemed slow in coming. Mills continued to close and
farmers continued to lose their lands. Rodney listened with a sense of
sheer irony as workers in his own plant complained about the situation
that surrounded them.

"Mr. Watson's farm is going on the block soon," one man cried.
And with no apparent sense of history, the man looked hard at Rodney
and innocently asked, "Can you imagine that? His family's been on

that land for generations and *BAM!*, just like that they lose it. Taken right away from them. Can you imagine that?"

Rodney had relayed the story with great pleasure to his family later that night.

"What did you say, Dad?" Ray asked.

"I just looked at him and smiled and said, 'Yeah, a thing like that can sure take the wind out of a person. Or a people.'"

The family laughed, except for Eunice, who stared down at her plate and needled her beans with her fork.

"What?" asked Rodney, seeing his wife's displeasure.

"I just don't think we ought to be laughing at this man's troubles," she said calmly. "I would think that this family, above all, would know better."

"But, Mom," Curley tried to protest.

"Nope, your Mom's right. I'm sorry, honey. I wasn't thinking, that's all."

"Well," Ray said flatly, "I think it's funny."

"Ray, you heard your Mom," Rodney said.

"But...."

"Ray, there but for the grace of God go we," Eunice said. "If you think that it can't happen to this family, you are very wrong."

"Aw, Mom, you know they can't run that plant without Daddy," he said confidently. Eunice looked at Rodney. The conversation ended on that note. She had decided that it was better to allow her children to feel safe than to let them in on the truth----that their father himself wasn't sure how much longer he would have a job.

But there was money coming in from another source in the Norris home. Curley was making money doing the only job he wanted, playing music. Over the first few years he had diligently put the money aside that he made at the Kiwanis meetings, the Chamber of Commerce dinners, and the numerous talent shows whose purse he had triumphantly walked away with. The money was carefully counted, folded and then unceremoniously stuffed into an old coffee can, which Curley kept deposited under his bed.

"The First National Bank of Norris," Rodney called it.

When he had accumulated enough cash, Curley went to his father and declared that he had finally decided how he was going to spend his money.

"It's time," he said, "for a step up. I'm going to order myself a new guitar."

Rodney whistled.

"Well that is certainly a big step there, son," he said. "But you've got the banjo-uke and there ain't nothing wrong with it. Isn't there something you actually need that you could buy?"

"No, Dad," Curley said adamantly, "this is something I need. I want a guitar like those fellows on the radio play. And I'm gonna get me a real nice case, too. Real musicians," he declared with a note of authority, "do not carry their instruments in a sack."

Rodney knew it would be hard to argue that point. He also knew that, since this was money Curley had made on his own, the decision on how to spend it had to be all his own as well. So he assented to the purchase of a new guitar and a real case to carry it around in. In many ways Rodney knew it was a good financial decision. His son was making money with his singing and playing. Tools were important to any trade, he guessed.

Rodney and Curley thumbed through the Sears and Roebuck catalog until they found the one that caught Curley's fancy. It was a Bruno six string acoustic and, additionally, it came with its own case. Rodney sent off the money and the whole family waited for the shiny new instrument to arrive. When it did, the Norrises all gathered around as Curley brought it from its dark black case and began strumming it. The neck was bigger than he was used to, so it took him about a week to really get the flow that he was used to going on it. But as soon as he did, he was out making money again, cheerfully accepting the compliments on such a fine new instrument.

That left the trusty old pawnshop banjo-uke to sit alone in the corner. But Curley was determined that the instrument, which he had become quite fond of and was surprisingly loyal to, would not gather dust for too long. Soon, that battle scarred instrument was in the hands of his brother Ray, whose quiet admiration for his older brother made him more than willing to take lessons and directions from Curley.

It didn't take long for Curley to decide and announce to the family that the little brother also had "it," a gift for music and a talent for performance that, Curley also said, was going to make the Norris Brothers famous all over Gastonia. No, check that, all over the entire state of North Carolina. This kind of assurance from the star of the family made Ray even more devoted to his older brother than he had been before. Soon Ray was tagging along everywhere with Curley. The personal appearances would include a set from Curley, then a few songs with Ray (introduced always as "the newest member of my family to take up the music bug") and then a final flurry of songs by Curley again. Curley planned on taking his time and teaching Ray every song that he knew, so that eventually the entire set would be performed by the talented and stupendous Norris Brothers. The young man had grand plans.

Against the backdrop of the depression that was closing in around them Curley and Ray made their way across the county, the new Bruno guitar and the old banjo-uke in tow. They found that they were able to make good money by setting up outside the gates of the local mills in between shifts. Especially on payday. That was when the workers were in the best mood and, frequently they found, the only time they ever had any money on them. So on every other Friday they would make their way downtown and wait for the whistle to blow. Then Curley would begin to strum and play and Ray would start his well-memorized lines.

"Ladies and gentleman, today for your enjoyment we would like to present a little musical entertainment featuring the talents of the Norris Brothers. On lead and rhythm guitar and lead vocals is Mr. Curley Norris." Curley had decided that the name he had always used at home was a more ear-catching stage name than the rather plain "Russell."

"And on banjo-uke and back up vocals is me, Mr. Ray Norris. We're gonna leave this here hat in front of us and we hope, if you enjoy the music, you might leave us a little that we can take home to our family. You know, every little bit helps."

Rodney was now constantly hearing on the floor of the mill about his talented young sons and how entertaining they were. He always smiled and thanked whoever had dropped the compliment. Sometimes he would sneak into a nearby corner and watch his boys play and sing. Every time he was filled with an excitement and pride that only a father can understand. After all, he was receiving what most parents never do: confirmation. Of course he and Eunice believed that the boys were terrific, but the overflowing cash and coin in the old felt hat he had lent them showed that they were not another pair of parents supporting a dreadfully average set of siblings. And his sons could both count some very influential people among their biggest fans.

The mill where Rodney worked was known as the Cramer Mill, after Mr. Cramer. The town also bore his name. Mr. Cramer had heard the boys one day as he himself was heading out for lunch. He had been impressed, he told Rodney, with their talent and, mostly, their salesmanship.

"Those boys know how to sell the most important thing in the world, Norris," he had said approvingly, "themselves. That'll get them a long way in this world of ours. I can guarantee you that."

Mr. Cramer was also impressed with the apparent innate business sense of the boys. The fact that they soon were only a fixture on payday and they conserved their voices and their energy until just before the change of shifts was a marvel to Cramer.

"I was thirty years old," he told Rodney with a chuckle, "before I understood as much about making money as those boys of yours know now. If that is something they were born with then I'll be damned if I can figure out why most Indians are so damned poor." Rodney decided to ignore the general offensiveness of the statement for three simple reasons. First, trying to correct entrenched ignorance was like spitting in the wind. Second, he was sure that Mr. Cramer had meant it as a compliment to his sons. Third, and most importantly, Mr. Cramer signed his paychecks.

Mr. Cramer's admiration for the Norris boys, and a respect and affection for their father, lead him to become a virtual patron of the boys. He would frequently come out of his office after the shift change was over, when the boys were resting and correcting any musical mistake they had made, and request songs. He would squat beside of them in his suits that were tailored and shipped straight from Wilmington and listen and watch their nimble fingers.

"I tell you boys," he had said once, "I would give my mill and most of my money to be able to have just a little musical talent. That's the truth. I've always kinda secretly wanted to be able to play and sing. Always."

"Ah, Mr. Cramer," Ray had responded, "its easy. We could teach you, couldn't we Curley?"

"Sure we could," Curley answered.

"Well, that's mighty nice of you boys. But the truth is I can't carry a tune in a bucket."

At that they had all laughed loud enough to nearly be heard over the rumble of the mill. And, as usual, when Mr. Cramer walked away he left them a hefty sum for their time. Curley and Ray came to love the sight of the white man with the gray wisps of hair walking towards them in his tailored suits.

"Let's kill this one, boy," Curley would usually say when he saw him approaching. "This one's for our dinner."

They apparently never disappointed, because Mr. Cramer was

always generous with his money.

But it wasn't long before the money appeared to be drying up. Soon Mr. Cramer stayed ensconced behind his large oak desk as if he was trying to keep the impending crisis at bay; and their were fewer and fewer workers coming and going at shift change. The workers who did still have jobs were less likely to part with their cash to support a local novelty act like the Norris Brothers. Curley and Ray learned that Wall Street could even affect the lives of journeyman musicians. It was a sobering lesson.

The Park Yarn Mill in Kings Mountain was the first to announce drastic reductions in its workforce. Soon the Sadie and Dilling mills were following suit. It wasn't long before the Cramer Mill was joining in the bloodletting of the local workforce. As if that wasn't enough, many of the local mill owners, those same smiling and confident men Curley had once entertained, came up with the idea of "gugaloo" money. This paper replaced cash on payday. The money was worthless anywhere except an all-purpose store owned and operated by the mill. It was a monopoly and a brilliant business enterprise for the struggling upper crust of Gaston County, but it left their workers engendered with a bitter memory of their lack of choice and the lack of say in how and where to spend the money they had earned. Soon the Cramer Mill was following suit in this way as well.

Rodney cautioned Eunice time and again not to complain too strenuously about the inferior quality of the goods he could bring home with his gugaloo cash. He was lucky, he insisted to still be employed. Both of them knew that their situation could worsen at any moment, and the stress and strain began to show in their marriage. For the first time ever they didn't always take their disagreements into the bedroom, opting instead now to argue their points in front of their frightened children. Many of the fights were over money and what kind of plans they should make to prepare for the worst. Rodney, who had already changed his mind numerous times about sending his wife into the workplace, was still adamant that this policy not change. They had more children now, he argued, and she was needed at home as never before. He said it was unfair to burden a sixteen-year-old boy like Curley with the duties of a mother and housewife unless things proved desperate. Eunice argued that if they waited that long, they might just find they had waited too long. Just as many of the fights were over petty things that were no more than the result of the constant fear of the unemployment notice. Rodney became more and more obsessed with the thought of having to return to Qualla with his "tail between his legs." Depression or not, the return of the Norris brood would not be viewed fairly or charitably. The thought kept him awake many nights. Under this pressure, he and Eunice frequently went days without speaking to each other over slights both real and imagined. When the ice thawed and they were talking again, they often found that they couldn't even remember what had started the quarrel in the first place.

Things came to a painful head when Rodney came home with the news that he had been dumped as a foreman. There just wasn't enough money in the till, Mr. Cramer had explained, to justify as many foreman as were currently on the mill's payroll. Rodney was still employed, but he was now no more than an average mill worker, one of the very men he had been ordering around and directing. For a man with his pride it was a bitter pill to swallow.

Eunice had tried to be supportive and put the best possible face on things for her husband.

"Well," she said with that brave smile Rodney had once loved so much but was coming unavoidably to resent, "we will just thank the Great Spirit that you still have a job to go to."

But those words were no comfort to her husband and she knew it. Sleep became a stranger to her husband. He understood that the demotion was only the first step in a painful process that could only end with him jobless. It broke Eunice's heart to see her husband when he came home from work now. His black hair was tangled with the white cotton that flew in the mill, it seemed to imbed itself in every pore of his body. His face was covered with the dust of the cotton.

"Meet me at the end of the driveway tomorrow," he had told her the night before going in to assume his new position. Eunice obeyed without asking him any questions. That next afternoon, when he came home, she met him. The sight ripped through her soul.

"What do you want me to do?" she asked him.

Rodney laid his lunch pail down and tried as best he could to dust himself off.

"I want you to pick this goddamned cotton out of my hair," he said. "Don't let my boys see me like this."

With the sun setting and dinner cooling in the kitchen, Eunice gently plucked each nasty piece from her husband's head, quietly crying the whole time.

They tried to keep the ruse up for a week, until Curley ended it one night at the dinner table.

"Dad," he asked in between bites, "how come you get Mom to pick your hair at the top of the driveway?"

Eunice looked up terrified and Rodney stared at his son, unable to manage a sound.

"Russell," Eunice finally said, "your Dad doesn't want to track that mess into the house, that's all."

Rodney looked back down at his plate. He could not meet his son's gaze.

"Oh, o.k.," Curley said absently, "as long as he ain't ashamed of what he's doing now."

Rodney and Eunice both looked up at their eldest son, bewildered.

""Cause we sure ain't." When he said "we" he motioned to his brothers. Ray and L.D. both nodded in solemn agreement. Rodney laid his fork down and walked out onto the porch. It was the closest his children ever came to seeing him cry.

That night Rodney lay quiet and still in bed. His usual tossing and turning was replaced by the motionlessness. It frightened Eunice. She was trying to find something to say, anything, when her husband finally spoke.

"I've been thinking," he said. His tone was cold and distant. Resigned.

"About?"

"The way things have been around here. And I guess..." He stopped. He drew in a deep breath and let it out slowly, letting the sound of his hesitancy fill the room.

"I guess, well, if you want to go and look for work....I guess that might be best."

"O.k.," Eunice said.

"I mean, I've been awfully proud, I guess. But we've got to look at things they way they are right now. And I'm scared Eunice. I see fewer and fewer faces around the mill these days. And what really scares me is that I don't see no new faces taking their place. I don't understand what's happening, but I know enough to know that we need to do everything we can to be ready just in case. And people might not always need the stuff we're making down at the mill. But as long as people are getting sick they'll always need nursing I reckon."

"Yeah," Eunice agreed, "they will."

Rodney sighed again as if the weight of the world rested on his all too mortal shoulders.

"So see what you can find. I reckon that's best."

"If that's what you think," she said. Rodney turned on his side to face her.

"I'm sorry, babe," he said, "I never meant to let you down this way."

"You have not let me down," she said.

"Ah, hell, I can't even provide for my own family."

"Rodney, these are tough times. I don't care what it takes, we are going to get through this. And you can be proud. You will always be the head of this house. Always." She leaned over and kissed him gently on the cheek. "We'll be fine dear one," she said.

"God, I hope so," he said. They drifted off to sleep clinging to each other. The world continued to tumble all around them.

But they still had each other.

CHAPTER TWENTY-FOUR

True inspiration is born of necessity.

It did not take long for Curley and Ray to see the necessity of pulling their weight around the house. Their father was seeming more frail and distant with every passing day he spent on the floor of the mill. His will to survive seemed, if not broken, at least temporarily dormant. He still put on his best face for the family and tried to be as attentive as he had always been, but for his two eldest sons it was clear that something was changing within him. He would ask them how their day had gone and then seem to drift away to a distant place when they began to fill him in. It wasn't until they stopped moving their mouths that he drew himself back into reality and smiled and nodded. The problem was sometimes they were telling him that they had just had a miserable day and were still met with that white, toothy grin. The boys had decided not to point out their father's mistake to him. He obviously didn't need anything else vying for space in his cramped and aching mind.

But the Norris Brothers still saw Rodney as a pillar of strength, a rock upon which the family could peacefully rest. It was the sight of their mother returning home from her first day of work that brought their illusions tumbling painfully down around their heads. The nasty little puffs of cotton that dotted their father's hair was something they had learned to accept---he was, after all, a man, and sometimes, as he himself liked to point out, a man had to do some unpleasant things for his family's well-being. But this was different. This was their *mother*. The respect and near-adulation that Rodney showed his wife was infectious, and both Curley and Ray looked upon her as a sacred being. They revered their Mom, and seeing her come home with her hands swollen and bleeding, her hair laced with dust and cotton, her smile weak and tired, was more than they could stand. They were both closing in on manhood now; and neither was complacent enough to stand by and watch their parents drive themselves into the cold Cramerton ground.

Still, even with all the apparent troubles swirling around them, Curley was unwilling to trade his guitar and pick to go and man some faceless iron machine in a cotton mill. He was young enough to boldly hold on to his dreams, even in the face of such poor odds. He remained convinced that he and Ray had something special, something that could turn a profit if they could only catch a quick break. There was no denying that they could no longer help their parents by playing supper clubs and street corners. There was no longer enough money floating around for that to be profitable. They had already seen the supper shows begin to dry up, and those that did still come in were paying considerably less that they once had. It was up to them to find the proper outlet, a way to turn their hobby into a way to take some pressure of Eunice and Rodney. The only problem now was that neither of them had the slightest idea how to do that. Ironically, it was their father's addiction that illuminated their path.

ଚ

Curley had decided that real musicians smoked, like the detectives in the serials he had seen at the movies. It just looked *cool*, he thought. Besides, there was a part of him that always thought his father seemed to look somehow smarter whenever he lit up one of his cigarettes. And when he stared across at you from underneath a canopy of thick, blue smoke, you knew that you were in some serious trouble. Curley wanted to be able to replicate that look. All he was missing, he decided, was the smoke.

His first cigarette came just after he turned fifteen. He was home that Saturday alone. His parents had gone with the other boys into town, and he had been allowed to stay. His plan for the time alone was far more ambitious than just sneaking a smoke---he was planning on composing his first original song.

The words to the first verse and the chorus had passed in and out of his mind like a dream for three days. He paid them little attention, assuming that he was remembering or thinking of some tune he had heard on the radio. After the second day, however, he realized that the words were his own, a realization that brought with it the full impact of inspiration. He immediately jotted the words down on an old envelope he had found lying on the kitchen table. Pausing only occasionally to allow his hand to rest, he quickly completed two more verses. On this Saturday he had taken his guitar into the den and begun to compose the music. He started with a G chord, but decided that was too bright for the lyrics, which were tinged with melancholy and the blues. He finally settled on an E minor, and from there the song seemed to write itself. When finished, he played the song through three times in its entirety to make sure he wouldn't forget it. Suddenly he was seized with the knowledge that there was no one around to share in this momentous moment. He wished Ray would hurry home so that they could properly rehearse the tune and debut it for their Mom and Dad. As he was skipping through the house and humming the new tune to himself his eyes fell upon the ashtray overflowing and sitting on the coffee table. He looked around guiltily and then moved closer.

There were several butts sticking out of the pile that had barely been smoked.

"No one would ever know if I tried just one," he thought.

He moved to the couch and sat down across from the table. It would be so easy. Just take one and light it up. If he didn't like it, he would stub it out with the others and that would be the end of it. And if he did like it, well, he could light up another one. It would really be so easy.

Curley decided to move into the kitchen and grab a pack of matches, just in case he chose to try one. He searched through the drawers until he found a pack that was already missing a few matches. He took the pack and moved back to the couch, resuming his vigil in front of the ashtray. Finally he went for it. He grabbed one of the hardly-smoked cigarettes and lit it up.

He felt the swirling smoke burn its way down his throat. He felt dizzy, and then numb. He didn't cough at all (a fact he would proudly relay to his incredulous younger brother). His eyes teared up reflexively and he felt an odd sensation that sent his nose twitching. But, he thought, he could learn to like this. He took another drag. Then another. Curley Norris had become a smoker. When Ray finally did get home that night, Curley couldn't decide which news to tell him first.

And to top it all off, Rodney and Eunice *loved* the new song.

શ૦

It wasn't long before Curley had initiated Ray into the smoker's club. And, since Ray was younger, it fell to him to keep a close eye on the ashtray and snag any butts that were dubbed "keepers" before Eunice had a chance to throw them out. It was a risky undertaking, because both of them knew that they would get a real beating if they were caught. But Ray proved to be as skillful at stealth as he was at rhythm guitar, and they never were caught in the act.

Once the butts had been retrieved, Ray and Curley deposited them in a small tin they kept under the steps that led to the front porch. When their parents were away at work they would take shifts, one watching the other brothers while the other went outside for a smoke. It was as essential to keep their siblings in the dark as it was their parents, especially L.D., who had a terrible habit of running to Eunice with any news he thought she should know. There were some serious, near-brawls when one brother went out to the steps and felt the other had smoked more than his fair share. But for the most part the arrangement was without conflict.

It was during one of these "shifts" that the idea slammed into Curley like a tornado. He burst into the house, terrifying Houston and L.D. and making Ray think that his brother had lost his mind.

"I've got it, Ray," he exclaimed. "By God, I have GOT IT!!"

"You got something alright, Curley," Ray said with a smile. He had become used to his brother's temperamental outbursts of ideas.

"No, seriously, Ray, I have figured out how we can help Mom and Dad."

"Start buying our own cigarettes?" Ray mocked. Curley frowned.

"I'm serious, Ray."

"O.k., o.k., let's hear it. What's your plan?"

Curley held up a smoked butt. Ray looked at him in terror and then ushered the younger brothers back into the den.

"That a cigarette?" asked L.D. Ray shushed him and shuttled him away.

"Curley, what in the world are you doing? Are you crazy bringing that in the house?"

"This is the answer." Curley smiled brightly. Ray gave him a confused look. "Well, don't you get it?"

"We gonna start growing tobacco?" Ray asked.

Curley laughed.

"No, you idiot," he scolded, "but we're going to follow the people who do!"

"Curley," Ray said, "you ain't making no sense. None."

"We've been sitting outside mills playing for people who ain't got no money, right?"

"Right."

"But if they had money, they'd give it to us. Right?"

"Well, sure. But they *ain't* got no money."

"Exactly. But why are we sitting out there like fools, waiting for them to get some? What we've gotta do is take our show on the road and find the people who have got some money. Tobacco farmers."

"You talking about trailing them old tobacco farmers to market?"

"That is exactly what I am talking about. You've seen those guys after they sell their crops. They are walking around like that money is just burning a hole in their pocket. Well, we'll be there to relieve them of some of it. Whaddaya think?"

"I don't know, Curley," Ray said, "I mean, some of those folks don't exactly like people like us. You know?"

"Well, Ray," Curley said, shaking his head, "the way I see it, it's either that or we get jobs in the mill."

Ray was silent for a minute.

"Let's try it."

Curley smiled.

"That's what I thought you'd say."

CHAPTER TWENTY-FIVE

Rodney stood for a moment in the center of the plant. It seemed that he was hearing the noise around him for the very first time. The machines twirled and rolled with thunderous precision. Rodney surveyed the faces of the workers. He looked for a smile somewhere, but found that the human faces were taking on the same uniformity of the machines that hovered over them. It was eerie how much all these people looked alike, the same expression, the same movements, the same way of shifting on the balls of their feet as they manned their own personal undoing. He took a deep breath and walked on. As the sound of the machines grew louder Rodney felt his mind fly away to Qualla. The rumbling underneath his feet suddenly reminded him of the coming of a thunderstorm in the mountains. He saw Molly's smiling face flash across the back screen of his mind. He took another deep breath and continued to walk. Home, he thought, was such a very long ways away. He wondered how he had come to be in this foreign place. Why had the Great Spirit placed him and his family here? Had he learned anything or imparted any knowledge to others that would make it all worth it? Yes, he thought, there had been something gained.

He smiled when he thought of his children, especially Curley and Ray. He was the proud father of two semi-famous children. There was no one in the mill who hadn't heard of the Norris Boys, and there were only a few cranky old bastards who had not contributed something towards their careers, either in the form of money or just a kind word. Maybe, when all was said and done, that had been the reason he had found himself in Cramerton. The boys had certainly had opportunities that they would not have found in the mountains.

He felt the twinge again and stopped walking. He closed his eyes and calmly said a quick prayer. He felt his thoughts fly away again, this time to the banks of the Occonoluftee. His mind's eye watched again as the summer breeze blew the hair of his young and beautiful bride. He thought of Eunice's shy smile and her tender touch. He reflected on how lucky he was to have found a woman like her, a woman who had seen past his outward self and seen the man within, the man struggling to be born in a world that always seemed to throw stones in his path. An awkward smile made its way across his drawn features.

"My love," he declared to himself. Then, as suddenly as it had started, the thunder faded away into nothing.

ಣಿ

Eunice was sitting in the floor, reading to her children when she heard the knock at the door. She glanced at the clock on the wall and thought about the fact that there was no one she knew that should be out visiting this time of day. She stood and walked quickly to the door. When she opened it, she was surprised to see Dell Matthews, one of Rodney's friends from the mill, standing at her door. Dell was holding his dusty, old felt hat in his hands, his sweaty hair matted down across his forehead. He was gulping down air like a man stranded in the desert might take down a tall glass of cool water. Eunice noticed that his eyes were nearly bulging out of his head.

"Dell Matthews," she said, trying to sound calm, "what in the world are you up to?"

"Mrs. Norris," he said, wheezing as he grabbed breath, "I'm afraid I have some troublesome news."

Eunice felt her heart sink. She clasped her hands behind her back and straightened her shoulders as if preparing to be slapped.

"What is your news, Dell?"

"Mrs. Norris," he said, "I'm awfully sorry, but, but.....your husband, Rodney, I mean, collapsed at work a little bit ago. Just fell right over. Mrs. Norris, I'm afraid it might be bad."

L.D. and Houston were gathered around their mother's knees now, listening intently to the strange man at their door.

"Boys," Eunice said quietly, "go back in the house. I'll be in in a minute."

When they had scampered back into the house, bickering all the way, Eunice turned back to Dell.

"Is my husband alive?" she asked.

"Yes, ma'am, at least I think so. He ain't opened his eyes or said nothing since he went down, though, so I can't honestly tell you that for sure."

"I understand," Eunice said.

"But, you know, this kinda thing happened about a month ago to Gerald Taylor, too. Just went down like a sack of flour in the middle of the back lot. And he was back at work in a week."

Eunice made no move to acknowledge the man's effort to soothe her. She appreciated the effort, but had no time to concern herself with his feelings at the moment.

"Dell," she asked, "where is my husband now?"

"Some of the men are bringing him here," Dell answered. "And we've sent for a doctor, too."

"Thank you for telling me," Eunice said. Suddenly finding her manners she asked, "May I get you something to drink?"

"No, thank you. If you don't mind none, I'm just gonna wait here for them to get here. I'll see if there's anything I can do then."

"O.k.," Eunice said, "I believe I'll wait inside. Will you please come tell me when you see them?"

"Yes, ma'am."

Eunice turned and walked back into the house. As she closed the door behind her she stopped and stared at the kitchen table. It seemed as though every word that she and Rodney had ever spoken to each other there came rushing back through her memory. She pressed her fist into her mouth and closed her eyes tightly. Now is not the time for tears, she thought. That time may come soon, but it had not yet arrived. She began to move quickly through the kitchen, making coffee. The men bringing Rodney home and the doctor would all want something good and strong to drink. Plus, it helped to do something to keep her mind occupied.

As she began to spoon the coffee into the old pot her mind reflected on how many cups of coffee she had shared with her husband. Suddenly the tears began to fall, sparkling like precious gems in her dark eyes. She pushed the coffee pot away and stood trembling in the afternoon sun. In the distance she heard the hum of a car engine.

ॐ

The doctor, a friend of Mr. Cramer's from Gastonia, stood by the bedside, prodding and poking, listening and, occasionally grunting.

The baby, Jimmy, was crawling around the floor of the den, trying now and then to stand on his own two feet. L.D. was keeping an eye on him and Houston for his mother. As he watched his mother disappear into the back room, he found himself silently praying for Curley and Ray to hurry up and get home from school. L.D. had seemed to grow ten years older when he saw his father's body being carried by these strange white men into the house like a sack of flour. They had come in Mr. Cramer's car, at Mr. Cramer's insistence. At Eunice's instructions they took Rodney back into the bedroom and stretched him carefully across the bed. Then they self-consciously removed their hats and retreated into the corner of the bedroom. Eunice had instinctively moved over and checked her husband's breathing and searched for a pulse. It was faint, but it was there. She breathed a small sigh of relief. There was still hope.

"Mrs. Norris," one of the men had said, "we're gonna go on outside now. We'll be right around the porch if you need us for anything. We're not going anywhere, o.k.?"

"Yes, thank you," Eunice answered absently.

"Doc Jenkins oughta be here any minute," another said. Eunice said nothing.

"Mrs. Norris, is there anything that you need before we go outside?"

"No, thank....wait, yes there is. Could one of you please bring one of the kitchen chairs in for me?"

"Sure," the first man said. Then they all filed out of the room and into the yard. They stood around, trying to remind each other of anything they could that would take the terror out of what had just happened. They seized on any bad habit or rumored bad habit of Rodney's like drowning men to a life preserver. It wasn't malicious; it was pure desperation. Even these poor men, men who had known the sting of death and suffering throughout their lives, did not want to acknowledge the random nature of their lives. So they spun tales and built dikes against the flood of their minds, searching for answers, trying to carve out some rhyme or reason for why this man, who they had all known and seen walking through the plant just this morning, was now laying in his bed fighting for his next breath.

Eunice sat in the chair beside the bed, rubbing Rodney's temples and moving the wet, black clump of hair out his eyes. She noticed his eyes twitch slightly when she did this, and she found herself desperately hoping that those eyes she loved might open and gaze into her own again. But the twitch ended and there was no more movement. She took Rodney's hand and held it to her lips, kissing it softly.

"Qua di ni," she whispered, "a qua da nv do, my heart, stay here with us. Stay here with me. You are still needed."

She felt the tears streaming down her face but she fought back the urge to make any noise. She did not want to frighten the children.

Eunice was pulled from her thoughts by the doctor. He had finally moved away from Rodney and was wiping his eyeglasses with a handkerchief.

"Well?" she asked impatiently.

"It looks like a heart attack," he said.

"How bad?"

Dr. Jenkins let out a slow and deliberate sigh.

"Very," he said. "I'm afraid it is very bad, Mrs. Norris."

The gasp was out of her mouth before she had even known that is was coming.

"There must be something that you can do, doctor," she pleaded.

"No, ma'am there isn't," he corrected. "I am afraid that it is only a matter of time."

"No," Eunice insisted. "I won't accept that. We must get him to a hospital."

"Mrs. Norris you're husband mustn't be moved. If you do that it will certainly kill him."

"But you just said that he was going to die anyway," Eunice nearly shouted.

"Yes, that is my belief. But I have seen people worse than your husband come back around. I don't want you to get your hopes up, but it can happen. However," he continued, "I feel certain that he will not survive any attempt to move him. Of course the decision is yours."

Eunice traced the outline of Rodney's jaw with her finger. She could feel that the doctor was right. Somewhere, below that spot where reality and dreams collide, she understood that there was no point in putting her husband through another move.

"Then we'll wait," she said. "And we will pray."

"Yes, we will do that. Now if you will excuse me, I am going to step outside and have a cigarette."

"Of course, doctor. There is coffee on the stove."

Doctor Jenkins left the room and Eunice found herself once again alone with Rodney. If only I could tell you I love you and have you hear me, she thought. She again took his hand and cupped it gently in her own.

"I love you, honey," she said, leaning in next to his ear. "I love you with all my life and soul and heart and mind. Please don't leave me. Not yet, Rodney. For God's sake, not yet. Please."

I don't know who I am without you.

The thought draped itself over her mind.

Rodney had never denied her needs before. As a lover, as a friend, he had always satisfied her needs. He had gone without many times for her and the boys. He had driven himself so that she could always have the best that he could give. Now all she wanted was him. One more time. One more smile.

I don't know if I can laugh without you.

I don't know if I know how.

Eunice placed her head in the crook of his arm and let the pain pour out.

"Don't do this, my love. Don't."

ꙩ

Curley and Ray stood quietly in the corner of the room. They could not pull their eyes away from this picture. Their father lay on the bed, broken, and there was nothing they could do to fix him. Their mother, the woman they had long ago placed on a pedestal, sat looking utterly human and scared. Curley felt the unwelcome weight of manhood resting on his shoulders.

"Mom, what can we do? What did the doctor say?" he asked.

Eunice did not look up from her husband's face.

"Your father is dying," she said.

"NO!" Ray cried, moving towards the bed. "He can't!"

"Hush," Eunice scolded. "Hush now. Your father doesn't need this. Not now. Russell?"

He walked to the foot of the bed, not feeling his feet or the steps that he took.

"Yes, Mom?"

"I want you to go and make sure those nice men have everything they need. And then I want you to bring me a cup of coffee. And look in on the boys, make sure they aren't killing each other. Take Ray with you."

"But...." Ray protested.

"Then come back in here as soon as you can," Eunice finished. Curley put his arm around his brother and led him out into the hallway.

"Ray," he said, "we can't do that again. No matter what happens, me and you have to be strong for Mom."

"But, oh god, Curley..."

"Promise me, Ray. Promise me."

Ray swallowed hard. He bit back the tears with all the effort he could muster.

"I promise I'll do the best I know how," he said.

"Good enough," Curley answered.

Curley found the men on the front lawn, standing vigil as they had been all afternoon. He offered them coffee but they declined.

"How's your ma?" one of them asked.

"She's holding up," Curley answered. "She's holding up." Curley noted the fact that none of the men asked about his father.

"They've already given up," he thought. "Well, they don't know my Dad."

He and Ray checked on the boys as their mother had asked. No one was killing anyone, much to their surprise. They then turned back into the kitchen to pour their Mom's coffee. They were surprised to turn and see L.D. standing quietly behind them in the doorway. They both noticed the stricken and terrified look on his face.

"Is our Daddy gonna die?" he asked. Ray turned away to stare out of the window.

"Listen, L.D.," Curley began.

"I heard those men talking with that doctor fella," L.D. continued, "and I heard somebody say that Daddy was gonna die. Is it true?"

"Yeah," Ray answered angrily, "he's dying. Mom said so herself."

Curley shot a devastating look at Ray to shut him up. He walked over and knelt down to look into his younger brother's eyes. He placed his hand on L.D.'s shoulder and gripped it firmly.

"Listen, partner," he said, "you keep that chin up. Our Daddy's a warrior, just like Geronimo or Crazy Horse. He's a fighter. He's gonna fight hard to stay here with us. I can promise you that."

"Can you promise me that he's gonna be o.k.?" L.D. asked, tears welling up in his eyes. "Please, Curley?" The little boy was pleading for reassurance with his older brother. Curley looked down to the floor and then forced himself to look back up and meet his brother's flooding eyes. He suddenly and forcefully thought of his Grandfather.

"I can't promise you that," he said solemnly. "I wish to God that I could. But we have to be strong. For Mom. O.k.?"

L.D. was crying hard now, his entire body convulsing with the tremors of the pain. But the little boy's head managed, somehow, to nod an affirmation. Curley felt his heart breaking within him.

"Be strong, little man," he said, "be strong."

He brushed his hand through L.D.'s thick shock of hair as he stood, and their eyes met again. Curley had been struck by the similarity of his hand's intuitive movement and that of his father's. The look on L.D.'s face made him believe that his little brother had felt it, too.

"My God," he thought painfully, "I might be your father by tomorrow morning."

He shoved the thought away and forced a smile at L.D. He motioned to Ray and they took the coffee cup and headed back into the bedroom. L.D. stood for a minute longer in the kitchen, listening the incessant moan of the men's voices in the yard. He quickly turned away and headed back to his brothers. He tried to think about Curley's words and the comforting feeling of his brother's hand on his shoulder. Curley and Ray were pulling themselves together for their mother. L.D. would hold himself together for his older brothers. He couldn't, he WOULDN'T let them down.

"No more crying," he promised himself. "Not no more."

ဆ

The clock in the den had just struck one in the morning when Eunice asked Ray to go and get the other boys.

"Let Jimmy and Francis sleep," she instructed, "but I think Houston and L.D. should be here."

Ray began to cry quietly. He knew what the instructions meant. His mother was calling the family into the room for the end.

Curley and Ray had taken shifts in the other kitchen chair that they had brought into the room. Eunice sat at Rodney's right, one of the sons at his left. The doctor alternately stood or sat by the foot of the bed.

Just before midnight Curley had become scared by the sound of his father's labored breathing. The sound was a wet, painful rattling that seemed to rip Rodney in half with each breath he took.

"Mom?" he had asked, frightened.

"It's almost over, Russell," Eunice had said quietly. The doctor had gone to take Rodney's pulse again. It was very, very faint this time.

"Not much longer now," he said.

Ray returned with the boys. He went and stood beside of Curley, the two boys went and gathered around their Mom. Houston's eyes had the vacant look of someone pulled unexpectedly from sleep. L.D. had been awake, waiting to be summoned to his father's bedside. They all stood in silence for a long time.

"Mom," L.D. asked, "can Dad hear me?"

"I think so," she answered.

L.D. moved hesitantly closer to Rodney. He looked up at Curley.

"It's alright," Curley said, "that's still Daddy."

L.D. moved close to Rodney's ear.

"I love you, Daddy," he said quietly and respectfully.

"Me, too," said Houston, following his brother's lead.

Eunice took her hands and gently pulled her boys next to her. She was crying softly now.

"Did he hear me, Mom," L.D. asked, "did he?"

"Yes, son," she assured him, "Daddy heard you."

Curley and Ray stood and moved over to their mother. Doctor Jenkins stood and took their place at Rodney's left. The breathing was becoming louder now; and there seemed to be an eternal moment between each one. Eunice reached out and again took Rodney's hand. Curley stood behind her with his hands on her shoulders.

Then the sound stopped. The room went peacefully quiet. Jenkins reached out and placed his hand under Rodney's chin. His hand moved quickly and thoroughly around several times, as if to assure himself before he spoke.

"It's done, Mrs. Norris," he said, "I'm sorry."

Curley felt his mother's shoulders begin to tremble and then shake. She bowed her head and placed it next to Rodney's arm.

"My darling husband," she cried.

L.D. and Houston began to cry too, and the sound of their grief seemed to make Eunice's tears come faster and harder.

"Come on, boys," Ray said. He looked up at Curley to make sure this was the right thing to do. Curley nodded at him. Ray ushered the boys out of the room and into their own beds. He sat with them, telling them they were all going to be alright, crying quietly in the dark as he spoke.

Curley pulled the doctor's chair from the foot of the bed and moved beside of Eunice, putting his arm around her shoulder and pulling her head to his chest. He hadn't even realized that he was crying himself until he tasted the tears on his lips.

"Oh, Russell," Eunice sobbed. "What now?" she asked.

"We'll be alright Mom," he said. "I promise."

"Rodney," she cried, "oh, my dear Rodney."

Curley pulled her closer. After awhile, Eunice's weeping slowed and she began to calm down.

"I'm going to miss him," she said, trying to force a brave grin.

"He was the best," Russell agreed.

They sat in the dark holding each other. Finally Eunice spoke.

"Son," she said, "go into the kitchen and look in my pocket book. There's a little money in there. Pay Doctor Jenkins and offer him some more coffee. I'm sure he wants to go home now."

"Yes, Mom."

Curley took a deep breath and headed towards the door.

"Russell?"

"Yes, Mom," he said, turning towards her.

"I love you, son. And you're father loved you very much."

"I know," he said, trying to control his emotions. "And I love you, too, Mom. And I promise you, we will be alright."

He left the room.

Eunice looked at her husband. There was peace on his face, a peace that she didn't think she had ever seen before. All the anger, all the drive was now gone.

She began to cry again in the dark.

CHAPTER TWENTY-SIX

As Eunice moved quietly through the sleepy house, she heard the faint calling of the whippoorwill in the yard. She felt the smile spread across her face as she listened. She walked into the kitchen and removed a slim, slightly used white candle from the pantry. She took it into the bedroom where L.D., Houston and baby Jimmy were sleeping and placed it in the window. She took the pack of matches from her housecoat and struck one, sticking its bright tip to the candle's bent wick. She had always been taught that, if you hear a whippoorwill and then stick a candle in your window, it will bring good and peaceful dreams. She moved quietly out of the bedroom and turned to look at her sons.

"They could use easy dreams," she thought.

The light of the moon was cascading down into the house, giving it a tranquil look that, although Eunice wanted to believe it, didn't really fit the overall mood of her home. Her sons were holding up remarkably well, showing the strength that she had always hoped they would have. But the underlying darkness would not be washed away by this harvest moon. It would only be washed away by the cleansing tears that were being shed privately, every night, in every Norris's own personal way. Eunice did not intrude when she heard one of her sons softly sobbing in their bed, crying themselves to sleep. They were healing, and it was not her place to try to stop the process. Despite what the whites thought, theirs was not a stoic people. They laughed as boisterously and with as little inhibition as any. And they hurt as deeply. But they did not, would not, do it for a show. Their victories and their defeats were not for public consumption. That was their way. And it was her way.

Eunice walked into the kitchen and sat down with a cup of coffee and a pencil and paper. She had been putting this responsibility off for too many days now. She could not prolong it any longer.

　She tapped the end of the pencil on the table, banging out a thin pow wow beat in the solitude of her thoughts. She closed her eyes and said a quick prayer for guidance and then began to write slowly and thoughtfully.

　My Dear Ma Runningwolf,

　　I must confess that I have put this off longer than I should have, but it has been difficult for me to find the words. I have also been trying to get over my own feelings that, once I commit these words to the page, the finality of the event of which they speak will come crashing down on my head and in my heart. But you must know, and the Great Spirit has seen that it is best that the responsibility of telling you falls to me.

　　The boy you raised, and the man we both loved, is no more. Rodney passed away one week ago tomorrow. You will be proud to know that he died as he lived: working to support his wife and his sons. I hope it will be some measure of comfort to you when I say that he did not suffer.

　　Rodney told me many times that you were both mother and father to him. He felt himself to be your son, and I know you feel the same towards him. As I look in the eyes of my own sons, I feel how little I could say or do to assuage the grief that this news must bring. But if there be any comfort at all, let it be in the knowledge of a life well and honorably lived. This, without doubt, was Rodney's life.

　　I cannot keep from tendering you the love and gratitude of an affectionate daughter-in-law who benefited daily from the values you taught the man I called my husband. It is my fervent prayer that I shape my own, precious children in the loving example you have set forth.

　　Tonight my husband's chair sits empty, yet I feel him all around me, as surely you do in your home and in your heart. His name shall never be spoken in this house in hushed tones or polite whispers. It will be spoken proudly and with due reverence. He was the love of my life and the light of my soul. My love for him will always be as deep as the ocean and as high as the stars. I miss him more and more with every breath I take. But I will carry on, as we all must, because that is the truest way to honor him and all he stood for. He managed to rise to the very heights of his dreams, and he never sank to the level that others, in their narrow-minded ignorance, prescribed for him. He was a man.

I must close now. I love you, Ma Runningwolf, as my husband loved you. I pray that the Great Spirit will grant you peace in the coming days, and I hope that you will remember me and my children in your prayers.

Your daughter,
Eunice Norris

CHAPTER TWENTY-SEVEN

Ray was sitting on his bed, gingerly working the F chord on his guitar. It was the chord that gave him the most trouble, and Curley was always complaining that the bottom three strings were still muffled when Ray tried to play them.

"It's passable Ray," Curley would say, "but it sure would sound better if you could manage to make them strings ring out the way they're supposed to."

So Ray worked every chance he got on making those notes "ring." Sometimes he thought Curley worried too much about little stuff like that, but there was enough sibling rivalry and flat out pride involved that he was not going to let the challenge go unanswered. So he laid his index finger across the strings, placed the other fingers in position, and strummed until he thought the strings had the proper tone.

"There, Curley," he said after one particularly nice strum, "let's see you find something wrong with that one."

"Not half bad," the voice said from outside the window. Ray nearly jumped out of his skin.

"Jesus, Curley," he said.

Curley shushed him.

"Be quiet before you wake up the whole house."

"Well," Ray answered, "if you want me to stay quiet, why in the Hell don't you come in through the door the way you're supposed to?"

Curley laughed.

"Because there is something that I want you to see and I don't want anyone else in the house to see it or know about it."

Ray was intrigued now.

"What've you gone and done now?" he asked.

"Meet me in the backyard and I'll show you what I've gone and done," Curley answered with swagger. "I think you will be pleased."

It was dark outside, but not dark enough to hide the look on Curley's face. Ray was able to read his brother like a dime store novel, and he saw right through the false bravado.

"Oh, God, Curley," he said, "you didn't. Please tell me that you didn't."

"Grow up, Ray," Curley snapped. "We needed a car and I got us one."

"But Curley...."

"No!" Curley cut him off. "What's done is done and I didn't bring you out here for no sermon. Tomorrow we hit the trail, and now we are going to do it in style."

"Is she going with us?"

She was Susan Muncie, a late thirty something widow who had attended a number of Norris Brothers shows and had let each of them know that she was available to take their fan club to a whole new level whenever they saw fit. Curley and Ray had both laughed her away. The only thing that Susan Munice had going for her was an automobile, a fairly nice one in fact, that had belonged to her late husband. It now sat unused in her driveway. She had told them often that it was theirs whenever they needed it to get to and from gigs. But both boys knew there would be a price.

"I oughta pound your face in," Curley spat, "of course she ain't going with us. Do you think I'm crazy?"

Ray arched his eyebrow in the same style that Eunice had perfected long ago when faced with a dumb question. Curley said nothing.

Ray walked around the car and glanced in. He didn't know what to say or what to ask. He kicked the tires just to kill some time.

"How far'd you go?" he asked without looking at Curley.

"Far enough," Curley answered.

Ray shook his head quietly.

"What?" Curley demanded.

"Nothing."

"No, what is it?"

Ray stopped his inspection and stared at his brother,

"What was it like?' he asked.

Curley shuffled his feet and watched the ground around his feet.

"It was o.k.," he said. "Nothing to write home about, I guess. But it was all right."

Ray shook his head again. He walked back around the back of the car until he was standing beside of his brother.

"Well," he said, "you don't look any different. Do you feel any different?"

"Yeah," Curley laughed, "I'm a little sore."

"Ah, jeez, Curley."

"Well, you asked."

"Yeah," Ray admitted, "yeah, I reckon I did."

"Look, Ray, truth is I ain't real proud of what I done tonight. But I just couldn't see no other way. And I figure there was no harm done, right? Me and Susan both had something the other wanted and we struck up a trade. Now we get to play our music. And that was what it was all about, right?"

Ray sighed.

"Yeah, Curley, I reckon so. But I guess you done the right thing by not driving up to the door. We cannot let Mom know about this."

"No kidding," Curley said. "I figured we could come up with some story to cover this up. We'll tell Mom that we're gonna hitchhike or something and just keep the car hidden. I think it would just be best to keep this to ourselves."

"I don't like lying to Mom."

"Well, neither do I," Curley said, "but I'd rather do it just this once than get myself killed before we even get out of town."

Ray nodded his agreement.

"Yep, 'cause if Mom finds out what you done, Curley, I'm gonna be the man of the house. And I ain't got no plans on taking that on just yet."

"So this is our secret?" Curley wanted to make absolutely sure that he had his little brother's complete agreement.

"It is our little secret. But Curley, let's don't make this a habit. Promise?"

"I promise."

Both boys felt the weight hanging over them in the cool night air. Lying to their Mom was not something either was comfortable with. Curley put his arm around Ray and they turned back towards the house. They walked quietly for a ways until Ray finally broke the silence.

"You know you have to tell me everything about it, right?"

Curley smiled.

"Well...."

The knock at the door surprised Eunice. She was expecting no one, and there had been precious few visitors since Rodney was buried. When she saw the familiar smile on the other side of the door she had to blink hard to make sure she wasn't dreaming.

"Little Reed," he said.

"Daddy!"

Lorenzo wasn't able to get anything else out of his mouth before his daughter had virtually leapt into his arms.

"There, there," Lorenzo said, smiling, "give your old daddy a chance to get in the door now."

"I'm sorry," Eunice said, remembering herself, "it's just so good to see you."

"Well, what about me?"

Eunice's eyes suddenly shifted behind her father to see Dora standing there.

"Dotie!" she exclaimed.

The hugging and smiling continued on the front porch until Lorenzo reached out his large hands and pulled his daughters into the house. He took a seat at the kitchen table and listened happily as his children chirped on about how good they looked and how kind the years had been. He remained silent and just listened to their voices. It was good for him to hear them, it reminded him of his legacy. Finally he interrupted.

"What's an old man got to do to get himself a glass of water around here?" he asked.

Eunice began moving around the kitchen with a speed and purpose that she hadn't had for what seemed like an eternity. Dora took a seat beside of her father. Eunice brought them each a tall glass of water and took her own seat.

"I, I don't even know where to start," she said. "I guess the most obvious question is how did you get here?"

"Took a train," Lorenzo said. "Decided to come see my daughter and all those new grandbabies."

"How did you get to the house?"

Dora let out a disgruntled moan.

"We walked," she said.

"Walked? All that way? Why?"

"Because Daddy insisted on it."

"Dad," Eunice teasingly scolded, "that wasn't necessary. If you had told me you were coming I could have made some arrangements or something."

"It was good for us. *Both* of us."

Dora rolled her eyes and then winked at Eunice.

"He insisted," she repeated.

"So, my Little Reed," he said, bringing the conversation back around, "there is much to tell?"

Eunice searched her father's eyes.

"That's why you came," she stated flatly. "You know."

Dora looked down at the table top, suddenly uncomfortable and very, very sad. Lorenzo met his daughter's stare and nodded. There was a moment of oppressive silence before Lorenzo spoke.

"We are sorry. I know you loved him. And I know he loved you and took care of you. I am sorry."

"How?"

Lorenzo reached into his old jacket and pulled out an envelope. He looked at it for a moment as if to convince himself it was really still there, then he reached out and handed it to Eunice. She recognized the handwriting immediately; it was Rodney's.

"What is this?" she asked, her hands visibly trembling. "Where did you get this?"

"From your husband," Lorenzo answered. "He sent it to me and asked me to come. He only told me that he believed you were going to need me. We left as soon as we could. I'm sorry we could not have been here sooner."

Eunice laid the envelope down without opening it. She didn't think she was up to reading it. With her slight finger she pushed it back towards Lorenzo who instinctively picked it up and returned it to his pocket.

"Why?" she asked. "Why didn't he tell me?"

"Eunice...." Dora began.

"He didn't know," Lorenzo interrupted. "He did not know anything for sure."

"He *knew*" Eunice corrected bitterly, "or he would not have sent that."

"He had a feeling, Little Reed. You know he did the right thing. There was nothing else he could've done. You know that to be the truth."

Eunice said nothing. There was the slight feeling of having been betrayed gnawing at her gut. She and Rodney had always told each other everything. They had been the closest of friends. He should have turned to her. Maybe they could have done something to stop what happened. Maybe he could still be here with her. She placed her head in her hands and began to weep. Lorenzo and Dora both went to her side and embraced her, providing a protective and comforting shell for her pain.

"I'm so sorry, Eunice," Dora said, her own tears cascading down her cheeks. Lorenzo said nothing. He just held his daughter and caressed her hair. Finally the pain began to retreat and Eunice pulled herself together. Her father and sister pulled back slightly and watched her.

"Thank you for coming," she managed. Lorenzo took his seat again and Dora followed his lead.

"So," he said, "where are all these little boys that I have not yet met?"

"They are in school."

The smile that spread across Lorenzo's face was electric with pride.

"How are they doing?" he asked. Eunice knew that he didn't want to know how they were adjusting to life without their father. It wasn't that he didn't care, he was just fixated on their education. It had been his mantra for a long time.

"They are doing very well," she answered.

Lorenzo's grin, if possible, actually widened.

"My boys," he cooed. Dora rolled her eyes again. "And Curley?" The affection is his tone was unmistakable. He had even leaned forward on his elbows when he mentioned the child's name.

"I'm sure he's gotten so big," he said.

"Yes," Eunice agreed. "He is a man now."

"Yes, yes," Lorenzo agreed.

"How are they dealing with things?" Dora asked cautiously. "Have they done o.k.?"

Eunice nodded.

"They have gotten me through it."

"They are fine boys," Lorenzo said. "How is Curley doing in school?"

Eunice felt a sudden lump in her throat the size of a boulder. In all the excitement and emotion she had not thought about breaking the news to her father that Curley would no longer be going to school. And Ray....

"Well?"

"Dad," she said, "that is something that you should know, I guess."

Lorenzo's eyes narrowed suspiciously.

"Russell isn't in school today. He and Ray left this morning to do some things over in Gastonia."

"And?" Lorenzo's tone was irritated and impatient.

"And they won't be going back to school," she said quickly. She had learned long ago that it was better to just hit him with the information and then deal with the consequences.

"What? Why? Is there trouble with the whites?"

Eunice laughed.

"No, no trouble. They have decided to be musicians. Guitar players."

"Guitar players?" Lorenzo exploded. "Where in the Hell did they get that kind of an idea?"

"Look, Dad...."

"Are you supporting this?" he thundered. "Are you?"

"Uh, Dad," Dora interrupted the storm, "I believe we came here to *help* Eunice, not beat her up."

Lorenzo suddenly looked deflated. There was slight twinkle of shame in his eyes. He took a deep breath.

"But...."

"But nothing," Dora said. "Calm down and remember that you are now in her home, not yours. And she is the head of this house now."

Lorenzo said nothing.

"Well," Eunice corrected, "I'm not exactly the head of the house now. That is the point. And," she continued, looking disapprovingly at Lorenzo, "if you will allow me to finish I think the story might make you rather proud."

Lorenzo cleared his throat and whispered, almost inaudibly, "Let's hear it. Go ahead."

The sisters looked at each other, acknowledging without words the new power that age and maturity had brought to them. It didn't seem like that long ago that an evil look from the man at the table would have sent them cowering in a corner of the room, but now they were standing together and staring HIM down. The knowledge was both exhilarating and sobering.

"My boys came to me yesterday," Eunice began, "and told me that they wanted to support the family now that their father was gone. Russell insisted that he wouldn't allow his mother to go and work in that mill anymore."

She saw Lorenzo's countenance soften as he visualized his grandson stepping up and claiming the reins of the family. Eunice related the rest of the story to her father and sister. She included in the story some background to bolster her son's claim of being able to make some money with their instruments.

"Well," she said when the story was ended, "not as bad or as irresponsible as you first thought is it?"

"I would rather see them get an education," Lorenzo replied, "but circumstances are what they are."

"They're good boys," Eunice said defensively.

"Yes," Lorenzo said, "I have no doubt of that. They have an excellent mother."

"And father," Dora added.

"Yes, and father."

They all sat in silence for a time, letting the weight of the matter settle over them.

"It's good to have you in my home," Eunice said to them. "I don't know if I have even told you that yet."

"It's good to be here," Lorenzo answered.

"This is a beautiful home," Dora added. She and Eunice then stood and walked through the house, Eunice proudly relating the details and stories behind each and every stick of furniture. Lorenzo stayed at the table, sulking just a little. He was now worried about his grandchildren. Lorenzo believed in the power of dreams, but he also believed in being practical. Although he knew very little about Cramerton, he began to try and think of other ways for this young family to keep it's head above water. He did not want to see Curley and Ray walk away from school. That was their real ticket to a secure future, he thought. Not some guitar from Sears and Roebuck.

He would find a way around this problem. School was everything. That much he knew. It was a tragedy that Rodney had died, but there was no need in compounding the tragedy by consigning his two oldest sons to a life of ignorance. As his daughters wandered through the house giggling and whispering Lorenzo turned the thoughts over and over in his mind. He had spent his life as a problem solver, and he reveled in the role. This problem was big, he granted, but not insurmountable. He would find a way around, he always did.

Lorenzo did not live in an age with quite enough spare time for over-introspection. He had spent no time analyzing his virtual obsession with education and the gifts it could bestow on the student. There was only one consideration for him, and it drove him more than even he realized. An educated Indian in America could at least rise to the level of second class citizen. An uneducated Indian could not realistically hope to be more than third class. It was a subtle distinction, to be sure, but one that Lorenzo thought it wise to reflect upon. And there was always the promise of change. That was the cruelest aspect of America: even when the nation stood absolutely still there was still the promise of growth, the promise of change. Jefferson continued to tease mercilessly from his hallowed ground of Monticello. And should America ever begin to live up to her promises, the Indian needed to be ready. Lorenzo's Indian would be standing there at the gate, having already laid the groundwork to make the most of the opportunity.

That meant knowing how to speak the white man's language and play the white man's games. And that meant education. If the day ever came when the white man did actually open up the gates of democracy and all its incumbent possibilities, Lorenzo thought Curley and Ray should be standing there with diplomas in there hands, not guitars.

"Dad, would like to see the backyard with us?"

Lorenzo turned and looked at his daughter.

"No, Little Reed," he said, "I think I will sit here and rest a bit."

Eunice reached down and took his hand.

"We're going to be fine, Dad," she said, "so just stop worrying."

"Who's worried," he asked smiling.

Eunice grimaced and walked out the door with Dora. Lorenzo went back to his thoughts, searching desperately for a plan.

CHAPTER TWENTY-EIGHT

Curley forgot himself. In front of his fan club of admiring little brothers and his mother, too, he simply forgot himself. He rushed into Lorenzo's embrace as if he were still six years old, with no thought of being cool or in control.

"Grandpa!" he shouted, "when did you get here?!"

Lorenzo pulled his grandson close to him. It didn't matter to him that Curley was now almost as tall and wide as he was, he was still going to treat him, at least for the moment, like the little boy he had watched drive away all those years ago. And it greatly pleased him when Curley didn't seem to mind.

"Today," he answered, "this morning. I thought it was high time I see you again and that I meet your brothers."

Lorenzo waved his arm over the boys who were gathered about his feet like leaves around the trunk of a great oak.

"And this is quite a brood," he remarked. "I understand that you are their fearless leader. You are their chief, huh?"

Curley blushed.

"Yeah," he said, "kinda."

"Well, aren't you going to introduce me to your friend standing back there at the door? He's the only one I haven't met yet."

Curley turned and saw Ray swaying nervously on the balls of his feet by the screen door. His hands were thrust deep into his pockets and he was wearing an uncomfortable grin. Ray had heard enough glowing tributes about Lorenzo from Curley over the years to feel like he was standing near the president of the United States. This was a moment he had long dreamed of, and now that it was here he was feeling something akin to terror. He was thinking for the first time about the possibility that his Grandfather would find him somehow lacking. He looked at Curley as if to plead for the best introduction he could provide. Curley complied.

"Grandpa this is my little brother and the finest rhythm guitar player in the state, Ray Norris."

Ray jerked his hands out of his pockets and offered one self-consciously to Lorenzo.

"Hey, Grandpa," he said, his voice quaking with electric excitement, "it's a pleasure to finally meet you. I've heard a whole bunch of really good things about you."

Lorenzo took the boy's hand and offered a tight, affirming handshake.

"And I you," he said, "and it is *my* pleasure to meet *you*."

Lorenzo took a seat on the couch as all the boys began talking and asking questions at once. L.D., Houston and Francis were all full of questions about their grandpa. Could he really make a slingshot with his own hands? Did he really hunt using a blow gun? Was he rich? What was it like to ride a train?

"Where are your feathers?" Houston asked. "Because at school they said that Indians wear feathers."

"Well, where are *yours*, then?" asked Lorenzo. He shot Eunice, sitting nearby and laughing at it all, a disapproving glance that told her immediately she was expected to go and raise some serious Cain about such silliness being taught to her children. Eunice gave him a wink to let him know that she was still capable of setting her children straight when the time came. Lorenzo made himself a mental note to have a long talk with all of these boys and remind them who they were and from where they came.

Little Jimmy trotted between his mother and grandfather, falling with every other step, but trying nonetheless to impress this imposing stranger with his newly acquired motor skills.

L.D. regaled him with stories of how well he was doing in school. It seemed to Curley that the child had memorized every nice thing any teacher had ever said to him and was now pulling them all out for Lorenzo's approval and validation.

And Lorenzo basked in it all. It was apparent that Lorenzo was to these children a conquering hero, a king returned to claim his throne. It was an idea that put a glow on Lorenzo's face; the unmistakable glow of the grandparent. At home things were, of course, different. Cora loved and admired her husband, but the long years of marriage had also made her a certified expert, as only long years of marriage can, of his many flaws and shortcomings. Dora also loved her father, but she had learned that to open up herself to him was to invite his advice and, too often, his condescension and scorn. He didn't see it that way, of course. He viewed it as a man doing his fatherly duties, steering his precious children away from the mistakes and pitfalls of his own life. But he had forgotten as only a parent can that he was trying to get his children to avoid the experiences that had helped to shape the very character he was now trying to impose, and that made Dora (and Eunice, when she had still been at home) turn away from her father and keep certain, important facets of her life closed to him.

And Chiltosky wanted nothing to do with Lorenzo. In the personage of his father he saw a beam set too high, a target placed impossibly out of range. In Lorenzo's stares he saw the apparition of dashed dreams and unfulfilled possibilities. Chiltos had not gotten an education, did not hold down a respectable job or a position of any importance. He was a drunk because he had learned very early that it was immeasurably easier to live up to his father's lowest expectations that to live down his disappointment.

But here things were different. Oh, so different. Here he was appreciated and revered. Here he was respected.

Here, he was king.

"You ever kill a bear?" asked Houston.

"You ever fight in a war?"

"You know how to use a real bow and arrow?"

Lorenzo answered each question with love and undivided attention.

For his part, Curley was impatiently reminding Eunice every five minutes that it was past these boy's bedtime. Eunice put him off, telling him that this was a special occasion in their home and one night wouldn't kill the boys.

"But, Mom," he implored, "they do have to go to school tomorrow, remember?"

"Yes, Russell," she chided, "but you will have to share your Grandpa a few minutes more regardless."

"Yeah, *Russell*," Houston teased.

"You and me will have plenty of time, Curley," Lorenzo comforted, "I'm not so old that I can't still stay up all night myself every now and then."

Curley smiled at his Grandpa, but it was insincere and everyone in the room knew it. He was unaccustomed to having his Grandpa's attention divided among so many people and he didn't like it. Besides, his Grandpa and Mom might think that there was plenty of time

available for them to catch up and talk about things, but Curley and
Ray both knew better. They had made plans to leave tomorrow, and
Curley was intent upon keeping to that plan. He would like to stay and
spend time with his Grandpa as much if not more than the others, but
he also knew that whatever money his Mom had was running out. She
hadn't told him or Ray this; she still insisted on not talking about
money to her boys, even if they were the heads of the house. But it
didn't take an accountant to know that she and Rodney had not put
much away for a rainy day. There had never been enough money
around to hold any back. So, whether he liked it or not, Curley knew
he was going to have to say goodbye to his Grandpa pretty early the
next day. There were tobacco markets waiting and money to be made.
The other boys could have him all to himself then. Tonight, he should
belong to Curley.

"Mom, can I see you in the kitchen, please?"

Eunice followed her son into the kitchen, where he was waiting for
her leaning on the counter with an angry look on his face.

"Don't look at me like that, Russell Norris," she said sternly, "I am
still your mother."

Curley quickly wiped the look from his face.

"Mom, Ray and I are leaving tomorrow."

"Tomorrow....why so soon?"

"Because we need the money and because the tobacco markets will
be starting up real soon. We ain't got much choice."

"You don't have much choice," she corrected habitually.

"Right," Curley said, ignoring the grammar lesson for the time
being, "so we have to get going."

"Well," Eunice sighed, "you know more about this than I do. But
Grandpa is going to be very disappointed."

"So am I," Curley said, working into his argument, "that's why I've
been after you to put the boys to bed. They're gonna have plenty of
time with him and I'm not. So, please, can you put them to bed so me
and Grandpa can spend some time together before I leave?"

Eunice nodded.

"Of course, I didn't know that was your reason. I'll put them to bed
right now and you and Grandpa can have some time."

Eunice turned and marched purposefully out of the kitchen.

"All right boys," she announced, "it's time for bed."

There was a collective groan and yell from the crowd.

"But, Mom...."

"Awwwwww, Mom c'mon....."

"See?" Houston announced, "we have to go to bed because Curley wants Grandpa to hisself! That's not fair!"

"That's not the reason," Eunice said angrily, "And Houston Norris you will do as I say."

Houston sulked over to Lorenzo.

"Goodnight, Grandpa Swayney," he said bitterly.

"Goodnight, Houston. I will see you in the morning and tomorrow when you get home from school."

Houston suddenly perked up and jogged towards the bathroom.

"G'night. Grandpa," he announced once more for good measure, "see you in the morning!"

Lorenzo tossed a hand in the air and called out a final goodnight to all of the boys. Eunice followed her sons into their rooms for prayers and kisses and, in a few cases, promises that there were no monsters lurking in the dark. Lorenzo, Curley and Ray were left alone in the den.

"Boys, what say we walk out onto the porch and take advantage of those nice rocking chairs that are out there, huh?" He stood and led the way out of the house and, just as importantly, out of earshot. He and Curley took seats in the rockers and Ray perched himself on the top step. They sat for a time just listening to the night as it called out stories all it's own.

"So, this is city life?" Lorenzo asked. Curley laughed self-consciously and studied his Grandpa's face.

"We have a movie theatre!" Ray exclaimed excitedly.

"Well, now, isn't that something?"

"You ever been to a picture show?"

"No," Lorenzo answered, "I guess I can't say that I have."

"They're great. Right, Curley?"

"Yeah, they're all right," Curley said, trying to sound less than enamored with what his Grandpa had termed "city life."

"Me and Curley used to go 'bout every Saturday," Ray continued enthusiastically. "That was before Dad died, of course. We haven't been since."

"What kind of pictures do they show?" asked Lorenzo.

"Oh, all kinds. They play lots of cowboy and Indian pictures. Me and Curley always root for the Indians. But they usually lose."

Lorenzo chuckled.

Ray continued, "I told Curley that someday me and him should make our own movie where the Indians win."

"That sounds like a good idea."

"Ah, that's crazy talk," Curley sneered.

"No crazier than being a guitar player," Lorenzo stated. Curley looked at his Grandpa with a mix of confusion and hurt.

"Mom told you?" he asked.

"Uh-huh. She says you boys are leaving school to try and make it as guitar players. Is that right?"

"Sure is," Ray shouted, oblivious to his Grandpa's unhappy tone, "we're pretty good, Grandpa. If I do say so myself."

"I'm sure you're good, Ray. But Curley, do you think it's wise to leave school like that? Couldn't you make money playing when you're not in school?"

"That's what we been doing, Grandpa," said Ray.

"Yeah," Curley interrupted, "that's what we've been doing. But we can't make enough money that way and support the family. And that is our job now that Dad is gone."

"I can appreciate that. But you're Mom isn't exactly helpless. Why don't you talk to her about trying her nursing down here. I thought when she left Qualla that was what she was going to do anyway."

"She tried that," Curley answered quietly. "I'm not sure what came of it, but I know that it didn't bring home any money."

"Why not?"

"I think you know, Grandpa."

Lorenzo went quiet. A look of bitter manhood had stretched across Curley's face. It was a look of knowledge and worldliness that threw Lorenzo off guard.

"The only way Mom can bring home money around here is to go to work in the mill. And my Mom is too good for that, Grandpa. Besides, her mill pay by itself wouldn't keep us up. I'd have to go to work there full time myself. And, at some point, Ray would, too. Dad was a supervisor at the mill, and neither me or Mom is going to get that kind of job or that kind of money. So, one way or the other, our schooling days are done."

"I don't accept that, Curley," Lorenzo said.

Curley found himself thinking suddenly about a foot race with his Dad. He and Rodney had always raced each other from the top of the hill down to the front porch on days when Rodney wasn't working. Some days, even when Rodney came home tired and dirty from a twelve-hour shift, Curley would meet him at the top of the hill and beg for a race. More often than not, Rodney would give in and they would "have at it." Rodney's long legs always carried him to the porch first, leaving Curley with the sweetest frustration a boy can know.

There were many nights when Curley would lie in his bed and dream of whipping Rodney in that cursed race. He would fall asleep with a broad grin on his face as he comforted his father with the same words he had heard so often.

"That was a good try, Dad," he would say as he placed his hand on his father's shoulder. He thought often about what a wonderful feeling it would be to win that race.

Then one day it happened. It was near the end. Curley had decided it would be fun to meet his depressed Dad at the top of the hill for old time's sake. Rodney showed up with grime on his face, cotton in his hair and a dejected, far-away look in his eye.

"What are you doing up here?" he had asked.

"Wanna race?"

Curley would never forget the sad smile that appeared on Rodney's face.

"Another time, o.k.?"

"Oh, no," Curley said, "that didn't work when I was little and it won't work now. You chicken?"

Rodney dropped his lunch pail.

"Your Dad chicken?" he asked. "You better be kidding."

"Then race me," Curley teased.

Rodney shook his head disgustedly.

"Boy, some folks just live for hurt," he said. "Are you ready?"

Curley turned and faced the porch.

"Ready."

Rodney managed himself into a crouch.

"On three?"

"On three."

"One...two...GO!"

Curley launched himself out of the gate like lightening from a cloud. Rodney's stride, still just a little longer than his son's, gave him the early edge. Curley sucked in wind like a mad stallion, his arms flailing at his sides. Suddenly, he felt himself move ahead of his Dad. Then he saw Rodney drop from the corner of his eye and he was on his own. With a mile of teeth paved across his face he flew onto the porch and turned, hopping on his feet and whooping with the sweet taste of victory dripping down his jaws.

Then he looked at Rodney.

His Dad was no longer running. He was walking painfully, with a look of agony on his face. For just a moment Curley had the terrifying thought that Rodney had let him win. The race had been thrown!

But one good look at his Dad's face told him that wasn't the case.

"You o.k., Dad?" he had asked.

Rodney forced a smile as he tried to draw in enough breath to respond.

"Guess I ain't the racer I used to be," he said. "There ain't much Jim Thorpe left in this body."

He climbed a few steps and then plopped himself down on the stoop. He looked up at his son with a tired smile.

"Well, boy," he said, "this is a big day. You finally beat me."

Curley could only nod.

"How does it feel," Rodney asked.

"Great," Curley croaked.

But it hadn't felt great. In fact it had been the most disappointing moment in his life. Standing on that porch, watching Rodney make his way slowly and deliberately to the finish line, he had not been struck by the knowledge of the man he had become. He was struck by the realization that his father was no longer the man he had *once been*.

"You have to accept that Grandpa," he said, pulling himself back from the memory, "because that's the way it is."

There. Another seminal moment. Unlike the race, Curley had never had any dreams of one-upping his Grandpa. This, after all, wasn't a foot race. This was life. Curley realized that he just wasn't ready for this torch to be passed. Not yet. Becoming the nominal head of the household was one thing, standing up to Lorenzo was something else entirely.

"Curley," Lorenzo said, "I respect every reason that you have given me for leaving school. And I can understand that you have no desire to go work yourself to death in those mills. Hell, I'd give you a swift kick in the head if you wanted to do that. But there are other ways."

"I'm sorry, Grandpa, I just don't see them."

"You're looking at one."

"I don't understand."

"Well, we may not have a picture show where I come from, but I do have a nice big house that could hold this family pretty well. And Me and Cora would both love to have you all there. And that would take care of all these worries about money."

"You mean...."

"I mean come home," Lorenzo said. "Let's talk your Mom into taking you home, where you belong. Come back to Big Cove."

Curley stood and walked to the edge of the porch. He stared out into the night. A few years ago, he would've jumped at this opportunity. But things have changed, he had changed so much now. To return to Qualla meant more than just giving up on his father's dream of making it here in the city. It also meant to abdicate his new position of authority. He knew instinctively that there was no way anyone but Lorenzo was going to lead in Lorenzo's house.

"This *is* home, Grandpa," he said without turning to look at Lorenzo. "My brother's don't know anything else. And the truth is, I don't think I want to go back, either."

"But, Curley...."

"No, Grandpa," he said, "that's the truth. I, we, have a responsibility to Dad's memory. He came here to make something of himself and to provide a better life for his family. Now I guess it's my turn to try and make that happen. Maybe you can't understand that. Or maybe you just don't understand why I want to make it happen through my music. And, God help me, Grandpa, I can't explain how music makes me feel. It's like a dream."

"Dreams are all well and good, Curley, but...."

"It's more than just that, though. Ray can tell you that."

Ray quietly nodded his assent.

"See, Grandpa, the thing is that music is the only thing I've ever done well that didn't cause some backhanded compliments or anything like that. We do good in school and it's always, 'Gee, he's smart for an Indian.' Or, 'Gosh, he sure catches on quick for an Indian.' But with our music it's just 'Wow they're good!' or 'Damn, those boys can play!' No 'for an Indian' to it. We're just plain good. 'Cause none of these white folks around here can play the way we do. And I like proving that every time I pick up my guitar and play a song. I like it a lot."

Lorenzo said nothing.

"He's right, Grandpa," Ray said, sensing that his brother needed some backup this time. Curley turned and faced his Lorenzo.

"We can do this," he said. "I know we can. Maybe Dad failed when it came to making his dream happen. But he died knowing that he had tried. And Grandpa, not a lot of people can say that."

Maybe he was losing his touch, or maybe Curley still constituted the biggest blind spot Lorenzo Swayney had ever known, but there was no argument left in him. The boy's eyes held so much confidence and so much desire that it melted Lorenzo's ability to see things in his usual pragmatic light.

"My God you are like your mother," he said, "I could never talk any sense into her, either."

Curley laughed.

"Maybe that's because we both had somebody tell us too many times that we could do anything we set our minds to," Curley responded.

It was Lorenzo's turn to laugh.

"Well who in the Hell told you that?" he asked sarcastically.

Seizing the moment Curley answered, "My Grandpa."

Lorenzo stood and motioned for Ray to do the same. Ray hopped to his feet, thinking that they were headed back inside. Instead, Lorenzo grabbed him and Curley each with one hand and pulled them to his chest and into his embrace. Ray looked at Curley in embarrassment but saw that his eyes were shut tightly. Curley was recording the moment in his heart for future reference.

"My grandsons," he whispered.

"Grandpa," Curley said. Ray wondered whether or not he should answer, too, but decided this wasn't really his moment.

Lorenzo let the boys go and turned away, momentarily ashamed of his weakness. Curley walked over and stood silently beside him.

"We leave tomorrow, Grandpa," he said.

"That soon?"

"Yessir. The tobacco markets will be starting up soon and we're gonna follow them, see if we can make some money that way."

"I haven't met a white man yet who parted easily with his money," Lorenzo said dryly.

"We're pretty persuasive," Ray said.

"I know, believe me I know. Well, I guess I should let you get some sleep then. Big day tomorrow and all."

"Yessir. We could probably all use a little rest."

The three of them turned and walked into the house without a word. Ray wished Lorenzo a goodnight and disappeared into the bathroom, leaving Curley alone in the hall with his Grandpa.

"Well, Curley, I will see you in the morning."

"Goodnight, Grandpa. I hope nothing I said tonight hurt your feelings."

"No, son. It didn't."

"Thanks for understanding."

"Oh, I don't understand, but I know that this is something you must do. And I accept it. But if things don't work out...."

"You'll be there," Curley finished.

"I'll be there."

"Goodnight, Grandpa."

"Goodnight, Curley."

Lorenzo turned and headed into the room he was sharing with Ray for the night. As he stood for a moment in the quiet hallway, he realized that he was really seeing it for the first and possibly last time.

Then the man of the house turned and walked into the darkness.

PART FIVE

TIGHTROPE

CHAPTER TWENTY-NINE

Ray registered his disapproval from the minute they walked through the door.

"Oh, Jesus Christ, Curley, you have got to be kidding."

Curley lost his cool.

"Goddamn it Ray, give it a chance, will ya? This place is exactly what you said you were looking for; it gives us a chance to keep making money and get off of the road for a while. It's just what you wanted."

"What I wanted?" Ray repeated sarcastically, "when did I say I wanted to play in a shithole every night?"

"Curley!!" The shout carried from across the bar and hit the boys like cold water. Big Joe Harrison was lumbering towards them, his plastic grin glued firmly in place. "I was startin' to wonder if ya'll was comin' or not."

"I'm sorry we're late, Mr. Harrison," Curley said, "we had a little car trouble. Mr. Harrison, I'd like for you to meet the other half of the Norris Brothers, my brother Ray Norris."

"The *better* half," Ray said, smiling and extending his hand for Big Joe to shake.

"It's a pleasure," Big Joe said, "and I see you and your brother's got the same amount of confidence. But, since cain't but one of y'uns really be the most talented Norris, I'll be lookin' right forward to seein' which one's a liar." Curley and Ray stared at each other, neither one of them sure how to respond. Were they being baited? Only Big Joe's raucous laughter eased the momentary tension. "Easy, boys," he chuckled, "I was just pullin' your legs."

Big Joe Harrison motioned the boys towards the front of the bar, to a small area he referred to as "the stage." The only thing that set the space Harrison pointed to apart from the rest of the bar was its lack of tables. It was just a cleared out corner.

"I'll let ya'll set up over there on the stage and then we'll get this audition started. Just call out when y'uns is ready." Big Joe patted Curley on the back and walked away towards the small office near the bar's restroom. When he was clearly out of earshot, Ray whirled to face Curley.

"Audition?" he asked angrily. "Are you telling me that we now have to audition to get a gig in a shitty little dump like this?"

"Ray...."

"Hell, no, Curley, I won't do it. I will not do it. We're too damn good to be playing here anyhow."

Curley sighed, too tired to fight anymore with Ray. The attitude had been this way since a disastrous corn shucking they had played a few weeks before. They had played hard for three and a half hours, only to be told by the man who had contracted them at the end of the night that there was no money for them, but they could take all the fried chicken home with them that they wanted. There was a hardness to Ray now, a cold distance that Curley didn't know how to bridge. The light in his eyes had been extinguished, and he now met every morning with a bitterness and anger that frightened Curley. He understood Ray's pain, but that didn't seem to matter. Any time he tried to say this to Ray he was pushed away. Life on the road had not turned out to be at all what they dreamed it might. There was no glamour. There was only constant driving, sleeping in the backseat of Susan Munice's car, and praying that the next gig would actually materialize. There was too much time in between, times when they ate little or nothing. Ray was already losing his patience with the entire endeavor, and he had been letting Curley know it for days on end.

This was why Curley was placing such high hopes on Big Joe Harrison and his bar, The Rooster. He was counting on the healing power of being stationary to resurrect Ray's spirits. Ray complained incessantly about life on the road--the bad meals, the constant crick-in-the-neck from sleeping in the car's backseat, the never ending search for audiences and cash. But Big Joe was promising them good money and a nice place to sleep every night. It seemed perfect to Curley, and it pissed him off that Ray was unwilling to give the place a chance.

Realistically, though, Curley was not blind to the shortcomings of The Rooster. No one really referred to the place in affectionate tones. Try as Big Joe might, he just did not own the kind of watering hole that inspired any loyalty or devotion. Every one of the men and women

who gathered there nightly knew that the passenger in the barstool
beside of them would rather be some where else.

The Rooster wreaked of urine. The mirror behind the bar was
colored with the accumulated cloud of countless smoldering cigarettes.
The wooden tables that dotted the "dance floor" were stained beyond
repair with a myriad of circles and spheres from decades of moist glass
bottoms. Lovers old and new had left their mark with knives and
heated utensils across every available surface in the bar. The bathroom
was never functioning, a real problem for a place whose greatest charm
was its cheap beer. The floor itself told horror stories with its gothic
blood stains which had dried into a macabre map of the city's seamy
and sinful side.

And yet The Rooster was never lacking customers. The very things
about the place, which insured it would never get a certain kind of
patron, also insured that it would always draw another. The place did,
after all, have character. And there were apparently enough people in
the city who preferred *low* character to *no* character to keep the joint
swinging deep into the Southern nights. They came to share their hard
luck stories and sorrows. Lost farms, lost fortunes, lost dignity. They
came over and over again because The Rooster never judged. They
came out of the hope that maybe one night someone would save their
soul before last call. It was the greatest of the ambitions left to them.

And then there was Big Joe, the burly owner of The Rooster. A
World War One veteran, Big Joe had left his right arm in Europe, but
not his ambitions. Upon his honorable discharge, he had roamed the
East Coast until landing in Raleigh, where he parlayed a gambling
talent into the ownership of a hardware store. Always mindful of
opportunity, Harrison's Hardware was soon famous for its two kinds of
screwdrivers. Running a speakeasy was dangerous work, but it was
also extremely profitable, and Big Joe was making good money within
the first year of his operation. Six foot three and barrel chested, Big
Joe was capable of using his one arm to toss out an unruly customer or
break up a drunken spat. And despite his handicap, he was gregarious
and charming, and more than a few local women had seen the first light
of day from his bed.

Curley took in the whole atmosphere of The Rooster with a sense of
detached amusement. There was something about the place, its sense
of last chance desperation, that both intoxicated and appalled him. Big
Joe, in his pinstriped, double-breasted suit with the right sleeve pinned
to the lapel, gliding across the floor with a surreal grace that was

comical and impressive. The painted women who milled around the front door, waiting for the word that The Rooster was open again for business. The waitresses in their tight skirts that would have been scandalous *outside* of the The Rooster's protective walls. The men with their careless appearance and hungry eyes, stepping in to buy a pack of cigarettes, sneak a peak at the night's waitresses, and then go back on the stoop to discuss the world and all its faults. Curley knew that he didn't want to spend too much time in this place, his instincts told him that it was the kind of joint that could suck you in and refuse to let you go. But he felt that it was a good place to collect their heads, make some money, and get a little rest from the road. He understood that, if something didn't give, the Norris Brothers were heading for a fiery crash.

"I am not auditioning for this job," Ray said derisively. "That's just all there is to it."

Curley took a deep breath, trying to prepare himself for one of his patented sales jobs.

"And don't try and give me one of your sales jobs," Ray said. Curley was suddenly angry that his partner was also family.

"Okay," he said, "no sales job. But can I at least outline for you the good points about playing here for a little while? Huh?"

Ray said nothing, so Curley decided that was as close to an agreement as he was going to get.

"All right," he started, "now promise me you'll hear me out without breaking in. Just give me that one chance?"

"Okay, Curley, I'll hear you out." The words seemed to pain Ray greatly, but he knew that he did owe his brother this one courtesy. "But I ain't gonna change my mind."

Curley sighed. Then why even hear me out, he thought.

"Well, just listen. Now I know same as you that this ain't like playing at the White House, but it is still better than being out on the road. It's like we been talking about, these tobacco markets ain't gonna run all year, and they are just about done. That means that we have to find a way to play and make some money at the same time, cause we know that we can't support Mom and the boys through street corner singing all through the winter."

"We could go back and get real jobs," Ray huffed. Curley ignored the remark.

"That's where this place comes in. It will provide us with a guaranteed income and a place to stay. Think about it, Ray. We could be making the most money that we've made since we left Cramerton, and we could be laying our heads down in the same spot every night."

"Above this damn bar," Ray scoffed.

"Yeah, above this bar. But its ours, and it is a little bigger than that damn backseat that you been complaining about for the last four months. Plus, Ray, we'd be making good money. Real good."

"How good?"

"Big Joe promised me that we'd get three dollars a night on Wednesdays and Thursdays, and five on Friday and Saturday. That's just the money he's guaranteeing us, Ray, we could always make more."

"Or less."

"No, dammit, you're not listening. This sixteen dollars a week is money that Big Joe is *guaranteeing* us, that means that we cannot get paid any less than that, but we could make more."

"I don't trust Big Joe," Ray said, spitting the bar owners name out with a nasty contempt, "I ain't so sure that he ain't a damn liar."

"Hell, I don't trust Big Joe either," Curley smiled, "but if he don't pay then we don't play. The worst we can lose is one night's worth of effort, 'cause I already told him that we expect to be paid nightly."

"And he agreed to that?"

"Yep." Curley leaned in close to Ray's face. "Sixteen dollars a week, at least, and no more nights on the road. You gonna pass that up just because you're in such a shitty mood?"

"I don't know, Curley, I just ain't sure about any of this anymore." Curley brightened to hear Ray's tone was softening, it lacked the belligerent defiance it had carried a few minutes before. Curley knew he was winning.

"Look, Ray, I know you feel real bad right now. And I know I ain't helped much. Maybe I push too hard sometimes. But I know that Mom is depending on us and I don't wanna let her down. The way I see it, playing here is the best way to do the right thing by Mom and you. We keep sending money home, good money, and you get a break from following these tobacco farmers around all the time. And if it don't work out then we pack our shit and we leave, simple as that. I promise. So whaddaya say? Give it a shot?"

Ray continued to frown but, just as he had known that Curley was working up a snow job, Curley knew that Ray's resistance was finished.

"Yeah, Curley, I'll give this ol' dump a try. But if we don't get that sixteen dollars a week or if I just plain don't like playing here, then we go. Right?"

"Right."

Big Joe Harrison bounded from the office, where he was still counting the previous night's earnings, and was surprised to see Curley and Ray had not yet even taken their guitars out of their cases.

"Whoa! You fellers ain't backin' out on me are ya?" Big Joe was studying their faces, looking for any sign of trouble. He had already figured that they were either Indian or some kind of mulatto, so when he saw that they weren't making any move to set up their instruments he began to contemplate the possibility that he was about to get robbed. Curley looked to Ray to find out what answer he should give.

"No, sir," Ray answered for him, "we're just moving slow today. We'll set up and play for you right now."

They ran through a mournful rendition of "Banks of the Ohio" and then stopped. Big Joe shot them his famous smile and whooped loud enough for the whole city to hear.

"I believe," he yelled, "the The Rooster is now the proud home of the Norris Brothers. Now, let me show you your new apartment."

They silently made their way up the steps in the alley behind the bar to their new home. Curley grinned all the way to the top. He had a really good feeling about this deal, much better than the one he had over the corn shucking. This rest was going to make all the difference.

All the difference in the world.

CHAPTER THIRTY

"Whoa, my sweet Lord I ain't never seen nothin' like that in all my days! Never, not ever!!"

Curley plopped himself down on the couch and took a long, delicious draw off his cigarette. He peered through the clear blue smoke at Big Joe, who was grinning from ear to ear and shaking his head in disbelief.

"I cain't believe what I done seen," he repeated. "That ever happened before?"

"Hu-uh," Curley answered, drawing more smoke into his throat and exhaling slowly. The sweat trickled down his forehead and into his eyes. He wiped away the dampness with his sleeve. Ray walked into the room and threw a pair of white cotton panties on the coffee table with a smirk.

"I believe these belong to you, brother," he said, squatting down in a corner of the room and lighting up his own smoke.

"And that ain't never happened to you before? You sure?" Big Joe was fascinated and incredulous. If this was really a first for the Norris Brothers, he was thinking, how were they remaining so damn calm?

"Nope," Ray said, "that was an absolute first time for us."

Curley leaned forward and reached out for the panties. He picked them up from the table and began twisting them in front of his eyes, studying their contour and shape.

"Well," he said finally, "at least they ain't extra large!" Ray cackled and Big Joe yelped with joy. He was coming to live vicariously through his young entertainers. Big Joe was a man who had experienced many things, but as he listened to the thunderous applause that came from just below his feet in the bar below, he couldn't help but envy the success of these two boys. The men all wanted to know them, to try and rub up against some of the greatness, to try and get just a little of whatever these guys had into their own system. The women, well, the women were literally throwing themselves (or parts of themselves) at the two musicians. Big Joe had never actually asked, but he was sure the number of long legs that had climbed these back steps was impressive by now.

"I just cain't get over it," he said. "Never seen nothin' like it." Curley tossed the panties over to Ray, who caught them and then playfully wrapped them around his head.

"Tecumseh!" he cried. "I am the great Cherokee warrior."

"Ah, yes," answered Curley, "the great Panty Head. You have ridden long." He and Ray both cracked up at their little play-acting. Maybe someday they would branch out into acting. Big Joe was still studying the drawers.

"You see who threw 'em?" he asked. "The panties, I mean?"

"Nope."

"Nope."

"Hey, Curley, just think, if we'd stayed in Cramerton we'd have been *making* these things! And now we're getting them thrown at us!" Ray twirled the underwear around on his index finger, staring at them as if looking into some strange and alternate future. Curley's face suddenly darkened.

"Not us," he said quietly, taking another drag off his smoke. "We had plans."

The roar below their feet began to wane and organize itself into a chorus of chants and yells. Curley sat up and stubbed out his smoke.

"You ready?" he asked Ray.

"Yeah, let's finish it out."

They stood up, wiped their faces clean of sweat, and headed silently out the door and onto the back steps.

"Bring it home," Big Joe called. They ignored him, moving silently and purposefully down the stairs. Big Joe studied the backs of their heads, bent confidently downward as they strode towards their stage. He promised himself that he was going to build them an actual stage. He was already hearing rumors that some of his competitors were thinking about trying to steal his entertainers away, so he would build them the nicest stage in all of Wake County. That would, hopefully, keep them at The Rooster a while. He pulled out his cigarettes and fumbled with the pack. When he had secured one with his finger, he flipped it into his mouth. Carefully returning the pack to his shirt pocket, he removed his lighter from his pants pocket and lit up. He

heard the low din of the crowd explode into excited, boisterous cheers
as Ray opened the door that led out into the alley. He watched his
"boys" disappear into the side of the building and out of sight. He
smiled knowingly and thanked the Lord for his own good luck.

The Norris Brothers had been one hell of a find.

ᚥ

Curley leaned into the microphone. He was seated in the center of
the cleared-out corner, smiling into the amorphous face of the crowd.
He couldn't make out faces, just the throbbing, bobbing mass in front of
him. A spot light had been set up in the back of the bar and it
effectively blinded him and Ray from actually seeing the people.
That's why neither of them had any idea who had thrown the panties,
although neither of them was all that curious, either. They had been
The Rooster's house band for three months now, long enough to know
that whoever had the audacity to lob their underwear at them during the
first set would undoubtedly have the "courage" to introduce themselves
after the show.

Ray had taken his seat beside of Curley. He fiddled with his guitar
for a moment, then frowned at the sound. He tinkered with the tuners
for a moment and then his face opened again. That was better. He
leaned close to Curley's ear so that he could be heard.

"Wanna tune?" he asked. Curley turned to Ray with a look of
mawkish amusement.

"Why?" he asked. Ray laughed and leaned back in his seat. There
was no arguing the point. This audience was discerning for rednecks,
but they were not likely to hold back their clapping because Ray's A
string was a little flat compared to Curley's.

"I guess ya'll ain't had enough yet, huh?" Curley teased the crowd.
A drunken roar went up into the night. They knew they were being
teased but pretended, as all audiences do, not to understand the rules.

"Play sumpin'," someone called, sending Curley and the crowd into
fits of giggles.

"Yeah, play *sumpin'*," someone mocked. Then the crowd took up
the chant: "sumpin', sumpin', sumpin'!"

"All right," Curley scolded teasingly, "cut it out." He glanced over
to make sure that Ray was with him. A slight wink set his mind at ease
and an impish grin spread out across his face like a favorite blanket.
"See if you like this one," he drawled, *"ONE, TWO, THREE FOUR,"*

and they were off: harmonies soaring to the ceiling and bouncing around the room. Melodies sinking their teeth into the night and sucking the marrow of the mood. Rhythmic fingertips easing through hair and harassing hardened hips into the groove. Ray's foot furiously stomped The Rooster's storied floor. Curley's eyes closed tightly as he coaxed moans and delighted squeals from his guitar. The women in the audience, even some who assuredly knew better, swooned and imagined.

"Oh," they thought, as they watched the musician's fingers move across the guitar's neck, "oh, my."

Some of them pulled whoever they were with a little closer, just to play it safe. They watched the hands, so knowing. One moment the fingers eased their way over the strings, gentle and loving. The soft whine that escaped from the guitar was replayed across the bar by numerous unwitting sighs. Then the fingers were speeding up, thumping the strings angrily, devotedly. Makeup ran and hair became mussed. And Curley and Ray smiled through it all.

"Thank you so much," Curley would announce when the song ended.

"Thank you," Ray seconded. It was all well scripted and rehearsed, but they worked diligently to insure that it always seemed fresh and spontaneous.

"Assume that none of these people have seen or heard us before," Curley said before each performance, "and then go kick ass."

They also worked to strike the perfect balance between rebellion and utter conformity. It was the essence of their appeal. While the music was going they both seemed driven by some inner demon, some subconscious need to let it all out. As they played they gave off an air of total confidence, of kick the bar over and take the waitress home bravado. But when the music died away they were perfect gentlemen, full of "thank yous" and "you're so nices." Although it was a tight and difficult line to walk, they succeeded more and more every time they took the stage. They were professionals now more than ever before, and every Friday and Saturday night, from eight o'clock until at least midnight, they were kings.

"You know," Curley said breathlessly as they wound down the night, "things are tough all over right now."

"That's right!" someone called. Curley picked up his pace with the ease, determination and conviction of an itinerant preacher.

"But they won't always be that way ("No sir," came the response).

No," Curley continued, "things are bound to get better. As a matter of fact, if me and Ray here can just hold out for about fifty more years (chuckles), then President Roosevelt says that everything will be just fine."

"God bless 'im," came the sarcastic call from the back of the bar.

"Yeah," Curley chuckled, "fifty more years and then ya'll will be working for *me*!" Curley looked at Ray and smiled broadly. "You ready over there?"

"I'm ready, Curley," Ray announced. He had to admit quietly to himself that, almost as much as the audience, he loved to watch Curley do this schtick.

"Then let's tell these folks what we are talking about. A-one, a-two, a-one, two, three, four...."

And then they launched into a blistering rendition of the Sons of the Pioneers' hit "When Our Old Age Pension Check Comes to Our Door," the number that they always playfully closed the show with. When they slammed their hands across the strings for the last chord, Curley and Ray both stood and bowed in sync. The Rooster's walls sounded like they were about to burst from the effort of holding in the jubilation. Curley and Ray smiled and mouthed polite "thank yous" to the crowd, bowed once more for good measure and then stepped out of the light and back into the cool, dark alley, their guitars slung over their shoulders. Ray headed up the steps first as Curley paused to light a cigarette. At the top, Big Joe Harrison pulled an envelope from his inside jacket pocket and smiled.

"Lotsa moola in there tonight," he said. Ray took the envelope and entered the apartment. Curley followed in behind him after shaking Big Joe's hand. This ceremony had almost become tradition for them all now. Big Joe was an intensely superstitious man, and he was not about to change anything now that he was rolling in sweet money. He stood in the doorway and watched the boys collapse into their respective corners. They seemed drained.

"Anything I can get ya'll before I head down for closing? Want me to send up some sandwiches?"

"Nah," came the reply. Normally Curley and Ray would have been more respectful, but the Saturday night crowd had pulled their most strenuous effort from them, and they were too spent to think of protocol or manners.

"Awlright," said Big Joe, "if y'uns change your mind just let me know. 'Kay?"

"Yessir, we will," Ray said. Curley seemed lost in thought as he drew the smoke into his mouth and stared out the window onto the street. Big Joe repeated that he'd get them something if they changed their mind and then excused himself. Ray carefully counted the money.

"Damned good night," he said. Curley mumbled something and went back to his thoughts. Ray lit his own smoke and dropped back against the wall. It had been a very good night.

"Dear Mom," Curley wrote, *"enclosed is the money from this weekend's shows. As you can see, we are doing even better than we was last week. Twenty-seven dollars and seventy one cents for two nights!! I told you you would be rich thanks to me and Ray! HaHa! Give my love to the boys and Grandpa and Aunt Dora and of course yourself. Write to us when you can. You know where we are at!*
    Love,
    Russell D. Norris

Curley slid the note into an envelope and sealed it tightlyHe wasn't crazy about sending money through the mail, but so far nothing bad had happened. The sudden knock on the door surprised him, Big Joe was apparently checking up on them tonight--something the bar owner had never done before. Curley walked to the door and opened it, surprised by the visitor.

She was not Big Joe. In fact, Curley had no idea who she was other than a short, pretty girl with red hair that clung to her head in tight, defiant curls. She was wearing a long, ankle length skirt and an extremely tight knit sweater that accentuated her personality.

"May I help you?" Curley asked, assuming that the poor girl was lost.

"I hope so," she cooed breathlessly, "I think you have something of mine?" She smiled a wicked smile.

"What? Why, I don't...." Then he caught the meaning of the smile. Even the seasoned musician could not suppress the blush that engulfed his features. "Oh," he said. The owner of the panties had shown up after all. She smiled again.

"My name is Lucy," she said, "may I come in for a little while?" Curley looked over. Ray was sound asleep in the corner, wrapped tightly in some of Big Joe's blankets. He turned back to look at the girl. The wheels of his mind began to spin out the scenario.

"Yes," he said, making a path for her into the apartment, "yes, you may."

As he closed the door he reflected on just how much he loved his job.

CHAPTER THIRTY-ONE

The plaintive strains of music still lingered in the air, rubbing noses equally with the greats and near-greats. These men and women stomped furiously and clapped with a wild enthusiasm in a vain effort to bring back the men with the instruments which gave them a brief respite from their worries and struggles. But the Norris Brothers weren't returning tonight, and Big Joe flipped on the lights to let the crowd know that they were now, once again, on their own.

Ray drooped onto the new couch that Big Joe had bought for their apartment several weeks prior, wheezing and spitting mucus into his handkerchief. Curley stood over him, feeling his brother's clammy forehead.

"You're hotter'n hell," Curley noted with concern.

"I feel terrible," Ray groaned, "and by head feels like a rock."

"That's 'cause it's full of rocks," Curley joked.

"Aw, c'mon, Curley, cut be a little slack, will ya?"

Curley tried to take Ray's arm and lead him over to the bed that Big Joe had also provided for them. Some nights they would share the double bed with the rusty "brass" head and footboard, but most nights one took the couch and left the bed to the other. Ray protested that he didn't think he could move that far, so Curley instead brought a blanket over and covered him up. Big Joe burst into the room with a grin and a boisterously positive review of the night's proceedings.

"Dammnit, you boys are even good sick!" he cried. Ray chuckled derisively.

"No, Big Joe," he corrected, "I am good eben when I'b sick. Curley'd be in bed for a week complaining and calling for our Bom."

"You know" answered Curley, "it's really a shame that you ain't too damn sick to talk." Ray grinned and leaned over to spit into the can Curley had deftly placed beside the couch. Big Joe rushed over to his side and felt his head.

"Whoooowhee," he cried, "you are burnin' up, son. You need a doctor?"

"Naw."

"You sure? I mean you are *really* hot."

"I'll be able to play tomorrow night," Ray said. A look of deep hurt and disappointment crossed the big guy's face.

"I'b sorry, Big Joe," Ray said quickly, "it's the fever talking. I dow you bean well." Big Joe was a man incapable of staying offended long, so he smiled again.

"That's all right. I know you're sick, son."

To Ray it seemed that room suddenly filled with a raucous and annoying laughter and a psuedo-concern that made his stomach turn flips. The room had brightened with the lightening-sharp grin of a predator. The air was thick with decadence and the sickening aroma of a false rebellion against the night. Lucy Jenkins had entered the room.

Curley and Lucy had been an item since their first night together over a month ago. She had chased Curley with all her might, and it seemed to Ray that his brother was entirely too trusting or too blind to see that he was leading himself closer and closer to a trap. They had fought over Lucy's intentions more violently than over anything else before. Ray had a great deal of Eunice Norris coursing through his veins, and he was unable to hide his contempt and mistrust of the trashy-looking white girl that had attached herself to their wagon. What made Ray truly angry was that his brother was not blinded by love, that would have given the whole sordid mess a nobility that it did not deserve. Curley was instead blinded by nothing more than lust, an emotion that clouded the senses and fogged the brain more than any chemical ever could. Curley frequently accused Ray of mere jealousy, arguing that his little brother was bitter that he had a girl and Ray did not. Ray wouldn't exactly qualify Lucy as a great catch, so he found the argument a little tedious.

"Oh my goodness, Ray," Lucy droned, "you just look terrible, honey. Are you all right?"

Ray coughed but said nothing. He felt the heat of Curley's stare even through his own fever. Still, he said nothing to the girl and he wouldn't. And Curley couldn't make him.

"He's pretty sick," Curley said.

"Pretty damn sick," Big Joe agreed. Lucy moved closer to Ray and bent down on one knee. She reached out to take his hand into hers, but

Ray quickly pulled away. It angered him that she could think herself able to pull off a gesture of such intimacy with him. She must know how he really felt about her. He had, after all, made no secret about his feelings.

"Ray," she asked, "is there anything that you need?"

"Peace and quiet," he growled. But it was no use, the girl was determined to bestow her unwanted kindliness upon him.

"Well, of course you do," she said, "and that is what you're gonna get. But first, would you like for me to fetch you some juice or toast or anything to settle your stomach?"

"Ain't nothing wrong with my stomach," he grumbled, "I would just like to be left alone."

"Look, Ray, Lucy's just tryin' to...."

"Now Curley, honey," she interrupted, "don't go gettin' on your brother tonight. He feels poorly and don't need your mess."

Curley fell silent, looking too much like a kicked dog for Ray's taste. He silently wondered what had happened to the fearless commander-in-chief of the Norris Brothers corporation.

"Yeah, honey," Ray said with a vicious smirk that seemed held to the corners of his mouth with tight strings of sarcasm. Curley's countenance told Ray that only Lucy's angel of mercy act was sparing him from another one of their battles. Lucy tousled Ray's hair and told him that she hoped he was feeling better by the morning. Prickly goosebumps raised themselves across Ray's body as a chill swept through him, a chill that had nothing to do with the fever. He could not resolve himself to her easy manner, the way she convinced herself that she was essential, integral, to their lives. The way she ingratiated herself into every situation. She had even taken to critiquing their sets now, telling them which songs worked and which ones, at least in her mind, didn't. It infuriated Ray because she knew absolutely nothing about the delicate balance that went into constructing a set list. And yet Curley listened.

Ray did not thank her for her concern or her words of consolation. He dug deeper under the blanket and turned his head from the room. Big Joe excused himself by telling Ray to just give a holler if he needed anything at all. The room fell silent until Lucy's alto began its ascent again. Ray tried to block it all out.

"Well, honey," she said, "I guess we should forget about that little shindig tonight at Tony's."

Ray's face involuntarily pinched into another look of disapproval.

Tony Williams was a good friend of Lucy's who was now also a part of their world. He was slimy and had eyes that were more shifty than a snake's, but Curley seemed to think that the sun shone from the man's asshole.

"Yeah," Curley answered, "I suppose we need to stay here with Ray." Ray shot up and spat.

"Oh, no," he said, "I need some rest, and I won't get none with the two of you hangin' around here makin' out. That'll just make me sicker. Please, go to Tony's place and just leave me be. Please."

"Are you sure?" Curley and Lucy asked in unison.

"Positive," Ray stressed, "I ain't never been so sure of anything in my life." Lucy smiled at what she mistook for a sweet gesture, but Curley's were engulfed with the flames of anger at what he, as family, understood to be a clear shot across the bow of his relationship.

"Fine," he said curtly, "we *will* go to Tony's, and if you need anything you can just call on Big Joe." Ray turned back to the wall and said nothing. He laid there until he heard the door close behind the lovers, and then he rolled onto his back and reached for a cigarette. Lying there in the stillness, he sadly wondered what was happening to the great Norris Brothers.

ಬ

Tony Williams's living room was drenched in smoke and sweat, and it was stale with the conversation of posers and pretenders. Curley was under the impression that he was there because they admired his talent and respected his craft. The truth was that he was only there to add an air of respectability and legitimacy to the gathering. He was the only person there who had been glanced with the finger of God, but he was not the only one there who tried his hand at calling down His glory through "art." There was Tony, of course, a former bootlegger who also, in his spare time, painted all manner of farmhouses and rustic scenes upon his canvasses, which he then hung ostentatiously throughout his own home. He wouldn't sell them to anyone, although he was thoughtful enough to occasionally give one to friends on special occasions. He refused to sell them for two reasons. First, he believed that America's avowed love of the free market would be its undoing (and the Great Depression swirling around him only added to his vehemence on the subject) and therefore would not taint his art by putting a price tag on it. Second, and arguably more important, no one in their right mind would ever want to buy his paintings. He was one of those truly rare artists that even death could not redeem.

There was also BoPete, a man whose penchant for verse made him a favorite at these gatherings. He had found a book of John Keats poetry as a teenager and had fancied himself the reincarnation of the English poet since. His poems were sophomoric and not very clever, but he continued to write and regale with passion because, since he *did* have the good sense to surround himself with other lesser geniuses, he continued to be urged on.

There was Milly Watkins, a Raleigh maid who wanted to be a great sculptor someday. She tended to spend most of her time sculpting naked men and women in conjugal poses because, in the aftermath of the roaring Twenties, she believed that made her open minded and sensual. She was a brooding fatalist who had seemed utterly heart-broken when she turned forty in perfect health.

And there were others, stragglers and wannabes, who came and went. And it was into this pretentious lot that Curley Norris waded, thinking himself suddenly urbane and sophisticated because these Raleigh types, these men and women who said things that no doubt would have left them dangling from the end of a Cramerton rope, paid him attention and doted on his ego. He was unable to see (and unwilling to hear when Ray told him) that they were not his equal and it was *they* who actually needed *him*.

"Curley, the working man," called Tony when Curley and Lucy strolled in holding hands, "how the hell are you?" Curley smiled and threw out his hand.

"Fine as wine, Tony, and yourself?"

Tony agreed that he was also doing fine and proceeded to ask about that night's performance and the response of the crowd. Milly swung by and took their coats and brought Curley an ashtray. BoPete was in the corner of the room, huddled by the fireplace with a piece of scratch paper and a pencil perched between his lips. Tony shared that BoPete had apparently been smacked by inspiration from something that Milly had said and had ran to the corner to compose. Curley nodded in serious appreciation and Lucy seemed enthralled with the prospect of being in the same room with an artist as he composed. Tony's phonograph cranked out Glenn Miller tunes and Louis Armstrong songs. Curley and Lucy excused themselves and began to dance in the middle of the room. Curley still wasn't quite used to the level of exhibitionism that came with the environment, but Lucy gyrated and jitterbugged as if no one else was in the room. Curley soon caught the fever himself. After all, he couldn't allow the others to get the idea that he was inhibited. That word, whatever it meant, seemed to be the greatest judgment they could pass on someone.

When the music died away, they all sat around on the three couches strategically placed in the room and talked about world affairs. Tony held court against the so-called "New Deal," which he called an affront to the common sense of Americans.

"Why won't Roosevelt just admit he's a failure?" he demanded. "Then we could all just get on with the business of the real revolution that this country needs." Someone gave him an academic amen and spurred him on: "The future of this country, hell, the future of the world, is socialism. And I just don't understand why that patrician in the White House won't or can't understand that!"

For his part, Curley was unsettled by the violent attack on the president. In his household, Roosevelt's name was spoken with a reverence second only to Jesus Christ himself. Curley knew nothing of socialism, so he decided that maybe Tony was right. Things didn't seem that much better with the New Deal. He shuddered as the thought passed through his mind. It was sacrilege, but he reveled in it.

"Roosevelt's a bandit," Milly offered, "and the country will see that soon enough."

"A bandit," Lucy agreed as she curled closer to Curley.

"What do you think, Curley?" asked Tony. Curley flushed.

"Well, I don't know. I don't spend a whole lot of time thinkin' about that stuff. I reckon I'm too busy supportin' my family to give the rest of the country much attention."

The crowd bellowed with approving laughter. Curley was confused for a moment, not entirely sure that he wasn't being mocked. Tony slapped his knee and wiped a tear from his eye.

"You are priceless, Curley Norris," he said, "you have just summed up the audacity of the New Deal in one sentence while I went on for half an hour!" Curley chuckled.

"Well," he said.

BoPete had suddenly emerged from his creative cocoon in the corner to premiere his latest masterpiece for them. He was just about to begin reading when Tony leapt from the couch and demanded that he stop the recitation.

"Wait," he cried, startling his guests, "this is a special moment. We are about to be present at the birth of a poem. This is a sacred moment.

Right, Curley?"

Curley nodded his agreement, although he wasn't sure what the big deal was really all about. As much as he wanted to admire these people, as much as he wanted to believe in their inherent greatness, he couldn't help but contrast this bombast with the simplicity of the moment when he and Ray worked on a new song. He saw his brother sitting in the corner of the apartment with a cigarette dangling from his lips and the banjo-uke in his lap, nodding his head as Curley played a new tune for him. He would call out suggestions and change a line here and there, they would complete the work, and then celebrate by playing the song through in its entirety, with no more fanfare than a fresh smoke. Curley felt suddenly guilty about all the songs they had shortchanged. He had no idea, and he was sure that Ray didn't either, that a new song was the equivalent of a birth and as such required such a celebration.

"See?!" Tony demanded. "See? Curley gets it! He gets it, man!" The others nodded their heads, trying desperately to get IT themselves, whatever IT was that IT was. "This moment is sacred and we are going to do it properly. Curley, tell them what to do!"

"Oh, no," Curley demurred, "this is your call, Tony."

Tony blushed furiously.

"My God, I am sorry. Of course. Of course it is. We are going to do this as Curley's people would. The Indians understood art as life, eh, Curley?"

Curley said nothing but sat there, suddenly terribly uncomfortable.

"Yes!" cried Tony, "they understood. I'll tell ya," he continued, driving a finger into Curley's chest, "this country would have been so much better if the white man had never come here. Never!"

Curley suddenly realized that he had never agreed with Tony more than he did at this very moment. Suddenly aware of his surroundings, he felt empty and alone. His thoughts flew to Ray and their apartment.

"Anyway," Tony continued, "we are going to do this Curley's way. The Indian way. Move these couches into a circle. Into the holy and sacred circle."

Curley stifled back a laugh and stood to help the others position the furniture.

"Jeez," he thought, "we're gonna have a pow wow right here."

With the furniture in place, the group sat in their little sacred circle and listened to BoPete recite his poem.

"Roosevelt wants a New Deal," he began, "but Christ gave us that on the cross."

"So far so good," thought Curley. It was obviously another anti-Roosevelt poem, but at least it was pro-Jesus. His discomfort began to subside.

"But just like that crazy Jesus/FDR just wants to be your boss."

Curley rolled his eyes and sat through forty more minutes of BoPete's "New Deal/Old Deal" poem, in which the avuncular part time teacher blasted FDR, Jesus, the Pope and all manner of religious and political subjects. Curley was struck by the fact that some of the verses rhymed and some didn't, and the ones that did were often stretches. When BoPete was finished the audience roared and jumped up to slap him on the back and assure him that it was his finest effort to date. BoPete thanked Milly for the inspiration and said that, thanks to Tony's example, he was dedicating his poem to the oppressed Indian in America. Lucy nudged her elbow into Curley's side and he forced himself to muster a weak "thank you" for BoPete's kind thoughts and words. They then spent an additional hour deconstructing the underlying meanings of the poem, most of which, Curley was convinced BoPete was not bright enough to have intentionally intoned. Slowly the crowd began to peel themselves away from their sanctuary and make their way back out into the night and the real world they so detested. Finally, it was only Curley, Lucy and Tony sitting alone in their little mock circle.

"This is some of the best stuff I have ever made," Tony said as he came from the basement with two large jugs under his arms. "I think you'll like it."

"I'm sure we will," Lucy said, "you make the best hooch in the county, Tony."

"Hooch?" asked Curley. "You mean that's moonshine you got there?"

Tony and Lucy looked at each other and grinned.

"Ah, the common man," Tony said. "Yes, Curley, this is 'moonshine.' And I think you will like it. I doubt you've ever had better."

"Well, I reckon I can guarantee you that," Curley chuckled, "'cause I ain't never had any at all."

"What? You've never drank?" Lucy seemed stunned.

"Oh, Lucy, grow up," scolded Tony, "of course he's pulling your leg. Who ever heard of a musician that never drank? Right, Curley?"

"Well...."

"See, Lucy? God you are gullible." Lucy shrugged her shoulders and giggled. She leaned in and planted an inappropriate kiss on Curley's cheek. Tony poured them all a drink and placed the glasses down on the table.

"There you go, working man," he said, "tell me what you think. If I get the approval of a traveling musician then I guess I will know for sure that nobody can touch my hooch."

Curley flashed a smile and took the glass into his hands. He tried to blot Eunice's voice from his head, where she was now, once again, imploring him to stay away from liquor. He remembered the horror stories she had told him about the evils of the white man's alcohol, the images she had painted of Molly Runningwolf and her violent husband. Lucy and Tony were both watching him carefully now, waiting.

"Well," Lucy asked, "ain't you gonna drink it?"

"Is something the matter?" asked Tony.

Curley raised the glass like he had seen actors do in the pictures he had seen and drained the glass. He felt the fire drip down his throat and ignite his insides, flashing violently into his throat and all around his tongue. A bitter aftertaste blanketed his tongue and his eyes watered.

"Ha!" yelled Tony. "Is that some good shit or what?"

"Yeah," Curley croaked, "good shit, Tony."

Lucy and Tony emptied their glasses and repoured. They talked and laughed into the night, until finally a heavy darkness swept over Curley and he passed out cold.

"You know," snickered Tony, staggering into his own bedroom, "you'd think he'd never been drunk before."

CHAPTER THIRTY-TWO

Danville, Virginia, was hopping with activity and flowing with the fresh money of the tobacco market. Farmers with money burning holes in their pockets made their way down the streets looking for presents for their children, trinkets for their wives, and diversion for themselves. The beer and wine flowed freely as they celebrated their success and thanked their Lord for getting them through yet another year of economic pressures. It was 1940 and the world seemed to be getting crazier and less stable all the time. Europe was embroiled in a horrific war and there was more and more talk about the possibility of American boys going off to die again in a far off land. But all that was only background noise to these men, who at this very moment were having nothing but fun and were determined to keep their own heads out of any "foreign entanglements."

The Norris Brothers were conveniently placed along the street outside of the market itself, flailing away at their own tunes and any song that the farmers felt an emotional need to hear. The money was as easily accessible as the old melodies they cranked out, and they were in terrific voices today, despite the underlying tension that accompanied them everywhere they now went.

Curley was still seeing Lucy Jenkins back in Raleigh, and Ray had been terrified that she would be go with them to Virginia. That was a silly concern, of course, because Lucy was by no means the only girl that Curley was keeping company with, and to drag her along on a road trip would have only cramped his style. Ray had become accustomed to listening for the sounds of his brother making his way home at night, stumbling through the alley-way behind The Rooster and fumbling his way around the dark, alternately cursing and giggling at the night. Despite numerous promises, Curley was not only still drinking, but he was now drinking an awful lot. He had struck a deal with Big Joe that allowed him to play on Mondays and Tuesdays, nights they typically had taken off to rest their voices and rehearse new material, in exchange for free drinks during the week.

Early on it had been a terrific deal for Big Joe. After all, Curley could have only a few drinks before he came close to teetering off the stool anyway. But as the weeks had gone on, Curley had developed a more professional tolerance for drink, and slowly Big Joe began to wonder about the wisdom of the deal, even if it did mean twice the customers on what had traditionally been "off nights."

Big Joe was also beginning to hear rumblings, for the first time, *against*, the charming Curley Norris. Some customers complained that, after a few drinks, the normally gregarious guitar man was abusive from the stage, mocking their requests and playing poorly. He also heard rumors of a volatile temper that came with the alcohol, and Big Joe himself had chased away a few jealous boyfriends and husbands who had come to The Rooster for the expressed purpose of taking home a scalp of their own---Curley's.

For his part, Curley thought that people were just jealous of his success. He couldn't help it if he had, on occasion, taken a married woman to his bed. It was their responsibility to stay faithful, not his. Hell, he didn't ask many questions before he leapt. And if these women did not offer the truth in advance, well, that wasn't his fault. As for the deal with Big Joe, Curley was enough of a businessman to believe that Big Joe was still getting the better and more lucrative end of the deal. The Norris Brothers had become synonymous with The Rooster, and he was going to make damn sure that he was well compensated for it. Alcohol seemed as good a way as any, because it erased any guilt he may have felt about dipping into the money that they were supposed to send home. As for Ray's contention that it was a terribly selfish deal, Curley was, again, not to be blamed if Ray didn't take advantage of his ability to call out to the bar for a beer himself. His little brother's puritanical streak was getting old as far as Curley was concerned.

They had seen the man in the grimy overalls before. He had emerged from the market with pockets bulging, smiling from ear to ear and slapping everybody he could find on the back. Curley and Ray had hoped he would make his way over to them and their hat, but he had instead veered purposefully to the right and into front door of a bar. He emerged two hours later, swaying like a willow in a hurricane, and made his way to them. There was a crowd of about twenty five gathered around them, clapping and singing along and, most

importantly, dropping coins and cash into their hat.   The man in the
grimy overalls pushed his way to the front and clapped self-consciously
when the song ended.
   "Beeyootieeful," he cried. "Oh, my that was good."
   "Thanks," said Ray.
   "Thank you," agreed Curley.
   "Do ya'll take spacial requests?" he asked.
   "Uh-huh."
   "Oh, fine," he said. "How much?" Ray and Curley looked at each
other carefully.   They had never put a set price on their songs.
Normally they just played them and waited to see what the customer
gave them. Curley saw their chance to make a nice payday this way.
   "A dollar for each request." Someone in the back of the crowd
whistled and laughed.   That price, they obviously thought, was
ridiculous.
   "Done!" cried the man in the grimy overalls. He dropped a dollar
into the well-worn felt hat and crossed his arms waiting. Curley and
Ray sat there in silence, not knowing how to proceed.
   "Well?" asked the man.
   "Uh, we still don't know what you want to hear," Curley reminded
the man. The crowd crowed at the drunken farmer, but he paid them no
attention. Instead his chest ballooned out and he jutted his jaw.
   "Maple on the Hill," he said proudly. "I want to hear Maple on the
Hill. Please." Curley nodded and turned to Ray for the count. They
began the song slowly and deliberately, coaxing the man to sway with
their music and the drink.

> *"Near a quiet country village*
> *stood a maple on the hill*
> *there I sat with my Geneva long ago.*
> *As the stars were shining brightly*
> *We could hear the whippoorwill*
> *As we sat beneath the maple on the hill."*

As the song progressed they saw the drunken farmer's bottom lip
begin to tremble and then his eyes welled with tears until they
overflowed onto his cheeks. Several of the bystanders, some of whom
had not even had a drop to drink all day, were also wiping their eyes.
In Curley's own eyes the man in the grimy overalls began to look a lot
like Rodney. Curley watched as the man's tears streaked his weather

beaten face and his crusty, tired but strong hands wiped away the water. The flecks of early gray and the overalls combined to bring back powerful memories. Curley saw Rodney's broken body lying across the bed at home. He saw Rodney standing at the top of the driveway, waiting for his son's little legs to get him there. He thought of the Saturdays that they had risen at the break of day to walk all those miles into Gastonia to buy Eunice something for the house or a modest birthday present. Curley felt the dry burning in the back of his throat that signified the coming of tears. He turned to Ray during what should have been a solo break and whispered to him his own request.

"I need you to take it home," he said. Ray nodded, confused but knowing what to do. Ray took the next verse and carried the song through as Curley managed to somehow bite back the tears.

"Don't forget me little darling
when they lay me down to rest
Just this little prayer I pray
As you linger there in silence
thinking, sweetheart, of the past,
leave your tears of sorrow on my grave."

When the song ended the man in the grimy overalls wiped his eyes again and flashed a brilliant summer of a smile.

"Yeah," he croaked, "that's the one." He chuckled and reached into his pocket, pulling out a pack of cigarettes and another dollar.

"Do it again, boys," he said, dropping the dollar into the hat. Curley's eyes became as big as saucers.

"Again, mister? Are you sure?" His business instincts had been overwhelmed by his sudden empathy for this man, and he was determined not to take advantage of the man's drunkenness.

"My money's good," the farmer answered.

"Oh, it's not that. But another dollar? Are you sure? Do you want another song?"

"Nope. Maple on the Hill. That's the one that I want. Please play it again."

And again.

And again.

When the farmer finally pulled himself away from the corner he had contributed twenty five dollars towards the Norris Brother's family maintenance fund and made both Curley and Ray sick of Maple on the

Hill.

"God," said Ray when the man walked away, "don't you ever ask me to play than damn song again, Curley Norris."

"Me either," Curley agreed. "How many tears can one man have?"

"Plenty, I reckon. Poor bastard cried every time you sang it."

"Yeah, he did. I guess that means you fellas are pretty good at what you do." A man in a suit had emerged from the crowd and was standing in front of Curley and Ray with his arm extended. "Here's my card," he said, placing the small piece of paper in Curley's hand. "The name's Delroy Hanson and I work at WBTM here in Danville. You've probably heard my show if you've been in town long enough."

"We got into town last night," Ray answered, "and we haven't heard a radio since we got in."

"You have your own radio program?" asked Curley, intrigued by the idea.

"Indeed I do," answered the man. "And a very popular one. And the radio station is heard by practically everyone in this area. WBTM," he repeated, "World's Biggest Tobacco Market."

Curley studied the card and then handed it off to Ray, who did the same. It certainly looked professional and on the level.

"Well, Mr. Hanson," Ray asked, "what is it that we can do for you?"

"Oh, no," the man corrected, "it is I who would like to do for you." Hanson scanned the area and smiled at the simplicity of the set up. "You fellas aren't street musicians," he said matter-of-factly and with a trace of contempt, "that is obvious. You are professional musicians. Am I right?"

"Yessir," Curley said proudly, "we are the house entertainment for a business establishment in Raleigh. Our boss gave us a few weeks off so that we could follow this tobacco market and make a little grub on the side. That's what brought us here to Danville."

"I knew it," Hanson asserted, "you're far too polished to be vagabonds."

"Well, thank you," said Curley. "But you haven't told us what you plan to do for us." The man's aristocratic air annoyed Curley, and he didn't like the implication that the man was about to offer them some sort of handout.

"Maybe it's another corn-shucking," Ray scoffed bitterly.

"Ha! It is quite another thing! I would like for you boys to come down to the station and play on my radio show tonight. We normally have two acts on a Saturday night, but one of the one's we had booked for tonight cabled that they couldn't make it and that has me in a helluva mess. You boys would be doing me a tremendous favor."

"And what do we get?" asked Ray.

"Well, the station will pay you ten dollars for two hours worth of work, and you will get wonderful exposure."

"Mister," Curley said, "we can make ten dollars in *thirty* minutes right here, and we don't have to move."

"No, but the market will be closed up by seven o'clock and I doubt that you will make a dime. Make your money here and then come down to the station and make ten more. Boys," he cautioned, "not everyone, even professional musicians, get the chance to play on the radio. Remember, it was radio, not Wildwood Flower, that made the Carter Family."

Curley and Ray did not need any more prompting. Everyone knew the Carter Family, and they had both heard that they got their start by doing radio programs. Suddenly, Curley and Ray realized that they just might be looking at their big break.

"We'll do it," Curley announced. "What time you want us at the station?"

⅋

Mack Crowe was an imposing presence in any setting, but none more so than the studio of a radio station. He had stood in a corner of the "booth" with his arms folded tightly across his barrel chest and scowled at the Norris Brothers throughout their set. He had smiled not once, even when Curley took off on one of his better guitar solos. When they had taken a break for a news story and Curley saw that his mike was turned off he had lit a cigarette and turned his own scowl on Mack.

"Can I help you with something?" he had asked accusingly.

"Nope, just listening," came the terse reply.

Ray's own response had been quite different. His own hands began shaking the minute the bright red "On-Air" sign was illuminated. It was intimidating enough to think about the fact that they were probably being heard right at that moment by more people than they had ever played for before (unless Hanson was pulling their legs). But it was even more frightening to think that they were, the moment they played that first note into the microphones, stepping into the well worn tracks of fellow musicians like Jimmie Rodgers and the Carter Family. And the withering looks from Mack only stiffened his limbs and made it even more difficult to make his fingers go where they normally went without coaxing.

They finished their set with a blistering version of "You Are My Sunshine" that Curley felt sure would elicit a smile from the stoic statue in the corner of the room. But Mack's features didn't even flinch, and as Hanson's mike sprang to life and he began talking about the Norris Brothers from Raleigh, the tall man moved gracefully to the spot Curley had warmed for him and methodically removed his banjo from its case, without even so much as a "nice job." A guitar player and a bass fiddler moved into position behind Mack. They made up the rest of Uncle Mack's Traveling Band and, like their leader, they said nothing to Curley or Ray as they moved into position.

"White sons of bitches," Curley growled as he and Ray stepped out into the hallway of WBTM for a smoke.

"Yeah," Ray agreed self-consciously, "what the hell was his problem? Jeez, Curley, he looked like he wanted to kill us or something."

"Jealous," Curley announced with too much certainty to be sincere. "I bet you he and them fellas with him ain't worth a damn."

They decided they would test the theory and they walked back into the studio to hear Uncle Mack's Traveling Band fall flat on their face. They had never been more disappointed in their lives.

When Hanson nodded to let Mack and the boys know they were on, a transformation occurred that stunned Curley and Ray. A broad smile broke across his face and a rich baritone voice announced that they were just "thrilled to pieces" to be in the fine city of Danville and the beautiful state of Virginia. Curley cursed himself for neglecting to say something like that himself. He also marveled at the soothing, immensely personable personage that this otherwise seemingly unfriendly man was giving off to the radio audience. Curley turned and saw from the quizzical look on Ray's face that his brother must have been thinking the same thing.

"Damn, he sure got friendly in a hurry," Ray remarked.

"Yeah, but let's see what he sounds like," Curley said, still hoping that the man would have no talent.

The first thing he noticed was that Mack Crowe did not count off at the beginning of his songs. He nodded his head and then, somehow, the whole band marched into the music as if mentally connected. Ray whistled softly at the impressive feat. Then they listened as Mack's fingers drove a furious pace and twirled the band around the melody. The dull thump of the bass fiddle gave the songs a heavy and sustained foundation, and the guitar player augmented Mack's playing brilliantly and effortlessly.

"Jesus," whispered Ray, "no wonder he didn't seem impressed by us. They're amazing."

Curley said nothing but stood mesmerized by the sound. He felt inadequate for the first time in his musical life and said a silent prayer of thanksgiving that he and Ray did not have to try and follow this man's act. They played for over their allotted hour, and Curley could not help but notice that neither Hanson nor the man they been introduced to as the station manager made any effort to stop them. Curley thought that a man who sounded and acted as professionally as Mack Crowe must have known the time. Curley was impressed by the fact that this man just assumed he and his Traveling Band was good enough to take all the time they wanted.

Mack tried to end his portion of the program with his signature "Wabash Cannonball," but Hanson requested "Banks of the Ohio" and Mack cheerfully complied. Curley and Ray both unconsciously edged closer to hear his rendition of a song they had previously thought they had mastered. Once again, they were blown away by the white man's proficiency with his banjo and the sultry and seething edge he gave the folk song about unrequited love.

"Well, Doug," Mack said when the lights of the On-Air sign dimmed out, "you earned your money tonight, son."

"Thanks, Mack," the bassist replied. "I think we were on pretty well tonight."

"Been better," Mack reminded, "but I ain't gonna complain."

Mack stood and headed past Curley and Ray into the booth with Hanson and the station manager. Curley watched as Mack made some small talk and then took a bulging envelope from the manager. He shook hands with the two radio men and was then quickly back in the studio, packing up his banjo.

"Oh, shit," Curley said, "I forgot to get our money."

He turned quickly and headed for the booth himself, hoping Mack hadn't conned the men out of all the money at their disposal.

"Hey," came the voice from behind him, "guitar man."

Curley turned to face Mack, stunned that the man even knew he was alive.

"Yessir?" Curley was angry at how deferential his tone sounded.

"When you're done in there I'd like to have a talk with you and your brother. That be all right?"

"Uh, yeah, yeah I reckon that's okay."

"Good," said Mack as he strolled towards the door, "meet me in the parking lot."

Curley nodded and went in to get their ten dollars, wondering what the evil looking white man wanted and feeling a good deal of trepidation at the possibilities.

CHAPTER THIRTY-THREE

At six foot four inches tall, "Uncle" Mack Crowe was quite a figure, towering over the heads of Curley and Ray. He was bald on top of his head with a ring of furry brown hair jetting around over his ears and across the back of his head. He had large blue eyes that seemed to take in everything around him, and his prominent nose added to features that were already regal. His legs were long enough to seem disproportionate against his average torso. He was barrel chested and had the laugh of an old sailor. Curley and Ray both lit cigarettes as he began to speak, more out of nervous energy than any real craving for a smoke. Mack reached into this own shirt pocket and removed a pouch of chewing tobacco and stuffed it into his mouth.

"So you two are from Raleigh, huh?" he asked.

"Yessir. We are the house band for a...."

"Which place?"

"Uh, The Rooster. I don't know if you've ever heard of it or not but...."

"Nope, never have."

"Oh, well, uh, that's where we play." Curley was stunned by Mack's brutal honesty. He didn't figure Mack would have actually heard of The Rooster, but he did expect him to do the decent thing and rub his chin and ponder over it for a minute before admitting that he had never heard of the place.

"What brought you boys all the way up here to Danville, then?" he asked. Curley was going to try and think of something that sounded clever and maybe even a little professional, but before he could Ray had already blurted out the answer.

"Tobacco market," he said.

"Tobacco market?"

"Yessir," continued Ray innocently and without pretension, "you can make some real good money following those folks around. In fact, that's how me and Curley really got our start. Ain't it Curley?"

"Yeah," Curley said with shame. Mack's "boys" turned to each other and giggled. "What the hell's so funny?" demanded Curley. The man with the bass fiddle started to say something when Mack cut him off.

"Easy boys," he said, "take it easy." Curley had taken all he was going to take from Mack Crowe.

"Look, Mister, I don't know what it is that you want from us, but I think I have just about known you as long as I want to."

"Now hold on, son...."

"No, you hold on," Curley continued, "you ain't been nothin' but rude since we laid eyes on you. Hell, you stood there during our set and stared at us like you wanted to bust our guitars over our heads and then ain't said nothing kind since. Maybe you're too big to be playin' tobacco markets, but we ain't. Not yet, anyway, and we have a family back home depending on the money that we send back. I reckon you can't understand that and that's just fine by me. But don't go puttin' us down. Not unless you're lookin' for a fight." A broad smile creased Mack's features. Curley thought it was the first time that he had seen the man smile without being on the air. "Now what's so funny?"

"Oh, nothing's funny," Mack agreed, "nothing at all. I apologize if you got the wrong idea up there. The fact is that I was just listening to you. Listening carefully. And when I do that I suppose I don't smile a lot at that."

"No," Ray added, "you sure don't."

"Well, I didn't mean to give ya'll the wrong impression. That fact is that I was sitting there thinking about how much I liked what I was hearing. I liked it a lot." Now it was Curley's turn to smile.

"Thank you, Mr. Crowe."

"Uncle Mack."

"Okay, thank you, Uncle Mack. Me and Ray was really impressed with ya'll, too."

"Yeah, you guys were something. Better than us," Ray added self-consciously and to Curley's mortification, "I know I was personally scared 'bout to death!"

"You didn't show it," Mack consoled. "Why in the world were you scared?"

"We ain't never been on the radio before," Ray admitted, "and truth is all I could think about was how we were doing stuff like what the

Carter Family done." Mack laughed loudly.

"The Carter Family? Well, now, they're fine people."

"You know 'em?" Ray and Curley asked in unison.

"Yes, I've played with them a few times. There's not a prettier voice on God's green earth than Maybelle's, I'll tell you that right now."

"And A.P. can write you a song at the drop of a hat," added the bass player. Curley and Ray stood slack jawed and wide eyed at the anecdote. These men actually knew the Carter Family!!

"I'm sorry, where are my manners," asked Mack. "I want to introduce you boys to my band. This here's Shifty Doug Reynolds, my bass fiddle player. And that's Randy Moore, my guitar player." Curley and Ray shook their hands and smiled, still in awe of the men that were lucky enough to accompany this great musician who knew even greater musicians.

"Randy there is actually the reason I wanted to talk to you two. But first let me ask you a question. Are either of you married?"

"No sir, we're both single," Ray answered quickly, fearing that Curley might mention the dreaded Lucy Jenkins.

"Plenty single," Curley added with a wry grin and wink.

"Good enough," Mack responded. "Well, Randy here ain't plenty single or just single, either. He's got himself a pretty little wife down in Charleston who just wrote him and told him that he's about to be a daddy."

"At least she says it' his," Doug added with a chuckle. Randy blushed but said nothing.

"And he has decided that he can't be a daddy and Uncle Mack's guitar player at the same time. So that leaves me, at least in three or four months, without a guitar player." Ray held his breath, thinking he knew what was coming but not wanting to jinx their luck by thinking it too clearly.

"So I been scouting talent everywhere we go, looking for a replacement. And I don't mind telling you I ain't heard a guitar player worth a shit in the whole damn South."

Curley stiffened, feeling another put-down coming.

"Until tonight," Mack added, "and then shit if I didn't run into two of 'em!"

"That's awful nice, Uncle Mack," Curley said.

"Shit, son, I don't say *nothing* just to be nice. I mean it. You boys are terrific. You need a little polish, and you need to get a few more radio shows under your belt, but I know good when I hear it, and you boys got it in spades. That's why I want to make you an offer. I want you boys to join my band. I want you to be a part of Uncle Mack's Traveling Band. What do you think?"

Curley and Ray turned to each other with opposite responses. For Ray this seemed to be a gift from God, but for Curley it seemed more like a devilish tease. As impressed as he had been with Mack's sound and his credentials, he had no interest in submerging the Norris Brothers under the umbrella of another man. Curley did not like sleeping in a backseat, and he did not want to live there, either.

"That sounds great," Ray said.

"Well, I think I can offer you boys...."

"We're not interested," Curley said curtly, "but we appreciate the offer."

"Now wait just a minute," said Ray, "I *am* interested. And I think we ought to hear what the man has to say." Uncle Mack seemed surprised at the disagreement, but no more so than Curley.

"Ray...."

"Uncle Mack," Ray said, turning his back on Curley, "I would like to hear what you have to offer. That is, unless you only want us as a package deal. Would you take one of us and not the other?"

"Ray!" Curley's tone was devoid of anger but full of hurt and shock.

"Well," Mack answered, "I had thought that I would hire both of you. A lead and a rhythm would fill out the sound, I think. But I guess I could settle for one of you."

"Oh, Ray, you ain't serious," Curley said. "You wouldn't split up the Norris Brothers."

Ray turned a cold, hard gaze on his brother.

"You watch me," he said plainly. Curley drew back and looked deep into his brother's eyes. To his terror he saw that there was no bluster there, no bluff.

"Look, boys, I think this a talk ya'll should have in private. Why don't you discuss it among yourselves and let me know something in the morning."

"I'm afraid that won't be possible," Curley said, "because we can't afford to stay in town tonight. We were going to hit the highway and get back to Raleigh by morning."

Mack reached into this pocket and fumbled around for a minute and then pulled out a shiny gold money clip. He pulled bills from the wad and handed them to Ray.

"This'll take care of the room tonight," he said. "I'll meet you at the hotel tomorrow around nine and see what you've decided. Is that okay with you both?"

"Yessir," Ray said, "and thank you." Curley said nothing. Uncle Mack and the band hopped into a shiny black car the likes of which Curley and Ray had never seen. Curley picked up his guitar case and moved silently towards their own, lesser means of transportation. Ray followed.

"Look, Curley...."

"Not right now," Curley snapped. "Not right now."

He cranked the car and headed into the highway. They drove to the hotel without a word, pulling in behind Mack's car and their own uncertain prospects.

CHAPTER THIRTY-FOUR

The air that hung around their heads and clung tenaciously to their clothing resembled a pool hall more than a hotel room from the massive numbers of cigarettes they had smoked in silence. They were supposed to be discussing Uncle Mack's proposal and their future, but the bitter divide between them precluded any real discourse. Neither brother had made much of an effort beyond inhaling and sitting up in their chairs as if they were about to begin the conversation, but then they each, in turn, slumped back in their seat and reached for a smoke. Ray was furious at Curley's tyrannical rejection of Uncle Mack's so-called proposition. He was irate that Curley had spoken for the two of them without even hearing the particulars of what Mack had to say. And he was tired of Curley speaking in for him, especially when then preceding months had left him so full of doubt that Curley really had both of their best interests at heart.

Curley's mind was still reeling from Ray's apparent lack of sentimentality or even loyalty. He could not, would not, believe that Ray would be so easily willing to throw away their partnership. His disbelief boiled over into anger at what he perceived as his brother's incredible ingratitude. Every time he started to speak, he realized that the words perched on the tip of his tongue, ready to dive and dice his brother's soul, were the kinds of things that, once said, he would never be able to take back. So he sat in silence, waiting for his rebellious little brother to make the first move. Finally, Ray did.

"So you wanna tell me why you ain't even willing to hear the man out?" he asked. "I mean, it seems to me that the least we could do with an opportunity like this is hear everything out and then weigh it. Who knows how much money he might go and offer us?"

"It ain't about the money," Curley corrected quickly. "It's about you and me. I thought you understood that."

"Well, I don't."

"Yeah? No shit." Ray took a deep breath.

"Then why don't you explain it to me, Curley? I'm listening."

Curley bolted up in his chair, suddenly charged.

"Okay," he said, "I'll tell you, even though I shouldn't have to."

Ray decided to let the shot go unanswered for the moment.

"Ray, this guy wants us to back him up. You know? No more Norris Brothers. We would be nothin' more than hired hands in this outfit. He'll be the star and we'll be the help. Would that suit you?"

"Hell, Curley, that don't sound too different to me than what I already been doin'." It was a remark that cut Curley deeply, and Ray regretted it almost as soon as the words had left his mouth.

"Then go join the asshole," Curley said, "and do what you want. But I ain't gonna be nobody's backup. That's bullshit."

Curley stood and stormed to the door of the room.

"Look, Curley, I just meant...."

"I know goddamn well what you meant," Curley shouted, "and I think it was a damn awful thing for you to say to me. And I also think that it ain't true and I think that, to top it all off, you know it ain't true." Curley turned the knob on the door and began to walk out.

"Where you goin'?" asked Ray.

"Out. I'll be back by morning to tell you and Uncle Mack bye." He stormed out of the room, slamming the door behind him for good measure.

৪৩

It was around five in the morning when the sound of the car horn ripped Ray from his tortured doze. He tried to blink away the sleep and swallow the cotton-mouth away. Then he heard the voice, floating heavily up the stairs and into the windows and door.

"Ray!! Hey, little brother?! My family!"

Ray threw the covers away and jumped out of the bed, grabbing for and tugging on his jeans. He ran out to the balcony without his shirt and saw Curley in the parking lot, leaning against the side of Susan Muncie's old car with a half-empty bottle clutched to his breast.

"Oh, Jesus," Ray whispered. "Curley," he called softly, "Curley, what are you doin'? Get up here and shut up!"

"What?" screamed Curley. "I can't hear a damn thing you're saying,

Ray. SPEAK UP!!!!!" Curley slammed the car door so hard it almost tipped the automobile over on its side.

"Ssshhhhhh," Ray called. "Hush, Curley."

"Oh, am I too loud?" Curley shouted. "Well, who cares? Let's wake up the whole damn place and tell them that the Norris Brothers are through. I think that's news worth waking folks up for. THE NORRIS BROTHERS ARE ALL WASHED UP, VIRGINIA," he bellowed at the top of his lungs, "DONE 'FORE THEIR TIME JUST LIKE THEIR DADDY!!!"

Ray winced at the cold reference to Rodney. Hotel patrons were now coming out on the ledge, clad in bathrobes and underwear, rubbing their tired eyes and trying to figure out what the commotion was that had interrupted their luxurious sleep. Ray recognized several tobacco farmers that had stopped and listened to them the previous afternoon, emerging from their rooms with cheap and painted women that Ray was almost certain were not their wives.

"Hey, buddy," one of them called, "how about shuttin' your fuckin' mouth and lettin' us get some sleep, huh?!"

"Kiss my ass," Curley yelled, "and go back to your little whore!"

"Why you cocksucker I'll cut your goddamn throat!" The man rushed into his room and disappeared. Ray assumed he was looking for his knife.

"Shit, Curley, shut up!"

"Hey, Ray," Curley called, "hows about if I let you play lead? Will that make it all better for you? Is that what you want? Huh?"

"Curley...."

"'Cause if that's what you want, you just say so. Don't let it bother you none that I taught you how to sing and play that shitty little banjer or that I practically raised you. Nossir, don't think on that none at all you fucking bastard!!!!" Ray felt hot tears streaming down his cheeks. He wanted to scream at Curley to close his mouth before he got them both killed, but his throat had dried up and just wouldn't respond to his brain's entreaties.

"Is that what you want, Ray? Huh? Is it?"

"Shut up!!" Cried someone else from the balcony.

"Ah shit," Ray heard someone say, "there's a drunk Injun in the parkin' lot." Ray was consumed with embarrassment for and deep resentment towards Curley.

"Hey, Injun Joe, shut your damn mouth!" Curley squealed a vicious curse at the man and hurled his bottle in the man's direction. The bottle slammed into the side of the building and exploded, spraying beer all over the wall and onto some of the gawkers.

"That's it, Indian," someone said, "you're dead now."

"Trouble?"

Ray whirled to find Uncle Mack and the boys standing at his side.

"Oh, good God yes," he said, "please help me get him up here in the room. Please, Mack, I'm beggin' you. They're gonna kill him."

Mack nodded and went into his action with Randy and Doug. Ray struggled to keep up with them as they flew down the stairs and into the lot.

"Let's go, son," Mack said, "I think you've put on enough of a show for one night."

"You bastard," Curley said as he lunged towards Mack's head, "this shit is all your fault."

Mack's reflexes were as quick in a fight as were his fingers on the neck of his banjo and he ducked away from Curley, grabbed his arm and twisted it behind his back. Curley yelped and began cursing and kicking wildly.

"Don't hurt him," Ray pleaded.

"Don't you worry none," Mack laughed, "I've had my share of experiences with drunk guitar players."

It took all four of them to get Curley up the stairs. When they had reached Curley and Ray's room they tossed him in like a sack of potatoes. Curley hit the floor with a dull thud and lay motionless. Ray thanked them for their help and entered the room by himself, closing the door behind him. Curley rolled over onto his back and giggled, then moaned.

"Ray, man that was a terrible thing to do. Sickin' those guys on me like that." He sat himself up on one elbow. "I guess you and Uncle Mack are closer than I thought."

Ray stood over his fallen hero and sneered.

"Curley, I don't know what to say to you right now. I think it would probably be better if we just got some sleep. Okay?"

Curley managed to pick himself up and teeter over to the dresser where he balanced himself.

"Nossir," he said adamantly, "it's not okay at all. We're gonna settle this tonight."

"Settle what, Curley," Ray demanded. "What is it that you could possibly think needs to be settled? Besides, you're drunk and stupid and I have nothing to say to you. Do you hear me, Curley? I have nothing to say to you tonight. Just rest up. Because when you wake up in the morning I will have plenty to say. Believe me I will."

"No!" Curley cried like a petulant child, stomping the floor with his foot. "I wanna know right now what it's gonna be? Is it Uncle Mack's Traveling Helping Hands or the Norris Brothers? Huh? Which is it, Ray?"

Curley's tone was getting loud again, and only the fear of the farmers figuring out what room they were in and coming in to make good on their threats kept Ray quiet.

"Not tonight, Curley," he said through clenched teeth.

"TONIGHT, GODDAMN IT!! I deserve an answer after all I've done for you, Ray." Ray stormed past Curley and grabbed his shirt and threw it on, missing buttons as he tried to close the front. Then he moved past Curley again and strolled purposefully to the corner of the room where he opened his case and removed the banjo-uke. Curley smiled the irritating smile of a drunk.

"Good," he said. "I'm mighty glad to see that you come to your senses. Breaking up the Norris Brothers was the dumbest damn idea you *ever* had."

Ray turned to Curley and smiled. Curley shuddered at the sight of Ray's humorless and chilling smile.

"The Norris Brothers?" Ray croaked through his sudden tears.

"Ray, look...."

"The Norris Brothers?" Ray demanded. He pushed past Curley and to the edge of the bed. "Curley this is what I think of the goddamn Norris Brothers."

And he drew back like a slugger and slammed the instrument into the hotel room wall, sending its pieces spiraling through the room and across the bed sheets. Curley screamed as if shot by a cannon.

"There's your answer Curley Norris," Ray barked. "You wanna be a fucking drunk? You wanna throw away your life and piss on your own flesh and blood? Well, you do it, Curley. You do what ever you goddamn well please. But the fucking Norris Brothers are finished. You hear me? THE GODDAMN NORRIS BROTHERS ARE THROUGH!" Ray grabbed his sack of clothes and his pack of cigarettes and exploded out the door and down the stairs into the Virginia night. Curley stumbled to the bed, too drunk to realize that there was no way to put that banjo-uke back together again. It lay in a million pieces all over the room, its lonely strings silenced forever. Curley dropped helplessly to the floor, weeping.

"Damn you Ray Norris," he blubbered.

He attempted to piece together the bits of banjo-uke around his feet almost until the sunrise, when he finally passed out.

CHAPTER THIRTY-FIVE

Uncle Mack had been banging on the door for almost twenty minutes when the ghostly sight of Curley pulled it open. Mack winced as he saw the puffy, drawn features of the young guitar player.

"Yeah?" Curley asked in a gravely tone. "What do you want?"

"Uh, may I come in?" Curley nodded but said nothing, opting instead to just move out of the way and allow Mack in. He dropped himself cross-legged on the floor and reached for his cigarettes.

"Shit," he whispered upon realizing that he had smoked them all the night before. Uncle Mack reached into his own pocket and pulled out an unopened pack.

"I thought you might need these," he said.

"Thanks."

Curley reached out and took the pack and proceeded to light a cigarette with hands that shook more than he had ever known them to before. Mack watched him and sighed. Curley paid the man no attention but sat on the bed, puffing and rubbing his temples.

"So," Curley asked finally, "when do you and my brother leave?" Mack seemed thrown by the question.

"What?"

"When do you leave?" Curley repeated.

"I don't know. Has he decided to join us?" Curley stared at the strange white man.

"Ain't he with you?"

"Son, I haven't seen your brother since we helped him get a hold of you last night in the parking lot." Curley groaned and stubbed out his cigarette. "I assumed he spent the night here with you," Mack continued, "I came by to see if the two of you had managed to come to any agreement last night."

"No, no we didn't," Curley answered. "And Ray ain't here. Fact is I don't rightly know where my brother is."

"Oh. I take it by the look of the room that you boys were into it last night, huh?" Curley nodded again.

"Mister, he was pretty well tore up with me last night," Curley said.

"Can't say as I blame him," Mack said reproachfully. "You gave him a pretty rough time."

Curley grunted.

"Mister, is my car down there?"

"It was a minute ago."

"Well, I reckon he didn't go far then. If you'll just wait around for a little bit I'm sure...."

"I ain't got time to wait," Mack said. "We gotta be in Baltimore soon. Besides, your car being out there don't mean a damn thing. There's a train depot not ten miles from here. Maybe he hopped and got the hell outta here."

Curley started to tell Uncle Mack that there was no way Ray would've just left town, but the little shards of wood around his feet reminded him that anything was possible. He placed his head in his hands and began to tremble.

"Christ, Mister, I ain't got no idea where Ray is. He might've gone any place as mad as he was at me. But I know that he wanted to join you. He.....he told me so."

Mack stood up and pulled out a piece of paper. He reached it out and Curley took it.

"What's this?"

"I'm gonna be cutting a record in Charlotte in a couple of months," Mack said. "If your brother decides that he wants to join my group *and* I haven't already found myself a guitar player, you have him call me there at the studio. If I ain't in they will know how to find me. Okay?"

"Yessir." Mack turned and walked out. As he got in the doorway he stopped and turned to face Curley again.

"You've got a lot of talent, son," he said sadly, "and the offer still stands for you, too." He placed an oversized gray fedora on his head and smiled. "And if I don't see you again, good luck to the lot of ya!" Then he walked out, closing the door behind him.

Curley tucked the paper in his guitar case and determined that he would deliver it to Ray and abide by whatever his little brother wanted to do. Against the pain in his head he began dressing quickly, deciding he had better find Ray and get out of Danville as soon as he could.

After all, he couldn't be sure what manner of trouble he had gotten into the night before.

PART SIX

THE STRANGER

CHAPTER THIRTY-SIX

It was an uneasy truce, but it held. Curley had not turned his back on the bottle the way he had promised Ray he would, but he had learned not to push Ray too far anymore and he acted accordingly. He would sneak his drinks before a show with the same stealth he had once applied to the butts of Rodney's cigarettes. And when he got really sauced, he made sure to do it only when Ray was no where around and on nights when he could get away with not coming home.

His new best friend's name was Tommy Dee. Curley had made the name up himself, and he applied it to any occasion when he was drinking. Most of the time Tommy's house was actually a night spent boozing and carousing. Sometimes it was a night spent in the hungry arms of Susan Muncie. But whatever the moment, the elusive Tommy Dee covered a multitude of sins.

Ray was no idiot, he smelled the tell-tale aroma of liquor on his brother's breath and he heard the stories that always seemed to lurk around the town on Monday mornings. But he was still madly in love with the image of his brother that he himself had created, and he decided to treat the gossip and innuendo as aberrations and not the definition of Curley Norris's present state of existence. He noticed the lines that were developing across Curley's features and the heavy duty saddle bags that sagged underneath his eyes. He saw the broken vessels in the nose that marred Curley's appearance. But he assumed that, since he hadn't seen Curley drunk since that awful night in Virginia, his brother was slowly calming things down.

Curley's love life was as erratic as his stunted reformation. He was seeing a new girl now, Emma Gold, and she had a car that she allowed them to use. Curley would often take Emma's car and date other girls in it, always claiming that he and Ray had a job. There had been several close calls when Emma had asked Ray how they had "gone over" (a phrase she picked up from Curley and mimicked mercilessly) the previous weekend or night and Ray had feigned ignorance. But Emma was crazy about Curley and, no matter how absurd his excuse, she bought into it with relish. On the few times that she pretended to be angry at Curley and refused him access to her wheels, he only had to make a quick trip to the Muncie home to get a way out of Cramerton. Rather than running Emma off, this knowledge only seemed to secure her devotion. It was all incredible to Ray.

Tonight they were speeding home from a small town named Cherryville, where they had played at yet another corn-shucking. In Bessemer City they saw an interesting sign that proclaimed a fifty dollar prize that night for the best amateur talent in the area.

"Damn," Ray sighed, "that makes me almost wish we weren't pros." Curley's face beamed.

"Yeah," he said conspiratorially, "it does, don't it?" Ray shook his head fearfully.

"Oh, no, Curley. We're too close to home. We'll get caught sure." Curley had wheeled the car to follow the arrows of the sign.

"Well, the worst they can do is throw us out."

He brought the car into a screeching halt in the parking lot of the local high school.

"C'mon," he said as he hopped out of the car and grabbed his guitar case.

"One of these days, Curley," Ray said, "you're gonna get us killed."

"Yeah," Curley agreed, "but not tonight."

The inside of the auditorium was filled with the smoke of nervous parents and the tinny sound of grandparents bragging about the family prodigy. Curley and Ray made their way up to the front and quickly signed up for the competition.

"See?" Curley said with satisfaction, "I told you there wouldn't be a problem. We've never played down in these parts."

Curley and Ray sat down in a pair of adjacent wooden seats positioned in the third row of the theatre. The first four rows were consumed with young men and women who had come to showcase their abilities and, hopefully, feed their family for a month. A tiny, spectacled white woman was sitting at a dusty old piano at the corner of the stage, prepared to accompany any artist who needed it. The town's mayor made his way slowly through the crowd, shaking hands and kissing babies all the way down the aisle. He took a microphone that had been set up for the talent show and welcomed everyone. A local preacher came forth and gave the invocation ("Lord, bless these young people and help them as they show us your divine gifts, Lord") and then the mayor was back at the mike, thanking local businesses and mills for contributing to this amazing purse that they were offering. The preacher came back and led the crowd in a hymn and then the mayor introduced the first act.

Curley and Ray sat in amazement as the people around them trooped, one after the other, up to the stage and blasted through their "divine gifts." Ray whispered into Curley's ear that he thought the night was anything but a show of talent. Curley laughed quietly.

"Curley, we can't do this," Ray said after hearing one young woman dissect Amazing Grace. "This is stealing."

"Ray," Curley asked, "if that was your fifty dollars, would you feel like you got your money's worth if any of these assholes took it home?"

"No, I reckon I would not," Ray agreed, "but we're professionals, Curley. And these people ain't. Shit, they ain't even close."

Curley shushed him and waited until finally their turn came. Ray clutched the Silvertone guitar that he and Curley had managed to buy to replace the banjo-uke. They took their seats and jumped into their version of "She's Giving Everything Away." The crowd, which had been lulled nearly into a coma from the parade of mundane mediocrity that had gone before, suddenly sat up and took notice. By the second verse, some of the people had begun to clap along. Curley and Ray watched as the tired and worried faces below them turned upwards into smiles and gleeful enjoyment. Some mothers elbowed fathers who were enjoying it too much, reminding them that these two "amateur" were about to take money away from their own wallets. But no amount of envy could stop the wave. The Norris Brothers were carrying the night.

They finished and departed the stage in a hail of applause and cheers. Even the preacher, who was less than impressed by their non-gospel selection, had to work extra hard to suppress a smile. Curley and Ray were forced to sit through the rest of the show, which included a guitar player who was incapable of playing chords and a ventriloquist who, due to the times, was forced to use his hand as his puppet. No matter, thought Curley. In the boy's apparent confusion he moved his lips more when he was supposed to be talking than when he hand was speaking.

When the last act had kindly stopped beating on the old piano the mayor took the stage again and said that the winner would be chosen by "audience response." Curley groaned, assuming that some local who had stacked the crowd with relatives was about to take off with their prize.

As the mayor went through act after pitiful act, Curley and Ray both noticed the lukewarm responses of the crowd. They held their breath when the mayor came to them.

"And everybody thinking the...uh," he checked his notes quickly, "that the Norris Brothers are the winner please...."

Before he could even finish with is request the crowd had erupted with applause and shouts. Curley and Ray smiled and slyly shook each other's hands. They had pulled it off. The mayor went through the last few names, but it was no contest. He walked over to Curley and Ray and pronounced them the night's winners. They smiled and turned to the crowd and waved like a couple of war heroes.

"Boys," the mayor said, "I can sweeten that pot by twenty five dollars if you'll do us a few more numbers."

"You got it," Curley and Ray said, grabbing their instruments and heading back to the stage.

"Ladies and gentlemen," the mayor announced, "I have got these fellows to agree to entertain us with a few more songs." The crowd clapped enthusiastically. "And I hope," the mayor added, "that you will all remember this come election day."

"This one's for the mayor," Curley announced gleefully. Then they ripped into "Don't Say Goodbye" and sent the crowd home with smiles plastered on their faces.

And the Norris Brothers took the seventy-five dollars and headed home, the best amateur group in all of Bessemer City.

CHAPTER THIRTY-SEVEN

"Thank you so much," the man cried into the microphone, "ya'll are great. Let me introduce my band to ya!"

The claps and the cheers were like a narcotic, easing away tension and sending the recipient on a high that took him across the moon and around the world. The bond between audience and performer was intensely sexual, as everyone leaned against each other, sweaty, dreamy and expectant, longing for the next hit. The musicians gasped air and rested their tired hands and voices. The crowd did not have to worry about the next town, so they celebrated with abandon, hollering and screeching. It was call and response. It was primal. It was salvation. It was music.

The audience was starry-eyed, gazing up at the stage as if they were watching a comet blaze its way across their sky. In many ways that was *exactly* what they were doing. That is the attraction of the traveling band, the chance to live vicariously and the opportunity to watch an event out of the ordinary, something that is solely yours for a few hours, and then is gone away into the night, gone to seduce others.

They provided melody for the dreams, soundtracks for the vision. As the amplifiers roared, some imagined they were returning from the coming war, decorated in ribbons and adorned in adulation. Some saw fading May sunlight and the appearance of their bride or groom at the top of a winding stair case. Others felt the hands of a lover, the caress of their mate. Music is poetry with a soul, and Uncle Mack's Traveling Band provided the brush strokes upon an otherwise dreary and opaque canvass.

"Now let me call your attention to the newest members of my group," Uncle Mack declared triumphantly. "They're known as the Indian Artists, and I'm proud to have them. First, on the rhythm guitar, Mr. Ray Norris!" The crowd bellowed their approval and Ray stood from his perch, smiled happily and shyly, and he bowed. "And on the lead guitar and the harmonica..." A dramatic pause and then: "Mr. Curley Norris!" Again the crowd threw up its voice and cheered. Curley smiled, without shyness, and bowed. He sat back down on the hay bale and waited for Uncle Mack to finish thanking the crowd and introduce the next tune. He forced himself to ignore his itchy backside, aggravated by night after night of placing himself on the hay. It was Uncle Mack's trademark road show, and Curley could not argue with its success. Mack always strolled onto the stage wearing denim overalls and a checkered flannel shirt. Curley found the pretense a little insulting, but Mack argued that to be loved by the people you had to look like them. Curley neglected to point out that the people adored him and Ray, but it was not because he failed to notice the irony. After taking the stage, Uncle Mack and his men sat upon bales of Hay. Plastic chickens littered the stage, giving whatever venue they played in the look of an old barn. That was Mack's precise goal. It was sometimes difficult to play those longing, tender ballads while being stared down by a fake hen, but the money poured in and the crowds got bigger and bigger with each city and town.

Curley had turned to Uncle Mack after returning to Cramerton. His name was no good in that city any more, and he recognized that to keep the musical dream alive any longer he was going to have to accept second fiddle for a while. He had courted Ray again, and for a third time found forgiveness. Ray believed that a professional like Mack Crowe could turn Curley around, so when he learned that Curley was going to join the Traveling Band he signed on as well.

Eunice had not been as supportive this time around. She had wanted her sons to stay close by and find regular work. Images of some tramp that her son had met on the road showing up at her doorstep with a squawling child clutched to her breast was itself enough to raise her ire and fill her full of doubts, but coupled with the knowledge that Curley was still drinking it made her even more apprehensive. She implored Ray to keep her constantly posted by phone and mail, and she instructed him not to leave Curley's side no matter what the abuses.

So they had met up with Uncle Mack in Charlotte and played their first gig at WBT radio in the Queen City. Then the tour really kicked off, as they barnstormed the Southeast, stopping for shows in Georgia and Tennessee and back to Virginia. The mobility made it next to impossible for Curley to find much trouble. He still drank and he still pushed the envelope, but they were typically back out on the road and far from the city limits when consciousness arose and damage assessments were made. It seemed the perfect scenario to Curley.

There was also more discipline. Uncle Mack did not presume to tell his musicians how to live their life or instill in them any morality, but he did demand that whatever they do in their spare time not adversely affect their playing, and that alone enforced a certain calm on Curley's rambling ways. Mack insisted that, on the circuit, one poor performance could end a man's career quickly. He was not about to allow anyone, no matter how talented, to undo all the hard work he done to cultivate his name as a family entertainer and top showman. Curley knew better than to bite the hand that fed him. He also respected Mack as a musician and a businessman, watching and learning as Mack debated fees and found ways to pack houses in communities where they were unknown. Curley enjoyed being schooled in the ways of the troubadour.

Mack ended his last banjo solo, thanked the crowd again, bowed one last time, and then made his way to the side of the stage, away from the eyes of the crowd, as the band continued playing. Once he was off stage, Curley stood, bowed, and trooped off stage beside Uncle Mack, leaving Ray and Shifty alone on the stage, playing a duet. When Ray was sure that Curley was out of sight, he, too, stood and bowed and made his way off of the stage. Shifty stood alone at the corner of the stage, a cigarette dangling from his lips, thumping out his lonely bass line. By this time the crowd was yelling and stomping furiously, trying to "coax" the performers back onto the stage. When they had worked themselves into a proper frenzy, Mack motioned Ray back out, and then they made their way out in reverse order of their exit. Once Mack was sitting again, they launched back into the last verse of "Big John" again---their encore. The process was carefully scripted and almost formulaic, but Curley never tired of pulling it off. He loved the way it brought the crowd to ecstasy when they returned, and he loved knowing that they had that kind of power at their disposal. When they had ran through the verse and chorus, they ended the show with a blistering double solo---Curley and Mack trading licks, and then a flourish, and then silence, followed by massive applause. They all stood, laid their instruments down, walked arm in arm to the lip of the stage and bowed in unison for the crowd. They departed the stage, smiling and waving, the way Curley had always dreamed of--- conquerors.

80

"We need to try that again, if we can, Hoop." Sam Hooper sighed.

"Mack, you know the policy. You're supposed to be rehearsed and get it one take."

Curley, Ray and Shifty watched the action in the booth, but they couldn't hear anything. It was clear from the look on Mack's otherwise taciturn face that they had not captured "it," that elusive and ethereal quality that made a record spring to life the minute the needle hit.

"Was it me?" Ray asked Curley. "Did I screw up?"

"It was all of us," Shifty said. "I think even Mack's pooped."

They had departed the Richmond show and headed straight for Charlotte, where Mack had booked some studio time. He was in a rush to get his new lineup and their new sound on record as soon as possible. But the schedule, following three months of life on the road, had taken its toll. Curley lit his smoke and passed one to Shifty. Ray declined.

"I still think it was me," he insisted, "I swear I think I messed up."

"You were fine, Ray," Curley consoled, "Mack just knows that we can all do it better than that. That's all."

Mack emerged from the control room looking tired and pissed off. He sat angrily in his chair and adjusted his mike.

"All right," he snarled, "let's do it again. We're paying extra for this one, so get it right."

Mack counted off the number with nods of his head and the band jumped in dutifully. Ray was tense, Curley and Shifty were so tired they could hardly keep their eyes open, and Mack was in a horrendous mood due to the extra money the technician was requiring him to fork over for the second take. All in all it was a pedestrian effort at best, and no one was any more satisfied with the second version than they had been with the first.

When the song ended, they all looked at each other and began to laugh the hysterical laughter of the truly tired. The man in the booth was surprised at the joyousness of the mood, he had expected Mack to dicker with him for another shot.

"Well, Hoop," Mack called, "how was that one?" The sarcasm caused the band to crack up again.

"Was it a keeper?" asked Shifty. Mack shook his head in resignation.

"This was my fault, boys," he admitted, "none of us is in the right mood to record. And as I learned from the Briar Hoppers, there is no use even trying any more if the mood ain't there. Hey, Hoop?"

"Yeah?"

"How about letting us come back tomorrow and try this thing again? Everybody knows you charge too much for this outdated equipment anyway, so how about it?"

Sam Hooper blushed self-consciously.

"I got one opening, Mack," he said, "for an hour starting tomorrow morning at ten. I'll give it to you for half price."

Mack grumbled. He looked at his watch and saw that it was already getting close to three in the morning.

"Can you make it noon?"

"Noon? Aw, c'mon, Mack, I'm booked solid for the next three days and...."

"Now, Hoop, don't make me remind you about who it was that sent the Delmore Brothers your way. I'd hate to pull rank on you, ol' pal, but I will. Now this song can't be no more than three minutes tops, you can work us, can't you?" Hoop sighed again and rubbed his eyes with his palms.

"All right, all right. Tomorrow from twelve to twelve thirty but not one minute more and you're paying me for the whole hour. Deal?"

"Yeah, yeah, Hoop. You got a deal. Let's go get some sleep, boys." Mack turned to Curley and Shifty. "And I mean sleep, dammit."

Curley and Shifty eyed each other and smiled. This was one night that Mack needn't worry about any extracurricular activities from them---they were as tired as Mack.

ဆ

"Hot dog!" Curley exclaimed. "We ain't never sounded better than that!"

Uncle Mack cheerfully agreed. It was a smoldering, solid effort that easily eclipsed anything they had attempted the night before. Even Sam Hooper was smiling.

"That'll get on the radio," he declared from the booth. "Hoop guarantees it!"

"You hear that boys?" Mack asked. "We have got Sam Hooper's good as gold guarantee that we will be on the radio. And I agree!"

The fitful rest of the night before had turned everybody's playing around, and the wax cylinder proved it. Sam Hooper promised to have the records pressed in a week, an amazing turn around time that showed everyone that his prediction had been serious. Uncle Mack and the boys packed their gear and said their goodbyes to Hoop.

Back at the hotel, Curley and Shifty cracked open beers to celebrate the successful recording session while Ray and Mack worked out the week's pay. Curley took his money and counted it. He started to complain, but realized that Mack had dutifully deducted the bail money he had forked over in Virginia for him. Curley counted out the money that he would need for food, smokes and, of course, drink, and handed the rest over to Ray.

"Give this to Mom," he instructed. Uncle Mack's baleful laughter surprised Curley, who wasn't aware that he had said anything amusing.

"Give it to her yourself," Mack bawled. Curley looked quizzically at his boss.

"I would," he said, "except I ain't gonna see her and Ray is."

"That's where you're wrong, Curley-boy," Mack said with a knowing smile, "not only are you going to see your mama, but we are *all* going to see the venerable Mrs. Norris." Curley decided to forgo the vocabulary lesson and find out instead what Mack was driving at. He registered the bemused look on his brother's face.

"What's goin' on here?" he asked.

"We got a job, Curley," Mack said. "And dang if it isn't right near your hometown. I believe you have heard of a place called Stanley?"

"Yeah. Yeah, I've heard of it. But there ain't no place to play there, Mack. That place is nothing."

"Maybe, but there is a place to play and Uncle Mack's Traveling Band is to provide the musicality. There's a man there, a man by the name of Jim Patton. He's a state representative, a good Democrat, and an old friend of mine. He's asked that we put on a personal appearance for him and his campaign down there and I have agreed. And, in order to cut our costs for the favor, your brother has been kind enough to arrange our accommodations. The whole band is being put up in the Norris household for an entire week. What do you think of that?"

Curley gulped. The thought of going home, with the band, seemed awful to him. The way his mother had treated him when he had returned to try and patch things up with Ray, not to mention his shady reputation throughout the county...all these things surrounding his boss's ears was not a pleasing proposition.

"Aw, Mack. Can't we stay someplace else? I mean, I got a wonderful family and all, but...."

"But you can't get away with your usual shit?" asked Mack rhetorically.

"Well," Curley said sheepishly, "something like that, yeah."

"Jesus, Curley," Ray said, "this is a chance for us to see Mom and you're worried you won't be able to get drunk? That's terrible."

"It's not just that, Ray...."

"I thought you'd jump at the opportunity," Mack pondered, "this attitude surprises me."

"Huh?"

"Well, you're going back home as a member of a successful musical outfit that is in the area at the request of a state representative. Seems to me that would be just the kind of homecoming a man would dream of. Don't it you, Shifty?"

"Why, hell yeah, Mack! I'd love to go home and look like a big shot someday." Mack nodded. Curley suddenly began to get new pictures in his head. Pictures of all those nay-sayers and doubters who would have to watch him pull into town as a lead guitar player for such an important and influential man as Mack, a man with such lofty connections. He could see the other men in town green with envy and the ladies lavender with lust.

"I hadn't thought of it that way, Mack," he admitted. "And, come to think of it, it would be awfully good to see Mom and Grandpa and my brothers."

"I thought so. And if any of your old pals come around, well, I guess I could even pretend that I was a proud member of Uncle Curley's Traveling Band. How would that be?"

Curley's eyes protruded from their sockets and his face brightened with the thought.

"Really, Mack? You'd do that for me?"

"Sure I would."

Curley smiled at Ray. They would go home, after all. And Curley determined to enter the city limits with garland and pomp, like a prodigal genius who was willing to lower himself just to prove he wasn't inflated with his success. This time he would return on his own terms and in his own way. And he would leave them with footprints across their horizon and tears in their eyes.

And, of course, with a smile on their face.

CHAPTER THIRTY-EIGHT

Jimmy and Francis darted across the living room floor and cowered behind their mother when Mack began flailing on his banjo. Curley, embarrassed by his brother's timidity, chastised them instead for their rudeness. Mack chuckled and told Curley to hush, that he supposed even he would be a little afraid at the sight of this big, bald white man playing the strange instrument. Eunice liked Mack, his manners, his easy-going ways, and the respect that he obviously commanded from both of her older sons. She was impressed with the trouble Mack took to see to it that he and his band were no trouble, even reprimanding Ray once for asking her to "fetch" him a glass of water.

"Your legs broke?" he had asked. Ray had blushed and gone for the water himself. Eunice quietly hoped that this man also was able to keep an almost parental watch over her boys, Curley especially. Maybe Mack Crowe could turn Curley's life back around. She had watched the man like a hawk in the week since they had arrived, and she had found no evidence of drinking or partying at all.

Lorenzo had not wanted to like Mack. The thought of a grown man who had never held down a "real" job in his life made him sick. It was all well and good to have a dream, but music was a hobby, not a vocation. Still, Mack's deference towards Lorenzo had melted some of the ice, and at no time in the week had Mack ever thought to impose his own will on the household, something that Lorenzo had expected from a white man and an "artist." He had even taken out his own fiddle and accompanied the group on a song or two, and Mack's effusive praise ("I see where you boys get your talent from") had not caused Lorenzo any pain, either.

The children were another matter. They were evenly divided in their attitudes. Houston and L.D. thought that Mack and Shifty might well be the most entertaining and wonderful human beings they had ever met, what with their stories about all the places they had seen and all the radio people they had met. Francis and Jimmy were simply terrified of the man. Where was his hair? What was that thing he played? Why did he have to sing so loud? But all in all, Uncle Mack and his Traveling Band received a very cordial reception and glowing reviews from the Norris home.

Mack put his banjo away, partly to placate the children and partly to save his voice and fingers for tomorrow night's rally.

"Boys, I say we call it a night musically. Tomorrow is a big day and I want us to sound as good as we can."

Curley, Ray and Shifty all put their instruments away dutifully. Curley and Shifty had eyed each other all night, each desperately wanting a taste of hootch before they turned in. When Eunice and Lorenzo announced that they were going to bed, Curley and Shifty made their way quickly out into the yard to put away their flask of whiskey. Mack cautioned them not to stay out too late and not to have too much to drink. Shifty grumbled that, in this town, that wouldn't be a problem.

"This is the last of the stuff, Curley," he said as they began to drink, "we've gotta find some more before I go crazy."

"Yeah, I know. Mom's been watching me like a hawk, and Mack's so worried about goin' over good tomorrow that all we've done is rehearse. I'll get away tomorrow, either before or after the rally, and round us up some good stuff. I promise."

Curley was embarrassed that he couldn't just announce that he was going to get some liquor for himself and Shifty. It made him look and feel childlike in front of the older and, at least in Curley's eyes, more experienced bass player. Shifty had complained incessantly for three solid days about having to ration the alcohol, and it was shaming Curley that he couldn't do something about it.

"Do they make good stuff around here?" asked Shifty.

"Oh, yeah," Curley assured him, "there's some really good moonshiners in this area. I'll make a point of getting the very best that I can. You'll be impressed, I can tell you that much."

"Don't tell me," barked Shifty as he pulled the last drop from the flask with his lips, "*show* me."

Curley nodded absently. Shifty excused himself and turned back to the house. Curley sat outside, dreaming about the next day's big political rally and hoping that everyone who had ever said anything bad about him in Cramerton would be there to choke on their crow.

The wooden stage was a sight to behold. It stood up off of the ground and was covered in flowing banners and bunting, adorned with pictures of President Roosevelt and Senator Patton. Flags waved in the chilly autumn air, and people young and old flocked back and forth with Patton buttons and hats, shaking hands and discussing the troubles at home and abroad. The band had set up their amplifiers and instruments earlier than usual, as part of Uncle Mack's nervous energy. Mack seemed more worried about their reception than Curley had ever seen him before, a sight which was not reassuring to Curley and Ray, both of whom were consumed with their own homecoming jitters. Mack knew that his friend was in a tight race, and he was convinced that, if he and his band sounded bad, the election would be lost. It was silly, of course. This election was revolving around the darkening skies over Europe, and over whether or not America had a role to play in that conflict. Patton was controversial because of his stance that yes, America owed it to the rest of the world to help stop the German menace---an attitude that was not playing well in Cramerton or the surrounding areas.

Most voters were only concerned with putting a stop to the Depression, and they could care less how many bombs were falling on Britain. But the Senator's stance was offset by his adherence to the party, and everyone knew that a Republican would have a hard time winning in the South, no matter what his Democratic opponent thought about the war. Patton had made a concerted effort to tie his opponent to Herbert Hoover, claiming that, like the former president, the Republican candidate was more interested in fishing than securing jobs and relief for the people of Gaston County.

Curley was impressed with the Senator's grace and easy demeanor. Patton had shaken hands with each member of the band and personally placed a "Patton for Senate" button on their shirts. He had embraced Mack and thanked him for coming, while Mack assured the politician that he and his "boys" were going to do everything they could to help him pull out a victory.

"Well, I appreciate all the help I can get. This election is very important for our state. Very important."

"Ah, you'll win," Curley said comfortably, "I ain't never heard of a Republican winning in these parts."

"I hope you're right," Senator Patton said glumly. "But the war seems to have scared people around here."

"Why?" asked Ray. "It don't involve us."

"That's what everyone wants to think," said Patton, "but we will have war here. It's just a matter of time."

The band decided to ignore the gloomy prediction. All of them, except probably for Uncle Mack, were young enough to fight, and they knew it. They agreed quietly, each to himself, that it would be better to concentrate on the music and not on world affairs today.

It was around two o'clock when the show started. A crowd of well over two hundred had gathered, and Senator Patton worked them with as much skill and delicacy as the band. Uncle Mack and his boys rose to the occasion, flying through their set and several encores without a glitch, impressing everyone within earshot, including Minnie and Essie Mae Abernathy.

CHAPTER THIRTY-NINE

"I can't believe you talked me into this."

Curley growled from the passenger's side of the car that Uncle Mack had allowed them to borrow. His brow was furrowed angrily and his fists were clenched at his side, causing him to look a great deal like his father. Over and over since the trip began he had repeated the phrase, like a mantra, "I can't believe you talked me into this." Ray ignored his brothers pleas, they meant nothing to him anyway. He could feel for Curley, he supposed, if he tried hard enough. But the truth was that he couldn't tear his mind away, didn't want to tear his mind away, from the image he was artfully creating of the coming evening. In fact, he immersed himself so thoroughly in his daydreams that he only occasionally caught what his brother was saying.

"Huh?" he asked.

"Jesus, Ray, the least you could do is act like you give a shit about the fact that I'm stuck with motor mouth for the next several hours. That is the very least that you should do."

"Maybe it won't be so bad," offered Ray. "Who knows? You might end up having a really good time with Essie Mae."

"You mean Assie Mae?" scoffed Curley with a nasty laugh. "I doubt it. Besides, I should be going out with Minnie tonight."

Ray whipped his head to look at Curley.

"How do you figure that?" he asked impatiently.

"Oh, come on Ray. Minnie wanted to go to that shucking with me and you know it. You just asked her before I got the chance."

"Bullshit!" Ray exploded. "God, Curley, you are the most arrogant piece of work I have ever met in my whole life. Really, you take the cake."

"You know I'm right. She wanted me to ask her."

"She did not," Ray insisted. "That just ain't so."

"You wanna make a wager on it?" Curley asked slyly. Ray studied his brother's face. The truth was that he most certainly did not want to place a bet on it, but he had been backed into a corner now, a corner that his honor and his own arrogance would not allow him to slink away from.

"Absolutely," Ray said confidently. "What do ya wanna bet?"

"Five dollars. I'll bet you five dollars that Minnie Abernathy would rather go to this corn shucking with me."

"All right, you're on. So, how do we find out who she wants to go with?" Curley frowned in thought for a minute and then perked up.

"I got it!" he cried. "I know what we'll do. You'll wait outside somewhere when we get near her house. Then I'll go in and tell her that you were sick and couldn't make it. Then I'll ask her if she'd like to go with me. If she says yes, then I reckon we'll know who she really has the hots for. Whaddaya say?"

"What about Essie Mae?"

"Screw Assie Mae," Curley asserted, "neither one of us wants her. So? You up for it?"

Ray sighed.

"Yeah, Curley. But you're gonna look really dumb, and you won't have anybody to blame 'cept yourself. You remember that."

"Oh, I will. I'll remember it."

ℬℭ

"That's too bad," Minnie said. Curley thought he detected a slight bit of insincerity in her voice, as if she were saying what she knew she should, but the words carried no deeper meaning, no hidden dissatisfaction. Curley's hopes began to rise. He had dropped Ray off behind a patch of bushes within sight of Granny Abernathy's small, brick home. Then he had proceeded into the drive and up the steps, planning his speech. He told Minnie that Ray was sick, just like they had agreed.

"I hope it's not serious," Essie Mae said.

"Oh, no," Curley said, "I think it is probably just a bug or something. He'll probably be better by morning."

"Well, it was nice of you to come all the way out here to tell me," Minnie said, positioning herself by the door as if she were about to see Curley out. "Give your brother my best." Curley took a deep breath and prepared for the payoff. He realized that, if his hunch was wrong and Minnie did not want to go out with him, then he and Ray would both be left without dates. He wondered if that thought had yet struck Ray.

"Well, I don't wanna leave you without a date at such short notice," he said. "I was wondering if maybe you'd like to go with me?" Minnie seemed taken by surprise and was suddenly speechless. Essie Mae also looked shocked---shocked and angry. This was supposed to be her date, not Minnie's.

"No. No, thank you. You and Essie Mae go on by yourselves and have a good time. There is plenty that I can do here tonight."

Essie Mae pouted and shook her head.

"Nope," she said firmly, "I don't wanna go. You and Curley go on. I'll stay here with Granma."

Minnie hesitated for a minute.

"Go on," Essie Mae barked quickly. "And ya'll have fun." She shot Curley a deadly and spurned look and excused herself from the room.

"Well?" Curley asked.

"I'll get my coat," Minnie said.

They got in the car and drove away. Ray tasted the dust cloud that engulfed the shrubs where he was hiding, and he stood just in time to see Curley and Minnie race off towards the corn-shucking. He jumped and down, screaming and cursing, until his wind gave out and he collapsed furiously to the ground. Minnie did not understand why Curley had driven away with his horn honking and a huge smile across his face. She only knew that he was more handsome than anything she had ever seen when he smiled like that.

And that was enough for her.

CHAPTER FORTY

The soft moonlight, glowing warmly against the autumn sky and illuminating their love and their laughter, shown down upon them like the glow of a candle held aloft by the Great Spirit for their path. They moved against the music and with the gentle wind, talking with people absently and crouching closer and closer to each other as the night progressed. Soon, they were walking hand in hand, showing off as a couple. Minnie didn't dance, she said she didn't know how and wasn't about to learn in front of him, so they perched themselves at a picnic table and watched the others boogie, snickering and admiring, holding their own counsel in all things, like the last two members of an exclusive club.

Curley was attentive, something that was new to Minnie and to him. He was used to being chased, and he was accustomed to being waited on, not the opposite. Minnie was no longer cold and distant, but she remained properly reserved. She marveled when he offered to go and get her some tea, and she reveled in his new-found chivalry when he waited on her cue for every move that he made. For the first time Curley was on a date, a real date. This was not a woman he had brought home from a gig, not some girl that he was using for wheels. And to top it all off, he knew, from her body language and her demeanor, that he was *not* going to get lucky tonight, and yet he was being nicer, and having a better time, than with any woman he could remember. The experience excited and unnerved him.

"So, is Curley your real name?" she asked as they watched the dancing continue.

"Oh, no," he laughed, "that's just my In, uh, my other name. My nickname. My real name is Russell. Russell Deveroeux Norris."

"Russell?" She sat in thought for a minute. "I like that name, it sounds very nice. Do you mind if I call you Russell? Instead of Curley, I mean?"

"No, I don't guess I do. That's what my Mom calls me. She hasn't called me Curley in years."

"Then I'll call you Russell," she said. Curley loved the remark, savored it, because it seemed to imply that they would see each other again.

"How did you get the name Minnie?" he asked. Minnie's face darkened and she seemed to draw away from him.

"I don't know," she said quietly. "My mom and dad aren't around much."

"Oh? I'm sorry, Minnie. I didn't mean...."

"That's okay. You didn't know. They're just troubled souls. That's what Grandma says. My dad drinks a lot and my mom....well, I don't really know what her story is." Curley felt a lump growing in his throat. He cursed himself for his over-sentimentality. He also realized how lucky he was to have a Mom like Eunice.

"My Dad's dead," he said. "That's why me and Ray play music. I mean, that and because we really like it. But we've been supporting the family for years now." Minnie smiled.

"What will you do when the music stops?" she asked. Curley started to answer her and then paused, realizing that he had never really thought about that. Not even Eunice had ever asked him that question, or even anything like it. Nor had Lorenzo.

"Whaddaya mean?" he asked. "Why would the music stop?"

"I didn't mean any harm," Minnie said, sensing his discomfort, "I just wondered if their was anything else that you had ever thought about doing. You know, just in case."

"Nope, I ain't never thought about doing anything else. Truth is, I don't know how to do anything else. I'm a musician and that's it. Is there anything wrong with that?"

"Oh, no. That's not at all what I meant." Curley pasted a quick, toothy grin across his face.

"Why are we talkin' so serious? I thought we were just supposed to have fun tonight."

"So we are," Minnie agreed. Curley stood and took her hand as the band began playing a slow song. Curley couldn't help but mentally critique the group's performance. They were okay, he thought, but they were no Uncle Mack's Traveling Band.

"Russell," Minnie protested, "I really can't dance."

"You don't have to dance, this is a slow song. All you have to do is move around in a circle real slow." Curley paused and looked deeply into her brooding eyes. "And you have to do that in my arms." He motioned for her to stand. He caught his breath as she hesitated--he felt like so much was riding on this one dance.

"Please," he said softly. Minnie looked back into his eyes, searching for any hint of mockery or deceit. Finding none, she stood and allowed him to lead her out onto the floor. She stepped awkwardly into his arms and felt the heat of his body seer through her cotton dress. He gently placed his hand at the small of her back and tugged her against him. Minnie felt the electric jolt of an untapped sensuality release inside of her. Curley felt her body tighten self-consciously.

"It's all right," he whispered, "I've got you." Minnie's tension eased and she laid her head down on his shoulder. Curley allowed the scent of her hair drench his senses.

"Don't let go, Russell," she said. "Just don't let go." Curley laid his head against hers and sighed. He bit back the fear welling within him and just enjoyed this new intoxication.

ৼ

The porch light was glowing, and the curtains moved back and forth every few seconds as Essie Mae tried to get a peek at what was happening. Curley stood across from Minnie, smoking his cigarette and telling her about most of his adventures in Raleigh. Her eyes filled with amazement and amusement, and she laughed at his stories. Curley loved to watch her laugh. She would throw her head back and make a loud, happy sound and then catch herself and toss her eyes down on her shoes, clearly berating herself for her lack of discretion.

"You have a great laugh," he said. He regretted it, of course, because the compliment only made her blush violently, as if he had grabbed her cheeks and viciously pinched them. "I'm sorry, I didn't mean to make you go all red like that."

"I guess I'm just not used to hearing those kinds of things."

"Huh? I guess the people in Stanley are dumber than I thought. I figured I'd have to get in line to say anything nice to you."

"Not hardly."

They stood quietly now, neither one sure how to proceed. In other circumstances Curley would have invited himself in, or at least gotten himself a good kiss before heading home. But this girl, like this night, was different.

"When are you leaving town?" asked Minnie. The thought had not struck Curley until this very moment.

"Next week sometime, I guess. I haven't really had that on my mind."

More silence; more confusion. Finally Curley summoned his nerve.

"Minnie," he asked, "could I see you again?"

"I'd like that. I really would. But Russell, I don't wanna be another girlfriend of yours. And you probably have one in every city."

"Well, not *every* city." He smiled, but she was staring sadly at her feet. "Look, Minnie, I was only pullin' your leg. I ain't no saint. Never have been. But I'm a good person. I wouldn't do you like that. Honest, I wouldn't." Curley wasn't surprised that he said the lines, he had, after all, said them many times before. The shock came in the realization that, this time, he meant the words. Curley heard the distinct sound of a door slamming in his mind and wondered if Minnie had heard it, too.

"Would you like to go to church with me tomorrow night?"

"Church?!" Curley asked. What kind of a date was that? Minnie looked up and straight at him.

"Yes, Russell, church. Tomorrow is Sunday, after all. If you have other plans...."

"No! No, I do not. And yes, I would love to go to church with you tomorrow."

"Will this get you in trouble with your brother?"

"Ray? Heck, no. He shouldn't have gone and got sick."

"Then I'll see you tomorrow. Around eight in the morning?"

"Eight o'clock sharp. Goodnight, Minnie."

"Goodnight, Russell."

She leaned in and gave him a small peck on his cheek. Then she turned and disappeared into the house. Curley leapt from the porch, bypassing all the steps (those were only for people *not* in love) and ran to the car.

In love?

Curley paused by the door. Is that what he thought? Is that what he was? In love? He opened the car door and slid inside. He cranked the car and pulled out of the drive. As he hit the highway he noticed that everything seemed to be going by him in slow motion. Was this love?

Curley decided to put the thoughts away. He didn't know what it was and he was damn sure not going to ruin it by thinking. Feeling and thinking had always been bitter enemies in the artist, and he knew which side he was rooting for this time. All he knew for sure was that

Minnie, this one woman, had managed to give him the same thrill, the same high, that it normally took a room full of applauding people to provide. One woman, he thought, with the same power of a sold-out and adoring audience. That was amazing and frightening and wonderful.

He didn't know if it was love.

He didn't care.

It felt good and it felt right.

And Curley Norris, Russell to some, was going with it, full tilt.

CHAPTER FORTY-ONE

Curley bristled against the prickly wool pants and the stiff dress shirt. The tie seemed determined to choke off all of his air and the shoes squeezed his toes with a malicious spitefulness. He wiggled and maneuvered, trying vainly to find some position, any position, that he could equate with comfort. Every now and then Grandma Abernathy shot him a withering glance and he settled down. Minnie tried to look around her grandmother's imposing figure to offer Curley a reassuring smile, but each time she did she felt the old woman's hands reach down and pinch her. Minnie recoiled and looked up to see her grandma frowning at her, as if to remind her that good girls did not smile in church. Curley was silently furious at the seating arrangement, with Grandma perched protectively between him and Minnie, but he knew better than to argue the point. It was, of course, a mortal sin to be even remotely sensual in God's house, and he was not about to break that rule on the very first day he met Grandma.

The preacher had worked himself up into a quality sweat of spirit, berating and cajoling the congregation to reach higher and act better. He reminded them that their nation had never been as low as it was now, nor the world in which they lived so dangerous. He warned against the evils of snuff, cigarettes, alcohol and dancing. Curley wondered if there was anything that he himself enjoyed that hadn't already been pronounced off limits. Just as the question popped into his head the preacher erupted into a tirade against the pleasures of the flesh, and Curley silently decided that, Minnie's affections not withstanding, this was not the kind of church for him. Still, it did provide the perfect excuse for his second date with Minnie. A date, that is, if only Grandma would get out of the way.

The discomfort had started before the preaching did, as Curley braved the stares and the whispers that accompanied his entrance into the church. There had even been some whispering and a few daring souls managed a barely concealed point or two. He had reached out for Minnie's hand, but she cautiously shuttled it away, knowing that would only intensify the speculation. He was the darkest colored person to ever enter the His Holiness Church of Stanley, and his mere presence as the escort of a good white girl bordered on the scandalous. Minnie knew the politics of the church well enough to predict what would be said of her: because all the local Christians knew the story of her parents, they had done everything but actually lay money down on how the girls would turn out. Minnie's arrival on the arm of an Indian would no doubt bring great joy to many of the people who had for so long been predicting her (or Essie Mae's) fall from grace. She shuddered to think what they would say when they learned of Curley's occupation.

Curley noticed the looks, but he had become almost desensitized to them by now. There was nothing new or threatening about them, so he spent more time taking in the environment of the church, a place he had not been to in years. The first thing that his eyes came down upon was the picture of Jesus that hung on the minister's podium. Jesus looked so clean, and so very, very white. Jesus was pale to the point of translucency, and his blonde hair and blue eyes made him seem so foreign, so unattainable. Curley couldn't help but wonder, "Is this the same Jesus that my Grandpa prays to? The same Jesus that my Grandpa has told me so much about?" Curley had once heard Lorenzo refer to Jesus Christ as the greatest warrior the world had ever seen. Of course Lorenzo had reminded the boy that Christ was a warrior for peace, but Curley looked intently at the picture of the white man's Jesus and wondered at how that man looked like he could never hold his own against anybody.

Curley also made note of the fact that the white man's Jesus had the hair of an Indian. Well, almost. Jesus's hair was a sandy blonde, but it hung just below his shoulders, the way the traditionals wore their hair back on the reservation. Curley knew that the missionaries and preachers on and around Qualla did not approve of their hair, so he wondered what they would think of this picture of their Lord.

Then there was the eyes and the gentle halo that spread from around the back of Christ's head. Curley thought it made him look so passive, so malleable. That was not the way Curley thought Jesus should look. He had always imagined Jesus as a real take-charge kind of guy, the kind of guy that you always wanted firmly between you and trouble.

But this Jesus just looked soft, like his hands would feel as smooth and silky as a woman's. Curley found it very disappointing and not at all inspiring.

Curley was deep in thought when he realized that the preacher had announced the morning's first prayer. He stood with the others and bowed his head respectfully. The preacher started the prayer, "Our dearest and most gracious Heavenly Father, we pray that you will...."

Then followed the "Yes, Lord....." and the church seemed to burst with requests and announcements. Curley raised his head and peeked to confirm what he thought: everyone was praying at the same time. And as if that wasn't confusing enough, they were all praying at the top of their lungs. Not wanting to be left out or appear less holy, Curley began to pray aloud himself. But it was no use, because he soon realized that he was praying for people he didn't know and things which meant nothing to him, picking up cues from the people around him. He beseeched the Lord to help his poor Uncle Henry, but then he realized that he didn't even have an Uncle Henry. That was the man behind him. He gave up when he realized that he was asking God to help him with the stubborn corns on his feet. That was Grandma Abernathy. Curley bit his lip and remained silent as the competition rose to a fever pitch and then ebbed as the preacher, miraculously throwing his voice over the congregation's, called "Amen." Curley thought it would have been more appropriate to have called "Time out," but he kept his opinion to himself. Then they all sat down at once and craned their necks to the pulpit, where the good reverend continued down his list of things that felt really good but were also clearly forbidden. Curley fought the urge to sleep and laugh successfully, and when the service finally ended he began the dance with Grandma Abernathy over who walked closest to Minnie.

In the yard of the church Curley, following the lead of some of the other men in the church, lit a cigarette. He saw the anger in Grandma Abernathy's face, but decided that it was too late to go back now and he was not about to waste a perfectly good smoke. Several women who looked to be the same age as he and Minnie came up seeking introductions. Curley nodded, bowed and smiled all in good order and with the greatest charm he could get going. Essie Mae had been kind enough to lead Grandma Abernathy back to the car, where they were waiting to go home for dinner. Curley quickly grew tired of all the forced politeness and began walking Minnie towards the car.

"Minnie? Minnie Abernathy, you wait a second!" came the cry.

Curley saw a clean-shaven young man sprinting towards them, his tie flapping in the breeze and his Bible clutched close to his side. Curley also could not miss the broad smile that came across Minnie's face when she saw the man behind the voice. He felt a pang of jealousy itch along his spine.

"Minnie, were you goin' to leave without introducin' me to your friend here?"

"Well, Michael...."

"Shame on you," he said. "You just ought to be ashamed."

"The name is Curley Norris," Curley said, stepping between Minnie and the fresh-faced man. "Pleasure to meet ya." Minnie moved around Curley and put her hand on his elbow.

"Michael Smith, I'd like for you to meet Russell Norris." Curley blushed, he had forgotten that Minnie did not like calling him Curley.

"Well, it is nice to meet you, Russell. Do you mind if I call you Russell?"

"Not at all," answered Curley, thrown off balance by the man's kindness and apparent respect.

"Are you from around here?" asked Michael. "Are you from Stanley?"

"I'm from Cramerton. Just up the road a piece."

"Yeah, I know it," he said. "I have some family in Cramerton myself. What brings you to our church?"

"Minnie," Curley answered flatly, wrapping his arm around her waist. Minnie smiled uncomfortably and eased her way out of the embrace. Michael smiled in a friendly way.

"Well it was good to have you here, and I hope that you will come back to visit with us again. I'm the assistant pastor here at His Holiness. If you ever need anything just let me know." With that he extended his hand, gave Curley a firm shake, and disappeared into the crowd of worshippers to shake more hands. Minnie walked coldly away towards the car without a word. Curley followed, wondering what he had done wrong.

಄

"He's in love with you," he said, trying to force a note of casualness into his voice. It didn't work.

"That's wrong. No, it's more than wrong, it's downright silly. Michael Smith is one of the finest men around here, but he's the assistant pastor and he is engaged to be married to a woman in Charlotte. He is most certainly *not* in love with me, Russell."

"I been around a lot more than you have, Minnie, and that boy is after you is all. I can tell these things."

"Are you sayin' that I'm too dumb to know?"

"Good God, no," he said, "but sometimes women can't see the truth. 'Specially about men." Minnie laughed.

"That's funny, Russell," she said, "because that sounds exactly like the little talk Grandma had with me today while we was doin' the dinner dishes. She seems to think that I am blind to the obvious where you are concerned."

"What?" Curley protested. "Why in the world would she think that, Minnie? I thought I was very nice to her all morning long. Why, even when she plopped herself down in between the two of us I was nice to her. Didn't say a word."

"Yeah, I know. Grandma thinks you're charming. That's the problem. She says a woman should never, ever trust a charming man. Plus, you're an Indian. And you're a musician."

"I don't see what in the hell my being an Indian has to do with anything. I am just as good as any white suitor who's come to court you, I'll guarantee you that right here and now."

"Russell, the point here is that Michael is not after me. That's what we were talking about." Minnie had changed the subject quickly. She did not want to get into a fight with Curley, and she did not want to hurt him, and she suspected that if he knew the vehemence with which her grandmother had objected, both would occur. She was also afraid, having only known him for two days, that he would be scared away. And, although she was determined to play it cool, she was becoming very fond of her Indian musician friend.

"All right," Curley conceded, not wanting to ruin what was left of their afternoon by arguing. He pulled his coat a little tighter around him, the late November sun was sinking fast and with it a frigid night was beginning to blow its frosty breath across the fields. "If you say so."

"I say so," she added emphatically. They sat huddled together on the porch steps. Curley wanted to throw his arm around her, but after the reception that move had received in the parking lot of the church he was uncertain. He hated the feeling. Normally, he was always quite certain about how to proceed with a woman, when and how to move next were not questions her frequently agonized over. But Minnie was different, and he was so confused around her, his head feeling filled with a thick, consuming fog. She nudged a little closer to him, sending him more strange signals. Did she want his arm around her in private and not in public?

"Are you embarrassed to be with me?" he asked suddenly. Minnie started from the question and looked carefully at Curley, trying to gage his seriousness.

"Why would you ask me that?" she asked sadly.

"I don't know," he answered, shuffling his feet, "it's just a feeling I get, I guess."

"If I was ashamed of you, do you think I would have asked you to come to church with me? This house and that church, they're my world. And I've taken you into both. Why would you think I was embarrassed?"

"Well, you didn't want my arm around you in front of that Michael guy today. And you pushed my hand away this morning when we was walking into the church. Now it seems like you want me to be closer to you. I don't get it. If it's because I'm Indian then I reckon you just better say so now, 'cause I ain't got no idea how I could stop bein' one. And I wouldn't wanna even if I *did* know how to change. So, if that's it, then you just need to say so right here and now. There won't be no hard feelins."

"Look, Russell, I...."

"And that's another thing," he added hastily, "why won't you call me Curley like everybody else? Curley's my Indian name and I hafta admit that I'm kinda partial to it by now."

"Russ....uh, I asked you and you said you didn't mind if I called you Russell. And it ain't because it's Indian, it just sounds, well, I guess I thought it sounded like a kid."

"And a stooge," Curley reminded. Minnie smiled.

"You told me yourself that your mother doesn't call you anything but Russell. And she's Indian, right?"

"Yeah."

"But if you really mind and you really want me to call you Curley then...."

"Nah. You're right. I don't really mind. But what about all that stuff at your church today?"

"Russell, you just can't act like that in church. Why, even the married folks there don't ever touch one another in public. It would just make people talk."

"Yeah? Well, let 'em talk," he said dashingly, "I'm used to it."

"That's all well and good for you, Russell, but I prefer to give them as little to talk about as possible. Okay?"

"Sure, Minnie, but it seems silly to me. What they don't know for sure they're gonna make up anyhow. Trust me." He put his arm around her and smiled. "Besides, they're just jealous of us!"

"Us?" she repeated. "I didn't know there was an 'us.' Is there?"

"Why, sure there is, Minnie. I'd say we're as close to bein' an 'us' as I've ever been. You?"

"I'd say so. But Russell, the way I see it, if there's to be an us, there can't very well be any others. Do you follow me?" Curley gulped. He followed her perfectly.

"Yeah."

"If that ain't how you want it then you tell me now and don't go wastin' my time. Like you say, there'll be no hard feelins."

Curley sat silent for a minute. The road stretched before him again, with all its charms and pitfalls. Uncle Mack's Traveling Band would be puling up stakes and leaving town again in the next few days, and he could only imagine trying to remain faithful to a woman on the road. God, he could hardly remain true to himself some nights when the loneliness and the booze and the frustration mixed with a willing woman and an empty bed. Then there was the adrenalin with which to contend. When they had "killed 'em," as Uncle Mack phrased it, and left the stage with the roar of the audience and the feedback from the amps lingering in the air, Curley felt like a conqueror. And he usually turned his attention to killing a fifth of something and conquering a woman. He had a hard time envisioning just packing his guitar case and going back to the hotel room, spending the night winding down through a card game with Mack and Ray.

"Russell?" Minnie's voice pulled him back. He blinked and turned to her. He saw that she was tensely awaiting an answer.

"Minnie," he said, "I will be leaving in a couple of days to go back on the road with the band. Would you be willing to wait on me to get back?"

"What happens when you get back?" she asked. "What then?"

Curley thought for a minute.

"I guess I don't know," he said, being as honest as he could. "Music is all I know. The road is all I know. I guess I'd have to leave town again before long. But, I would come back again. And again and again." Curley smiled, but even in his own ears it sounded like a miserable offer. Minnie's brow had creased and her face had darkened with thought. Curley's first thought was that he had lost her and that he should say something quickly to pull her back. But anything else he could say, anything that would take the sting of uncertainty out of his life, would be a damn lie. So he sat in silence. Waiting.

"All right, Russell," she said finally. "If you really want me to, and if you meant what you said about you and me being an us, then yes."

"Yes?"

"I will wait."

The ridiculous look that crossed Curley's face caused Minnie to break out into laughter.

"Don't look so surprised," she said. "You're not that bad of a catch."

"Well, you're the first person who thought that," he said, not counting the still murky motives of one Lucy Jenkins. He pulled her close to him and gave her what he was sure was the biggest and most important hug of his life. He reached up with his hand and lifted her chin, looking seductively into her eyes as he did so. He leaned in slowly to kiss her, and he felt her warm and hungry mouth press eagerly to his own. They kissed for a few seconds, until Minnie realized that she was perilously close to losing control and pulled away.

"What?" he asked. "I do something wrong?"

"Oh, good God, no," she said through a giggle, "you did *nothing* wrong. I just thought we might better cool it a little." Curley fought off the urge to grin. He was disappointed that she had pulled away, but ecstatic that she had felt something hot enough to warrant cooling off.

"I better be gettin' home," he said. "I'd like to see you again before I leave. We'll be rehearsing all day tomorrow, but if I can sneak away in the evening.....would you be free?"

"Yes," she answered, "and I'd love to see you." She stood and placed a tender kiss on his cheek.

"Give my best to Ray," she teased, turning to go into the house.

"Oh, no. I'll save your best for me. But I will tell him that you said hello."

She gave him a sly wink and ducked into the house. Curley whirled gleefully around and skipped to the car. He shook his head, he was skipping a lot these last couple of days. And he was making many promises. He cranked the car and silently resolved that he was going to keep every one of them.

No matter how hard it was.

CHAPTER FORTY-TWO

Curley would have been willing to swear that women were able to instinctively smell the difference between a man with a commitment and one without.

And it was becoming more and more obvious which one was more attractive.

His battles against the flesh were a source of continuing amusement to the others in the band, who watched in stupefied amazement as he managed (sometimes just barely) to rebuff the advances of the women who flocked to their cars after the show. Curley would grumble and crawl into the car and beg Mack or Ray to rush him back to the hotel, where he usually tumbled headlong into a bottle and swam until he passed out. Curley had decided that, as long as he was unconscious, he couldn't break his promise to Minnie. He doubted that she would have approved of his methods, but at least the promise remained intact.

Mack and Ray tried their best to convince him that it was nothing more insidious than the fact that they were playing better than ever before. The respite and the home cooking they had acquired at the Norris home had done them all good, and their music reflected their freshness. But Curley thought their reasoning wreaked of bullshit. Yes, they were playing well now, and yes it was probably the best they had ever sounded. But that could not be enough to explain his newfound popularity. Curley had never lacked for female admirers before, but suddenly they seemed to be crawling out of the woodwork to get their hands on him.

"You'll be beatin' 'em off with a stick before too long," Mack had teased, but Curley thought there was some truth to the remark.

And it wasn't just that they could sniff out the guy with the girl in the group---they seemed to be able to gauge the seriousness of the relationship. Curley thought about how, when he supposedly "belonged" to Lucy Jenkins, he had not had this problem. That was a reflection, he decided, of the relationships of the chasers. They were probably attached, just as he had been, to people for the companionship of convenience. To rip apart a relationship so much like their own would not have been an accomplishment, it would have been a travesty. But the sight of a man clearly smitten with one of their sisters was too much to bear, and they seemed hell-bent on bringing this faceless sister to her knees. If they couldn't find true love, they weren't going to let someone else get it, either.

"Ya know how womenfolks'll go to the toilet together?" observed Uncle Mack. "Well, it's the same way with love. If they catch one of them veering away from the herd of unhappiness, why, they go after them full-tilt."

Curley couldn't have agreed more.

Meanwhile, Ray tried to count his own blessings where his brother was concerned. By all rights, he was still convinced, the lovely Minnie should have been his girl. But he was almost willing (although not quite) willing to dispel all bitterness for the half-victory that was Curley's newfound morality where women were concerned. His brother now seemed less likely to get stuck with a Lucy Jenkins or killed by a jealous boyfriend or husband. And, although the drinking was still excessive and often out of control, that was still progress.

On nights when Curley did not drink himself into oblivion, he and Ray sat up talking deep into the morning. With the lights out in the room, and only the tips of their cigarettes to illuminate them, Ray thought their relationship better than it had been for years. As pissed as he was at his own missed opportunity, Ray couldn't help but like Minnie for bringing his brother this far back to him. He listened with a mix of awe and incredulity as Curley weaved out his new fantasies, fantasies that were far more domestic than any Ray had ever heard from him. With his finger stabbing the air and his hand slashing through the blue smoke, Curley painted the perfect picture of what his home life would be.

"And she won't work," he declared. "'Cause she won't have to."

"Where are you gonna live?" asked Ray. Curley sat up on his elbow in the bed and thought for a minute.

"Where's the Grand Ole Opry?"

"Tennessee. Nashville, I think."

"Then there," Curley said as he laid back down. "We'll live in Nashville because by then the Norris Brothers will be the hottest goddamn ticket on the circuit." Ray chuckled.

"Well, at least I'm glad to see that Minnie hasn't pushed me out of the picture entirely."

"Of course not," Curley insisted. "Our music is what'll keep her from ever havin' to work. I'll get her the best maid in all of Tennessee. And you can live with us. Yeah, of course you will. And Mom and the boys and Grandpa and Grandma."

"Hafta have a big house," Ray noted.

"The damned biggest," Curley said. "It'll be the biggest damn house you've ever seen."

"What about kids?" Ray teased.

"Oh, I want a house full, same as Mom and Dad. Imagine that," he said, becoming extra animated again, "you'll be somebody's Uncle Ray!" The thought cracked both of them up.

"You're really crazy about this girl, aren't you, Curley?"

"Man, Ray, she's just not like any of the others. You know? I mean she's decent. Really decent. And, I don't know, something about the way she makes me feel. She makes me feel like tryin' to be better. She makes me feel decent, too, I guess."

"Hell, Curley, you're better'n decent. Always have been. You just kinda forgot is all. And you still need to quit that drinkin'."

"One sin at a time, Ray," Curley said with a grin, "one sin at a time."

ဆ

Curley stood in the wings at stage left, shifting on the balls of his feet and waiting for the Master of Ceremonies to quit his introduction and let them get on with the playing. Bristol, Tennessee was jumping for their annual Christmas Fair, and the boys and Uncle Mack had been contracted to be the main attraction. It was a cold December Sunday afternoon, and the good folks of the town had come straight from church to celebrate the coming of their savior. The Fair had begun in 1932 as a way to make the people forget their economic troubles, and had quickly turned into a tradition. Although the economy was no longer in the dire straits that it had been in the fair's inaugural year, the people of Bristol were unwilling to part with the fun.

For Curley and the rest of the band, it meant a big payday and a chance to play in a top-notch auditorium. Plus, they were contracted to do live shows at the local radio station, WOPI, for the next three nights, which meant even more money for fewer miles---a proposition that was pleasing to them all.

"So, in the spirit of Christmas and fellowship, let's give a warm Bristol welcome to this afternoon's entertainment-----Uncle Mack and his Traveling Band!!"

There was polite applause as they took their places on the stage. The stage lights seemed extra-hot here, Curley thought, as he sat upon the bale of hay that a local farmer had provided at Uncle Mack's specifications. The heat would make his ass itch even worse than it normally did from the hay. Curley found himself hoping that there wouldn't be many encores tonight. The money was guaranteed, so he wanted to get going as soon as possible.

"Thank ya'll for having us here at the famous Bristol Christmas Fair," Uncle Mack exclaimed. "We hope that we play something you like today."

"Us too!" came the reply from a drunken man in the crowd. Mack laughed heartily. Curley and Ray exchanged worried glances. The audience laughed in embarrassment. They assumed that these musicians, like all musician types, were worldly and urbane, and they sincerely hoped that their neighbor had not made them appear to backwards.

"Well," Uncle Mack said, "I'll send this out 'specially for you." He pointed to the man and winked good-naturedly. "'Cause I reckon you're gonna be my toughest customer tonight." The crowd laughed and clapped, and Uncle Mack flew into his banjo with a single-minded determination. Curley, Ray and Shifty quickly followed his lead, and by the second verse the crowd was enthusiastically clapping along, almost in rhythm. Someone near the front, a man, was singing along, off key but clearly having the time of his life.

"Ahhh, now do it, Curley-boy," Mack called, sending Curley into a guitar solo. His fingers flashed across the fret board, bending and coaxing the strings, making that piece of wood cry. When he was finished, Mack leapt back into the vocal, sounding like a man who had never seen a dollar bill in his life. Curley could almost hear Mack saying, "Sing for your supper boys," as he breathed life into the microphone.

"Now let me hear that harp," Mack bellowed passionately, "and I mean really give it to 'em good!"

Curley leaned in and attacked the harp, going down on it like a hungry man on a sweet and willing woman. His head shook from side to side, causing his naturally curly hair to shimmer and shake. Sweat dripped from his forehead and gathered as evidence on the floor in front of him. His excitement caused him to begin to speed up the tempo, at which point he heard Ray's boot heel thudding against the wooden stage floor. Curley raised his eyes and saw Ray smiling, but nodding to remind him that tempo was everything. Mack didn't seem to notice any of it, his eyes were closed and his head rocked back and forth on his shoulders. Finally, Curley lifted his head, relinquishing control of the crowd back to Mack, who played a torrid banjo solo before drawing the song to a rollicking and explosive ending. Ray and Curley burst into laughter, and the crowd squealed with delight.

"Easy on them hands," Mack teased, "it's a long show!" Then he turned his attention to the drunk. "Well?" he asked. The drunk staggered to his feet.

"Goddamn!" he said before collapsing back into his seat. The crowd again roared with applause and laughter. Mack turned to Curley and winked, and then they were off onto another song. Another story.

ಬ

Curley was wiping the sweat from his face when he noticed the MC out of the corner of his eye. Mack was cutting up with the audience and did not see the man. Curley nodded at Ray who turned and saw the man too. Curley thought the man looked as if he had seen a ghost. His face was ashen and his eyes were rimmed in red. He was waving a sheet of paper and motioning for Mack's attention. Uncle Mack, in full character, did not see the man at all and began the count for the next song.

"Mack? Hey, Mack!" Curley called. Mack turned his stunned gaze on Curley. This was an unacceptable breach of protocol.

"What Curley? What in the world is it?" Curley nodded his head towards the side of the stage, where the MC had now moved into full view of the audience. Mack saw him and waved him over.

"Everything all right?" he asked.

"No," came the man's terse reply. "May I use the microphone?"

"Sure," Mack said, raising himself from his own hay bale and standing aside for the shaken MC.

"Thank you," the man whispered as he moved past Mack. He cleared his throat and leaned into the mike.

"Ladies and gentlemen, I am afraid that I have some very terrible news," he said, the hand holding the yellow sheet of paper visibly trembling. Curley leaned his guitar against the hay and sat forward. "I just received word from Eddie at the radio station." The man stopped again, clearly trying to hold fast to his composure. "It seems, uh, that is, well......ladies and gentlemen, the Japanese have bombed us."

There was a pained gasp from the crowd. Ray looked at Curley, who looked at Uncle Mack, who stood straight but stricken, his mouth hanging ajar. Curley heard the frustrated questions, "Why?", "How?", fly through the otherwise stagnant air. It seemed that everyone had just stopped breathing. Curley remembered Senator Patton and his dark prediction of a month before.

"They bombed...uh, I believe it is called Pearl Harbor, which apparently is in Hawaii somewhere." He took another deep breath. "They say several of our ships were sunk, and as many as a thousand of our sailors have been killed."

The auditorium erupted in cries for swift and terrible vengeance. The MC sulked from the stage, apparently utterly drained from his duty. Curley sat dumbfounded, staring into the glare of one of the stage lights.

"What in hell does this mean?" he wondered. There would be war. Of that there was no longer any doubt. Would there be a draft? Would he have to fight? What about Ray? How had the Great Spirit let something like this happen?

Mack's voice interrupted his fears. He was not sitting, he was standing there, talking into the mike.

"Ladies and gentlemen, we have enjoyed being here with you fine people. And, as much as I hate to cut the show short, it seems to be totally inappropriate to continue." Curley heard some people agree through the sniffles that moved like a wave through the still crowd. "Again, our thanks for the invitation, and I hope we can all do it again some time real soon. Meantime, let's all say a prayer for them sailors and for our country tonight." With that, Mack moved gracefully away from the mike and began packing up.

ಬ

The most immediate effect of the bombing of Pearl Harbor for Curley and the band was purely financial. The promoter had decided that, since they had played an abbreviated show and thereby broken the contract, he did not have to pay them.

"You have gotta be kidding me?!" Mack protested. "Boy, where in the hell is your good sense. We quit playing because of what happened. You want me to try and follow news like that with a goddamn banjo song? You've gotta be nuts!"

"Mr. Crowe, I will not be talked to in that way."

"And I will not be cheated. Do you hear me?"

Curley watched in dismay as Mack fought with the promoter. He wanted to go over and shake the man to his sense, or at least until he himself felt better. But he knew that Mack would not appreciate any help in a business matter, so he kept to himself, watching the weasley man squirm and rationalize.

"Mr. Crowe you did not live up to your end of our agreement. Therefore...."

"Are you blaming me for the Japanese attack?" demanded Mack.

"No, of course not."

"Well, that is why we quit playing. Nobody was in the mood to play or listen after that news. God, can you not see that?"

"Mr. Crowe a contract is a contract. There is nothing that I can do. I am sorry." Mack stood silent for a minute, deep in thought. When he scratched his nose playfully, Curley, Ray and Shifty all knew that he had found some angle in that head of his, and that he was ready to move in for the kill.

"Mr. Hadley," he said, "to have continued playing music today, to have brazenly gone on with the show on a day like this, would have been disrespectful to the honor and memory of those young men who died this morning. And it is my belief that the good people of Bristol would and will see it that way. We'll know tomorrow---because when we play that show at WOPI, I intend to tell them all that you wouldn't pay us because we stopped to honor those dead. Let's see how popular you are tomorrow evening." With that Mack turned and started to enter the car.

"Mr. Crowe, wait," called the promoter. "Let's don't be hasty."

"I'm tired of fucking with you, Mr. Hadley," Mack retorted, employing a word that he almost never used, "either pay me all that you owe me or take your chances. What'll it be?" The promoter grumbled as he reached into his suit jacket and pulled out a bulging envelope.

"Here," he said, tossing the envelope onto the hood of the car, "I hope you enjoy it."

"Just a minute," Mack said, stopping the man. He pulled the cash out of the envelope and counted it meticulously. "All right," he said, satisfied that it was all there, "been a pleasure doin' business with ya."

Hadley grunted and stalked off. Mack and Shifty hopped into their car and Curley and Ray into theirs. They drove away silently, into a terrifyingly uncertain dusk.

CHAPTER FORTY-THREE

Curley, Ray and Shifty sat in their hotel room, waiting for some news. Mack had driven into town to check with the manager of the radio station and see whether or not there was any reason for them to stay in town. With the whole world turned upside down, Mack sensed that there might not be room for him and his band on the radio over the next few days.

Curley prayed that wouldn't be the case. The money from the station was okay, sure, but what he really wanted, what they all wanted right now, was the diversion. It would be just what the doctor ordered to immerse themselves in their music and forget about all the fear and doubt. But he sensed that Mack was probably right---he doubted there was going to be any show.

Ray was fumbling with his guitar. He tossed out series of chords without actually playing any recognizable melody. The sound seemed harsh against the strained silence, and it annoyed Shifty.

"Christ, Ray," he said, "either play a song or put that damn thing down." Curley mumbled his assent. Ray sheepishly began to play a song.

"I was dancin', with my darlin', to the Tennessee Waltz, when an old friend, I happened, to see....."

"Oh, shit," cried Shifty, "could you have picked a sadder song? Goddamn it play something fast, will ya?"

"Yeah, Ray, for God's sake cut the slow stuff out. It gives me the creeps right now."

Ray placed the guitar back in its case and sat back in the chair. He didn't feel like playing any up-tempo songs, so he gave in to the quiet. The room, filled with cigarette smoke, was at least beginning to smell better than it had when they arrived. Shifty was eyeing the two of them warily now. Ray noticed that he seemed to be debating some very important issues as he measured him and Curley up.

"What are you looking at?" Ray asked testily. Shifty blinked, as if he hadn't even realized that he was staring.

"Oh, sorry," he said. He paused a moment and then moved to what he was wondering. "I gotta question for ya'll," he said finally.

"What is it?" asked Curley.

"Well, ya'll are the Indian Artists and all...."

"Yeah?" Ray didn't like where this might be headed.

"So how come ya'll seem so nervous about all this war talk? I mean, I don't mind admitting that I'm scared shitless, but I don't get it from you two. I thought for an Indian to really be a man he had to be considered a warrior and all that shit. So how come ya'll two ain't jumpin' at the chance to go out and earn your feathers or something?" Curley's laughter competed with the smoke and filled the room.

"Jesus, Shifty," he said, "where in the world did you hear that shit? I ain't in no hurry to go and get my ass shot off in Japan. And I can't think of any Indian who would be."

"Ain't that the truth," Ray added. "Where *did* you hear that crazy shit?"

"In a picture show, I think," Shifty said innocently.

"Well, don't believe everything you see in the picture shows," Ray scolded, "especially when it comes to Indians."

They sat quietly for a few minutes, Shifty allowing his new knowledge to sink in while Curley and Ray separately tried to process the way the white man's mind worked. Finally, Curley broke the tension.

"Got anything to drink?" he asked Shifty.

"Nope."

"Nothing at all?"

"Not a thing, Curley. My cup is empty."

"Wanna go find something? It'll be a while before Mack gets back from that station."

Shifty stood and threw on his coat without even bothering to answer.

"You guys don't go gettin' tanked," Ray implored. "Mack won't be gone that long."

"Why don't you come with us, Ray?" asked Curley. "You ain't gotta drink nothin', but it beats sittin' here by yourself singin' them sad songs and worryin'."

"No, thanks," Ray answered. The truth was that he did not want to sit in the hotel room by himself thinking about being sent off to die on some war, but he also hated watching Curley poison himself with alcohol. "I'll stay here and wait on Mack."

"Suit yourself," Curley said as he and Shifty disappeared out the door. Ray leaned down, picked up his guitar, and went back to doing the Tennessee waltz.

ℵ

Mack sat with his head in his hands, waiting for the news like the rest of the country. The station manager, Chris Connally, had told Mack that he was deferring the decision until after he heard the president's address to the nation.

"Let me hear what President Roosevelt says, and then we'll make the call. From what I hear, he's expected to declare war on the Japs. Maybe on Germany, too."

"Anybody figured out why they bombed us?" asked Mack. "I mean, I heard about Hitler and Germany and them troubles, but I didn't even know that Japan was mad at us."

"Oh, they're crazy," came the answer. "The whole damned world is crazy."

So Mack sat in the booth with Chris and the DJ, a man named "Wild" Willie Madison. They smoked and talked about music and sports and women. They tried to avoid any mention of the grander purpose that had them all in the booth in the first place. It seemed that everyone wanted to know more, but no one wanted to talk about it. When the address finally came from Washington, their worst fears were confirmed. Roosevelt called the Japanese attack unprovoked and vicious. And he asked the Congress of the United States to declare war on Japan and Germany. Mack dropped his head into his hands.

"Ah, shit," he said in complete resignation. "Here we go again." Mack's attitude contrasted sharply with the others in the booth. This was news, BIG news, and they were ready to pounce on the story with both feet.

"I'm sorry, Mr. Crowe," Connally said finally, after making preparations to do a live show on what it all meant for Tennessee and the country, "but we won't have time for you and your band today. If you wanna stay in town a few more days, I'm sure we can get you in at some point."

"Thank you, Mr. Connally, but no. I reckon we'll be getting back on the road. Thanks for the invitation."

Mack left the station and walked back to his car. He drove back to the hotel, trying to fight back the tears that wanted to stream down his cheeks. He had planned his whole life for fame and fortune, for the day when he would spend more time in a house that he owned than he would in hotel rooms. And with this new lineup, with Ray's rhythm and Curley on lead and harmonica, he had felt the finger of God and the smile of fortune. Fame, he had been sure, was just around the corner, and his days on the circuit were numbered. Uncle Mack's Traveling Band was going to be huge----he could just feel it.

But now there was to be a war. Another European war. And Mack was a realist. Shifty was twenty six. Curley was in his early twenties, and Ray wasn't far behind. His band would certainly be called to arms. His chance was fading. He pulled into the parking lot of the Happy Days Motel, weighing the possibility of finally joining Curley and Shifty in one of their binges. Why not? He no longer had anything to lose.

ଚଠ

Curley and Shifty left the bar early. They had a good buzz going, but they had pulled away before getting drunk just in case Uncle Mack returned with news that they were going to be playing a radio show that night. Mack would not accept their assuming anything, especially if it cost him any money or caused him to lose face by having to cancel a gig.

They stepped out into a chilly but bright afternoon. Curley pulled his coat tight and buttoned it. Shifty wrapped his scarf snugly around his neck and lit a cigarette. They turned a corner and headed back toward the hotel. As their boot heels clicked against the pavement they saw a young man dart from the side of a building across the street with an armload of thick newspapers. He ran to his destination at the corner and began to bellow out his message to the pedestrians passing by.

"EXTRA! EXTRA! PRESIDENT ROOSEVELT DECLARES WAR ON GERMANY AND JAPAN!! PRESIDENT CALLS ALL GOOD MEN TO COME TO THE AID OF THEIR COUNTRY!!!!"

Curley smiled a humorless and bitter grin. When the chips were down, he thought, the country suddenly belonged to *"all"* good men, and not just the white ones. The thought made him nauseous. Without a word he threw his arm around Shifty's shoulder and they turned and headed back into the bar.

Surely Mack would understand.

ॐ

"Jesus, Mack, what does that mean?"

"It means that we're at war now," he answered, "and for the near future."

Ray slumped back into his seat and sighed. Okay, so they were at war now. That much he could figure out for himself. But what did that mean? Would the army be enough to win the thing or would FDR be expecting others to flock to the cause. And, just suppose, enough people did not flock to cause, would that mean that people would be made to go and fight against their will? Would he be made to go to fight?

"I don't understand," he said, "how could something like this happen these days?" Mack shrugged. "Mack," he asked again, "what does this mean for us?"

"It means that the band's over," Mack said sadly. "Don't get me wrong, they ain't gonna want nobody like me. But you and Curley and Shifty? Huh, I guess they'll be after you fellas in no time at all. That's just what I think."

"Well, maybe not. Maybe it won't come to that. Right?"

"Sure, Ray. Maybe not."

Mack's demeanor scared Ray. The man had become far more than a mere employer to him in the last months. He had become an almost surrogate father. Curley had abrogated those responsibilities and Ray just didn't have the closeness to Lorenzo that Curley did, so Mack filled the void. When Curley and Shifty escaped to paint the town, Ray and Mack were left behind to play cards and philosophize. Mack loved learning everything he could about Curley and Ray's heritage, and Ray picked Mack's brain for all the knowledge he could regarding business and finances. But to see him like this, so forlorn and seemingly without a prayer, it made Ray even more nervous than before.

"C'mon, Mack, don't sound so hopeless. Who knows what might happen? Why, with President Roosevelt in there we might win this thing in six months."

"He ain't even whipped the money troubles yet," Mack observed caustically, "and now he's got to add this on top of it all. Jesus, I don't know how that man can do it all. I just don't know, Ray. Things look bad from where I sit. They really do." He paused and took a deep breath. "Where's your brother and Shifty?"

"They went to find something to drink. I figured they'd be back already, seein' as how they didn't know whether or not we was playin' tonight. Maybe they just forgot the time."

"If they went into town they've probably heard the news and decided to really hit the bottle hard. And I can't say as I blame 'em one damn bit." Ray bit his lip. "You might wanna start drinking too, Ray," he said, "'cause we're all gonna need it."

&

Curley leaned forward, pulled out his wallet and scanned. It was a truly sad sight. As usual, he had already pulled most of his salary aside and handed it to Ray to be sent home. And now here he was, in danger of only getting half-wasted, and he was all out of cash. It was a horrible situation. Shifty had left an hour ago, saying that the noise in the bar was making him more nervous. Curley cursed his luck---if Shifty had stayed he could have borrowed the money.

"You look sad," came the sultry, if slightly slurred, voice. Curley turned. She looked to be about thirty or so, with dirty blonde hair and grey eyes. He captured the look immediately. She was on the make.

"Yeah," he said, "I'm running a little low at the moment. And I ain't as drunk as I would like to be. Not for this occasion, anyway."

The woman gave him a satisfied smirk. That was all the information that she really needed.

"Um-huh, things are getting crazy, I guess." From the tone of her voice, Curley wondered if she even knew that there was a war to be fought. But then he realized that it didn't really matter. After all, it wasn't her firm grasp of foreign policy that he was after.

"Crazy," Curley repeated, "and it seems a shame to stay sober during a time like this." He winked.

"Well," she offered, "I could lend you some money and you could get drunk. But I'd probably never see my money again."

Curley stared to protest that he was good for whatever she loaned him when she unexpectedly continued.

"Or, we could go back to my place and finish the job together. And you could, I am sure, find some way to pay me back."

Curley's mind immediately threw up Minnie's face, and their promises. He was one-half of an "us" now, and that should have changed things. But then he thought of the newspaper boy and his cries. All good men. War. Curley decided that now was just not the time to go hedging his bets.

"Lead the way," he said as he pulled on his coat. "I'm all yours."

CHAPTER FORTY-FOUR

Uncle Mack had decided that the only thing to do was to cancel the rest of the tour. With things happening so quickly, it seemed that no one could think about anything but the war. It was obvious that no one felt like sitting through their music. Not right now. So he had sent the boys home and he had returned to Charlotte to stay with Sam Hooper. He told them that he would be in touch as soon as he figured out what to do. He paid them for their work, and he even paid them what they would have likely made for the rest of the tour. It was generous, and the boys all promised to remember it and remain faithful. They gave Mack their word that they would not contract out to play for anyone else until they had heard something from him.

Curley and Ray figured that they had enough money to last them through the rest of the month and probably into the new year, but 1942 was looming, and they both knew that work had to be found. Curley's first thought was a CCC camp, but Ray refused to go and Curley was not in the mood to go it alone. There was always the WPA, Works Projects Administration, but Curley thought he would keep looking before he went that route. He had seen some of the WPAers doing their work, sweating as they repaired the roads and fixed the local bridges. Curley decided to file that option away as a last resort. There had to be a better, or at least an *easier* way, to make ends meet.

The clear upside to the sudden vacation was the time he was able to spend with Minnie. In what seemed like no time at all the two of them had become almost inseparable, a fact not easily lost on Curley's family. Eunice watched the whole blooming relationship with skepticism. On one hand, she was more than happy to see her son beginning to show some of the signs of manhood, some of the traits of maturity. On the other hand, she knew that the "love bug," as Cora called it, would have had to have bitten Curley awfully hard to have him behaving this way. Eunice also couldn't help but resent the new woman in Curley's life. It filled her with jealousy to know that this Minnie Abernathy was able to work some kind of magic on her son and make him want to straighten up his act---something that Eunice herself had not been able to accomplish.

Not that Curley had suddenly become an angel. Even the strange and growing feelings that he had for Minnie could not bring about that radical a transformation. In fact, his relationship with Minnie only meant that he had to work all the harder to keep his drinking a secret: now he was hiding his habit from two strong willed and disapproving women. That meant that his excuses had to become more elaborate, and he was having to rely on Ray's cover stories more and more.

Minnie took in laundry to help make ends meet in her home. She normally finished her work around six in the evening, when Curley would arrive and they would go out on their date. Uncle Mack had taken one of the "band" cars, Shifty the other, leaving both Ray and Curley wondering how they would adapt to getting places on foot again. But they had arrived to find that Lorenzo, once again refusing to be outdone, had purchased a second-hand but nice looking automobile which was now at their disposal. It helped that Eunice steadfastly refused to drive the car to work every day, insisting that the automobile was going to make America a country full of fat people. That left the car to Curley, who gave his grandfather his word as a gentleman and a Swaney that he would never, not ever, drive the car while drinking. For the most part he had kept his word, and the car was still in one piece.

So he would arrive around six, the battered old muffler announcing his arrival almost ten minutes before he actually got there. Grandma Abernathy was typically waiting for him, perched in her rocker which she moved out to the porch everyday around five thirty, unless it was raining. The temperature didn't matter, and Curley had to marvel at the old woman's persistence. She clearly hoped that, if she met the boy at the door every day with a hateful scowl and a bitter aside, he would stop courting her lovely grand-daughter. Of course, Curley was just as determined not to give in, so the battle turned into no more than parlor amusement for Minnie and Essie Mae.

Minnie was in love and everyone around her knew it. That was the only plausible reason for why she had suddenly found the courage to disobey her grandmother. Essie Mae pestered her constantly with entreaties to be fixed up with Ray ("that little brother of his"), and

Minnie had broached the subject with Curley, who had told her simply that Ray's pride would never have allowed it. Curley had already developed the good sense to not state anything bad, even the obvious, about his girlfriend's family. Minnie now talked only of Curley, nothing else, and drove everyone around her crazy.

Grandma Abernathy forced herself to be civil to Curley when he came. Of course, to her being civil meant only that she had not pelted him with any flying foreign objects. She despised the very sight of the boy---from his cocky, self-assured walk to his sly, sideways smile. The way he nodded his head towards her when he passed by on the porch. The way Minnie "acted like the fool" whenever he entered the room. The silly little things that they said to each other. It was all, as far as she was concerned, so much bad news. Grandma Abernathy believed that love was supposed to be practical. A person could follow their heart only as far as their good senses would take them, and if the heart tried to go any further it was that person's obligation, as a Christian, to yank it back. Minnie had been taught this since she was a child. Grandma Abernathy had held up her son and daughter-in-law as prime examples of what not to do; they had ran off in a blaze of passion and collapsed in a heap of broken promises and unfulfilled dreams. That was the price of passion, and Minnie had been taught that it was a price not worth paying and a chance not worth taking. But the girl wasn't listening. God only knew what she saw in Curley, because Grandma Abernathy couldn't find anything good in the boy besides his looks and his charms, one of which would fade and the other of which would only get more dangerous with age and practice. He was a traveling musician! That was no job. And, in times like these, to be running around the country singing and playing? As far as Grandma Abernathy was concerned, that did not speak well of the boy.

But there was just no convincing Minnie of any of this. The girl was slap blind to the truth. The sideways smile melted her, the charm intoxicated her. It was more than Grandma Abernathy could take. It made her physically ill---she had taken to her sickbed upon learning that Curley was back in town---and she became more and more terrified for her innocent young granddaughter.

The fact was the Grandma Abernathy had plenty of reason to worry. Curley was as in love as was Minnie, that was not the problem, that was not any trouble. But, as Curley was beginning to find out, he was not totally in control of himself any more. He promised himself over and over that he would leave the booze alone, that his drinking days were behind him for good. Then he found himself with a little time on his hands and a horrendous craving that left his stomach in flames and his mouth bone dry. The rationalization followed closely, and before long he was cruising the streets seeking just a drop of the stuff that quenched his thirst. The drop turned into a downpour, and he found himself staggering away from yet another near-miss with the wrong woman or the law. Since the screw-up in the Bristol bar he had remained faithful to Minnie, but he had also remained faithful to the bottle, and he knew damn well that the two were bound to crash into each other before much longer. And he also knew that, when it did happen, it would not be a pretty sight.

Most of their dates were church functions. Curley was becoming more comfortable with Minnie's church, and they seemed to be getting more accepting of him (at least they rarely stared now). He didn't have a problem with the religion thing, in fact it reminded him of his own childhood. Of course, Rodney and Eunice had not subjected Curley and his brothers to much "organized" churching, most of their faith was instilled through quiet family times on Sunday evenings. Curley remembered some of the kids at school once telling him that he and his family were going to Hell because they did not go to church. Frightened, he had gone home and found his father laying in the grass in the backyard.

"Dad," he had asked, "are we going to Hell?"

"Not so's I know of," Rodney replied, "why in the world do you ask that?"

"Just something I heard."

"No, Curley, we ain't goin' to Hell."

"So how come we never do go to church?" he asked. Rodney had raised himself up and grinned, fanning his arms out in the wind.

"Because I feel much closer to God out here," he had remarked. Curley had never forgotten that. He also understood it better now. There were some good people at Minnie's church, but everything seemed so formal, so tight. They talked about God as if He just sat up there in Heaven, watching people and waiting to knock them for a loop. Curley wondered where all the love had gone. He knew there had been plenty of love in the stories Lorenzo and Eunice had told about Jesus, and he wondered why these people seemed so determined to make God seem scary. Curley was convinced that you couldn't frighten a man into doing the right thing, you could only do that by loving the person and setting an example. The only example most of these people

seemed intent on setting was how to dress fashionably. The farm
families and people who were poor beyond even pretense sat self-
consciously in the back of the church, apparently trying to hide from
God's discerning eye. It bothered Curley a great deal, but he said
nothing for fear of offending Minnie.

But now he was preparing himself for a completely new kind of
date. He was surprised at how nervous he was. Things would be fine,
he reminded himself, there was nothing to worry about at all. Minnie
was ready, he was ready, the timing was perfect. The next step, after
all, had to be taken at some point. No time like the present, he
counseled himself.

He would pick Minnie up on this Sunday and they would actually
miss the church service. They were going in the other direction.

It was time for Minnie Abernathy and Eunice Norris to meet.

CHAPTER FORTY-FIVE

"It is such a pleasure to meet you," Minnie said as she entered the house. Eunice stepped forward to measure the young girl up, to see if she could find the spark that had lit up her son. The first thing she noticed was Minnie's hair. It hung in loose curls down around her shoulders, not the typical tight curls of white people, the kind that made whites always look like their face was being pulled too tightly against their skull. Minnie had, without her own knowledge, scored a silent point.

The second thing that Eunice noticed was Minnie's modest dress. It was a simple blue and white pattern, made of soft cotton. It dropped to a proper length below the knees before displaying the girl's skinny legs and bony ankles. She was wearing very little make-up and no jewelry, the only accessory being a beaten, black leather purse that she carried in her gloved hand.

"This is a pretty girl," Eunice begrudgingly thought. Still, she was no fool. Curley had walked hand in hand with more than his share of pretty girls, and Eunice wanted to see what lay beneath the surface. She wanted to know what it was about Minnie Abernathy that caused Curley to beg her to press his shirts and pants before he saw her. He wanted immaculate creases and would not accept a single stray wrinkle. Curley had always been a clothes horse, but he had never been this fastidious about his appearance. Never.

"It is nice to meet you, finally," Eunice said.

Curley stepped back and watched the action, amazed that the two women were finally in the same room together. It felt strange watching his two very distinct worlds come into contact with each other. This was more than the awkwardness of staying at home with the band. That had been about appearances; this was about emotions. And although he would never have spoken it aloud, the summit had the

distinct feel of a changing of the guard. A passing of the baton. If
Eunice could accept Minnie, if she could only see what it was that
Curley saw, then she could lovingly and in good conscience pass off
the mantle of responsibility for her son. For Curley, it was a moment
pregnant with symbolism and sentimentality.

Eunice felt the moment as well. Not at first, but as they sat in the
den and chatted, with Curley and Minnie side by side on the couch and
Eunice alone in the rocker, she began to feel change. And she did not
like it. Curley had caused her so much pain over the course of the last
few years, but that didn't matter now. In fact, it had never really
mattered. When she looked at him she could still feel the cool,
cleansing waters of the Occonoluftee. She could still smell the wood
stove, burning in the backroom of Don Tyson's store. She remembered
all the days when she had sat on the porch, watching Curley, Rodney
and Ray romp through the yard and play catch. She was not ready to
relinquish him. Not to Minnie or any other woman.

It wasn't a long jump from this realization to the inevitable search
for flaws. Eunice Norris was certainly not the first mother to seek out
short-comings in her son's mate, but she began it with an intensity and a
thoroughness that was unmatched. The modest cotton dress soon
became a cheap garment. The lack of jewelry and make-up, along with
the apparent poverty that that suggested, turned Minnie into white
trash. The tattered purse only served as further evidence of this
conclusion.

Lorenzo had once told Curley that a white man's vicious hate was no
match for an Indian's polite aloofness. Curley began to understand that
statement as the meeting progressed. Eunice was not rude, she would
never be rude unless provoked, but neither was she the picture of
hospitality. Her answers were curt, and she gave no more information
than was specifically asked. She smiled wanly and, with the most
determined control, bit back even the slightest trace of animation.
Curley shifted and squirmed, hoping that Minnie would just think that
his mother was the quiet type. He tried as best he could to pry his
mother's attitude, but nothing worked. He had forgotten what an iron
will this woman possessed.

"As much as I hate to end this lovely afternoon," she said
eventually, "my Dad, Russell's grandfather, will be returning home
soon with my other children, and I really should begin to make their
dinner. These boys won't let no one but me cook for them." Curley
blushed at the obvious broadside: I'm number one to them, she was

saying, so don't even try it. Minnie just smiled and nodded.

"Thank you for letting me come by," Minnie said, "it has been a pleasure." Eunice said something from the kitchen, but it was purposefully inaudible. Curley helped Minnie put on her coat and he walked out with her. Without a word to Eunice.

&

Curley was pushing the old Packard hard, driving much faster than usual, gritting his teeth. He was seething. He had dropped Minnie off without incident, although her quiet demeanor in the drive back to Stanley was considerably more subdued than the trip to Cramerton had been. Curley could feel her disappointment; it steamed off of her like rain drops on hot pavement. He avoided even mentioning the disaster until he had kissed her goodnight on her front porch.

"I think it went good today," he had said. "I really do." Minnie had only mumbled a tacit agreement. It was clear that she knew better. She was no fool. As Curley watched her walk into the house, her shoulders drooping, he felt more angry than he ever had in his life. How could his Mom have been so inconsiderate? Why had she been so hateful, when Minnie had bent over backwards to go over well? He was determined to find out just those answers. And that was the reason he pushed the car. He wanted those answers.

He stormed the steps like a general staking a conquered hill and threw open the door. Finding the kitchen dark and empty, he plowed his way into the den, where the sounds of his brothers gave away their location. He scanned the room, but there was no sign of Eunice any where. Ray walked into the room, fresh from shaving.

"Hey, Curley."

"Where's Mom?" Curley snapped.

"Dunno. What's wrong?"

"Where's Mom?" Curley demanded from Houston.

"Backyard," he answered. "Why? Watcha need?"

Curley bolted past the boys without another word. He opened the back door and its screen and stepped back out into the night. He saw Eunice sitting under the elm, facing away from the house and towards the field that lay outback. She wasn't wearing a coat, and the night was cold. Curley walked up behind her, some of his anger dissipating.

"I know you're angry," she said without turning. Curley stopped in his tracks.

"How'd you know it was me?"

"I know your walk. I know all you boys' walk. Why, you could blind fold me and I could tell you which one of you entered or left a room." She patted the ground beside of her. "Sit," she said. Curley knelt and then sat beside of her.

"You should have your coat on," he said.

"Big Cove nights are a lot colder," she stated. "I think I can handle this."

"Hell, Mom, you can handle anything."

"Don't curse, Russell. It isn't nice." Curley apologized. The words had become a part of his working vocabulary now, and sometimes they slipped out when he spoke to his Mom. It wasn't intentional, he still had too much reverence for her to ignore her sensibilities. "Have you cooled off any since you left?"

"Some. I guess. But I don't understand why you acted that way. I don't understand that at all. Minnie couldn't have been any nicer to you. Or more respectful. So, I just don't get it. I thought you'd like her."

Eunice turned and faced her son. The look of hurt that he wore ripped through her. She knew that she was the reason for the look and, more importantly, the hurt. She dropped her head, allowing her chin to rest on her chest. She sighed.

"Mom? What's wrong?"

"I'm sorry, Russell. I had no right. And I never meant to hurt you."

"Mom, why did you act like that way? What do you have against Minnie? I mean, you just met her. Why don't you like her?"

"She's not good enough for you," she said, looking up and back at her son. "I just don't believe that she is right for you."

"Don't you think that should be my decision?" he asked sharply. Eunice said nothing. There was a little voice inside of her head that was singing in mockery. She had come full circle. She didn't want to think about how long ago it had been that she had been the child with the "unworthy" love, and she refused to see herself in the same role that her father had played. This was different, she thought. Curley was still drinking and, quite obviously, searching for something. The boy was vulnerable and he had been every since Rodney's death. He wasn't thinking clearly. And this Minnie Abernathy was ingratiating herself by stepping into the void. She was taking advantage of the boy. It was as plain as the nose on your face.

But the excuses rang hollow as she looked into her son's face. Not at it, but really *into* it. All the disappointment and anxiety. The hurt from the rejection. He was in love with this girl. Eunice had suspected it for weeks, but seeing him now she was certain. She had lost her son to this interloper.

"No, I don't think it's your decision at all, Russell. Because judging from your track record, I have absolutely no faith in your ability to make this kind of decision. Good Lord, Russell, can you blame me?"

"Sure, I can," he said, "because you're a smart woman, Mom. And just as sure as you knew that Dad was a good man, I think down deep you know that Minnie is a good person. In all the time I've known her, do you know I ain't done nothing but give her goodnight kisses? Now don't that tell you something?"

"Yes. It tells me that you're a fool for thinking that that qualifies you for some kind of respect. And from your reaction I'm guessing that every other 'girl' you've been out with has been considerably faster. No wonder you think she's something special, she's probably the first decent girl you've seen. But," she added emphatically, "you do not have to marry the first decent person you meet."

"You did," Curley fired back.

"This girl," Eunice insisted, "is not your father."

"Mom, listen to yourself," Curley said, his patience waning. "You sound like you hate her. And you've never even given her a chance. I deserve better than that, no matter what mistakes I've made in my past."

Curley stared at Eunice and waited for a response. She sat quietly, her head lowered again and resting on her chest.

"Mom, why do you seem so sad?" he asked. Suddenly, it hit him. Like the force of the first electric light in Gaston County it illuminated the corners of his mind and cast away all shadows from his mother's angry denunciations. "Oh my God," he said cheerfully, "you think you're losin' me! Don't you?"

"Don't be ridiculous," Eunice whispered. "You can be so arrogant when you...."

"That's it! Oh, Mom, how could you even think something like that? Mom don't you know me better than that?" He reached his hand out and laid it on her arm, which she quickly jerked away.

"I told you that isn't it." Curley put his hand back, this time refusing to allow her to yank it away.

"Mom, I want you to look at me," he said. Slowly, grudgingly, Eunice turned to her son.

"What?" she growled.

"I love you, Mom. You're the greatest, strongest, most wonderful woman I know. Why, the way you've held this family together without Dad. The way you've always tried to make us wanna be the best people we can be. The way you cut me and Ray free to let us chase our dreams...."

"That is not at all what I did," she corrected, "I have never 'cut you free.'" Then, as if she herself could just now see it she said mournfully, "Maybe   that's   the   trouble."

Curley reached out his hand and brushed the hair out of Eunice's eyes, just the way he had seen his Dad do whenever she was sad or worried. Eunice shot him a warm smile as if to acknowledge.

"This isn't a competition, Mom," he said. "No woman could ever take your place in my heart. Not even Minnie. We've been through too much together, you and me. I'll never forget all that you've done. Not ever."

Eunice sighed.

"Do you love her?" she asked. Curley swallowed hard.

"Yes, ma'am, I do. I really do." Eunice nodded thoughtfully.

"And you say she's a good woman?"

"Yes, ma'am. A real lady. You'd like her------if you gave her a chance."

"Uh. Well, I suppose I can do that. For my son." Curley leaned in and embraced her.

"Thank you, Mom."

"I haven't promised to like her, Russell," Eunice said, wanting to hedge her bets just a little. "I have only promised to give her a fair hearing."

"That's all I ask. That's all we'll need."

Eunice shuddered. He was talking about them as 'we' now. He was up and walking back to the house before she could say anything more. Curley was getting out before she could change her mind. He was a man, now. You could even see that from his stroll, so full of the world, yet still set apart. That was the Indian. He would find his way, like his father had, in the world. And maybe a white girl could help him. But that was asking for so much trouble and grief. Eunice wondered if either of them had thought about that. Was their love strong enough to withstand the judgmental glare of the world?

She stood and shook her head. Only they could know that, and only time would truly tell. Eunice wished them well. There was nothing more that she could do.

CHAPTER FORTY-SIX

"You ain't lost any of your chops, son," Mack said proudly, "you're in fine form." Curley nodded appreciatively.

"Thanks, Mack," he said. "I gotta admit I was a little nervous. I ain't played as much as I should have."

"Yeah, I guess neither one of us has practiced all that much since the last tour," Ray agreed.

"Well, it doesn't show," Mack said happily. "You boys still hit those fills like pros. And I'm glad for it, because I'm trying to put a little tour together to get our name back out there. And make a little money."

"That sounds great, Mack, 'cause the money's 'bout all gone," said Curley. "Nobody's payin' for music these days."

"No, that's the truth," Mack agreed. "Everybody's worried about appearances and don't want to seem to be having a good time while the boys are overseas. That'll wear out, though," he promised, "'cause people can't be restrained for too long. It just ain't in their nature. Meanwhile, there's still the radio. And that's what I'm thinking. I've already booked out three radio shows in Charlotte and I'm working on a few more in Georgia and Tennessee. You boys still interested?"

Curley and Ray nodded quickly. They had been hoping for weeks that Mack would call before the WPA did.

"How about Shifty?" asked Curley. "You talked to him?"

"Talked to his Dad," Mack answered, "and Shifty won't be coming with us."

"How come?"

"He went off and joined the Navy." Curley and Ray exchanged shocked glances. It was hard to imagine Shifty getting behind any cause, no matter how noble. He was not the responsible type, and he was certainly not the kind of man who didn't mind getting shot at.

"The Navy? Mack, are you sure?"

"Positive. He's done shipped out. His Dad said he thought he was about to get drafted, so he just went on down there and signed up. His folks are tickled to death. I reckon it sounds better to say that your son is off saving the world than that he's off with Uncle Mack's Traveling Band."

"Yeah," Ray said, "but at least you don't get shot at in Uncle Mack's Traveling Band!"

"Well, not by Nazis anyway," said Mack, eyeing Curley suspiciously. "Her husband wasn't German, was he Curley?" Curley blushed and shook his head.

"I didn't hang around long enough to find out," he answered caustically.

"So how about it, boys? Can I count you in for sure?"

"Absolutely," they answered without pause. "We're in."

"Great! I'll search around for us a bass fiddle player, and then I'll be in touch with dates. I'd like to be on the road by the middle of next week." Mack paused. "Either of you heard anything from the draft board?"

"No. Should we have?"

"Oh, no. I just wanted to make sure."

With that he crawled back into the car and drove away. Curley and Ray shook hands and headed home themselves. The road called again.

80

Minnie had been quiet since dinner. Curley had picked her up and taken her to a nice Italian restaurant. The checkered table clothes and the thick, bright candles provided a romantic atmosphere. Curley had hoped that the fanciness of the surroundings would make up for the news that he brought. He had hoped that, with the promise of money and therefore many more fancy meals, Minnie would not mind his leaving again. He had been wrong.

She pointed out that fancy meals were almost worthless if he wasn't there with her. She had no desire, she said, to go out to eat by herself. Besides, she had never had those material things before, and she was sure she could do without them now. What she didn't want to do without was him. She had become used to seeing him everyday. She watched the clock with anticipation as she ironed and washed, waiting for the minute when she could put down her work and jump into his car, where they would drive away from the rest of the world and keep

each other in sacred company. What would she do now? Curley
pointed out that she had known how he made his living when she first
met him, why was she getting angry at him now?

"Yes," she agreed, "I knew what you did for a living. But I didn't
know that I would fall in love with you."

Curley's eyes grew to prairies.   They had never used that word
before. Whether or not they felt it, whether or not everyone around
them knew what they were feeling and freely labeled it, they had never
used that word. And now it was out, hovering over the table like a leaf
caught in the summer winds.

"What did you say?" he asked, wanting to make sure he had not
imagined it.

"I said I did not know that I was going to fall in love with you. I
love you, Russell." He reached across the table and took her hand. He
saw the tears gathering in her eyes.

"I love you, too," he said. "But this is what I do. Minnie, I'm about
broke. And me and Ray have to help out with the family. You know
that."

Minnie nodded sorrowfully. They stopped talking. They pretended
to eat, but nothing tasted very good to either of them. Curley paid for
the meal and they drove home in a heavy silence. He walked her to the
front door without taking her hand. His feet felt like they were filled
with lead, every step a struggle. He was relieved when Minnie faced
him before going in.

"Well," she said, "I guess this is goodbye for a while."

"Yeah," Curley agreed, "but not for too long, I promise." She said
nothing. "look, Minnie, you know that I'll come back for you. I always
have."

"That don't mean you always will," she said glumly. "I can only
guess what gets thrown at you when you're out on that road. I ain't
crazy or stupid, Russell. I know what some women can be like."
Curley tried to stamp down the guilt that he was afraid glued itself
conspicuously across his features.

"Minnie, it ain't that bad," he managed.

"See? You see? Even right here you can't tell me that it ain't bad.
You say it ain't 'that' bad, but not it ain't bad. Oh, Russell, I don't
know. Maybe Grandma's right."

"Now just wait a minute," he fumed, "just because I'm going out on
the road to make some money for my family you're all of the sudden
ready to say that your Grandma's right about me? C'mon, Minnie, you

know me better than that. You know that I am better than what your
grandma says."

"I know that. That's not what I'm talking about. I just mean about
us being from different worlds. Maybe she's right about that."

"All she means by that is that I'm a dirty Indian and she don't want
her grandbaby seeing no Indian. That's all she means."

"Well, your mother thinks that I'm white trash," she shot back.
"Maybe they're both right."

"Maybe," he said.

"I'm going in now, Russell."

"Fine." She turned and walked into the house without the usual
goodbye kiss or even a kind word. Curley cursed under his breath and
stomped back to the car. How was it possible that on the same night
that they had admitted that they loved each other they had also broken
apart? He backed out of the driveway with a terrible ache in his heart
and his stomach rolling. Losing her hurt more than he would have even
imagined. He set his mind to mending fences in whatever way he
could.

୫

Minnie was startled from sleep by the sound of something rapping
against her window. She sat up and pulled the covers up to her chin,
terrified. Was it her father? Sometimes he would sneak up to her
window, wreaking of beer and wine, and ask for money. After the
night that she had just been through, she was not up to facing this
again. She had cried herself into a light slumber, waking every now
and then to the lonely room and the sounds of Grandma Abernathy
snoring, a sound which filled the house and, it seemed to Minnie,
probably the entire neighborhood. She heard the clock in the living
room chime four. Then the sound of an object hitting the glass of her
window. She pushed aside the covers and pulled on her old housecoat.
It no longer really fit her, it had been too little for over a year now and
was getting more so with each passing week, but it was all she had.
Crossing the room she came to the window and prayed softly for
strength. She raised the window and felt a cold blast of air hit her. She
shivered as she peered out into the yard. She saw no sign of her father.

"Psst! Hey, Minnie." She turned and saw Curley crouched beneath
the pine tree that towered over the small house. "God I'm glad that was
your room," he said with a relieved grin, "I just knew it was gonna turn

out to be grannie's."

"Russell? What in the world are you doing here at this hour? Have you lost your mind?"

"Nope," he said as he stood and crossed over to the window, "I just now found it."

"Huh?"

"Minnie, I ain't been home yet."

"Russell!" she said disapprovingly. "Your mama will be worried sick."

"Maybe. But I couldn't go home. I drove around a while and then I just parked and sat and thought."

"What did you think about?"

"Us," he said confidently. "I thought about how you make me feel. And I thought about how much I love you. And I thought a lot about you telling me tonight that you loved me, too."

"I do love you, Russell. But sometimes that just ain't enough to make it all right."

"I reckon that's true enough. But it's a helluva lot more than lots of folks have. Minnie, some people go through their whole life without ever being in love." Minnie couldn't help but think of her father when Curley said this.

"Russell, I don't know what you're talkin' about. You just ain't makin' any sense."

"Then just listen," he said. He reached through the window and took her hands in his. "You think that I'm gonna go out on the road and fool around and not come back to you. That's crazy as hell, but I know it's what you think."

Minnie felt the waterworks turning on again. He was right---that was exactly what she thought.

"Well," he continued, "I am coming back to you. I'll always come back to you, honey pot. And I know just how to prove it." Her eyes turned down into his. Curley, no novice to the dramatic moment, paused for just a minute. "Marry me," he said. "Marry me tonight, Minnie."

"What?!"

"I want you for my wife. I wanna be your husband."

"Russell, I, uh, I just don't know. That's crazy."

"What's crazy about it?" he demanded. "I love you and you love me and the rest of a marriage ain't nothin' but real hard work, and we can't start that until we say 'I do.'"

"But----my Grandma, your mama. They'll kill us."

"No they won't. They'll probably yell and cry and yell some more. But they'll get over it. They have to. Please, Minnie. Say yes."

She looked at his face. It was handsome in a boyish way, but nothing in his demeanor suggested a boy beneath the face. She looked into his eyes. They were as black as the night, and they burned with an intensity that she had never seen in another man---especially when he was dreaming and spinning great plans as he was now. Was this traveling musician Indian the man that she wanted to spend the rest of her life with? Was this the man that she wanted to be the father of her children? Did she love him that much, the through sickness and in health kind of love?

"Yes," she said. "I'll marry you. Now tell me what we do."

CHAPTER FORTY-SEVEN

"Ray? Ray? Damn it, Ray, wake up!"

Ray rolled over onto his side, facing the doorway that led from his bedroom into the quiet hall. He smelled the coffee that was brewing and wondered if he had slept too late.

"Huh? Jesus, Curley, what time is it?"

"Don't worry 'bout that none," Curley whispered. "Listen, I need a favor."

"What? Uh, sure, sure Curley. Whaddaya need?"

"I need to borry your nice dress shoes. The black patent leather ones? You know the ones I'm talkin' about?"

Ray sat up in the bed and studied Curley's face. He noticed that his room was still dark---the sun had not yet risen. Curley seemed curiously impatient---he had the look about him that told Ray whenever he was up to something.

"What the hells goin' on?" Ray demanded.

"Look, just trust me," Curley pleaded. "Trust me and tell me where in the hell those shoes are. Please?" Ray could see that whatever was motivating Curley was something important. Curley was not wearing that impish grin or even his best Clark Gable smile. He seemed utterly sincere and curiously serious.

"You promise to have 'em back by five? I got a date." Curley smiled.

"I promise." Ray pointed to his closet.

"They're under the set of sheets Mom keeps in there." Curley shuffled across the room, knelt momentarily, and then drew back, his right hand clutching the shoes. He gave Ray a happy wink.

"I'll be back by five," he said.

"And then you'll tell me what the hell this is all about?"

"Yeah. I tell you all about it." Curley practically floated across the room and ducked out the window. Ray dropped back onto his pillow and pulled the covers up to his chin. Whatever the reason, he felt sure Curley's story would be entertaining.

໖

They sped in silence towards the South Carolina border. Once across, they would find their way to the bustling little city of York, where a couple madly in love or deeply in trouble could get themselves quickly hitched. Every once in a while Minnie would look out of the corner of her eye to glance at Curley. The car's interior was filled with the soft light of morning as the sun rose to greet them. It seemed to Minnie that Curley must have asked her how she was feeling every other minute. She smiled at his courtesy and told him that she had never been happier in her life. She couldn't help but think that she must not have sounded convincing, because Curley continued asking her.

Impetuous by nature, Curley could worry all he wanted or needed to about Minnie's feelings. He was not one to second-guess himself or his decisions, especially the ones that he managed to make when he was sober. He had asked this woman to be his wife and she had consented, there was nothing else to think about except possibly the honeymoon. But he knew that Minnie had not made many snap decisions in her own life. In fact, he wondered how many decisions she had actually been allowed to make on her own at all. Grandmother Abernathy was not a woman who took to dissent, and Minnie did not possess the fire of a rebel. Curley marveled at how calm she seemed, and decided with a measure of pride that this only proved the wisdom of his decision.

"York.....ten miles," Curley said gleefully as they passed the road sign. Minnie inhaled deeply and let the air out slowly, as if it had a taste that she did not want to relinquish. "Are you all right?" he asked again. She nodded quietly, without the confidence she had shown him only minutes before.

"Fine," she croaked. Curley pulled the car over onto the side of the road and turned to face his bride. Minnie looked ashen and shaken. She tried to manage a smile as he she returned Curley's look, but it was crooked and weak.

"What's wrong?" he asked softly, laying his hand on top of her knee. "What's the matter?" She stared blankly at him for a moment, seemingly far away. When consciousness returned to her eyes, wide and innocent as a doe's, she forced another smile, this one as pathetic as the first.

"I just thought about it all," she said with a resigned giggle. "What we're doing, I mean." The terror spread slowly and wickedly through Curley, freezing him for the moment.

"You just thought about it?" he repeated. "You just thought about it......just *now*? Jesus, Minnie!" She laughed at him, a healthy and confident sound that allowed Curley to dare to dream again, allowing the hope to return. She leaned across the seat and kissed him, then she sat back in her seat.

"We must be nuts," she declared. "I mean, we must be just totally nuts."

"Nah," Curley said, starting the car and pulling back out onto the road, "we're just in love is all."

"Same thing," she answered. Curley thought for a minute and decided there was no arguing the point. The difference between love and insanity did seem awfully slim as they drove closer and closer to York. "I'm white and you're Indian. You been all over the place and I never left Stanley. We must be nuts."

"We ain't all that different," Curley responded. "I mean, we are on the outside. But in the inside, we're kinda the same, you and me. You know? I mean, you know me better'n anybody except maybe Ray and Mom, and you know me as good as they do and you ain't known me half as long. I reckon that tells me all I need to know." Curley emphasized this final point with an emphatic shake of his head that sent a wayward curl into his eyes. Minnie reached out her hand and brushed away the hair.

"Do you know any married people who are happy?" she asked shyly, sadly. Curley turned from the road long enough to see the pained look in her eyes.

"Yeah. Why you askin' that?" Minnie paused and fumbled with the hem of her dress. She stared at the floorboard as she spoke.

"'Cause I don't," she said. "I ain't never seen happy married people. My folks ain't talked in years....can't even be in the same room with each other. Grandpa Abernathy was a mean drunk who beat Grandma when he'd tied one on. And that was *if* he even came home at all." Minnie sighed. "I've heard Grandma say she didn't know whether to want him home or wish him into another woman's arms. I just ain't never seen people who was married who was happy. Never."

"Well," Curley said, "you shoulda seen my Mom and Dad." Minnie turned a with a hungry look in her eyes, wanting to hear something to ease her fears.

"Really?"

"Oh, yeah. I mean they couldn't keep their hands off'n one another. It used to make me and Ray get so embarrassed. And they talked. All the time, like they was still gettin' to know each other. And they did this right up to when my Dad died. Me and Ray could hear 'em in there in their room, talkin' and laughin'. We'd hear Dad strike a match and the clink of ice in their drinks. It was real peaceful. And happy." It was Curley's turn to sigh.

"She must miss him," said Minnie.

"Yeah. She don't talk about it much. That wouldn't be Mom's way, but I reckon she does."

"Well, she's still young."

"Oh, that don't matter none," Curley corrected, "she says she'll never marry again and I'm inclined to believe her. Not that she couldn't. You'd be surprised at some of the white men who come to call on her. But she turns 'em all away. She says she's had her turn and that she had the best, now let the rest of 'em find their own. And I reckon she means it, too."

"So it can happen," Minnie said, as much to herself as to Curley. "I suppose you just gotta get lucky."

"Oh, no. Luck ain't got nothin' to do with it. I mean, after you meet a girl you like, whether or not she likes you back, I reckon that's luck. But after that it ain't nothin' but damn hard work. That's all there is to it."

"That's it, huh?" Minnie asked, poking fun at how easy Curley made it all seem. "It's just that easy?"

"I didn't say nothin' about it bein' easy," Curley corrected. "Fact is that sometimes I think Mom and Dad wanted to wring each other's necks. But if you love each other enough then you find a way to muddle through somehow. You have to....you don't get many chances at love."

Her husband-to-be's philosophy was too cute; Minnie found herself blushing as she made the mental leap from the aisle to the wedding bed. Curley saw her look and smiled mischievously. He could see right through her.

"We'll get to that," he smirked, "but first things first." Minnie's keen sense of propriety took hold and she looked away and out of the car window to watch South Carolina begin to pass by.

They stopped at the jewelry store which was conveniently located across from the courthouse and Curley bought a set of rings for a whopping twenty five dollars. He silently thanked Uncle Mack for lining up this new concert tour--he was going to need the money. Minnie balked at the price and demanded that Curley not pay it.

"That is highway robbery," she griped. Still, as Curley reminded her, they had no rings without this set, which was one of the most "reasonably" priced in the entire store. Minnie gave in, though not without a parting shot at the "thief" behind the counter. They crossed out into the street and a bright, beautiful day. A brisk wind slapped against them and made sure they were wide awake for their big moment. Hand in hand they bounded up the courthouse steps and made their way to the office of the Justice of the Peace.

The good Reverend E. Geddys Nunn was presiding this day. Nunn was a stickler for the word of God, and he had agreed to work an occasional shift at the courthouse so that he could be a witness for the Lord to the young couples that came there seeking marriage. He had made it his own personal crusade, and he was good at what he did, even if he was pushy at times. He was an impressive figure, standing well over six feet with a beak-like nose which sat prominently on his face and held up his wire rim glasses. He had a thick shock of bright red hair which, no matter how hard he tried, always looked gloriously unkempt. His rich, deep bass voice added a solemnity to whatever proceedings over which he presided and had made him a favorite on the local funeral circuit. It was said that he gave the best send-off the town of York had ever seen.

Curley and Minnie stood in the hallway and read the sign. Five dollars for a license. That was no problem. Witnesses. Curley told Minnie not to worry, they would corral someone before they went in. Parties must be eighteen or be with their legal guardian before entering into the holy sacrament of matrimony. Check; that was no problem.

"Uh, Russell," Minnie interrupted as Curley continued down the list.

"Huh?"

"We might be in trouble."

"How's that?"

"Well, see, I ain't eighteen yet." Curley's jaw dropped.

"You ain't?" He hadn't even thought to ask.

"No. I just turned seventeen." Minnie began to tear up quickly.

"Now, don't cry," he pleaded, "we'll figure somethin' out."

"Oh, Lord," she moaned, "we spent the whole night together in that car. If we don't come back married I'll be ruined. *Ruined*. Ooooh, Lord!" Curley paced back and forth. He had come this far, he was not about to be undone by this little technicality.

"Well," he said after some thought, "we will just have to lie." Minnie stared at him in disbelief.

"That's it?" she asked impatiently. "That's your plan?"

"Yep. That is my plan. There ain't no way that the justice of the peace is going to know how old you are. Hell, I thought you was at least eighteen myself."

"And what if he does know?" Minnie demanded. Curley smiled. He could tell that she had never broken the rules before.

"He won't," he assured her. "Trust me."

The door to the office opened suddenly and a man who looked shell-shocked exited with his bride, who looked as if she had eaten something which really didn't agree with her. Curley grabbed the man's arm as they passed.

"What the------"

"Easy, bud," Curley said, "I was just wonderin' if maybe ya'll could be our witnesses. We come all the way here from North Carolina and ain't brought no witnesses. Ya'll don't mind, do ya?" The young couple looked at each other and nodded. Sure, they'd do it. In fact, it seemed to make them feel a little better just knowing that there were two more people willing to go through this process this morning.

Reverend Nunn welcomed the young couple into the office with a hug and a "good morning." He did a double take over Curley, wondering what a nice looking young white woman could want with this man, but decided not to press that issue. There was only one question he wanted answered this day.

"Are you with child?" he bluntly asked Minnie.

"What?" she and Curley asked simultaneously.

"Are you with child? Is that the reason for the wedding?"

"Look you," Curley said, his voice gradually rising along with his temper, "I ain't about to let you talk to....."

"Reverend, I am not with child. In fact, there is no possible way that I *could* be with child, if you follow my meaning?" Reverend Nunn nodded and chuckled pleasantly.

"Well, praise the Lord," he said. "I am glad to perform this kind of service." He asked them the pertinent questions and they answered. Minnie breathed a hefty sigh of relief when Reverend Nunn quickly moved past the age requirement, apparently just assuming, as Curley had, that she was of age. They took each other's hands and basked in each other's glances. They repeated their vows dutifully, and the ceremony whirred past them at the speed of light. Suddenly, seemingly as soon as the service had started, Curley heard Reverend Nunn's closing remarks.

"Then by the power vested in me by the state of South Carolina and the good Lord above, I now pronounce you man and wife. You may kiss the bride." Curley leaned in cautiously and kissed Minnie deeply. When he pulled away Reverend Nunn slapped his hands together and exclaimed, "Mr. and Mrs. Russell Norris! My don't that sound nice?" Curley grinned at the preacher as he pulled his bride into his grasp.

"It sure does, preacher. It sure does."

CHAPTER FORTY-EIGHT

Grandma Abernathy was crossing the yard to dump the slop bucket when she heard the familiar groan of Curley's motor. She dropped the bucket by her feet and turned to face the car as it pulled easily into the drive. Curley was the first to get out, Minnie paused to gather herself and summon all of her courage. The deed was done, at least, so there was nothing that her grandmother could do. Except kill them, of course. Minnie tried not to think about that very real possibility. She watched Curley's back and drew some comfort from the strength in his shoulders and his confident stance. That was her husband. She no longer answered to Grandma Abernathy. She was one half of her own family now. She was Minnie Norris.

She slowly eased her way out of the car and tossed a warm smile at her grandmother. The old woman grimaced and her eyes slithered from Curley to Minnie and then back again. She leaned down and spat a long brown stream of snuff into the bucket without taking her eyes off Minnie. Curley was awed and shaken by the ease and accuracy of the woman's aim. He hoped she wasn't as good with bullets as she was with snuff.

"Morning," she called out sarcastically. The bitter edge of her voice tingled across Minnie's face and chilled her courage. Curley answered with a 'morning' of his own when he realized that his bride wasn't going to answer. He turned to Minnie and nodded, trying to prod her into breaking the news and getting it over with. But Minnie seemed breathless and empty. Curley moved to her side and placed his hand on her shoulder. He didn't see the evil squint that crossed Grandma Abernathy's face, but he saw the terror reflected in his wife's eyes.

"C'mon, honey," he said, "it'll be all right. You want me to tell her?"

"No," Minnie managed, "I want her to hear it from me." She stepped away from Curley and took several steps into the yard towards her grandmother.

"Decide to come home?" Grandma snapped. Minnie nodded.

"I have something to tell you," she said.

"Get in the house," Grandma ordered. "And you," she said, pointing to Curley, "you better get outta here while you still can, while you're still all in one piece." Curley swallowed hard and instinctively took a step backwards.

"I say I have something to tell you," Minnie repeated. Grandma's eyes had not left Curley, though, and she didn't seem even remotely interested in what Minnie had to say.

"Told you to get outta here, boy," she repeated harshly. "I ain't gonna tell you again. Are you proud of yourself? You won't goin' to be happy until you'd ruined her, were you? Well, you done done it. I reckon now you can crawl back under that rock from where she found you and stay clear of here. You hear?"

"Grandma," Minnie implored, "don't talk to Russell like that!"

"What? Mind yourself, child. I'm still your Grandmama and you're bound to...."

"And he's my husband," Minnie said quickly, cutting off Grandma's advance and any hope she may have harbored for retreat. The old woman stumbled back as if she had been physically struck, her eyes bulging in her head and her hands grasping downward for the bucket. She needed something tangible, even if it was full of slop. "Me and Russell just come back from South Carolina," Minnie continued. "We got married down there." Grandma looked at Curley and Minnie and was clearly stumped. Of all the things she had feared about Curley, his running off and actually marrying her granddaughter was not one of them. She had just not pegged the man as the marrying kind. This was not news for which she was prepared. Without a word she reached down and picked up the bucket.

"Grandma?"

"Congratulations," she said as she walked away to dump the slop. "I hope you know what you're doing."

And that was it. No screaming, no ranting and no throwing objects. Curley put his arm around Minnie and they watched the woman, her back bent awkwardly, head to the back of the house where she disappeared to leave the bucket's contents for the ground to dispose of.

"Well," Curley said, "that wasn't so bad." Minnie looked up at her husband.

"No," she agreed. "Let's hope your family takes it that well."

જી

Eunice had not paced the floor. She had not even posted herself as guard at the kitchen table. Not so long ago, she reflected, she would have been worried sick over Curley staying out all night. But there was so much water under the bridge now, and so many things had happened that she didn't have the energy to worry about him. He had proven himself to be exceedingly good at getting himself into trouble, and yet he also seemed terribly good at extricating himself from that trouble. Curley was a survivor, of that much she was sure. So if he stayed out all night, she reasoned, the worst that could happen would be mild embarrassment for the family for a week or two---just long enough for someone else in the community to make the gossip circuit. She had handled that before, she could handle it again.

The sound of the car wafted into the house and she put aside the dust cloth she had been using to clean the coffee table in the den. She picked the ashtray up from the floor and laid it carefully down on the table. She took several deep breaths and reminded herself that she had resolved months ago that she was not going to let Curley upset her so badly anymore. Lorenzo believed that Curley would calm down eventually, and she had to believe it, too. She heard the screen door pop shut behind her and Curley's footsteps across the kitchen floor. Eunice also took note of the other footsteps. Those were foreign to her, she only knew it wasn't a member of her family. She turned and faced her son and Minnie. There was a moment of surprise, which she tried to conceal from them. It was not all that hard to believe that Curley had stayed out all night with this trollop, but it did strain credulity to think that he would bring her back home the next morning. Eunice was deeply offended and suddenly angry. The deep breaths had not worked.

"Mom?"

"What is she doing here?" Eunice asked bluntly. "Isn't it enough that you shame this family constantly with your behavior, Russell? Now you've taken to rubbing our noses in it?" Eunice saw Minnie blushed and wanted desperately to reach out and slap the child. What kind of woman stayed out all night and then feigned shame over words?

"It's not like that, Mom," Curley said, "there's something that we need to tell you. You might wanna sit down." Eunice studied their faces and their strained stances.

"I take my news standing, thank you. Good or bad. She pregnant?" Minnie turned as red as a beet this time, and Eunice again felt that desire to lash her against the wall.

"No," Curley insisted, "that ain't it. This is good news. Honest."

"Well," Eunice said dubiously, "it would certainly be nice for you to bring some good news into this house for once. Let's have it."

Curley took the deepest breath of his life and reached over to take Minnie's hand. He could feel it trembling beneath his own. Eunice watched their fingers intertwine and knew at once what their news was.

"Oh dear God, Russell," she said, "please tell me you haven't gone and married this girl. Please." Her voice was desperate and pleading, causing Minnie's eyes to fill with tears. Curley was now shaking himself, this time with frustrated rage.

"Look, Mom...."

"God almighty, Russell, tell me you haven't gone and married a white woman. Tell me!" Eunice was demanding now.

"I'll be good to him, Mrs. Norris," Minnie said with a quivering voice, "and I'll make him happy. I promise I will." Eunice's derisive laughter tore through the room like a tornado.

"Happy?" she barked. "Of course you'll make him happy. For an hour or two. And then it'll be on to the next one. Miss Abernathy that is how my son works."

"That ain't right," Curley said through clenched teeth.

"What?" asked Eunice. "What isn't right."

"It's not Miss Abernathy. It's *Mrs. Norris.* Same as you, Mom." Eunice took a step towards him but stopped herself. She was going to keep one promise which she had made to herself: there would be no more violence in this house.

"Get out," she said quietly and calmly. She turned her full attention on Minnie, who cowered backwards from her new mother-in-law's vicious stare. "There is only one Mrs. Norris in this home, and that's me. I *earned* the name and managed to keep it all my life. We'll see how long you have it." She turned back to Curley. "Now, Russell, take your white wife and get out of this house. Now!"

Curley turned Minnie and they walked out of the house. Minnie began sobbing in the front seat as Curley got the engine going. He let her cry---there was simply nothing he could think of that was worth saying. He couldn't promise her that his Mom would come around. He had seen her hold fast to beliefs long after they ceased being comfortable, and he saw no reason to believe this one would be any different. Curley tried to push away the look in Eunice's eyes when he had referred to Minnie as Mrs. Norris. His mom had looked as if she had been completely betrayed. Sold out and cast aside by her eldest son. Resentment settled over him quickly. Minnie was the first decent woman that had come into his life. Why didn't Eunice see that? Why couldn't she be thankful for that?

Eunice peered from the kitchen window and watched the car speed out of the driveway and down the road. When they were out of sight she bowed her head and began crying quietly. She had handled the absences with the band. She had handled the slow disintegration of their relationship that the booze had brought on. She had handled every thing that Curley had brought across her threshold---both the good and the bad. But now her son loved another woman. Minnie Aber--- *Norris*, was now first in his life and she commanded his emotions. And for the first time Eunice felt like she had really lost her son.

The newlyweds sped down the road towards Gastonia. They had thought of everything and managed to get themselves wed. But as the noon day sun broke through the clouds their honeymoon remained mired in limbo.

Curley had a wife now, but he had no where to take her.

The newest Norrises were homeless.

PART SEVEN

REDEMPTION

CHAPTER FORTY-NINE

Curley turned over and studied the form sleeping peacefully next to him. He quietly watched the side rise and fall and listened to the contented, slight moans that slipped out from under the covers every now and then. The noises of the well loved. He reached out and fingered the unruly edges of hair that teased his face and tickled his nose. The world was not yet awake, the curtain had not been raised on the day. He snuggled closer to the warm body beside of him, throwing his arm around the hip and hugging her towards him. The smell of her hair filled his senses. This was heaven.

"You think you're gonna find this on the road?" she asked playfully. Curley was startled—he had not known that she was awake. He laughed at her joke.

"Sure I can," he answered, "I just don't get to snuggle as long." She rolled over quickly and punched his chest.

"Russell Norris you better be kiddin'!" she yelled. She was grinning, but Curley got the feeling that there was some honest concern behind the teasing.

"Aw, c'mon, Minnie," he assured her, "you know that you are the only one for me." He leaned a little closer and kissed her tenderly on the cheek, then on her neck.

"What do you think you're doin'?" she asked, pretending to push him away.

"I think," he said, "I am getting a proper send off from my wife." Minnie sighed and tugged the covers over them, shutting out the world and the thoughts of goodbye for a little while longer.

Curley tossed his guitar in the trunk of Uncle Mack's car and faced his wife, who was doing an admirable job of holding up, considering the circumstances. She had helped him pack and was even trying to help him load the car, although Mack and Ray were doing their best to make sure she didn't actually do any manual labor. Once the car was fully loaded, Mack and Ray slipped into the car without a word to allow Curley and Minnie a more private farewell.

"You be careful out there," Minnie said with a fake smile. Curley hugged her and ran his hands through her hair.

"Trust me," he said without mentioning why he had said it. He didn't have to—they both knew what was running through her mind at that moment. The truth was that it was running through Curley's mind, too, but there was no way he was going to admit it to his wife. That was the last thing she needed right now. Still, she knew him well enough to make him worry and wonder if she smelled his own fear. Curley knew what the road was like, and he knew better than anyone the temptations that would be brought to bear on him this time out. Sure, they had been there before, and he had, for the most part, survived them. But this time there was no room for failure. If he screwed up this time, it didn't merely make him a sorry excuse for a boyfriend, it made him an adulterer, and while he had not spent a great deal of time within the walls of any church, he knew well what *that* meant. It was a great deal of pressure for a man not known for his self control and will power. From behind them, Curley heard the not-so-subtle clearing of throats.

"You'd better go," Minnie instructed, "before they change their mind and leave you here."

"Not a chance," Curley bragged. "You gonna be okay? I mean, going back to your Grandma's house ain't gonna be easy." Minnie nodded.

"No, it won't. But I'll be fine. Honest. You go and make enough money so that *we* don't live with Grandma when you get back." Curley cackled at the thought, then he pulled Minnie close to him.

"Grandma ain't never heard such racket as all that," he said wickedly. "She'd have the preacher on me in a second."

"Or the police," Minnie cracked. The throats started clearing again and Curley kissed her long and sweetly.

"See you when I get back," he said, assuring her that he was taking the fact for granted. He turned and walked to the car. As he opened the door, Minnie rushed again to his side and kissed him passionately.

"There," she said as she drew away, "if that memory don't keep you true then there ain't a thing I could do about it anyway." Curley laughed and hopped into the car. Minnie waved as they pulled away and headed out. She turned and went back into the house to pack her own suitcase and wait for Essie Mae to come and get her. She tried not to think about the aching hole in the pit of her stomach, but it was no use.

She missed him already.

Curley didn't know what he would have done without Mack's kindness. That awful day when they had broken the news to their respective families had left both of them shaken and adrift. Curley had turned the car around in Gastonia and headed for Charlotte and Mack's house. Mack had welcomed them and made them feel at home, giving them as much privacy as they needed and as he could, allowing them to at least have the semblance of a honeymoon.

On their second day of marriage Ray had stopped by for a visit and to offer his congratulations on the nuptials. Eunice had angrily informed him of the event, and her anger was still great enough that Ray had been forced to come up with a lie to cover his real destination.

"She's tore up, Curley," he had informed them. "I ain't never seen her this mad. "Curley had shushed his brother, but it was too late. Minnie had heard the news and was exiting the room in tears. Curley dispatched his brother to act as an ambassador for his marriage. The hope was that if Ray could just give Eunice a since of how happy Curley was and how deeply hurt they both were by her refusal to recognize their wedding, she would come around and welcome them in her home. Unfortunately, Ray returned with word that Curley was always welcome in Eunice's home ---- as long as he came alone. Clearly, Eunice was not budging. With little choice, Curley and Minnie set up house in a backroom in Mack's house, waiting for the day when the traveling band lived up to its name.

The situation was not what either of them had dreamed of, but it had the happy result of only bringing them closer together. As each night set in, Curley would lie beside of Minnie, both of them naked and perspiring from their love making, and paint pictures of their future on the bedroom wall. His finger traced the imaginary and mystic outlines of their home; the large wooden porch with its padded swing. The sprawling yard with its lush green grass. The little creek that bubbled and giggled along the edge of their home. The children, brown and beautiful, that darted back and forth across the yard, calling for their mother's and father's attention. As Curley called forth the vision and spread it across their bedspread, Minnie fell deeper and deeper in love with this man she now called her husband. In the midst of their troubles, as they were forced to rely on the kindness of friends and as family turned their backs to them and their commitment, somehow in all of this mess Curley was able to make her believe that they were going to conquer the world. It wasn't that hard, she supposed. He clearly believed it himself.

"Hey, where you at?" Curley's head snapped up and he saw Mack and Ray both turned and starring at him, bemused looks on their faces. "I got a feeling the reason for them noises that been keepin' me up at night's the same reason for that silly look!" Ray announced his cheerful agreement.

"Man, Curley, I sure never would've thought it. You a married man. Damn!"

"I never woulda through it, either," Mack agreed. "I was convinced you'd be swingin' long after you shoulda settled down. Hell, I figured you'd meet your end at the hands of a jealous husband."

"Well, boys," Curley said, puffing himself up and acting older than he was, "this is what happens when you meet the greatest woman on God's green earth. It don't feel so much like settlin' down as it does like winnin' a race. That's the truth." Ray and Mack faked vomiting, filling the car with the sound of melodramatic gags.

"That's so sweet," Ray mocked.

"It's beautiful," Mack said through convincing emotion. "Ray," he cracked, "reach in that bag there and get me a hanky. It's getting' to me." Curley sank deep into the backseat, trying to shield himself from the taunts. Mack and Ray were chuckling with relish. Curley wanted to curse them, but their laughter was infectious, and he couldn't help but join in after a minute. When the laughs subsided, he sat back up in the seat and became suddenly serious.

"You guys do like her, don't you? I mean, it ain't just me is it? Ya'll think she's pretty, too, right?" Mack and Ray glanced cautiously at each other – they tried desperately to give each other the power to control their laughter, but it was no use, the care was quickly filled again with the sound of their laughs. Curley shot up higher in his seat and demanded to know what was so funny. The obvious anger in his voice and demeanor only made things seem funnier. It was several minutes before Mack was able to formulate an answer.

"Jesus Christ, Curley, what in the hell do you care what we think? You're the one that has to go to bed with her every night for the rest of your life."

"Yeah," Curley agreed, "but you know how it is. I mean, I think she's definitely a looker, but I guess I just wanna make sure ya'll agree with me. I mean, its always nice to have your friends think that your girlfriend is pretty."

"Wife," Ray corrected, "she's your wife now, Curley."

"Alright, that just makes the question even more important. Do you? Do ya'll think that Minnie's pretty?"

"Yeah, Curley," Mack said in his most soothing voice, "I think that Minnie is damned pretty. In fact, I ain't sure what in the hell she's doing married to a mutt like you!"

"And I agree one hundred percent," Ray chimed, "she would've been so much better off to have kept that date with me. But, it's her loss." Curley smiled.

"I don't think that she sees it that way, little brother. I'm pretty sure that she don't see it that way at all." Curley folded his arms and sat back in his seat, giving off the air of a monarch who has just had his domains praised by a rival sovereign.

"Well, *I* sure do think she's pretty," he said, as if someone had dared to disagree with him. "Prettiest girl in that dump of a town."

"Yep," Mack said. He looked sideways at Ray and winked. "Course, the only trouble is leaving a girl that pretty at home all alone while you're on the road. That could be tough."

"Oh, yeah," Ray agreed happily, "that's just askin' for trouble."

"What kinda trouble?" Curley asked. His face had drawn into a knot at the mention of trouble. "What do ya'll mean?"

"It's just that she is in fact so pretty. I mean, I wouldn't want to leave her behind all alone. Somebody's bound to make a play for her. I mean, how many folks even know that ya'll got married? I just think it could be trouble," said Mack. Curley flashed a cocky smile.

"Oh. Well, I ain't worried about that none," he said. "I trust Minnie. She ain't about to stray." Ray groaned. "What?" Curley demanded.

"Huh?"

"You think different you better just say so." Ray cleared his throat.

"Gosh, Curley, I don't mean nothin' against Minnie or nothin'. It's just that, well, like Mack says, she is so pretty and all. And then, like you done told me, there's already been guys after her. Like that preacher fella. What was his name again?"

"Michael Smith?" Curley asked incredulously.

"Yeah, yeah," Ray said, "that's the fella, ain't it? The man that was after her for a while?"

"Shit, Ray, I ain't worried about *him*." Ray shook his head, looking concerned.

"Okay, Curley. I'm just saying…"

"Well you can quit saying it," Curley snapped, "cause that little white preacher ain't worryin' me none. Shit, you should just look at how he walks."

"Huh?" Mack asked. Ray knew exactly what Curley meant and chuckled.

"He walks like a white man, Mack. Like he's got something heavy and thick stuck up his ass. You can just watch a man like that walk and you just know he can't please no woman. Trust me." A look of sheer terror crossed Mack's otherwise placid features.

"Is that true?" he asked Ray, deciding this was not the time to go trusting Curley. Ray nodded solemnly.

"Yeah, Mack, it is," Curley added, "your walk ain't bad. But Michael Smith's walk? Nah, I ain't worried about him."

"We're just kiddin', Curley," Mack said, "she's a fine girl. You ain't got a thing to worry 'bout."

Curley dropped back into his seat again and began humming a tune. Ray instinctively picked up on the tune and added a harmony part. Soon Mack chimed in with a third part and they were working out their trio act. Curley missed Minnie, but it was good to be back on the road. He trusted her, probably more than he trusted himself. But he was going to remain true. Mack and Ray would help him – they would be there every step of the way. Curley stretched out as best he could and laid his head on his coat. As he drifted off to sleep he instructed himself to dream of his wife. That would make it seem, at least for a minute, like she wasn't so far away. Until he awoke, that is.

CHAPTER FIFTY

The encores weren't as dramatic as they had been in the days when Shifty plucked his bass lines alone in a cloud of cigarette smoke, but they still felt awfully satisfying. It remained Curley's favorite part of the show. Their sound had suffered somewhat by the departure of their bassist, but Curley and Ray enjoyed the newest challenge---trying to close all the possible "holes" in the songs with their strumming and their fills. Mack seemed pleased enough by the crowds and the responses, and without Shifty the Norris Brothers were entitled to a bigger piece of the gate. As a man with a wife now, Curley found that part of the arrangement much to his liking.

There was still his Mom and the boys to think about, though. Ray's take of their earnings was not nearly enough to keep the house running, but Eunice had made it clear that she would accept nothing from her eldest son. Accordingly, Curley and Ray lumped their money together when they sent it off to their Mom, allowing her to think that the money all came from Ray. Curley decided that the best arrangement for his pay was to send half of it to Eunice and the boys, a fourth of it to Minnie, and keep a fourth for himself out on the road. Minnie was at home with Grandma Abernathy, and since they had no children to worry about her expenses would not amount to much. Curley was sure that what he sent her each week was more than enough for her to get by on. Besides, he may no longer be able to enjoy the company of other women while on the road, but that didn't mean he couldn't still enjoy *himself*. And war or no war, there were still many ways to do that.

Ray and Mack just assumed that Minnie had known about Curley's drinking when she married him, so they didn't ride him too hard about his occasional excesses. Mack's only stipulation was that he not have to visit the inside of any more strange jails to bail Curley out. That seemed reasonable, so Curley managed to keep himself just out of reach of the long arm of the law. There were, as always, some close calls, but nothing counted against him as long as he didn't get caught. And he was doing everything in his power to insure that.

He dropped letters off to Minnie whenever he could, keeping her informed of their movements and trying to get her to use the money he was sending to get a telephone at her Grandma's home.

"I miss the sound of your voice," he wrote, "and would like to hear you say you love me again. Words on a page aren't the same."

Of course, he didn't even have the luxury to read anything from her hand. Their conversation was totally one sided because, traveling as they were, there was no way Minnie could have gotten a letter to him anyway. So he did all that he could in an effort to say everything they would have said to each other had they been in the same room. He filled the letters with rambling declarations of his undying love for her and his complete and total devotion to her. He didn't say it (because that would have been imprudent even for him), but each time he wrote a letter he was proud of himself for not having cheated or otherwise done something to ruin his marriage. The fact was that Curley's good behavior surprised no one more than himself. When he wasn't assuring her about his love, he was playfully teasing her about the things he was planning to do when he returned home.

"I hope Granny Abernathy is not reading my letters," he wrote several times. He could just imagine Minnie's face turning a deep crimson as she read about his dreams and desires, and the thought made him want her even more. He also entertained himself with thoughts of Granny actually getting her hands on the letters. The old woman, if she even knew what Curley was talking about (and he doubted that she did) would have keeled over on the spot. "If she should see any of this," he added as a postscript after one particularly steamy passage, "please assure her that it is the Irish in me talking---*not* the Indian! Maybe that will make her feel better."

It seemed that war fever followed them wherever they went. Curley was surprised to see how gung-ho so many people were to jump on a boat and go fight in Europe. As far as he was concerned, these mouthy white boys were welcome to it. They could have all the war they wanted; just leave him out of it. Curley and Ray talked often about the possibility that they would have to go and fight eventually. Things were not going particularly well for the United States and her allies, and anyone who had once believed that there was the possibility of a quick resolution to the war was now freely admitting their mistake.

Ray was convinced that it would all be over with before the government came looking for them, but Curley wasn't as confident as his younger brother. The more he heard about the fighting the more he believed it could go on forever, and that meant eventually someone was going to call their number.

They also ran into some serious hostility because they were obviously young and able, but they had not come to the aid of their country---they were out playing music and chasing women. Uncle Mack had been forced to cancel several shows because of rumors which reached him and indicated that his "Indian Artists" safety might be in jeopardy. Curley and Ray were able to laugh off the danger. These were not the first white folks who thought the world would be a better place without them, but Uncle Mack was not used to the animosity and wanted to avoid even the possibility of trouble. He did not want to have to explain to Mrs. Norris why her sons weren't coming home anymore.

The night air slapped Curley smack in the face as he threw open the stage door and walked out into the alley. Mack and Ray followed closely behind carrying their instruments and the night's purse. They loaded the car and scrambled into it, cranking it quickly and driving away into the night, leaving behind more satisfied customers.

"Nice show," Mack observed in a tired voice. They had worked hard for their money tonight, forced to win over a crowd not disposed to applauding anything but gospel, and then only on very special occasions.

"Yeah," Curley agreed, "I guess. Those folks sure was cranky, though." They drove on in silence, enjoying the quiet, allowing the ring from the amplifiers to subside in their ears. It was a beautiful spring night with a high, full moon splashing light across the highway. Curley watched the stars as they drove forward, wondering what his wife was doing now. It was late, she was probably getting ready for bed; if she wasn't there already. He thought of the smell of her hair, the way her hands brushed it away from her face in an effortless, supremely graceful and alluring motion. He sighed and pulled his attention back inside the car, away from the tormenting dream.

"Where we stayin' tonight, Mack?" he asked.

"Don't know yet," Mack answered with a good-natured and shy chuckle. "I forgot to make those arrangements. I reckon we'll drive 'till we find a place and then we'll just bunk there."

"Try to find a place near a bar, will ya?" Curley joked. Mack groaned and Ray grumbled something disapproving. Curley laughed at

them. "Like a couple of goddamn old women," he shot. "You two
tryin' to be deacons or something?"

"No," Ray chided, "just tryin' to 'keep your Indian ass outta jail is
work enough for both if us, we don't need no more responsibilities."
Mack nodded his agreement and Ray turned to make sure that Curley
caught the proud look on his face. That had been a good one.

"Yeah, funny as hell, Ray."

They drove on, keeping their eyes peeled for a place to lay their
heads and get some rest before heading to the next song.

༮

The sign said only "Motel" and "Cheap Rooms/By the Night or the
Hour." It was an intriguing way of drawing customers, although Mack
wondered aloud exactly what kind of customer it attracted and whether
or not it was safe. But the night was getting away from them, and they
had reached a point of fatigue where a dirty bed was better than no bed
at all. Mack pulled the car into the lot and to a parking space near the
office door. There was an eerie, yellow light which escaped onto the
pavement from the nasty window. The sound of a radio was barely
audible; the sound of a man singing jubilantly and off key could be
heard for miles. Ray leaned into the backseat and shook Curley awake.

"Huh? What is it?"

"C'mon, Curley, we're checkin' in. We found us a place for the
night." Curley licked his lips and rearranged his pillow.

"Ya'll go on in and come get me 'fore you go to the room." Ray
sighed but moved obediently. There was no prodding a dozing Norris.

Mack signaled for Ray to hurry. He had been driving since they had
left the gig and was getting ornery. Ray jogged over and they entered
the motel's office together. The room was musty and wreaked of cigar
smoke. Behind the counter sat a very large man reading a magazine.
He did not look up when the little bell which hung by the door rang to
announce their arrival. He merely licked his fingers and flipped the
page of his reading. Ray saw that it was some sort of girly magazine.
He smiled as he thought of this fat, sweaty white man sitting alone in
this hole-in-the-road dive imagining he was lying down to make love to
one of his magazine's models. Ray thought it would take an
exceptionally strong woman to survive being under that pile of love.

Mack stood up to the bar that separated the clerk from the customers
and waited. And waited. He looked at Ray who could only shrug his

shoulders. There was no way the man could not know they were standing there. His chair was less than five feet from where Mack stood.

"Ahem!" Nothing. The man licked his fingers again and turned another page. Ray wondered if they were interrupting a special moment---perhaps it was the first time tubby had ever seen a naked woman. "Ahem!" Mack tried again but with no more success than the first time.

"Excuse me, mister?" Ray said, raising his voice to a level that would have been rude under other circumstances. "Hey, pal?!" The man sighed and folded the top corner of the page he was being forced to abandon. He turned and measured Ray. There was something strange about the look, something that made Ray feel uncomfortable, as if the man was saying something that he didn't want to hear. The light which flickered behind his eyes suggested recognition, although Ray was certain the two of them had never met.

"Mister, we were wanting to get us a room," Ray said, quieter now that he had the man's attention. The man squinted and leaned over in his chair, spitting a brown stream of snuff into the can sitting beside of him. Still he did not speak. Ray began to wonder if perhaps the man was deaf. "Nah," he thought, "who would leave a deaf guy in charge of a motel in the middle of nowhere in the middle of the night?" Mack closed what gap there had been between himself and the man and leaned in.

"Can you hear me son?" he asked. The man shifted his eyes from Ray to Mack. Ray saw that the look that had so unnerved him was gone when he looked at Mack.

"'Course I can hear you," the man retorted as if it were a stupid question. "You want a room." Mack grimaced and rubbed his hand across the stubble forming on his chin.

"Well, then, what do we hafta do to get one around here?" The look returned to the fat man's face as he turned and again looked at Ray as if he were trying to size him up. An evil and dirty smile crossed the man's thin lips. Mack, whose patience was already running low, slammed his fist down on the counter with a thunderous thud. "Goddamn it," he cried, "what in the hell is the problem? Now are you gonna rent me a room or not?" The man returned his eyes to Mack's.

"Sure," he said, slowly turning in his chair and pulling a key off of a large wooden board. Mack breathed a sigh of relief. He would be in a warm bed in no time. He reached in his pocket and pulled out a wad of cash.

"There'll be three of us," he informed the clerk, "so charge me whatever that would be. Just one room, though." The man coughed harshly into his hand and then leaned over and spat again.

"Two," he said through shallow breaths. Mack eyed him warily, mentally deciding that the man was retarded.

"How's that?" he asked, trying to muster some inner reserve of patience.

"Two," the man repeated, "there will be two of you in the room."

"No," Mack said, speaking slowly this time and making sure to enunciate every syllable clearly this time, "there-----will----be----- *THREEEEEEEE*----of us in the room."

"Two," the clerk repeated. "This here," he said, tilting his head absently towards Ray, "will just have to sleep in the car." Ray and Mack exchanged nervous and confused glances.

"How's that?" asked Ray, moving closer to the counter.

"I say you'll have to sleep in the car." The man tossed a finger towards a hand-painted sign behind them. "No Dogs and No Niggers," the man read with grim satisfaction. "You ain't white is ya?" Ray tried to speak but found that his voice caught in his throat. Mack recoiled in shock, finding himself as speechless as Ray. He felt the blood rush to his face as the embarrassment from the actions of one of his own began to settle in.

"Well?" the man asked again. "You ain't white is ya?" Ray was about to answer when the hollow *ding* of the bell went off behind him. Curley was standing in the doorway with his satchel in his hand.

"What the hell's takin' so long?" he asked. "We ready or not?" The man hunched up in his chair to peer around Mack. Upon seeing Curley, he shook his head in disgust.

"I take that back," he said to Mack, "looks like they won't be nobody but you in that room tonight."

"Now hold on," Mack protested, "my money's as good as anybody else's is. We need a room."

"Then keep driving," the man snapped. "Ya'll ain't stayin' here." Curley was trying to gage the situation, searching Mack and Ray's demeanors to figure out exactly what was going on.

"Are you tellin' me that you won't rent us a room?" Mack asked indignantly. "Is that what you're tellin' me?"

"No," the man said, "I ain't exactly sayin' that. I am sayin' that *you* can rent as many rooms here as you want. But these two niggers here...."

"What the fuck did you say?" Curley asked, dropping the satchel and storming towards the man. "What did you say you fucking fat bastard?!" Mack stepped in front of Curley and stopped his progress towards the clerk.

"Easy, Curley," he said, "he ain't worth it, son." Curley stared at Mack.

"That ain't for you to decide," he answered curtly. "You ain't the one bein' called that shit. You ain't the one been called that all your life, Mack. So don't tell me who's worth it and who ain't." Mack started to answer when he heard the cock of the hammer on a pistol. Suddenly Ray was standing by their side with eyes wide and hands pointing.

"Let 'em come on," the clerk said, aiming the gun towards Mack and Curley. "Let the nigger come on!" Curley gritted his teeth and balled his fists. There was no way he was dumb enough to charge a man with a loaded gun---no matter how fat and slow that man might appear. He felt Mack's grip around his biceps.

"Let's go, Curley. Save that energy for when the odds are better." Mack turned quietly and nobly towards the clerk. "Thank you," he said in a voice as taught as a hangman's rope, "but I think we will patronize another establishment. Sorry to have bothered you." Mack turned Curley around and gently urged him towards the door. Ray was already under the bell. As he stood in the doorway Mack heard the clerk call from behind.

"Damn nigger lover." Mack did not turn. He walked out into the parking lot and entered his car. Curley and Ray sat mute and sulking. Mack cranked the car without a word. But there was something different, something had radically changed. Before they had all been musicians, a proud and selective race all its own. Now, however, they were painfully aware of their differences----differences which had existed before but had been submerged under the camaraderie of the road. That was gone, now. The car no longer felt like the private domain of Uncle Mack's Traveling Band. Now they were two young Indians and an aging white man, thrown together through a curious mix of talent, need and circumstance. Mack felt the unmistakable urge to scream, to rant against the injustice and the bad luck, but he knew that would accomplish nothing beyond making everyone feel even more uncomfortable. They had been forced to confront their differences, and things would never be quite the same.

Curley said nothing. He wanted to bite back any and all anger or resentment towards Mack quickly. Implicitly he understood that, of course, Mack had been right to intervene. In fact, Mack may have saved his life. But feelings were not so easy to control, and no matter how hard he tried to remind himself that Mack was one of the good guys, one of the world's last true gentlemen, the anger threatened to boil over. He wasn't mad at Mack, but that didn't matter. He was mad, no, he was furious, at white and everything that stood for in his world. That curious mix of supreme arrogance and utter insecurity that made up the psyche of all oppressors was what he wanted to shatter. Mack didn't act like the clerk. But he was still a white man, and he still thought it was his responsibility to keep Curley in line and look out for him. Hell, white men had been "looking out" for Indians for years now. In fact, as Lorenzo liked to quip, white men had looked the Indian clean out of the entire continent.

"Hey, fellas," Ray said, breaking the heavy silence, "there ain't no sense lettin' that lard ass get us down. We'll just find another motel and get a good night's rest. That's all we need, right?"

No one answered. Curley seethed and Mack regretted as Ray tried to soothe. It made for an interesting, if almost completely untenable, dynamic. Ray turned away and stared mournfully out of the window. It had taken so little to turn their night into a living hell.

CHAPTER FIFTY-ONE

Curley rolled over quietly on the blanket, trying his best to find a comfortable position before the sun rose and ended the battle once and for all. The grass underneath him made for soft bedding, but it was no replacement for a well-stuffed mattress. Mack had driven for over an hour after the run-in with the motel clerk before deciding that accommodations were not to be found. With the consent of Curley and Ray he elected to pull the car over as soon as they found a nice field, and they would content themselves with a night under the stars. It was certainly not the first time they had made nature their own expansive motel suite, not the first time the band traded in the roof of a cheap room for the stars of the night. But things were different tonight. The three men were tired and beaten in a way they had never been before. Mack struggled with himself to try and find something to say, anything, which would offer some comfort to his friends and, in some small measure at least, redeem his own race. But he recognized an emotional mine field when he saw one, and it seemed more politic to avoid even mentioning the events in the hotel's lobby. Ray recognized the expression on his brother's face: the tightly wound anger, the bitter resentment festering just below the surface. He knew in a way that Mack could not that there was nothing to say. Ray also wanted to find the words that might assuage some of what Mack was feeling. Although he could not relate to it himself in the same way, Ray saw the look of pained devastation that Mack wore. It made him all the more angry at the stupidity in the world.

Curley remained distant from the other two, maintaining his own space and avoiding anything which would open the doors to Mack's pity or Ray's preaching. Tonight he wanted to hate, and he didn't care whether that was right or wrong. Mack and Ray had done nothing to him, but he knew better than to allow them to get in the way of his mood. Misplaced anger was just as devastating as anger well earned. Curley was not going to let the fat man from the motel cause him to hurt these two men with whom he had shared so much and come so far. As a matter of will, he was not going to let that happen.

Curley heard Ray mumbling something in his sleep. He rolled over again, this time moving too far and landing squarely on a rock embedded in the soft ground. He cursed and sat up, reaching under the blanket and feeling around for the stone. Once he had found it and dispatched it deep into the field, he rolled onto his back. Propping his head underneath his arm he watched the gradual encroachment of the horizon. Morning would be coming soon and he hadn't had the first moment's sleep. He cursed again quietly and rolled back onto his side, forcing his eyes shut and determining to sleep.

The sound of the car blurred into the background at first, barely warranting his attention. There had been the sounds of passing motorists off an on all night, it came with the territory. It wasn't until he realized that the car had stopped and was idling near the ravine that he sat up, peering into the darkness to see who or what was lurking out there. The sound of muffled voices came down through the bushes towards his ears, alerting Curley to the fact that, whoever it was, they were sneaking around. He looked over to see if he could reach Ray without moving too conspicuously. He had moved too far, though, when he had rolled away from the pesky stone under his bedroll. Curley glanced around. If he could find a stick that was long enough he could prod Ray awake.

The snapping sound of a twig breaking underfoot froze his search. They were coming closer now. They were coming towards the campers. Curley felt his pulse beginning to quicken. He grabbed a small stick and tossed it at the back of Ray's head. It found its mark, but with only enough force to cause Ray to toss around momentarily and grumble something vaguely profane. The sound was enough, however, to halt the progress of the people sneaking around. Curley heard the voices lower, then a sustained "Sssshhhhhhhhh," and then the footsteps began again. They weren't car thieves, that much was clear. Car thieves would have hot-wired the engine and been careening down the highway already, they would not have risked getting ambushed by greater numbers the way these folks were doing. Curley wondered if the field in which they were laying might belong to one of the voices he heard. Maybe they were trespassing.

The moon peeped from behind some billowy clouds and gave

Curley a little more light. The shapes of the figures coming towards them became clearer. Curley could tell from their walk that they were indeed men, ending his slight hope (and fervent dream) that a group of lost and beautiful women were stumbling into camp seeking directions and hungry for love. Although the light was slight and dancing, Curley thought he counted at least four. They moved at a deliberate pace and in a low crouch. They looked, he thought, as if they were searching for something.

Or someone.

Curley had seen enough. Ray and Mack were going to have to be yanked from their sleep, and the quicker the better. Curley ruefully wondered if he had already waited too long---by the time they had cleared the sleep from their eyes and the cobwebs from their heads these men would be upon them. He decided that the quickest way to get them awake was to startle them. And, in the balance, he hoped that maybe the action would also frighten away the shadows that were creeping ever nearer.

Having decided, Curley took in a deep breath and quickly asked the Great Spirit for a little help and a lot of luck. Then, as quickly as he possibly could, he rolled onto his knees and shot up like a bolt from the blanket. As he jumped he let out a blood curdling scream and threw a handful of dirt and pebbles towards the figures.

"GET OUTTA HERE!!!!" he screamed at the top of his lungs. "GET ON OUTTA HERE NOW!!!!!"

From beside him he heard Ray lumbering towards consciousness, dutifully inquiring from Curley what the trouble seemed to be. Curley didn't bother to answer, opting instead to continue his screams with another bellow designed to make these stealthy creeps fall back on their heels. Curley heard Mack, apparently fully awake, hop up and yell as well. Ray, still confused, was begging to be let in on the secret.

Curley was dismayed to find that all the noise, while temporarily stunning the men and halting their forward progress, did not keep them at bay for very long. Instead, they collected themselves and pounced upon the camp with a vicious and overwhelming ferocity. Curley felt the slam of thick wood against his side, sending the air retreating from his lungs. He gasped for air, filling the night with his dry heaves and desperate, hacking gulps.

From beside of him, Curley heard the sickening sound of flesh being pounded by flesh, the unmistakable sound of one human being thrashed by another. As the two by four slammed a second time into the side of his head, he realized that it was Ray who was being pummeled. All of his instincts, familial and animal, cried within him, demanding that he defend his kid brother. The world was ebbing and flowing around him, and consciousness was trying to fade away. Curley felt the ground rushing up to meet him, but he managed to catch his fall and sit up on one knee. He became vaguely aware of someone's voice punctuating the thuds and smacks with exhortations and brutal commands. Curley heard Mack's voice, crying desperately. There was another, metallic sound, and Mack went silent. Curley was sure he had just heard the band leader murdered. There was no time, now, he told himself. He had to save Ray. He had to. The wooden plank crashed against his jaw. His mouth filled with the acidic taste of his own blood. He gagged, choking momentarily on several of his teeth. He collapsed to the ground. He rolled over onto his side, his survival instincts reminding him that blood was still gushing down his throat. He felt someone tugging at him and realized he was being dragged across the ground. He tried to fight, but it was no use. He had no strength left. He closed his eyes and prayed for his wife, about to become a young widow, and his family. He thought of his mother. How would she handle losing two sons at the same time? Then the movement stopped. Curley heard the soft moaning beside of him and struggled to raise his head. He saw Ray, bloodied and horribly bruised, lying next to him. He was alive at least.

He felt the body drop onto his, heavy and wet. Curley managed to roll Mack off to the side. There was no sign of life in him. Curley tried to crawl closer, to feel for a pulse, but a hard kick to his ribs stopped him cold.

"Be still, boy," came the gravelly voice from above. Curley complied. He tilted his head just enough to watch the men as they ransacked the camp. After a few minutes, the men walked closer and inspected their handiwork. The toe of a work boot prodded at Curley cautiously until he made the desired noise.

"Ain't none of 'em dead," one man said. Curley noted that he sounded disappointed.

"You sure?"

"Yeah. Not yet, anyway. Might be a different story in the mornin'." An evil chuckle rippled through the group, which Curley had now counted at six.

"This them?" one of the men asked. Curley saw the silhouette of a large man creep closer and bend down, inspecting Ray's face by the waning light of the moon. Then the man stepped over Ray and knelt down to look at Mack. He grunted and then stepped again to Curley. He dropped to his pudgy knees and looked. Curley met the man's eyes, momentarily startling him. The fat motel clerk quickly (or, as quickly as he *could*) stood and backed away from Curley. His petrified motion caused the other men to laugh and taunt him.

"Shit, Dale," one man said, "he ain't gonna hurt ya now!"

"Careful, Dale, he might breath on ya hard!" Curley tried to whisper a bitter "fuck you," but he had neither the energy nor the air. His struggle amused his tormentors, who pointed and laughed as he gasped and tried his best to refuse to be broken. Realizing that he was no danger, the fat clerk, who Curley now knew was named Dale, walked in a pretentiously bold stride to Curley's side and kicked him in the ribs. The dough white man's foot landed softly and without injury. He didn't have the strength to speak, but that didn't stop him from smiling through his bloody lips. The grin, full of mockery and pride, sent a chilling message down Dale's mousy spine and caused convulsions of merriment in his redneck friends.

"Sumbitch is laughin' at ya!" one of them exclaimed. Dale uttered a curse and stepped away from Curley. One of his partners moved close to Curley and knelt, crouching on his knees between Curley and Ray, who was beginning to show signs of life. The man turned Ray onto this side, so that the Norris Brothers were now facing each other. Curley was stunned to see Ray's haggard face, with its flesh hanging limp on the skull. A gash across his forehead bled profusely, oozing a red river down Ray's features. The terror was all the more striking when Ray, struggling to retain consciousness, managed to open his eyes. The sharp and horrific contrast between the pearly whites which surrounded the stormy brown pupils and the crimson tide seared itself in Curley's mind. His pride and determination could not hold back the tears, which poured now unabashedly down his burning cheeks. Curley cried from anger and pain; he wept with fear and loathing; he broke in two with frustration and bitterness. Sickened with himself and his weakness, he tried to end the sobbing, but the flood gates had opened. His chest heaved and his shoulders shook with the force. Snot and blood clogged his nose, forcing him to lean over and vomit. He felt the furry chunks hurl over his tongue and past his teeth, splatting on the ground and then rolling gently down the slope and across his shirt and pants. From somewhere far away he heard the sound of laughter. Curley realized that he must have passed out. He shook his head and forced his eyes wide. Ray was staring at him helplessly. His mouth worked back and forth, without forming any words. Curley wasn't even sure that Ray was *trying* to say anything.

"Goddamn you," Curley said, "leave my brother alone." The man kneeling next to him did not respond. Curley wondered if indeed he had actually said anything at all. Suddenly, the man's hand lashed out, slapping Curley's face and ricocheting across his jaw. Pain, like a bolt of blue summer lightning, streaked across Curley's mind.

"Are you with me, boy?" the man was asking. "Can you hear me? Huh?" The man reached into a pocket and pulled out a pocket knife. He opened the blade and leaned closer to Curley, holding the knife to Ray's side. "Answer me, son. Can you hear what I'm sayin'?"

"Uh..........uh-huh."

"Good. Now you listen good. I don't know where ya'll from and I don't rightly give a shit. But around these parts, our colored folks know how to behave themselves. You ain't all nigger is ya?" The man leaned close to hear the response.

"Uh." Curley licked his lips and took a deep breath. "In.....Indian. Indian." The man nodded thoughtfully.

"We got a few of them left in Georgia, ain't we boys?"

"A few," one of them answered solemnly.

"Well, Indian, colored, whatever, there's just certain things that a boy like you ain't gonna get away with doin' around here. You unnerstand? Dale there tells me that you and your friends was kinda mouthy tonight when he wouldn't let ya'll rent out a room. I reckon you didn't know no better. But now you do." The man's tone dropped quickly from conversational to menacing. "I suggest that, if ya'll ain't dead by mornin', you get the hell outta our town."

"And maybe our state," someone added.

"Yeah, you might wanna think about that, too. Ain't no where in Georgia that's gonna let a colored boy talk back to no whites. We're keepin' things the way they oughta be. Ya'll just get on back up north tomorrow. You hear me?" Curley nodded and Ray groaned. Curley suddenly realized that he was looking at the man's shins, he was no longer faced with the man's glare.

"Wanna try it one more time, Dale?" someone asked gleefully. Curley became aware of the sound of lumbering footsteps and moved in time to see the clerk jogging towards them. He ran up to Ray and delivered the best kick he could to Ray's gut. A pained "ooof" escaped Ray's lips. The sound of applause echoed in Curley's ears.

"Time for the encore," he thought. The footsteps vanished into the sound of a car's motor, and that, too, soon disappeared. Curley dragged himself to Ray.

"You......are you all right?" he asked. Ray nodded in a definitive negative and then smiled sardonically. Curley draped his arm over his brother and they passed out together, the sound of crickets fading in their ringing, stinging ears.

CHAPTER FIFTY-TWO

"Owwww, goddamn it, ouch! What the hell is that shit, man? It hurts!" Curley's head snapped up in a reproachful stare, full of concern and sprinkled with contempt. Ray withered under it, thinking to himself how much Curley could, at times, resemble their mother.

"Be still," Curley said. "I gotta do this."

The sun had risen on the scene of the Great Motel Clerk Massacre to find that, mercifully and miraculously, there were three survivors. Wounded and sore, Curley had taken charge quickly and driven into the nearest town where, even despite the confused and accusing looks of the locals, he purchased bandages and cigarettes, antiseptic and beer.

"You sure this is what you want?" asked the attendant at the grocery store as he rang up the cans of beer. "Looks like you had a rough night."

"I want it," Curley said testily. "You gonna sell it to me?"

"Take it easy, pal. I's just askin' is all."

Curley returned with the goods and began doctoring. When he had felt Ray and Mack were taped together enough to warrant traveling, he had carried each of them to the car and dropped them in the backseat like sacks of dirty laundry. He had then gathered up what could salvaged from the camp and packed the car. As soon as that was accomplished (it hadn't taken long, the rednecks had cleaned them out with the same diligence and attention to detail that they had applied to the ass-kicking) he had driven away from the site, hoping he never had to see that stretch of highway again in his life.

Mack faded in and out of consciousness, but Ray grew more lucid with each passing mile. Curley debated with himself whether or not he should attempt to find a hospital or doctor for Mack----there was no way for him to know the extent of his boss's injuries. There could be internal bleeding, or there could be something broken that Curley couldn't see or feel. Still, he had to believe that the redneck attackers from the previous night were the rule, not the exception, in rural Georgia. Right or wrong, that assumption was the only safe way to insure their survival. And if that was the case, taking Mack to a local doctor might be more dangerous than the risk *not* taking him entailed. Curley decided to stay as far away from local whites as possible. At least for a while. In the meantime he prayed for Mack with all his faith and power. The feelings of resentment and mistrust had faded. Mack was now a victim as well, beaten to within an inch of his life for no reason other than his friendship with Curley and Ray. Curley resolved not to forget that fact. Mack may be as white a white man as Curley had known, but he was now lying in the backseat, covered in his own blood and pus, because he had remained loyal to two brothers with dark skin.

"Where we headin'?" came the weak, shaky voice from the back. Curley's eyes shot to the mirror, which he had positioned so that he could watch his patients. It was Mack!

"Good mornin', captain," he cried, trying to sound as cheerful as possible, "it's so good of you to finally wake up and join us." Mack struggled to sit a little higher in the seat, but quickly found the effort too difficult for him. Sighing, he dropped back with a grunt.

"Where we goin', Curley? What's goin' on?" Mack was clearly dazed. His eyes wandered around the car, seemingly taking everything in for the first time. His face registered his shock when he turned and saw Ray, who was dozing again beside of him. Mack emitted a slow, steady stream of air and looked back at Curley.

"I look as bad as him?" he asked. Curley laughed. It was good to hear Mack joke, it made Curley feel more confident that they were all going to make it.

"Shit, man, you wish you looked that good!" Curley teased. The annoying sound of his s's whistling through his mouth filled the car. Curley found himself missing those teeth that he had swallowed along with the tiny pieces of the two by four.

"I told ya to brush after every meal," Mack said, "but you wouldn't listen, would ya? Now look at ya.....losing your teeth. And at your age!" Curley shook his head and chuckled. Mack began to laugh along as well. Suddenly he was gripped with a racking, violent cough. Curley peered at him through the mirror.

"You all right?" Mack shook his head bravely. Then the coughing intensified and he was pushed up from the seat by the force. Ray, startled, opened his eyes and looked around.

"Who's there?" he asked, apparently still half asleep. "Who is it, Curley?" Curley started to answer but had his attention pulled back to Mack, who was spitting up blood, unable to keep it from oozing down his chin and across the already tattered front of his denim shirt.

"Oh, God, Curley," he said, "I think I'm dyin'. I'm dyin' back here." Curley whirled the car off onto the side of the road and jumped out. He sprinted around the front of the car and threw open the back door. He caught Mack and dragged him towards a small grove of trees. Carefully, trying to be as gentle as he could, Curley propped the band leader against the fat trunk of a pine tree. The coughing began to slowly subside. Mack's face, covered with a thin film of sweat and darkly purple, began to soften. Curley sat down beside him and placed his head in his hands. Ray began crying from the back of the car.

"Curley!" he cried. "Curley....help me! Curley, they're comin' after us again!" Curley was on his feet in no time, ready to rush to the car and beat the hell out of anyone he saw. But what he saw was only the fragile form of his little brother, limp and asleep in the backseat, wracked with troubled dreams. Curley fell to his knees and wept. From behind, he heard Mack's terrible gurgling and choking. Cursing, he picked himself and steadied himself to play nurse or begin a death watch----whichever proved necessary.

ဢ

Curley couldn't help himself---the irony was simply too rich not to be noticed. He had been absolutely convinced that Uncle Mack Crowe, beloved entertainer and all-around good guy, was going to die. By all indications, Mack had been seriously, even fatally injured. Curley had believed that right up until he had procured a motel room for the battered trio. The very act that had been the cause of all this misery was now the very thing that seemed to revive Mack's spirits and health. By the time Curley had cut off the denim shirt and washed away most of the dried blood and mucus, Mack was again trying to cut up and was asking for food. Curley breathed a sigh of relief and thanked the Great Spirit for an obvious miracle. He had become concerned that Mack might die for selfish reasons----if a white man died in the company of two Indians, Curley wondered if anyone would listen to his version of events before stringing him and Ray up from the highest tree they could find. Mack's recovery made that less of a possibility.

Ray was also stronger now, able to stay awake for longer periods of time and able to hold a real conversation. His head did not seem weakly tethered to his shoulders anymore, and the eyes were beginning to regain their lively sparkle. Of course neither man was ready to return to the stage, and Curley was still concerned about what the morning held. Every time a pair of feet passed by their motel room door, he tensed and waited for someone to come crashing in, guns blazing. He also worried that the "recovery" of his patients was only temporary. It had not yet been even twenty four hours since the attack, and the peak-valley effect of the day could always bottom out again. He tried to push the thought from his mind, telling himself that worrying would only break his own spirits, and Mack and Ray were both totally dependent upon him right now.

The night brought him no rest. He had literally put Mack and Ray to bed, tucking them in and reassuring them with the gentleness of a mother hen, and then sat out on the front stoop of the motel, smoking and drinking his beers. He held himself to only four, knowing that if anything should happen in the middle of the night, if Mack or Ray should take a turn for the worse, he didn't want his head full of alcoholic clouds. He watched the stars climb into the sky and twirl themselves around the horizon like well groomed ballerinas, teasing mortals and reminding them that the night, not humans or their famous follies, formed the real basis of inspiration. Curley wondered how many different poets, how many songwriters, had compared the night sky to the face of God. He was certain it had to number in the thousands, or at least to easily qualify the thought as a cliche. That wasn't a problem for Curley, who pulled out the pad of paper he had with him and began jotting down the words for a new song. He didn't mind clichés as much as most people seemed to think that he, as an artist, should. He was just too damn practical for all that. As he saw it there was only one requirement for something to be considered clichéd, and that was for it to be the hands-down best way to say something. And if that was the case, what the hell was the point in avoiding using it? Shaking his head, he resolved once more that he would not ever understand white folks----even the ones he liked.

White folks! What a strange breed they were, with their funny walk and their strange speech and their little eccentricities. Of course, to refer to anything about white people as "little" seemed almost a contradiction to Curley. There was, after all, no denying that they were an ambitious people, a people with one eye always on the future and what they called progress. Curley wondered, though, if they ever took the time to look behind themselves, to just quickly glance over their shoulder, at least once in a while, to see where it was that they were coming from. Of all the whites that he had come into contact with, Curley reflected that they all seemed to be missing something, something spiritual which their goods and their God did not seem to fill. They had no ancestors. That was where they failed, he decided. They never really knew who they were, and that was why they seemed so unstable. Why in the hell else would a group of grown men drive out in the middle of the night to chase down a couple of Indians whose crime was no more than to have "talked back" to a white motel clerk? Talk about too much time on their hands! Curley wondered why those tough motherfuckers had not rushed down to their local recruiting station (of which, it seemed, every town had at least one these days) and joined up to fight in a real war. The answer was obvious. In a real war, the enemy often knew that you were coming, and he almost always got off a few shots of his own.

Curley ripped the sheet out of the small notebook and tucked the lyrics into his shirt pocket. He stubbed out his cigarette and walked back into the darkened room. He undressed without turning on the light. Ray and Mack were sleeping peacefully, which was a small measure of comfort to Curley, who had feared their screams and nightmares would keep him awake all night. He had placed them in the same bed, a large double with enough room for them to lay spread out without knocking each other around in the process. That was his one selfish indulgence for the day----he was going to have one bed all to himself. Giving everything else he had been through and done that day, Curley felt very little guilt over the arrangement.

He crawled under the covers and rubbed his legs back and forth, feeling the soothing cool of the clean sheets against his skin. It felt good to be indoors tonight, with a locked door between himself and whoever might be on the other side with less than friendly intentions. He felt a small twinge of homesickness, not really for Minnie or Eunice or even Lorenzo and the boys, but for the community as a whole, that small mill town where people went to church or school or visiting without locking their doors. That kind of security, he thought, would feel awfully good this night.

He rolled onto his side and closed his eyes. He had assumed that sleep would not be a problem, it had, in fact, been chasing him all day. But once the silence penetrated his thoughts and he was left alone with only the sound of breathing coming from the next bed, he found that rest was running in the other direction. He cursed and dared sleep to stay away. He tuned his mind into the sound of Ray and Mack's breathing, thinking that would surely lull him into relaxing. But the more he listened, the more panic-stricken he became. Every breath sounded like it was their last, and his imagination began to make each one sound more and more like the death rattle he remembered from his father's bedside. Curley tried to shut out the breathing, taking the opposite side of where he had just been. That didn't work, either. The more he tried *not* to listen, the more his mind told him he should pay close attention---just in case one of them needed him in the middle of the night. He felt his eyes moistening again, but he managed to swallow down the fear and frustration that were taking on the form of more salty tears.

"No," he whispered, "no more fuckin' cryin'."

Sometime before dawn he passed into the dream world, hoping to become refreshed and stronger. Survival was the only option. And it was up to him. Just before his dreams began to unroll, like the warm sound of violins across the radio dial, Curley realized that he had spent so many years as the survivor. The protector. And, his myriad of mistakes not withstanding, he was good at it. Damn good.

Even with all he had been through, a smile spread across his face, giving his face a more peaceful and rested look than was truly merited.

CHAPTER FIFTY-THREE

The protector.

Those words had haunted Curley all day long as he had once again passed the hours as nurse, bandaging and cleaning wounds, and cracking jokes to try and keep the best face on their situation. It had not been at all easy. Although both Mack and Ray had survived the night, they had awakened only to prove the veracity of the old wive's tale---they were twice as sore on the second day as they had been the day after the beating. Curley kept them both well doused in ice and full of water, which he had always heard could cure just about anything. His most difficult chore was not the doctoring of his patients, but trying to conceal his own foul mood from them. Mack and Ray knew him well, and it took a virtuoso performance to pull off the deception.

The morning had started poorly, following as it did on the heels of a number of nightmares. As vivid as a walk through real time, Curley's dreams had seemed determined to chastise his failure to stop the beatings, his inability to warn the other before it was too late. Over and over he played it out in his mind, the precious seconds he had wasted while trying to decide who was coming towards them and what their business could be, as if they could have wanted anything other than trouble. What could he have been thinking, laying there as the seconds slipped away? He believed it was his fault, and his dreams clearly agreed.

The worst of the dreams was, of course, the last, the one that would embed itself against the back of his eyes and linger all through the day. In it, Curley stood watching as the rednecks beat Ray almost beyond recognition. He could feel Eunice's hands on his back, urging him forward. He heard her yelling at him, begging him to please, please, intervene and find a way to save her son and his brother. But for some reason, he stood still and mute, watching the action as a dispassionate observer. He felt compelled to act, to do something, but an all consuming laziness got the better of him and his feet, and he stood watching, taking everything in like a scientist who had no vested interest in the outcome. Eunice's voice grew louder and the force of her shoves stronger as Ray's face began to melt away under the pounding of white fists. Finally, a particularly vicious shot sent Ray's head flying off of his shoulders. The redneck cackled madly and Eunice, who Curley still couldn't see, bawled fiercely. Curley awoke in a cold sweat, his mouth dry and his entire body shaking like the leaves on a tree. He had crawled out of the bed and walked to the bedside, where he had stayed long enough to satisfy himself that Ray was, in fact, still drawing breath. Then he had walked back out onto the porch of the room and smoked until he heard Mack wake up. He had gone through the remainder of the day like a zombie, not allowing himself any thoughts or reflections.

He put Mack and Ray to bed the same way he had the night before. Walking outside for a cigarette, he sat and watched the cars zip by. He wondered what it must be like--to travel in your own country with impunity, afraid of nothing more than fate. It must be nice, he thought, to be able to go and come as you please, without deferring to anyone for any reason. He felt the anger and ambition rising again, the same way he had felt it time and time again. He thought of all the apologies he had made, all the times he had said that he was sorry. Sorry for what? For offending someone's racial sensibilities? Who the hell worried about offending him? Or worrying him?

Curley looked down and realized that the tips of his fingers were bleeding. Without thinking about it, he had been biting his nails. He had ripped them away, tearing them to the quick and drawing blood. He sighed and stood. He checked the doorknob to make sure that it was securely locked. He needed a drink as badly as he had ever needed one in his life. Deciding Mack and Ray would be all right for an hour or so, he jogged lightly out into the parking lot and to the car. He promised himself that he wasn't going to get drunk.

Just good and numb.

The night sped by Curley at an alarming rate, making him fear that the sun would rise before he had time to extract the sweet juice of vengeance. That was what motivated him, that was what kept his eyes open and drove him long after the toll of the day should have laid him prostrate on a clean bed. He could smell revenge, he could smell the delicious fear of the bastard on the other end of his hate----it smelled unique and fresh, not unlike the dewy and intoxicating smell of a woman's excitement. Curley knew that smell well, and he was determined to be as familiar with its less prosaic cousin before sunrise. That was why he drove so fast, like a madman trying vainly to escape the responsible reach of anyone who would puncture the fantasies with cold, hard doses of reality. He didn't worry about the possibility of being pulled over by a police officer, and he didn't worry about losing control of the wheel and losing his life in an anonymous Georgia ditch. No, the voices of the elders ringing in his ears assured him that was not his fate. Listening as closely as he could, Curley knew that those voices were not assuring him that he would live through the night; only that he was going to make his destination. Beyond that, Curley supposed that he was on his own.

As he drove, he thought about his wife at home. She was probably sewing, or cleaning up the dishes of a late supper. Maybe she was sitting out on her porch, watching the stars the way he had done, thinking about this touch, his kisses, his scent. Or maybe she was reading her Bible. Curley remembered that Minnie liked to do that in the fading light of dusk. He thought about the words of that Bible. Vengeance, it taught, belonged to God. He would get to it in his own sweet time. Curley marveled that something like that could be the tenet for the white man's religion. Whites, who were more impatient than any Indian had ever been, were supposed to wait and allow their God, to take revenge for them. Curley decided that he just couldn't wait that long. There were some things which he believed God left to humans. This was one of them. Besides, what if the offender begged for forgiveness? As Curley understood things, he was bound to receive it if only he asked and repented. But who could honestly tell the heart of a man? And, let's say, what if he did mean it? What if the offender was actually sincere? Curley did not believe that merely asking to be forgiven should be the end of the discussion. Like most things peddled by whites, that answer was too easy. Someone had to make amends. And, tonight at least, that someone was Curley Norris.

The motel was not very well lit, Curley was surprised that Mack had been able to see it from the road at all. It looked more like a converted house, with a small sign in the front that sat under a row of small light

bulbs. "Cheap Rooms" it promised. "Pay Upfront." Curley watched as
a young man and woman left the office and made their way down a row
of cars and in front of a dingy brown door. The woman stood,
shoulders stooped, to the left of the man, waiting obediently and
without apparent enthusiasm, for the door to be opened. The man
glanced over his shoulder and then, taking the woman by the elbow, led
her into the darkened room. Curley noted that the drapes were quickly
pulled before the inside light was switched on. He chuckled.

"You oughta be home with your wife," he said with mock
apprehension, "and them little babies of yours."

He turned his eyes back to the office. There was, of course, no way
of knowing whether Fat Dale was working tonight or not. If he wasn't,
then it was going to be a wasted trip and wasted gas. Curley took a
deep breath and tried to slow down his racing heart. He watched for a
few minutes more, trying to be as sure as possible that there weren't any
more customers in there----innocent people who could get hurt or assist
Dale and turn the tables on Curley. Once satisfied that no one else
lurked behind the thin glass screen door, he emerged from the car and
the shadows and began to stroll purposefully towards the motel. The
wind whipped against the side of his face and caused his jaw to throb
and ache, painfully reminding him of the reason for the dark journey.
His boots thumped on the chunky asphalt, echoing across the lot and
sounding vaguely like the drums of Big Cove. He got a few feet from
the door and peered in. Behind the counter, again immersed in a
magazine, sat Dale, chocolate smudged across his chin. Curley noticed
for the first time the slimy, greasy appearance to the man. He
wondered what ran through this man's mind when he sicked a group of
rednecks on a sleeping camp, all for no reason except that he had no
real sense of his own manhood. Curley wondered if Dale even ever
took the time to think about his own motives. He doubted it. Someone
with the capacity for thought would not have done the deed in the first
place. Curley again took a deep breath and pulled the screen door
open, stepping into the office.

It must be his way, Curley thought as he crossed closer to the
counter. Dale, in the same aloof manner as he had displayed the other
night, did not bother to look up from his magazine. His meaty hands
obscured the title, but Curley felt sure that it was once again one of
those flesh mags which are only read by people who have no hope of
seeing the real thing. Curley stood in front of the counter with his arms
folded across his chest. With the patience of a warrior, he waited. Dale

made no moves other than the occasional shift of a page or weight.

"May I help you?" he asked finally, still without looking up. Curley said nothing, instead allowing the silence to coat the room in a thick blanket. Curley began to feel hot and realized that tiny beads of sweat were forming on his brow. He hoped the fat man would not take that as a sign of fear. He did not want to be denied total control of this situation, even by Dale. Curley waited for the clerk to look up.

"Look, pal, if you don't talk I can't know what you need now can I?" Dale asked, his voice dripping with contempt. Still Curley waited. The room was filled with the sound of the ticking clock and his own heartbeat.

"Not very talkative are ya, pal?" Dale asked.   Finally giving in to his disgust he looked up from his reading and straight at Curley, who smiled wickedly and with great satisfaction.   Curley saw the unmistakable look of terror spread across Dale's round features.

"Huh," Dale said, as if emerging from a deep thought, "now ain't that funny? I don't remember ordering no wooden Injun." He smiled, but it was no use. The corners of the grin trembled noticeably, giving lie to the feigned bravery.

"How you doin', Dale?" Curley asked. "I ain't seen you in a while. And I didn't really get to talk to you the way I woulda wanted the other night. Ya'll left in such an all powerful hurry that I just had to come and see ya once more before leavin' town for good. Hope ya don't mind. And don't you worry none, boss man, I ain't gonna be askin' afor no room! Nossir, I reckon you done taught me my lesson but good on that count!! Yessir, you sure did." Curley closed the distance and leaned over the counter. Dale pushed his chair back, trying to get away from Curley. He traveled the small distance to the wall behind him and then came to a crashing halt. The jolt caused his blubbery stomach to jiggle, sending waves like the ocean up and around his belt. Curley laughed good-naturedly.

"What the hell's the matter, Dale?" he asked. "Goddamn if you don't look plum scared. Why is that? Ain't nobody here but an old friend." He winked at the clerk. "Ain't that right, man?"

Dale took a hard swallow, so hard in fact that it was audible to Curley, who smiled even wider at the clicking noise in the fat man's throat.

"I said, ain't that right, man?" Curley asked, more menacingly than before. Dale, unable to speak, simply nodded meekly. "Yeah," Curley continued, "that's what I thought. And, since I am such an old friend,

I'm surprised that you ain't asked me how I'm feelin'. Or about how my brother or my friend is feeling. 'Cause the last time you seen 'em they weren't doin' so good. Ain't you even a little worried?"

"S----s--sure I am, mister. I was just about to ask you if they made out all right. 'Cause, you know, that shit wasn't my idea. I swear to God it wasn't. Them fellas, Otto and the others, they come by here not long after ya'll left and, you know, in the course of the conversation I think I mighta mentioned what happened with ya'll and all and the next thing I know they was sayin' how we all had to go so's that we could teach ya'll some manners and I was sayin' how it won't no big deal and how we ougta just stay here and drink or play cards or somethin' but they wasn't hearin' it, they was real mad........"

"Bullshit," Curley said calmly, "that's bullshit and I think you know it. Don't lie to me, fatboy. I swear to God, if you lie to me I'll cut your fuckin' heart out. You hear me?" Dale shook but said nothing. "YOU HEAR ME?" Curley screamed. Dale, terrified and trapped, panicked and made a move for his rifle. The fat clerk was far too slow, however, and Curley leapt in a cat-like motion over the counter and sent his boots thrusting deep into Dale's fat stomach. The clerk dropped the rifle and turned crimson, gasping for breath. Curley stood up and grabbed him by his collar.

"You fuckin' nobody," he sneered, "I'll show you why people don't fuck with me and my family." Curley balled his fists and slammed them repeatedly into Dale's contorted face. The soft flesh almost padded the hits, and Curley was almost thankful, knowing as he did how rough punching someone could be on a musician's hands. Blood spurted out of Dale's nose and mouth, and Curley slammed his fist into Dale's front teeth, determined to extract some of the clerk's own pearly whites.

"Please," Dale cried, "please don't. Please." But Curley was lost in the moment, utterly consumed by the rage and the hurt and the burden. He couldn't have stopped even if he had truly wanted to stop. And he did not.

Dale tumbled to the floor in a limp heap, crying and making soft guttural noises. Curley leaned away and caught his breath. A voice inside of his head began urging him to leave, not to press his own luck too far. No one had come in during the beating, but someone might stop by at any time and, if they did, Curley figured he was as good as dead.

"You know, Dale," he said, "I hate we had this falling out. I think me and you coulda been real good buddies. Hey, tell ya what----next time I come through these parts I'll stop by and we'll try it again. You know, get us a fresh start. Whaddaya say?" The pained grunt from the floor below him made Curley laugh. "You mean you'd think about lettin' me have a room?"

"Ugh."

"Half price?"

"Ugh."

"Goddamn it, Dale, I don't care what they say about you, I think you are a damned fine fella. I really do. And, I might just take you up on that offer, I really might. Next time I'm in Georgia I will make a point to make a beeline for your door. Okay?"

"Ugh."

"Yeah, I'll miss you, too. But don't cry. I'll come back, I promise." Curley became aware of something kicking his leg, rhythmically jolting against his shin. Turning his eyes to the floor, he noted with some alarm that Dale's leg was twitching in a queer way. Curley looked from the foot to Dale's face and back again.

"Oh shit," he thought, "I've killed the asshole." The thought had no sooner passed through his consciousness when Dale raised his head and spoke.

"Muck oo," he said, blood drooling down his chin, mingling with the chocolate. "Muck oo......mucking nig....mucking nigger redskin ass...." Curley had heard all he needed and he pounced on the clerk with more ferocity than he had known himself capable of feeling or producing. He was screaming now, at the top of his lungs. He didn't care that people were around----fuck 'em. Let 'em come. He'd kill them, too.

And that was exactly what he was now trying to do---kill the clerk. It was no longer going to be enough to hurt him, he wanted to watch the man die, he wanted to stand over the obese body and watch the life slip away. Nothing else would quench this thirst. Nothing. Dale was trying to fight back, but that was a silly effort which only further enraged Curley.

"You wanna fight it out, you white trash bastard?" Curley screamed. "I'll give you more of a chance than you gave my brother! You at least seen me comin'! That's more than you did for us! I'll fuckin' kill you, you bastard!!!" Curley pummeled Dale with all the might he had. Finally he had to stop, just to get his breath. Beside of his foot he saw the magazine. He reached over and picked it up. Curley had never seen anything like it before in his life----it was more than pictures of naked women, it was pictures of men and women having sex with each other. Leave it to white people, he thought, to come up with something like that. He turned and stared down at Dale.

"You like lookin' at these pictures?" he asked. Dale had rolled onto his stomach and was looking at Curley through his left eye. The right one had swollen shut and would, eventually, close itself off from all light. His look was full of resignation. All his fear had been beaten out of him and he now only longed for Curley to finish the job, to put him out of this miserable pain that flashed throughout his body every time he moved.

"Well, do ya?" Curley repeated. Dale remained motionless. Curley tore a page from the magazine, causing Dale to flinch. "You like lookin' at other people do it? You like that? I betcha you like eatin' pussy, too, dontcha, Dale? And a fella your size must have a helluva an appetite, huh?" Curley crumpled the page into a tight ball and dropped himself on Dale's chest. "Well," he said, "eat this!" He stuffed the paper into Dale's mouth, the clerk's eyes bulging in disbelief. Dale gagged and thrashed around, trying to get air through the tiny gaps between the paper and his mouth. Curley ripped away another page and repeated the process. "You fucker," he whispered through his teeth.

Somewhere off in the night a lonely dog howled. Curley stepped away from the clerk, who lay without moving for what seemed like an eternity. Finally, with a wrenching gag and a burst of blood and vomit, Dale the Clerk sprang back to life, if not quite to consciousness. The fat man rolled there in the floor, crying and moaning under his breath for help. Curley thought he had never seen someone seem so broken. He was filled with a bitter pride. He walked back to the clerk and knelt beside of him. Dale stopped moving, waiting for the final blow.

"That, Dale," Curley said tightly, "is what we niggers call Indian justice. Try not to forget it. Or I'll be back."

Turning on his heel, Curley disappeared into the night, driving away into the night, into the sound of the dog.

CHAPTER FIFTY-FOUR

The rest of the tour, such as it was, never really recovered from the Massacre in the Georgia Field. Curley had rushed home from his second (and far more satisfying) encounter with Dale the Clerk and dragged his patients out of bed and into the car. He had hit the road before sunlight, and driven without pause until the middle of the next night, when he had been safely across the border and away from the arm of the rednecks, who he felt certain would make every reasonable effort to catch up to and kill him. He never told Mack or Ray the reason for the sudden departure, but their looks told him that they suspected some foul play on his part, although their few remarks seemed to indicate that they were assuming it was trouble with a local girl. Curley decided it was better to allow them to go on thinking that way---it would make things simpler for him. He felt no remorse for his attack on the fat man, and he did not want to sit through any lectures about the danger of the course he had taken. That would sap the event of all its enjoyment. He wasn't about to let Mack or Ray ruin his revenge by throwing on the cold water of reproach. If ever they found themselves in a similar situation and the Great Spirit saw fit to leave one of them in charge, then they could act as they saw fit. Curley had done what he thought was necessary, and he wasn't apologizing to anyone for it---ever.

Still, the sweet taste which had filled his mouth as he had driven away from the motel office had evaporated quickly, and without quenching his thirst. Curley found revenge's healing qualities to be fleeting and unfulfilling. He did not feel like the hallowed warrior. He was not impressed with the crossing of some sudden threshold of manhood. Quite to the contrary, he found himself feeling more empty than before, and more bitter. As Ray and Mack grew stronger and healthier, Curley seemed to slip closer to the edge of his own luck and fortune. His days and nights became a tribute to decadence, a gradual descent into some previously unknown level of desperation. Far from getting a chance to really thank him for all that he had done in nursing them back to health, Ray and Mack were quickly reduced to praying and worrying for Curley's own safety and his own sanity.

It was the bottle that sped the fall. Curley was hitting the liquor with a determination he normally only applied to his music. And with his drunken spells and sprees came the requisite lapses in judgment. The parade of women in and out of his hotel rooms or dressing rooms stunned Ray, who knew his brother well enough to know that Curley's protestations of love for Minnie had been sincere. And yet he seemed bent on proving that he could bed any woman he wanted, any time he saw fit. Not that any of the girls he scored were exactly prizes, they were the easy love types, the kind of girl any man can have if the light is right and, more importantly, he goes through the trouble of asking. Mack called the girls Curley's "grudge fucks," acknowledging that Curley was merely using the women as a weapon against some perceived or real slight. Unfortunately, if that had been Curley's plan it failed miserably, as Mack could have told him it would. With every new woman, with every new expression of his vitality and "manhood," Curley felt more and more pressure to assert his humanity. It was a vicious cycle which left Curley looking considerably older than his years.

The effect on the band could not have been more striking. The truth was Uncle Mack's Traveling Band rarely sounded like anything but shit anymore, and both Mack and Ray held Curley directly responsible. Oh, he still made all the rehearsals. He still arrived at the gigs on time and, for the most part, sober. But his actions had driven a thick wedge between himself and his band mates, ruining the chemistry which they had, over a million nights and across a thousand stages, perfected. Ray did not speak, sickened as he was by everything which his brother and one-time hero now stood for. He knew what Curley had waiting for him at home, and he watched in agony as he mocked all which that stood for by his bedding of every piece of trash he could get his hands on.

Mack, although still fond of Curley and possessing a real desire to reach out and help him, also wrongly felt responsible for the free fall he was witnessing. He was convinced that it was his own fault for having been so blind to the ways of the world, especially when it came to his admittedly "Indian Artists." He was the band's founder and leader, and it therefore should have fallen to him to shelter the boys from the kind of abuse which he had actually subjected them to when he pulled into that motel's parking lot. He should have left them out in the car and taken care of the arrangements himself, and he would have avoided all the heartache which had followed. His self-reproach led to a major depression which, in addition to taking its own affect on the quality of the music, also caused him to withdraw from Ray and Curley, which did nothing to alleviate the internal tension or improve the waning relationships.

On this morning, the car slipped through the early morning fog, slicing through the low lying clouds and splashing aimlessly through the street puddles as it made its way back to the motel. Its motion gave the appearance that the passengers were carefree, as if they drove with a happier purpose or a more noble destination. But inside the car, there was no conversation, no movement except for Mack's feet as he worked the peddles. Curley was slumped in the passenger seat, his head leaned against the cool glass of the window. It felt good, easing the throbbing beat in his head and slowing the train chugging across his temples. He had called Mack to come and bail him out one more time. And, as usual, Mack had complied with a minimum of fuss or sermonizing. Curley had fumbled his way through the parking lot and was thankful that Mack seemed even less inclined than he was to have a conversation on this gray morning.

The arrest was silly and had been over nothing bigger than a misunderstanding. Curley had spent the night with a young woman he had met after their show. Her name was......he realized that he couldn't actually remember her name. Alice? Alicia? It didn't really matter, of course. The point was that he had gotten his own motel room (with no problems this time) and they had enjoyed what was left of the night by sharing several bottles of Scotch and a couple packs of smokes and, well, and their own hungry bodies. Then something had gone terribly wrong.

She had been trying to compliment him. That much he remembered. She had said that she thought he played the guitar very well. In fact, she had said that she thought Curley was good enough to play for......who was it? It had been her favorite musician. What was that guys name? Oh yeah, Glenn Miller. She said that Curley was good enough to play for Glenn Miller. She was only trying to be nice and Curley had known that, but something about her tone and the tilt of her head had really pissed him off. And that was when things had gone south.

He had told her that, despite what she may think, he played a style that was completely different than the stuff Glenn Miller's band played. Besides, he said curtly, when the time came he was going to be heading up his own band. His greatest ambition was most assuredly not to spend the rest of his life as a second banana hired hand.

"Don't be dumb," she had told him, "playing with Glenn Miller would be a big break and you know it. Who wouldn't wanna play in Glenn Miller's band?"

"I wouldn't," Curley had answered proudly.

"Don't be stupid." He had turned on her quickly.

"What did you say?" he asked, the threat implicit in his tone.

"I said don't be stupid," she repeated with impunity.

"Don't call me that," he said tightly. "Don't ever call me that. Take it back." She had laughed at him, mocking his anger.

"Anybody who tells me they wouldn't wanna play for Glenn Miller? Why, I wouldn't know what else *to* call them!"

That had been all Curley could handle, and before he realized what he was doing he had summarily tossed her out of the room and into the parking lot. And she was still quite naked. She had made a terrible scene, banging on the door and screaming and yelling and cursing. She had kept that up until the police arrived and forced Curley to open the door. Upon taking one look at him and then another look at her, they had tossed him into the squad car and taken him in. And that was when he had called Uncle Mack.

The car slowed to a crawl as Mack turned into the lot and then eased into the parking space situated just across from the room. Mack turned off the ignition and opened his door without a word, without even looking at Curley, who slowly pulled himself out of the car. His head was hurting badly, an occurrence that he wasn't used to---he rarely experienced hang-overs anymore. He silently blamed it on the Scotch, a drink he wasn't accustomed to downing in any appreciable quantities. That had been her idea, he thought with a twinge of anger. He still couldn't remember her name.

"Thanks, Mack," he drawled as they stood in front of the door. Mack keyed open the lock and then entered the room without acknowledging that Curley had even spoken. Curley wondered if perhaps he had whispered his thanks due to the head pain.

"Thanks, Mack," he said, this time louder. Mack crossed the room and dropped into the chair which sat opposite the bathroom. He looked so tired. He looked....he looked defeated. Curley was filled with a sudden, gnawing worry.

"Hey, Mack," he said, "you okay?" Mack leaned down and pulled off his shoes. Still he did not answer. Curley waited, expecting Mack to respond. But Mack said nothing, in fact he wouldn't even look at Curley. He kept his eyes purposefully pinned on the floor, safely away from Curley's own. He sighed, and Curley saw that his breaths were coming in short and shallow waves. Curley scanned the room and found no sign of Ray.

"Mack, what's happened? Is Ray all right? Has something happened to Ray?" Mack finally looked up, directing his eyes at Curley. There was a sad, awful smile spreading across Mack's face. He looked so old. "Answer me, Mack," Curley said, forcing a measure of politeness in his voice. "Is Ray okay?"

"Ray's fine, Curley." Mack's voice was gravely and strained, trembling with obvious stress and an overload of emotion. Curley sat down on the bed, facing him. He waited for an explanation, but Mack had gone mute again.

"Where is he?" he asked.

"I don't know," Mack answered. "I told him that I was going to bail you out of jail and he said that he was going to go for a walk. Said he needed to cool off a might before he saw you." Curley chuckled.

"Ah, hell, Mack, is that all? Jesus, you scared me to death. Ray's pissed off at me for gettin' thrown in, huh?" Again Curley chuckled. "Well, I reckon he'll get it over it soon enough. You know, Mack, that's somethin' I been meanin' to tell you for a while now. I really appreciate the way you get me outta jail when you have to and don't preach to me or make me feel like a kid. I appreciate that." Mack's eyes went back to the floor. "Oh, don't worry," Curley continued, "I'll pay you back for this here bail. Same as always. You know you can count on me. You'll get your money, Mack. You ain't worried about *that* are ya?" Mack sighed and shook his head. "Good, 'cause you know I ain't never forgot to pay you back any of the bail money that you've shelled out." Curley looked closely at Mack and saw that, no matter how hard he was trying, something seemed to be eating Mack alive, slowly and from the inside out. "Mack, I think maybe you best tell me what it is that's botherin' you." Mack folded his hands in his lap and sat back in the chair. He seemed to be trying to summon something, although it did not look like courage to Curley.

"Curley, I have a lot on my mind right now. I can honestly say that I don't know which way to turn right now."

"Well, Mack," Curley said in an attempt to be helpful, "why don't you just tell me what the trouble is and I'll see if I can help you out with it." Mack inhaled deeply.

"The problem, Curley," he said, "is you." Curley felt the jolt shoot through him.

"What? What do ya mean I'm the problem?"

"Curley, I can't let things go on this way. Everything has gotten out of hand. I'm sorry, but this just will not work any longer."

"Mack, what are you talkin' about? What ain't gonna work out anymore? C'mon, Mack, you know I'll pay you back, you just know I will." Mack stood from the chair and began to pace in front of the bathroom door.

"Good God in heaven, Curley, I ain't worryin' about no fucking bail money. Jesus, son. can't you see nothin' at all? Curley, you're headin' for a real bad place, and you seem bound and determined to take everybody with ya. I ain't worked my whole life to have you run around and get me killed or ruin my name. Son, even a guitar player as good as you are ain't worth all that. Nobody would be."

"Mack, you don't mean that. This whole goddamn thing this mornin' wasn't nothin' but a misunderstanding. It was just bullshit is all. If you'll just give me half a chance I can explain the whole thing to ya in no time flat."

"I don't even wanna hear it, son. I don't wanna hear one thing that you have to say because I have heard every promise and every excuse and every possible thing from you over the last year or so and ain't none of it made a flyin' fuck of a difference." Curley recoiled from the intensity of Mack's anger. He had never heard the man cuss this much, not in the entire time that he had known him. Mack was still pacing, moving across the floor like a caged animal seeking a weak spot in the fence, his face a contorted road map of veins and vessels.

"Mack, you ain't said nothin' to me before about...."

"Don't start that, Curley," Mack interjected, "don't even try turnin' this around on me. I don't know how many times I begged you and Shifty to get your shit together and settle down. You thanked me a minute ago for not preachin' to ya, for not makin' ya feel bad whenever I'd come on down and get your drunk ass outta jail? Wellssir, the way I see it I haven't done you any favors. Not any at all. Curley, the fact is that I've let you get by with too much and I'm ashamed of myself for it. All the way down to that station this mornin', do you know what I was thinkin' about? I was thinkin' about your mama. Mrs. Norris is one of the nicest, plain out best women I believe I have ever come into contact with. And she trusted you with me, Curley. You and Ray. And how have I repaid that trust? By lettin' you throw away everything and act like a damn fool in every town we enter? Well, that day is done. It stops now, Curley. It all stops right now, right here in this town, in this room." Curley straightened. The throb in his head was subsiding now, buried beneath the strain of the moment.

"What are ya sayin' Mack?"

"Curley, when I first met you, you was a powerfully talented musician who partied a little every now and then. But now? Well, Curley, now you're a man who parties all the time and just dabbles a little in music. That's a tragic thing for me to watch, son. But that's the all out truth."

"Mack," Curley repeated, "just what are you sayin'? Are you firin' me?" Mack stopped pacing and returned to his chair. He folded his hands, then unfolded them and leaned towards Curley, resting his elbows on his knees, allowing his hands to dangle between his legs.

"Curley, you are a helluva guitar picker. One of the best I have ever had the good fortune to know. But," he paused and took a deep breath, "I do believe it has come time for us to part ways. I hope you understand."

Curley wanted to be angry---that would have been so much easier. But he saw Mack again for the first time at that moment, and he remembered all the things they had been through together. All the little towns, all the faces and the applause. He thought of all the times that Mack had arrived at a jail in the middle of the night or early in the morning to save the day. He thought of all the times Mack had advanced him money to send home. All the memories, all the music. They all flooded in like storm waters. Curley felt the burning in the back of his throat and the subtle gathering of tears around the edges of his eyes.

"Mack," he croaked, "please.....you're all I've got. This group, this is my life. You know that."

"No, Curley. The bottle is your life, and it has been for too long now. Besides all that, you've got a little wife now waiting for you back home. Curley, I ain't no saint, but I can't sit by and watch you screw around on that girl every time the goddamn sun goes down. Son, you just can't handle the road. Curley, this hurts me like hell. Why, when you and Ray come on board I thought for sure I had stumbled upon the combination that was gonna take me straight to the Grand Ole Opry. But Curley, some things is just more important than making it big. I won't, hell I can't, watch you rip yourself up into little pieces over and over. I'm sorry, son. But you're fired." Curley felt the tears streaming down his cheeks now. Mack looked away quickly. He had never had children of his own, but the banjo picker understood at that moment how it must feel to lose one.

"Jesus, Mack," Curley pleaded, "don't send me back to work and die in no mill like my daddy. Please." Mack stood slowly and walked past Curley, pausing in front of the door but not turning to face his guitar man.

"Curley, I'm going right now to wire Charlotte for some cash money. When it gets here, probably day after tomorrow or so, I'll be able to get ya a bus ticket on back towards Cramerton. Don't know that I can get you all the way back, but I 'spect you can find your way on in from Gastonia or even Charlotte if'n you hafta."

"Mack.....oh, Mack, please gimme a chance." Curley turned and looked at Mack, whose back was still turned to him. Although Mack did not turn to face him and made no sound, Curley could have sworn that the big man's shoulders were shaking. Curley thought Mack was crying.

"I'm sorry, son," Mack said softly. "I wish things was different, God knows I do." He walked to the door and took the knob in his hand. "Good luck, son," he said, "I wish you nothin' but the best in this life."

Mack opened the door and disappeared out into the lingering fog, taking Curley's dreams of stardom with him. In the distance, Curley could hear the faint rumblings of coming thunder, and he thought how strange it was---how much thunder sounded like the inside of a cotton mill.

CHAPTER FIFTY-FIVE

With no real plan of action to speak of, Curley went home to his mother before he went home to his wife. It was easier, though not at all easy, to face Eunice first. She knew well enough to know that something had fallen apart somewhere, but she was not likely to press him on the subject, satisfied as she was these days to merely have him return home in one piece. When he told her simply that things had not worked out with Mack, she had only sighed and spoken softly.

"That's a shame," she said, "I thought he seemed a fine man." The look she wore let Curley know that she was full of disappointment and an infinite sadness. She was kind enough to stay away from the most obvious point of contention, the most blatant weak link in Curley's simple tale----that Ray had not yet returned home. Things, apparently at least, were working out just fine between him and Mack. That seemed to leave the blame for the explosion on Curley. Her raven eyes betrayed her, and Curley could see that Eunice had not missed this point. Still, she allowed him to hold tightly to what remained of his pride by letting the deception slide.

Eunice also did not apply any pressure on her son about his marriage, and the wife who waited on him up the road. Eunice was no fan of the arrangement, and she was no fan of her new daughter-in-law, but she still believed Curley had responsibilities which he was bound to face sooner or later. But she could see, anyone could have, that Curley was dangling, in danger of losing himself at the slightest provocation. If he needed time, home was the place to find it. If he needed rest, home was the place to lay hold to it. And if he needed to grasp and struggle, then Eunice would make damn sure that home was the place where he could come and get some measure of the peace of mind her son had been struggling so long to achieve. If he needed her counsel, she would be there for him, as she always had. Eunice couldn't help but see progress in the fact that Curley had come to her, not Minnie, when his dream had shattered. She desperately wanted their old relationship back, she wanted her son and their friendship back, and she saw a rebirth implicit in the ashes of his music. Or, at the very least, it gave her something more tangible for which to pray.

For his part, Curley was virtually a non-entity in the Norris household. To his surprise, L.D. and Houston were the powers around which the household now revolved. L.D. had blossomed into a tall and confident sixteen year old man, with broad shoulders and a confident stride that even Curley had a hard time matching, especially these days. In fact, the emergence of L.D. only served to further depress Curley, who had not expected to come home and be forced to actually look up to his younger brother. And, with his loss of physical stature came a commiserate loss of status in L.D.'s eyes. That sense of wonderment and awe did not permeate his every glance as it once had---in fact he now seemed convinced that Curley, older brother or not, was only human. It was not the morale boost which Curley normally looked forward to upon a trip home.

The change had been painfully, though nearly comically, apparent from the moment Curley had come home. First nights back had always been something that Curley and Ray had relished, those moments when Eunice and the boys (and sometimes Grandpa and Grandma) gathered around and hung on their every word, on every adventure the road had brought to them. That wasn't the case this time, not even close. Curley had entered the house with a false smile and a determination to put the best face he could on his troubles. He was determined not to lose any esteem in the eyes of his brothers. He knew that he couldn't fool his Mom, but he felt confident in his abilities to pull the wool over the eyes of his siblings.

The fact was, however, that they hadn't cared why he was home or what he had been up to while away. L.D. had smiled and given Curley a quick and thoroughly obligatory hug and then excused himself for a date. He was seeing some local starlet and had no time for catching up with Curley. Houston, although home all that evening, was engrossed in a cowboy novel and didn't seem any more interested than L.D. had been. In fact, when Houston deigned to speak to Curley it was only to extol the virtues of their brother L.D., who now could almost make the sun rise and set out of his ass. It was all very disconcerting for Curley, who had nurtured a belief that, as breadwinner and eldest, he would always command the ultimate loyalty and respect from his brothers.

But only little Jimmy seemed to even really take notice that he had returned home from another tour.

With Spring approaching, Curley spent many of his evenings sulking on the front porch, a piece of random wood perched in his hands as he fumbled with a kitchen knife in an attempt to carve out some rhyme or reason, to will something creative and artistic from the stick. He tried, but his gift with the strings of a guitar did not extend to a pocket knife, and the project turned into nothing more than a way for Curley to pass the time. He would drag one of the kitchen chairs out and, leaning against the wall, watch the world pass him by and the sun sink into a memory. He would barely notice when L.D. darted out of the screen door and down the drive on his way to a date, throwing his hand absently over his shoulder.

"See ya, Curley," he'd call. "Don't wear yourself out, hear?" With a nasty little giggle he would disappear in a cloud of testosterone induced dust, unable to hear Curley's bitter rejoinder. After all his sacrificing and all his work to keep the family afloat, that was all the thanks he got? Not even a little respect from the brother whose very survival he had made possible? It all made Curley's head spin and his stomach lurch. No one in the house, not even his mother, seemed to understand what he had been through for them, and they didn't seem to care about what they didn't know.

"What are you doing?" Eunice walked out onto the porch, dragging her own chair behind her from the kitchen and dragging Curley from his thoughts.

"Nothin'," he answered without emotion.

"Huh," grunted Eunice, "truer words were never spoken." Curley shot her his nastiest glance, but she did not flinch. She was aging, but she was not wilting.

"Did you need something?" he asked impatiently.

"Why? Am I bothering you?" Curley looked back down at the stick, deciding that to answer was only to invite a fight. Eunice, sensing that she was being dismissed, pressed ahead. "Russell, you want to tell me how long you think you can go on living like this? Son ,there are certain things that you just can't run from."

"Not now, Mom. Okay?"

"No, it is not okay. Russell, you've been here for almost three weeks and you haven't called on your wife, and you haven't called about a job. Son, that isn't going to work out." Curley was stung by the choice of words, it sounded as if he was now getting fired by his mother.

"I'll be about it in a few days, Mom," he said, "just as soon as I get my bearings." Eunice studied him, holding him in her gaze as she sized him up. "What?" Curley demanded, blanching under the heat of her eyes.

"Russell, if you haven't gotten your bearings about you by now, after all these years...."

"You don't mean that," he snapped. "I know you don't, 'cause that ain't even a little bit fair. I've worked hard for this family and you know it. Jesus, Mom, I've been the man of the house since....."

"Since your daddy died," Eunice finished. "You've been the man of the house since your daddy died. And I know that it has been a terrible burden. And I know that it hasn't been fair. But Russell, you go up there to that little welfare cemetery where your father is buried and you talk to me about fair. It wasn't fair that I lost my husband long before I should have. It isn't fair that Jimmy never knew his father. It isn't fair that boys as smart as you and Ray never got to finish your education. Son, life isn't always fair. But you don't question the wisdom of the Great Spirit and you make the best of what you're given. Russell, we've come through some lean years in this family, and all you boys are healthy, your grandparents are healthy, we still have our home......good God, son, can't you see all the blessings around you?" Curley didn't answer. He wouldn't have known what to say, even if he could have made his tongue work. Eunice waited patiently, allowing her son enough time to get out his words if he wanted to. When she was satisfied that he wasn't wanting to speak, she plowed ahead. "And as for the rest of your responsibilities, well, that was your own doing. No one in this house, least of all me, was putting even the least amount of pressure on you to go out and get yourself a bride. That was all your doing, Russell."

"I love Minnie, Mom. I really do."

"Then go to her," Eunice said, chastising him. "Go to your wife, Russell, let her know that you are at home and that you're not going back on the road. Make a home with her if that is what you have chosen to do."

"How?" he asked bitterly. "You just tell me how to make a life for me and her, Mom. You just tell me how to make a home for my wife and goddamn it I'll do it. I've lost everything. Can't you see that? Huh? All them years I spent on the road, payin' my dues, and I ain't got a thing in this cotton pickin' world to show for it. I've seen the inside of damn near every jail on the East coast and played 'till my fingers bled. I've sung 'till my throat felt like it was full of broken glass to entertain all them smilin' white people. And what've I got to go and show for it? Nothin'! Little brothers who look at me like I got the plague or somethin' and a Mom who tells me to just up and go make a home for me and my new wife. I didn't play this long for nothin', Mom. Where's my break? I've earned a little respect and I've earned some loyalty. But what do I get? Fired by a damn white man who's past his day and can't even admit to it. I'm sick of these white people keepin' me down, Mom. I'm just sick to death of it and them all." He looked at her. He had laid out his case as best he knew how. He tried to read her face, but couldn't. Her expression was one which he had never before witnessed her use on him or towards him. He didn't realize until after she spoke that it was pure contempt.

"White people?" she repeated with thinly veiled disgust. "White people?"

"That's right," Curley repeated emphatically. "I am sick of answering to these white people, of paying my dues with them and to them and then not getting anything out of it. All the money I made that Uncle Mack Crowe and he goes and fires me like I'm just some unknown picker off the street?"

"Russell," Eunice interrupted, "have you forgotten that that is exactly what you were when he found you." Curley felt his blood rising.

"He didn't make me," he snapped. "I was a big help to him. Hell, he's still got Ray, and that's thanks to me. But after all we went through and he just fires me like that? Like I'm a nobody? Just like a white man."

Eunice took a deep breath and held her son's eyes for a moment. Then she leaned in, close to him, her eyes sparkling with the pure vibrancy of the truth.

"There wasn't any white man pouring beer down your throats all those nights," she said coolly, "that was all your doing." Curley pulled away and stood. He walked to the edge of the steps, his mind debating whether to turn and have it out with her or run for his dignity. It was clear that Eunice was allowing no quarter this time.

"That ain't fair, Mom."

"Humph."

"Well, whaddaya want me to do?" he asked, whirling to face her. "You make it all sound so easy! What would you have me do to make this house and take care of my wife? Huh, Mom? My music playin' days are over. So what do you expect me to do?"

"I expect," she said, her voice calm and utterly controlled, "for you to get yourself a job." Curley's eyes widened and his jaw stretched into an incredulous smile.

"Oh," he said, "you can't be serious. You......Mom, you can't mean that you expect me to go to work in one of these damn mills. That can't be what you mean." Eunice's eyes closed into narrow rivulets of shame.

"Why not? Your father did, and, believe me Russell D. Norris, you are no better than your father." Curley swallowed hard. "You asked me for the chance to go after a dream and I gave that to you. You have had years of chasing that dream. That's more than your father or I ever had. Now it is time for you to do the hard thing. You have a wife, son. And besides that, I can't keep you up here, not with all my other responsibilities. I expect you," she said as she stood from her chair and headed back into the house, "to go tomorrow and see about a job." She stopped in the doorway and turned to face him, looking every day of her age and full of that bitter grief. "Russell, if you think you are too good to work, then there is no place for you in my home. I love you, son. So stand up. It's past time."

With that she was gone, back into the house and back to the litany of chores which tied her days together. Curley stood, stunned and reeling, watching the shadows dance across the kitchen floor. When he was finally able to feel his legs again, he walked slowly down the stairs and towards the bridge, where he would look for inspiration and settle for contentment.

CHAPTER FIFTY-SIX

The house wasn't much. It wasn't that mansion in Nashville. In fact, it wasn't even a mansion in Cramerton. But it was home when he could convince himself that it did not represent a surrender of all that he had held dear; when he was able to out run the annoying little voices which devilishly accused him of selling out and turning his back on the dangerous vocation called dreaming. He had gone to work at the Cramer Mill, stepping in through the same door which his father had been carried out. He had not told Eunice that he was going to even apply there, his sense of pride and personal dignity would not allow him to admit to her that she had been right, or to see that he was throwing in the towel and taking the exact course which she had prescribed. He knew that there was always the chance that he would run into her on the floor, or outside during a break, but he was willing to take that risk. They would both be working if that happened and, surrounded by their coworkers, Curley felt confident that his mother would not cause him any humiliation by saying, "See? I told you so." She wouldn't want to chance causing him to turn tail and storm from the plant and the county.

He had sat in Mr. Cramer's office, praying that the man would have the good taste (and better sense) not to mention the "old days" when Curley and Ray had entertained his troops during their breaks for whatever money they could spare. Of course there was no real chance of that. Mr. Cramer was a ball of energy now that the war was improving business and the clouds of the depression were lifting. He had money to burn again, and hiring Curley was something that he was happy to do----after reminiscing.

He couldn't believe how Curley had grown. He wanted to know all about the places Curley had seen. What, he asked with a crooked smile, were the women like "up North?" How come Ray hadn't returned to Cramerton yet? He sure was sorry that things hadn't turned out the way Curley had hoped, he had been sure himself that those boys were gonna be famous.

"'Spected to hear you on the Grand Ole Opry," he said sadly. Curley swallowed his pride and thanked Mr. Cramer for all the kindness he had always shown their family. Then he explained that he had recently been wed (Oh, how utterly marvelous!) and was in need of work. A look of studied seriousness crossed the old man's face, and he began a speech which Curley was certain had been cooked up and debuted long before he had even been born.

Mr. Cramer extolled the virtues of work in general and, of course, textile work in particular. Yes, mill work had provided the back bone for families in this area for generations he said, and he was always glad to see the "tradition" passed down. He talked about what a fine man Rodney had been and, more importantly, what a good worker. He told Curley how hard Eunice worked, and how dependable his parents had always been. In fact, he pointed out, Cramer Mill itself was like a family of sorts. As the man droned on, Curley honestly wondered several times if Mr. Cramer was going to break down and weep at the sweetness and beauty he saw in a son following his father's footsteps into his mill. It was a speech worthy of the greatest capitalist, or the most ambitious politician.

But Curley was not moved. He was not sitting in that office because of any sense of tradition or history, he was sitting there, listening to the bullshit being shoveled around him, because he had failed in his quest for his own dreams and because he needed a place to regroup and rethink his life. He wondered if Cramer was really oblivious to that fact or if the man was merely trying to put the best face on a difficult situation. Or maybe Lorenzo was right when he had said that most people just didn't think poor people had dreams. Anyway, after the feel-good session Mr. Cramer had, in fact, offered Curley a job and Curley, with no enthusiasm, had accepted.

After a month of solid performance and prompt arrivals, Curley was notified that he was now eligible for one of the mill houses owned by Mr. Cramer and rented out to employees of his mill. In the past, it would have taken longer to move up the list, but the circumstances were changing. Many of the male employees of the mill were already en route for Europe, and once they left Mr. Cramer felt no need to allow their spouses to stay in the homes they rented from him. Those houses were for mill workers, not military wives. Accordingly, he turned many of the women, with their children in tow, out into the streets. He couched his decision in terms of strict religion and morality---arguing that women left alone should return to their own parents or, if that wasn't possible, her in-laws. There was too much temptation, he argued, to allow women to live alone in those houses and run the risk of falling prey to their desires or the slick entreaties of the men and boys who were still at home. It didn't matter to Curley how the house had become available, only that it was now empty and awaiting him and his bride.

So he had packed his things and moved out of his mother's home. Even knowing that he had surrendered to her wishes, he couldn't help but feel a jolt of pride and satisfaction that he was moving out on his own, into his own house. The move told Eunice the secret, all the mill houses were in the same area, but by then it hadn't mattered. He admitted he was now part of the mill as he walked out of the door, thereby avoiding any unpleasantness, any nagging or, more to the point, any gloating. Then he had made a beeline for Stanley and retrieved his wife, who was both shocked and delighted to see her husband home so soon and, apparently, to stay. With a certain degree of resignation and a smaller degree of happiness, a second Norris household was set up in Cramerton, this time with Curley as more than just the nominal head--- this time he ruled the roost in name and in deed.

The house wasn't much---a small living room, a cramped kitchen, and a bedroom shoved off in the corner almost absently. There was no real furniture to speak of, except the few items Curley had been able to rent from Mr. Cramer (who, conveniently, also had a furniture selection for the employees who rented his houses). Curley had settled for the essentials. There was a small couch, a tiny iron bed, a kitchen table, and, of course, a radio. The clerk had assumed that, like most young men, Curley would sit glued to the sound waves and pray for a quick Allied victory and thereby avoid military service. The truth was that Curley wanted, needed, to be able to hear the latest music and try to learn it, to make sure that his chops didn't desert him. He was able to survive his shifts in the mill by convincing himself that this was temporary. Curley had not given up a return to the road and another reprieve from Ray and Mack. It had, after all, happened many times before.

Minnie did what she could to make the place seem bigger and more open. She fell easily into the role of housewife, it was a minor variation on the role she had been playing for years. She sensed

Curley's distance, and she felt that something was missing. The spark, that little twinkle which had been so intriguing the first time they had met, was buried now under a mountain of resentment. He spoke viciously of Mack's betrayal and dismissed Ray's ability to make anything happen without him there on the road with him. He complained about the people he worked with and said little or nothing about his mother and brothers. Each time Minnie suggested that they should go by and visit he turned the idea away with a deep bitterness which surprised her. There were times when Minnie began to wonder if she was the reason for his simmering anger. But Curley always assuaged her fears with a stroke of her cheek or a smile. Coupled with a sincere "I love you," Minnie was sure that, whatever was bothering her husband, it wasn't the fact that he had married her. She decided that Curley must be missing the adulation he had received on those tours with Uncle Mack. She tried to fill the void with her own, more sincere brand of admiration. If he still seemed restless and bitter, she would just try harder. Time and again he gave her his word that she was not the problem. So she continued to love him, and waited for the day when the mood would pass and the man she fell in love with would return.

What scared Curley the most was that he wasn't sure that man would *ever* return. He hated every goddamn second he spent in the mill. The sound and the stink, the whirl and the buzz all made him feel adrift and burdened. He tried to maintain the stance of a loner while at work---all he wanted was for those people to leave him alone and allow him to do his job and go home. But they all wanted to be his pal, to hear what exciting stories he had to tell (and the rumor mill said he had many stories at that). He was one of them now. He had failed and was therefore no longer a threat. He hadn't gotten out, he hadn't outdone them. Despite his best efforts, the world had beaten him and brought him home to work in the same factory in which his father had worked. So now they could be fascinated with him and with what he had tried to do when he walked across that county line the first time. It was safe now, from a distance, to vicariously live and listen to the almost-star describe the outside world. In fact, it almost felt good, because they could revel in his experience and still go home knowing that they had made the right decision when they had accepted their lot and not fought against destiny. At least their way meant they had reached a compromise with life, instead of having life whip them into line.

But Curley avoided them every time he had the chance, leaving himself open to the charge that he still thought he was better than they were and the occasional threat, stating that just maybe somebody needed to learn that uppity Indian a lesson. Curley always managed to keep his cool, though, and walked away whenever things became too heated. If there was no chance for escape, then he would reluctantly regale whatever crowd gathered with his stories and then sneak away, back to his position and his job. It wasn't living, it was surviving, and Curley felt it with every cotton-laden breath he took. Still, it allowed him to make a home with Minnie while licking his wounds and thinking up his next move. He was going to find a way back out of the mill and out of Gaston County.

It was just going to take a little time. And, right now, time was all Curley had anyway.

CHAPTER FIFTY-SEVEN

Minnie had not asked how they were suddenly able to afford the new set of kitchen chairs and curtains that Curley had brought home. She had not asked where he had found the money for the lovely new bracelet he gave her on her birthday. She looked the other way when he came home with an updated version of the battered radio they had been listening to---this one with a genuine imitation wood grain finish that matched their new coffee table. Minnie was still blissfully naive enough to think that, if there was something she really needed to know, her husband would of course tell her. And Curley was still jaded enough to think that his wife didn't need to be privy to all that he was up to. Ignorance was bliss, they said, and Curley was determined to keep Minnie blissfully happy. Besides, the truth, he felt certain, would either wreck his marriage or get him killed, and he wasn't fond of either option.

He wasn't stealing, so in that sense it was still honest money. But that was the *only* sense in which the money could really be considered honest. Curley had traded in his guitar for car keys---he was making his spending money by running bootlegged whiskey into the surrounding dry counties. He didn't know the name of the moonshiners and he had no interaction with them at all. That was the way everybody wanted it to be. He picked up the goods at a designated spot and then dropped them off at a designated spot, and he was paid later by an accepted intermediary. It was all very secure and secretive, and Curley thought the overall plan seemed damn near fool proof.

He had been recruited by Steve Elliot, an older man he worked with at the mill. Elliot promised Curley all the drink he could ask for, plus a nice chunk of change in return for the risks involved. When Curley learned that he would even be provided with an automobile for the runs, he was ready to sign on. He had already been arrested enough to know there was nothing to fear in the county lock up as long as there was always someone around to post your bail, and he was assured by Elliot that plenty of important locals wanted to see the enterprise succeed---a subtle way of letting Curley know that he wouldn't be allowed to rot in jail should the law catch onto or up with him. Steve assured Curley that he had personally made many "runs" himself without ever even getting a whiff of the police. The same could have no doubt been said about Curley, had he not driven his second load while also fully loaded himself.

The car had been swerving for nearly half an hour, several times coming perilously close to careening off the side of the road and into the ditch. Somehow, Curley managed each time to regain control and whip it back into the lane, giggling harder each time. He was aware that he was breaking the cardinal rule of any good bootlegger---don't touch the merchandise until you are well out of the reach of the law, but Curley didn't care. He had originally intended only to sample a small taste, but Elliot had been right, this was the best moonshine Curley had ever tasted. As a result, that one swallow quickly turned into ten and that was soon half a jug. By the time Curley had reached the limits of Cherryville, he was as drunk as he had ever been. And, he thought, as happy. In fact, he was so happy that he continued to giggle even when the car flipped several times before coming to rest in a corn field, and he was laughing riotously when the police pulled him from the wreckage and shoved him carelessly into the back of their waiting car.

୫

Minnie mumbled for Russell to get up and answer the door, she needed a few more minutes sleep. When the merciless pounding continued, she forced herself awake and rolled over to find the bed empty on his side. She remembered that he had told her he was going to work a double shift and that he probably would not be back until later in the morning. She drew her eyes into focus and read the clock. Quarter of seven. That was probably her absent-minded husband at the door making all the fuss. Minnie tugged her housecoat around her and padded down the hall, silently rebuking him for forgetting his keys.

She was stunned to find Eunice standing in front of the door, a look of exasperated impatience etched in her face.

"Mrs. Norris?"

"What in the world took so long?" Eunice snapped as she brushed past her daughter-in-law and into the kitchen. "I ain't crazy about this neighborhood these days, and I sure don't like waiting out there with it almost dark."

"Well, uh, I am sorry, Mrs. Norris, I had no earthly idea it was you or I'da come a whole lot quicker'n I did." Eunice gave Minnie a caustic glance and then peered down the hallway, as if on some secret search and rescue mission. "Mrs. Norris, are you all right?"

"No. No I am not. Russell's not here, is he?"

"No, ma'am, he ain't here yet but...."

"Does it not worry you when your husband doesn't come home at night, Minnie? That would sure worry me." Minnie straightened herself and tried to untoussle her hair. She recognized that she was on the defensive now, and she did not like the insinuation Eunice was making.

"No, it don't worry me none," she said confidently, "because, number one, I trust my husband. And, number two, I know exactly where he is and what he is doing." She tipped her head at the end of her response to let Eunice know, with as much respect as the moment would allow, that this time they were on Minnie's turf, in Minnie's house.

"You know what he's doing?" Eunice asked. The tone, anger laced with sheer disbelief, through Minnie off for a moment. For the first time she began to think that something was terribly wrong.

"Y--yes. Yes, I believe I do." She cursed herself. *You believe?* Oh, that sounds really confident.

"You were aware, then, that Russell was out all night bootlegging?"

"Wha----"

"Running whiskey, child. Russell was running liquor. That's why he isn't home. I thought," Eunice added with thinly veiled contempt, "that you *knew* where your husband was." Minnie made it to the table just in time to drop heavily into one of her new chairs.

"There, there must be some mistake. Russell knows better than that."

"Oh, my dear," Eunice laughed, "Russell knows better than a great many things. But Russell does not always choose to act on what Russell knows."

"But why? How? I mean, I don't understand." Minnie looked up at Eunice. "How did you find this out?"

"Because your husband, my son, is in jail."

"*JAIL?*" Eunice chuckled sadly.

"Yes, dear, jail. And it is not the first time."

"Oh, my God." Minnie doubled over and placed her head in her hands. Rocking back and forth, she tried to hold back the vomit. Eunice pulled out a chair and sat across from Minnie without a word or any movement to ease the wave of nausea. She watched in detached amusement as the young woman's head shook back and forth, as if she could unmake the truth with the vehemence of her protest. "I don't understand," she said finally, steadying herself against the edge of the table. Her world had begun to swim away from her.

"What is there to understand? Russell didn't want to work in the first place. At least not in the mill, and I guess this just means that he was able to find an easier way to make some money. Minnie," she asked delicately, "do you even know why Russell is back here? Without Ray? Do you know what happened?" Minnie's horrified stare told Eunice all that she needed to know. She sighed. "Do you have coffee in this house?"

"Ma'am?"

"Where do you keep the coffee?" Eunice had stood from the table and was already shuffling through the cabinets.

"Second from right," Minnie answered, still a little confused, "from the edge of the stove." Eunice found the can and chuckled.

"I see you're drinking the Cramer Mill brand, too," she said with good humor. Minnie didn't know whether or not to laugh, she had no idea what this woman was up to now.

"Mrs. Norris," she asked as Eunice began to fill the pot with water and set it on the stove, "shouldn't we see about Russell? I mean, we can't just leave him down there, no matter what it is he's gone and done." Eunice shot Minnie a look of impatience.

"We'll see about him," she said curtly, "in our own time. That jail's become a second home to Russell, I think he'll survive." Minnie decided not to push the question, although she had heard such terrible stories about jail that she was rocked with fear for her husband's safety, even if, as his mother claimed, he had been in there many times before. Eunice was obviously going to make coffee and take her time. Eunice turned and read Minnie's look of concern.

"Look," she said, "I've jumped up and ran after that boy time and time again, and the truth is that I'm tired of running. Now we'll go get him soon enough. I promise. Okay?" Eunice's tone was beginning to soften, and Minnie hoped that signified a thaw in their relationship.

"Mrs. Norris," she asked, "did I cause this? Is it something I done?

Or ain't done?" Eunice paused, leaving her back to Minnie. Minnie saw the shudder as it passed like a bolt down Eunice's spine. The question had brought something hidden into the light, and Minnie tensed as she waited for her mother-in-law to turn on her. But Eunice took a deep breath, composed herself, and took a seat across from Minnie. She sat still for a minute, obviously measuring each word carefully.

"It's not you," she said finally. "I'd like to blame you, but I can't. Russell lost something a long time ago, and it's been eating away at him for years now. I didn't see it for a long time, so in many ways I guess this is all my fault. I turned him loose into the world before he was ready to handle it. When his Dad died, Russell and Ray were both determined to support the family, and they both insisted that I not go to work. I did anyway, but those two were so proud that I had to do it behind their backs." Eunice smiled the broad, satisfied smile of a mother. But it vanished quickly into a sad look of defeat. "There was really no choice. I couldn't support them on my own, and I was just too proud to go home again. It's a wonder this family has come as far as it has," she said wistfully, "given some of the choices we've made. We've worn our pride around our necks like an anchor, and we're still trying to swim upstream. My husband and I took Russell, took all of our sons, away from our people and everything we knew, all we were about really, because we wanted to give them a better life. We thought we could make a better way. And, whose to say that we wouldn't have, had Russell's Dad lived? But things changed so fast. I think Russell is still trying to catch up with the cards life dealt him. Or maybe we were fools." Eunice looked deep into Minnie's eyes, making certain she had her full attention. "You cannot raise a family," she said, "detached from their ancestors." She sat back in her chair, clearly tired from the conversation, from the outpouring of the load she had held within her for so long. Minnie sat in stunned silence---this was so much to process at once.

"You think I'm making excuses for him, don't you?" Eunice asked after a few minutes had passed.

"No, ma'am," Minnie said, "I don't think that at all. But I do think that Russell has to make some choices. He ain't the only one that had to grow up before he wanted to, and he ain't the only one who's been handed a tough life. I see that all around. Mrs. Norris, I ain't had it as easy as you might think," she said, "and I ain't out runnin' moonshine."

"It sounds like you've given up on my son already," Eunice fired.

There was a twinge of knowledge in her voice, as if she was telling Minnie that this was what she had expected from the very beginning. "You married an Indian, young woman," she instructed, "and all that goes with that. An Indian man is proud and weak all at once. Strong and tortured. Filled with more honest laughter, and more *hate,* than you can imagine. It's hate that drives them. Some, like my father, use it to drive them to great heights. Others, like my brother, allow it to drive them....."

"Over cliffs?" Minnie met Eunice's stare this time, refusing to look down or away. Eunice's lips parted into a crescent moon smile.

"Something like that," she answered. "You have no idea what they carry on the inside. The memory of generations of women and children they couldn't protect, ways of life they weren't enough to preserve. Russell's godmother once told me that an Indian man smells fear and gun powder every night before he falls asleep----the Great Spirit reminding him not to sleep too soundly, because in the morning his whole world could be gone."

"And how do Indian women handle these men and all this?" Minnie asked.

"Oh, we're still working on that," Eunice said with a grin. "But we love them hard, I'll tell you that. And," she added, "we don't ever, *ever* let them push us away." Eunice cocked her head at Minnie. "Do you understand that?"

"I do. Believe it or not, what you just described ain't all that different from what a lot of poor white folks live through." They sat quietly for a time, listening as the world around them began to awaken. Finally, Minnie pierced the silence.

"Mrs. Norris," she said, raising herself from the table, "you can stay here and have that coffee if you'd like. But I'm goin' to get my husband back from that cliff." Eunice smiled and, without answering, turned off the burner and walked into the living room, where she would wait while her daughter-in-law changed into her clothes.

They would go to the jail together.

CHAPTER FIFTY-EIGHT

Curley wasn't exactly sitting. He was mostly draped over the couch, his legs slouching over the stuffed arms and his hands alternately holding the hot towels Minnie brought from the kitchen for him to lay on his head. He didn't think the booze had caused the headache---he was convinced he was immune to that. But the bawling out and the constant nagging that he had received from the double team of Eunice and Minnie, was enough to cause any man to plead for silence and beg for forgiveness. Neither, however, would be quick in coming.

He had tried everything. He moaned as if he were in excruciating pain. Still they bitched. He tugged at his temples as if he were in the throes of some demonic possession. Still they bitched. He crumpled to the couch and made strange gurgling noises as if he were about to be sick. And still they bitched. Curley wondered if he was losing his skills as an actor. And the disturbing fact was that he couldn't even hope to simply wear his accusers out----this time there was two of them, and they relieved each other, working in shifts to get the maximum mileage out of their anger and disappointment.

Minnie hadn't even looked at him since they had bailed him out. When he had first heard her voice, he had felt a sudden urge to rip down the iron gate and strangle his mother. He had called Eunice because (besides the obvious fact that he and Minnie couldn't afford and therefore didn't have a phone) he wanted to keep his little trouble away from his wife. And here his mother had gone against his wishes and brought Minnie with her. The catcalls from the other drunks in the tank only made matters worse.

"Hey, sweet cheeks!" someone cried.

"Um-um, come on in this here cell with me, baby!"

"I got the old one," came one taunting jeer, which sent up gales of laughter from the others.

"Ya'll shut your goddamn mouths!!" Curley had bellowed, forgetting that both his mother and his wife were within earshot.

"Fuck you, pal!"

"Yeah, you can't handle two women, can ya?!" More laughs, more snide remarks. And things only got worse when Curley saw Minnie and Eunice turn the corner and walk towards him. They looked so sweet and pure, so completely out of place. Even Curley thought how odd it looked that two women such as these could know someone stuck in the Gaston County drunk tank. For the first time in a long time, he was filled with genuine shame. They were walking down this hallway, being degraded and jeered at, because they had come to fetch him, to get him out of jail. Of course Minnie and Eunice would not normally be seen in a place like this. In fact, they would never be seen somewhere like this if it wasn't for him. Curley managed a Philistine smile, but that only seemed to darken his rescuer's mood. He wished, not for the first time, that Lorenzo had not been called back to Qualla on business.

Minnie looked at him, her emerald blue eyes sparkling with bold tears. Eunice stood just behind her, her smoldering black eyes devoid of any kindness or understanding. Minnie stared intently, as if trying to read a book she had understood the night before but, upon picking it up in the morning, found it written in some foreign tongue. She seemed controlled, calculating. But under the surface Curley sensed a pain that rattled her bones and curdled her blood. Eunice looked at her son as if he was a threatening cloud---expending itself too quickly to nourish anything below.

"Jesus, Minnie, I'm really sorry. I didn't mean for you to have to come down here this morning, honest I didn't."

"No?" she demanded. "No, I guess you think it's better to lie to me some more, to let me just keep on livin' this lie?"

"Huh? No, no it ain't like that at all. It's...."

"You'd rather your mother come out here for you? Drag her away from her family to bail you out, to spend money she doesn't have, money we don't have, to pay for your stupid, selfish mistake? Is that what you had in mind, Russell?" Curley bristled as the other inmates began to laugh at his predicament.

"Minnie, can we not do this *here*?" he asked. "Let's save this for home, huh?"

"Whatever you say, Russell," she said coolly. "I wouldn't want to dare embarrass you in front of this fine group of men you're keepin' company with." Behind his wife, Curley saw Eunice's face break out suddenly into a look of sheer enjoyment and approval.

"Great," he thought, "*now* she likes my wife." The irony was not lost on him. The guard yelled at Curley to "gather up your shit" and then unlocked the door. Curley stepped out and tried to take Minnie's hand, but she drew it away quickly and without any attempt to hide her response. The guard took Curley by the elbow and led him away from the women, to the desk where he could be processed out. He glanced over his shoulder to make sure that he couldn't be heard.

"That your wife?" he asked.

"Uh-huh," Curley mumbled. The guard stopped and suddenly threw Curley against the wall, his forearm thrust violently into Curley's Adam's Apple. "What th...."

"You dirty bastard," the guard drooled through clenched teeth, "I hate seein' your kind draggin' down white gals. You keep your fuckin' nose clean, you hear me?" he demanded. Curley tried to respond but found that he couldn't even draw breath. "If I catch you in this jail again, on my shift," the guard said, "you won't leave here in one piece. That clear, boy?" Curley nodded an enfeebled affirmative. Then the guard allowed him to breath again and shoved him into the outer office.

And, in retrospect, that had been the easy part of the morning. That redneck guard's forearm was nothing compared to the blistering assault Curley had faced from his wife and mother. He found himself almost willing to take his chances with the jailer. They called everything into question: his love for them, his good sense, his manhood. Nothing was off limits. Nothing. And there was nothing that Curley could do, he had brought this all on himself and he knew it; all he could do was listen to their anger, absorb it, and try to survive it.

The sun was a mere memory when Eunice finally left them alone. Minnie had walked her out onto the small porch. Curley listened as the screen door creaked to a slamming close, and he strained to try and hear what they were saying. As absurd as it was, he was worried that Eunice might actually say something which would hurt Minnie. He squeezed the towel, sending some of the hot water streaming down his face like an invasion of lonely tears. He was worried that his Mom might cause Minnie some pain? No, he had caused all the pain that was going to be felt today, and there was nothing he could do to change that. He glanced up when he heard Minnie come back into the house.

"Honey pot?" Nothing. She walked past him without a trace of emotion or concern. Hell, she didn't even ask if his head was easing off any. He heard her in the kitchen, slamming pots and pans, every move a thundering reverberation in the echo chamber of his head.   He groaned loudly---loud enough for her to hear him and stop. Suddenly she was standing over him, a frying pan in one hand and a butcher's knife in the other. Curley felt sick as he remembered the stories about Molly Runningwolf.

"I'm sorry," she said, "am I botherin' you with my housework?" Curley knew better than to even attempt any answer at all. A "no" would cause her to tell him to keep *his* groaning and moaning and a yes? Well, a "yes" would likely send that knife through his skull. She stood, patting her foot, waiting for an answer. Curley brought the towel over his eyes---a clear signal of surrender.

"You broke my heart today, you know?" she asked. Curley heard her voice tremble, and the sound cut like a knife through his heart. He took the towel away and sat up. He patted the couch, motioning for her to sit down beside of him. But she didn't budge.

"C'mon, honey pot," he cajoled, but to no avail.

"You broke my heart. When your mother came into our house and told me that my husband, that you......" her voice trailed away. There were no tears, and Curley wondered if it had been pain or anger which had forced her to stop.

"I'm sorry," he whispered through the rows of cotton which had sprung up in his mouth.   "You just don't know how sorry I am." Minnie's face did not look up from the floor.

"Russell," she said, "did I marry I lie? Our love, all them promises, all them things that you said to me......was all that a lie?" Curley stood and walked towards her, but she backed away and raised a hand in protest, the hand that was holding the knife. Her eyes widened and she dropped both the knife and the pan. Curley remembered her stories--- the violent fights that she could still recall her parents having in the days before she came to live with her Grandmother Abernathy. Some nights she still awoke in a cold sweat, dodging the plates, the ashtrays, which hurdled towards her head in her dreams. She cried out and turned away, running down the short hall and slamming the door behind her. Curley heard the sound of the bolt being thrust into the wall. She had locked him out of their bedroom.

He thought of running after her, but decided that would only bring on more panic. She needed time to herself, he guessed, and he was going to give it to her. He fell back on the couch and rubbed his temples with his index fingers. He wondered what had happened to that pack of smokes he had? Were they all gone?

"Boy," he thought, "you sure have screwed up this time." He felt himself missing his father. He had dreamed of Rodney while in the jail. They were running and racing, enjoying themselves again and without a care in the world. Of course, there was a part of Curley that gave thanks that Rodney was not around to see the shape he was in. But there was another part, that part of him that, like all men, would always be somebody's son, that assumed his father would know exactly what to do and say to make everything okay again. Curley stumbled out into the yard and began walking.

He had no where to go, and he could go anywhere. Anywhere except home. Home was chaos and pain.

Curley decided to track down a beer.

CHAPTER FIFTY-NINE

Curley came home, handed his paycheck over to Minnie, jogged to the bedroom where he retrieved his guitar, and then bolted out the door. This had been the pattern for months, and Minnie no longer asked when, or even if, he would be coming home. She had developed a stoic outlook, a sad and beaten resignation towards her husband. In her quiet moments she thought about how right Grandma Abernathy had been. Marriage was a prison, a disaster wrapped in ribbons and trimmed in lace and then sold to each generation of women as if it were a vital necessity. She had escaped the stifling oppression of her grandmother's home, only to step blindly into a world where total loneliness came disguised as independence. She no longer wondered where Curley was or who he was with. It wasn't that she didn't care. No, she still loved him with a searing intensity. That was, in fact, the point. She decided not to care so *actively*----in the hope that that would ease the pain. It didn't, but she had found no alternative.

He left home and headed, as she knew he did, for the bars. That was the reason for his guitar. He no longer played for the love of the music; now he was playing for the need of the beer. He took his instrument and found a bar which needed some entertainment. Usually he rotated among the same three or four little dives, places where he couldn't be found and wasn't likely to be bothered. He struck up an agreement, much like the one he had procured at The Rooster an eternity ago, whereby he played and brought in customers and was then rewarded with booze. The owners realized that they had nothing to lose by agreeing. After all, if Curley didn't win over customers then Curley didn't drink. And Curley was able to assuage any guilt he might feel about blowing his family's cash on hootch. He dutifully turned in his paycheck and then got his drinks through his gift. As far as Curley was concerned, everyone was a winner. And, thank God, Minnie had stopped complaining and nagging weeks ago.

Tonight he pulled up into The Clover, a rowdy but friendly little joint owned and operated by Delbert O'Kelley, a flamboyant Irishman with flaming red hair and a rumored sexuality to match. Curley had heard enough stories around town about O'Kelley's predilections to avoid being alone with him, but the man's private life was not enough to keep Curley away from his bar. O'Kelley was bright enough to keep his dalliances private, so his bar flourished by selling cheap beer and providing the occasional music. Curley had been given a trial run at first, and his guitar and harmonica work had proven so popular that he had been offered a permanent position. Curley wanted to keep his options open, however, and had demurred. So now he came by every now and then. If O'Kelley already had someone lined up for the evening then he moved on down the road. If not, he stayed, played and drank. It may have lacked the glamour of the Uncle Mack touring days, but it served his purposes---it kept his skills sharp and beer in his belly.

He was in luck tonight---the trio from Gaffney had come down with the stomach flu and couldn't even sit up, there was no way they could sing. Curley took his spot by the door, lit a cigarette and began tuning. As the crowd slowly filtered in, he warmed up his voice and jumped into a song. As the notes drifted out, he could already taste the beer.

 භ

Minnie had been smiling for forty five minutes straight, with such a dedicated effort that her entire face was beginning to cramp. She felt the sides of her lips twitch now and then, and she silently prayed that her guest couldn't see it--she was certain it must look like a deformity when the sides of her mouth began to dance. He droned on incessantly, smiling happily himself, asking innocuous questions, and filling her in on all the latest news from the community. It wasn't gossip, he didn't do that, it was only the good news, the silver linings that he came to share. Normally it would have been the kind of conversation, just the sort of visit that she would really enjoy. But these days it was just another on a growing list of things that no longer brought her joy. She just wanted him to leave.

He didn't seem to notice that she was uncomfortable, or at least if he did he was kind enough not to say anything. Instead he managed to talk rings around the issue, gently prying, trying to figure out what he needed to know without being imprudent enough to actually ask. When he realized that he wasn't going to get anywhere, that the information was not going to be forthcoming, he pulled his Bible from the leather satchel he carried with him, read a passage about, conveniently enough, perseverance in difficult times, and then had a short prayer with Minnie. Even in her quiet sorrow, she couldn't help but think that some church was going to be awfully lucky to get Michael Smith as their pastor. As he began putting his Bible away and preparing to leave she told him so.

"You know Michael, I am going to hate to see you move away from here and take on a church in some big city, but I reckon that's what'll happen, huh?"

"Oh, I don't know," he said as he drained the bottom of his coffee cup, "we might set up house in these parts. I've come to really love the people around here. It just all depends on where the Lord leads me. In many ways the decision is not in my hands. But that'll be off in the future."

"Don't be silly," she protested, "I'm sure churches have started calling on you already. Why, Essie Mae was tellin' me that a pulpit committee was there when you preached two Sundays ago, and I hear they ain't the first."

"Oh, that's true enough," he said, blushing slightly, "but I won't be taking any of them jobs for a time. I have other plans. I'm going off to Europe soon, Minnie."

"What?" she asked, stunned and horrified. "Michael, have they drafted ya?" The thought was enough to paralyze her. She had heard that people were being drafted all the time, but this was the first person she actually knew who was getting called up.

"Oh, no. I'm volunteering to serve as a chaplain. I figure, why, I couldn't be needed any place as much as I am over there. I've heard some pitiful tales about what it's like. I want to do my duty."

"Well, I don't know what to say. I mean, I sure do admire what you're doin'. But, well, I hate to see you do that. What does Ethel say?" Michael laughed ruefully.

"She didn't speak to me for about a week. Said I was trying to be a hero, said I'd seen too many pictures." He shrugged. "She ain't happy about it, but she knows that I've prayed about it and that I think and feel that it's the right thing. So," he sighed happily, "she's standing by me."

"Well, that's just wonderful." Michael squinted---just a little---but enough to let Minnie know that he had heard the subtle dip in her tone, the emotional catch in her voice. He seemed so happy, his words made love sound like the foundation for such a magical partnership. Minnie shuddered as she reflected that, just a short time ago, she would have quickly agreed. The knowledge of all she had surrendered made her bitter and hopeless. And her voice betrayed her.

"Minnie," he asked softly, "are you all right?"

"Yes," she croaked, "I am. Why? Why would you ask that? I mean, I hope I didn't.....I wouldn't want to...." then it was all over. She collapsed into a heap of fury and tears. Taken aback, Michael stood frozen and mute for a second before he regained his composure and knelt beside of her. She was in her knees in the floor, crying and shaking.

"Minnie.....Minnie, talk to me. What's happened? What's wrong?"

"It's all falling to pieces," she sobbed. "It's all been a lie. Oh, Michael, I don't even know that man I married. He was so sweet, so gentle and kind and funny and wonderful. I had no idea that......that....."

"That what?" he asked. "Minnie, what has Russell done?" She took several deep breaths and allowed Michael to help her back into her seat. He pulled a handkerchief from his pants pocket and handed it to her. She dabbed her eyes and waited for her tears to slow down.

"I don't even know where he is," she said plaintively. "I mean, I ain't got no doubt that he's in a bar somewhere, but I don't which one or where it is. I don't ask anymore. Thursday, Friday and Saturday nights---sometimes more----he's off drinkin'. Sometimes he comes home sloppy drunk, sometimes he stays away until he's 'bout sober enough to get by. Michael I'm having to watch my husband do just exactly what I had to watch my Daddy do all them years. And," her voice became distant, "and it's killin' me. I love him so much, and there ain't nothin' I can do for him. Nothin' I say matters. Nothin' I do helps. I'm losin' my husband and my home," she cried, "and I never even had the chance to make it work. It ain't right, Michael, and it just ain't fair." She wanted to cry, she couldn't help but feel that was the only thing appropriate in this case. But there were no tears left. She had been crying for weeks. Now she was just so tired.

"Minnie," Michael consoled, "I am so sorry. I thought things were going good for you and Russell. I mean, you had the house and all, I just thought things were settling down."

"No," she said with a wry chuckle, "I ain't so sure they ever will. I'm not sure that things are gonna get better, Michael."

"Now, Minnie, you know that you've got to hold fast to your faith. Why, it's in times like this that our faith is the very most important thing left to us, it's the weapon God left for us when everything, and everyone, else falls to the wayside. You know that."

"Michael, how can I have any faith right now?" she asked despondently. "I don't have anything left to cling to. Can't you understand that?" Michael sat quietly, his eyes cast down to the floor. He was trying to find the right words or think of the right passage that might help, but his own fury was blinding him. He couldn't stop thinking about the night he had seen Curley in the back booth of a bar, drunk and cuddled up with some bar tramp. Why hadn't he gone to Minnie the way he thought of doing? He had given Curley the benefit of the doubt, and it was clear now that had been a mistake.

"Minnie, do you want me to talk to him? Would that make you feel better?"

"Thank you, that's a very sweet thing for you to offer. And I do appreciate it, but no, I don't think that would help any at all. He doesn't listen to me, his mother or his grandpa, so I don't think he'd listen to you."

"Sometimes it's easier to see and hear the truth when it comes from someone not as close to you," he said. Minnie shook her head.

"Thank you, but no." Michael took her trembling hands and prayed with her again, this time more fervently and with more conviction than he had shown before. His work in the community and the church had made him familiar with Minnie and Essie Mae's history. He knew of the abuse and the alcohol, the bitterness and the violence. He could encourage her faith until he was blue in the face---but within even he was questioning why God would allow such a cruel repetition of history. He concluded his prayer and walked to the door, pausing to don his hat.

"Minnie, if there is anything that you can think of that I can do for you, please let me know. I think the world of you. And I'm sorry that you are going through this."

"He's a good man," she said, more to herself than her guest. "Down deep where his heart is, he's still the man that I fell in love with. He just forgets how to be that way sometimes. Michael," she added sadly and with desperation, "please pray for him and for us. We need some help so bad......so very bad." He hugged her.

"You're always in my thoughts and prayers. Always." He turned to walk out. "And if you think of anything?"

"I'll call," she answered. He stepped onto the porch and then down the stairs to his waiting car. Minnie closed the door and walked towards the bedroom where, once again, she would get ready and then go to bed alone.

CHAPTER SIXTY

Curley fell out of the car and landed with a dull thud on the frozen ground. He swung absently at the air, as if it were trying to personally knock him senseless, as if it had singled him out for its cold edge. He heard someone laughing and he called out a mild obscenity, an act of impotent defiance that only made the laughter grow louder.

"Cocksucker," he muttered under his breath. Then he felt the supportive arms slide underneath him and he heard the soft, feminine voice.

"Come on, baby," she said, "we better get you back inside." Curley grinned.

"Minnie?" he asked. "When'd you get here?" Suddenly the arms which had been stabilizing his world and helping him get right-side-up were gone, and he plopped back to the ground with a force that took away his breath. He grunted and rolled onto his side, casting his eyes up to look at his wife and find out why in the hell she had dropped him like that. "What the....."

"I ain't no 'Minnie' you dipshit," the woman spat, "and you're askin' me where I came from? Fool!"

"Huh?"

"Hell, I been with you in this car for the last half hour. What're you? Stupid? Who the hell is Minnie anyway, Curley? You told me I was your girl." Curley sat up with no little effort and planted the palms of his hands into his eyes, digging at them in an attempt to clear away the cobwebs. It was all coming back to him, now.

"I'm sorry, uh, uh," he decided not to risk screwing things up worse by getting the woman's name wrong, "I'm sorry, darlin', I just had a little too much to drink."

"A little?" she mocked.

"Yeah, a little. Now, help me up, will ya, Minnie?" It had slipped out before he knew it was even coming. The woman sent her purse, which must have contained bricks, crashing down across his back, neck and head. Curley stood quickly and managed to grab it from her. "Goddamn it," he yelled, "cut that shit out!" She grabbed her purse, yanked it away from him and stormed into the bar. Curley saw the form of the man who had been laughing at him earlier. He was perched against the side of the building, grinding his hips against some woman Curley thought might be a waitress on her break. It didn't matter, at least the guy was too consumed to have seen the battle. Curley straightened himself as best he could and trooped into the bar.

"Stitches" was about as far from being a classy establishment as one could possibly imagine. It was frequented by the lowest of patrons, and it tended to bring out the worst in even them. But, like many other local bars, they welcomed the Indian troubadour who had traveled the country and made his living as a musician, and they were happy to pour beer down his throat as long as he didn't mind being marketed and auctioned to the general beer-drinking public. And, of course, Curley didn't.

He caught up with his angry "friend" just inside the bar. She had just started telling the story to her shocked and appalled buddies when Curley took her arm and jerked her around to face him.

"I'm sorry," he yelled over the noise of a hundred conversations and come-ons that were clinging to the sticky bar walls, "don't be sore, okay?"

"Screw you," she hissed, tearing her arm away. She whirled away from him and back to her friends.

"So, can I call you?" Curley called after her with a gravelly giggle. Women.

"I have an idea," came the voice, "why don't you try calling your wife?" Curley turned with his fists cocked.

"Who the fuck is....." He stopped. He had not expected to turn and see a smiling face. But, then again, he wasn't all that surprised to find Michael standing behind him, looking like a pale and cherubic shadow. This was the third time this month that Michael had arrived in a bar with Curley, smiling and preaching.

"Evening, Russell," he said.

"You know, preacher," Curley snapped, "me and you are gonna have to stop finding each other this way. People are gonna start thinkin' we're queers or somethin'." Curley grinned. "Buy ya a beer?" Michael shook his head patiently.

"No, thank you, Russell. I'll pass."

"Well, you just do that. But I done played hard tonight and earned it, so I think I'll have me one. 'Scuse me, won't ya?" Curley tried to push past the good reverend, but found that Michael was standing his ground. The preacher was surprisingly solid. "Uh, excuse me, preacher."

"Do you mind if I tag along?"

"Look, preacher, I don't bother you when you preach, do I?"

"No."

"Okay, then. How about leaving me alone while I play my music."

"But you aren't playing music," Michael shot back. "You're just drinking. Do you mind if I tag along?" Curley, understanding that the night wasn't getting any younger, relented.

"Sure, but if you ain't gonna drink I don't see why you don't just go on home. I told you the last time that I wasn't interested in hearing anymore of your preachin'." He turned and looked at Michael, his eyes flashing violence. "And that still stands tonight!" '

"Just wanted to sit with you a while."

Curley went to the bar, got his bottle and sulked back to the tiny table the owner kept for him near the toilets. Curley hoped the smell would drive this do-gooder home, which would allow him to drink in peace. He took his seat and began to drink his beer. He didn't even acknowledge Michael's presence.

"Why do you do that?" asked the preacher.

"Do what?"

"Drink," said Michael, tilting his head towards the bottle. "Why do you drink?"

"Because I'm thirsty," fired Curley.

"Water'll take care of that. And it's much cheaper." Curley gave Michael a wary stare. "Sorry. I just don't understand what would possess a man to leave his wife at home alone to come to a place like this. That doesn't make sense to me."

"You left a fiancee to be here didn't ya?"

"Well, she's not at my home, if that's what you mean. But I did sacrifice a date with her to follow you. Yes." Curley chuckled.

"Well, preacher, I reckon we're even. 'Cause I don't understand *that*. Now, if you don't mind, I'd like to finish my drink alone."

"What about the rest of your life?" Michael asked darkly.

"What the hell's that mean?"

"Do you want to finish the rest of your life alone? Because that's the way you're headed. You're losing your wife, Russell, and either you can't see it or you don't care."

"I am not losing my wife," Curley answered. "Minnie don't believe in divorce. She ain't leavin' me."

"Is that it? Do you think that, because Minnie loves you so much and wants your marriage to work, do you think that gives you the right to put her through this hell? Is that it?"

"Preacher," Curley said, his voice rising, "my marriage is my business. Keep your goddamn nose out of it. Besides," he sneered, "I don't believe for one goddamn second that you'd shed the first tear if me and Minnie went our separate ways. Would you?"

"I have no idea what you're....."

"You've had your eyes on her since I first met you, you bastard."

"Russell, I...."

"Well, she's my wife, and don't you forget it!!"

"I am not the one who seems to have forgotten," Michael said quietly. *"You* are." There was an interminable pause, and Michael wondered whether he had pushed too far. Curley's eyes smoked with rage, then suddenly cleared. A smile spread across his ruddy face.

"I admire you, preacher," he said. "It takes balls to come in a place like this. What is it that makes you think I'm worth all this shit?" Now it was Michael's turn to smile.

"Russell," he answered, "you are a child of God. And I think all of God's children are worth any amount of, well, shit." Curley cracked up at the difficulty Michael had with the curse word. But then the good humor faded and he was angry again.

"Child of God, huh?" he asked. "Where was God when my Dad dropped dead on the floor of the mill? I would like to hear an answer for that, preacher. Because, so far as I can tell, God quit takin' an interest in me and my family a long time ago."

"Russell, I am sorry about what happened to your father. But the Bible says that rain falls on the righteous and the unrighteous. I can't explain it any better than that."

"That's the problem with your religion, white man," Curley fumed, "it has more questions than answers. I want answers."

"You won't find them in that bottle," Michael said. "That much I can tell you with certainty. Russell, God loves you. And he walks with you everywhere you go and he sees everything you do. Russell, God only wants whats best for you."

"Ha! Do you hear the shit you're shovelin'?" Curley demanded.

"How can you sit there and say that shit to me, preacher? Have you ever heard of the Trail of Tears? Huh?"

"Well, I...."

"You ever heard of Wounded Knee?"

"Listen, Russell...."

"Have you ever had the fuckin' shit kicked out of you because of who and what you are?" Michael said nothing. "ANSWER ME!!" Several of the customers had turned and were watching, itching for a good fight to top off their evening.

"No, Russell. That has never happened to me. Russell, the Bible says that all those who cry 'Lord, Lord' shall not enter the kingdom of heaven."

"What the hell does that mean?"

"It means, Russell, that a lot of things are done in the name of our Lord that the Lord has nothing to do with." Curley studied the minister's face. There was something so sincere about it, and there was something about what he said---Curley found himself wanting to believe it.

"Fuck you," he muttered.

"Russell, you can keep running all you want. Eventually, I'll give up. Eventually, Minnie will give up. Eventually, your family will all give up on you. But, Russell, the Lord will never, *ever*, give up on you. And you cannot run from Him forever."

"Fuck you."

"How many people have already given up, Russell?" Curley's mind threw Ray's face at him. He was startled and shaken. Michael saw him flinch and knew that he had hit a nerve. "How many?" Curley took a deep breath and turned to Michael, who saw that his eyes seemed to be brimming with tears. The preacher did not think it was the alcohol.

"Preacher," Curley said, struggling to juggle the pain and the anger and still maintain control, "I have heard you out. You have followed me around and I have been patient and kind and I haven't been nothin' but nice to ya. But that's over now. I've heard my wife and I've heard my mother, and they both have said the same things that you're sayin' here tonight. But my Grandpa told me a long time ago not to trust a white man or his God, and I aim to listen to that advice. You have no right to preach to me because you have no idea what it is like *to be* me. Preacher, leave me alone. Leave me alone, or I will not be responsible for what happens. *Do.....you......understand.....me?!*" His eyes narrowed and he stared directly into Michael's. The preacher stood from the table and slipped his hands into his pockets.

"Okay, Russell. I have done everything I know how to do. I'll be praying for you, Russell. I just wish you knew what a lucky man you are. There's pain everywhere. You are so, so lucky." He turned and walked away.

"Hey, preacher!" Curley called. Michael turned.

"I tell you what----you get that God of yours to give us back Georgia and we'll talk some more." Curley threw back the rest of his beer and then began to laugh uproariously. Disgusted and frustrated, Michael turned and walked away.

Now he was ready to give up, too.

CHAPTER SIXTY-ONE

Lorenzo listened to the story without showing any emotion. Michael tried his best to hide his trepidation and to control his nerves. The tall, regal looking man across the table was an intimidating and imposing presence, even for someone who was used to communing in the presence of God Himself. The young minister's voice quivered slightly, and his hands were less than steady as they reached out and grasped the coffee cup placed in front of him. It was the kind of performance that would have normally left Lorenzo looking for an exit, full of mistrust and uneasiness.

But his instincts, as sharp as they had ever been, were telling him something different. There was something earnest about this white man's unease. There was something in his manner which betrayed a noble heart. Rather than throw him out on his head, Lorenzo decided to hear him out. He knew enough to recognize the truth, no matter how painful, when he heard it.

Lorenzo had only recently returned from Qualla, where he had gone to arrange to have more of his belongings brought to Cramerton, while also checking in with old friends and up on his children who remained on the reservation. Stitching together the stories he had heard upon his return from Eunice with the new ones he was hearing from Michael, it seemed that his grandson's world was collapsing---caving in on the boy while he continued to pull down the walls. First, and most incredible to Lorenzo, Curley had married a white woman. The old man knew that this was not the first white blood injected into their family story, but they were no longer sheltered by the loving shadow of the mountains. They were fully exposed in the white man's world now, and he feared for the safety of the new family. He wondered if Curley had even thought of this possibility when he had taken the step. It was one thing to promise "till death do we part," but it was quite another to court death itself by making the vow.

And then there was the question of the drinking. Lorenzo had known, of course, about his grandson's drinking when he had left for Qualla. But like everyone else in the family he had assumed things would work themselves out. Curley wasn't going to become an alcoholic because they were going to will him to wellness. They loved him too much, literally, to even entertain the idea that they were losing him. If they kept thinking it *couldn't* be true, well, then, maybe it *wouldn't* be true. Besides, when Lorenzo had embarked for Qualla he had thought Curley was off on another trip with that Uncle Mack fella and Ray---which meant that he was trying to turn things around. He had expected to return and find things were back to normal.

But, then again, maybe this *was* normal. Maybe alcohol and trouble were the only two things an Indian could count on any more. Qualla seemed awash in booze. Chiltos was lost to all---Lorenzo had confirmed that with this last trip. The son looked more aged than the father---broken blood vessels lining his face, drawing a map for anyone who wanted or dared to trace and follow every disappointment, every misstep, the boy had ever taken while searching out the man. His back bowed with the weight of the years, his step heavy beyond his years, he was a stranger to the love of his family. They could not even claim to know him anymore. And Chiltos was only one of many. Others, fathers, drank to try and forget that their sons were being snatched away and shipped off the fight in defense of a democracy they weren't benefiting from. Boys, some so young that Lorenzo doubted they even had received their short hairs yet, could be found passed out along the road in Big Cove, unable to make the last leg home. Lorenzo had left with his heart heavy, and his hopes high that things were going to be better where he was heading. He had been wrong.

Michael had summoned all the courage available to him before making the drive to the Norris home---the original version---to talk to the grandfather of whom Curley had spoken. It seemed to Michael that every time he began to get next to Curley, every time he began to see the defenses crumble, the name of the grandfather was invoked as a talisman against the white man's religion, and more specifically, against this white man's concern. Michael understood that he was just begging to be insulted, but he had to visit the source itself. He prayed for weeks about the decision, and finally decided it was the only route open to him. Minnie had told him how much Curley loved his grandpa and, she believed, how much Lorenzo adored Curley. If that was indeed the case, Michael did not believe the grandfather understood that the weight of his words was being used to justify his grandson's slow suicide. Armed with the power of the Holy Spirit he would just tell Lorenzo that, no matter how hard it might be. The Holy Spirit was a powerful ally.

But sitting in the kitchen, under Lorenzo's ironic gaze and piercing brown eyes, the Holy Spirit seemed to be so far away. And Lorenzo, well, he was right *there*. Michael realized that if he said the wrong thing, if he went too far, it wouldn't take long for Lorenzo to pound out an apology.

"So, Mr. Swayney, that's the reason I decided that I must speak with you. It is obvious that Russell thinks the world of you----he clearly idolizes you. But, with all due respect, sir, he seems to think that you would somehow approve of what he's doing, of the life that he is living. I thought, perhaps, if you knew that, maybe you could help me to find a way to convince him that he is on the wrong track. Mr. Swayney, sir, I don't believe your grandson can live long at the rate he's going."

Lorenzo coughed and watched Michael. He wanted to see if this white preacher looked away or down after making such a sweeping statement. Michael answered his gaze intently and did not flinch.

"I know you're sincere, Reverend Smith," Lorenzo said, "but I am not making the same connection that you have made. You say that my grandson always uses me and things that I have said to ward you off when you are trying to follow him into these bars and stop him from having a drink?"

"Yes, sir, that's right."

"Well, I don't see how me telling him not to trust white people or missionaries is the same as telling Curley that it is okay to be a drunk." Michael laughed. Lorenzo was obviously a quick debater.

"It doesn't make sense, sir," he responded, "but for Russell, or Curley, it is the only way out. He uses you to push me away. I won't lie to you, I would like to bring Russell back to the Lord, but that's not my goal right now. Mr. Swayney, right now I am just trying to save his life. I know how you feel about Christianity and Christians and I suppose that I can't really....."

"How's that?" asked Lorenzo, snapping to attention.

"Huh?"

"You say you know how I feel about Christianity? Is that what you said, young man?"

"Uh, yes, yes, sir, it is. I mean, I know that you don't believe the same way that we do and....."

"Is that what Curley told you?"

"Well, no sir, not exactly. But, I mean, he did certainly make it sound as if you wanted nothing to do with people like me, preachers, I mean, and...."

"Reverend Smith, could it not be true that I want nothing to do with people like you, but that I am myself a Christian?" Michael sat dumbfounded, trying to find the answer. Lorenzo waited for an answer.

"Sure," Michael said finally. "Sure it is." He paused. "Mr. Swayney, sir, does that mean, I mean, are you telling me that you *are* a Christian?"

"Well, of course I'm a Christian," Lorenzo snapped impatiently. "My whole family is Christian, Reverend. Curley was raised Christian. I hate to disappoint you, but we aren't heathens that you can come and win to Christ. And," he said sarcastically, "we don't buy our groceries with wampum, either." Michael felt the blood explode to his face.

"I'm sorry. I didn't mean anything ...."

"Oh, I know," Lorenzo said with a dismissive wave of his hand. "I'm not angry. Not at you, anyways. Reverend Smith, Curley knows better than to act the way he is, and he has never heard one thing from me that would indicate to him my approval of what he's doing. Ever since that boy's daddy died he's just gone near crazy. His mother---my daughter---has done the very best she knew how. It's not her fault. Curley knows better," he repeated to himself. "I was rough as a young man, too," Lorenzo continued, lowering his voice slightly. "I did some wild things. I made booze and sold it. I drank like a fish. But that phase came and went for me. My son, on the other hand...." Lorenzo's voice cracked and he cleared it with an emphatic huff. "Well, something must be done. Do you have any ideas?"

"You were my idea," Michael said with a tired smile. "I thought if I could somehow come here and convince you to stop encouraging Russell, then maybe we'd have a shot at getting him to think about what he's doing. But, it seems I was wrong about you being the problem." Lorenzo chuckled.

"I hope so, son. Tell me about my grandson's wife," he said. "Is she a good girl? Does she love him?" Michael nodded solemnly.

"She is a fine and beautiful girl, Mr. Swayney, and a dear friend. And yes, she loves Russell more than you can imagine."

"Oh, I don't know about all that," Lorenzo said, his voice traced with

pain, "I can imagine loving that boy quite a bit." He smiled a wistful
smile that carried years of struggle and survival on its edges. "I'm
getting old now, Reverend," he said, "and I'm coming to the days when
I start to think a lot about my dying day." He gave Michael a
conciliatory wink. "Don't worry, there's not gonna be any death bed
conversion here. I made my peace long ago. Besides, we Indians aren't
afraid of dying. It's as natural as being born. What's that the Bible
says? Cry when their born and rejoice when they die?"

   "Yes sir, that's what it says."

   "That's the truth. I've never tried to find the difference between your
Holy Spirit and my Great Spirit. I don't think I could. God is God
reverend."

   "Yes, sir, I agree with you."

   "Huh," said Lorenzo, "most white folks wouldn't. Anyway, I think
about dying more than I used to. But my son-in-law, Curley's dad, he
probably never thought of it. Never really had the chance to. The
Great Spirit---God---took him early. But he's left me around. And I've
seen a lot, reverend. *A lot.* Curley's in pain and he wants it to stop and
thinks drinking and whoring around, if you'll excuse the phrase, might
make the pain go away. He was taken away from us when he was just
a boy and thrown into a world where he was always gonna be different,
a world where he was gonna always have to be just a step faster and a
hair smarter if he was gonna get anywhere. That kind of pressure can
eat a man alive. Slowly, sometimes, but it eats away nevertheless. And
underneath that there is the fear, that one constant for Indians, that he'll
never be good enough, no matter what he does. Reverend, it doesn't
matter if you cut off all that savage hair and put on a nice pair of
britches---you're still gonna be an Indian, and they're still gonna expect
the worst. Some men use that, it pushes them to spend their whole life
trying to prove everybody wrong, to show everybody up. But other
men, reverend, men like my grandson, they take all that they can and
then they just give up. They figure since the world is always going to
think the worst of them, well, the least they can do is live up to it. And
it's the living up to it that kills them. When he was still small enough to
think that I knew everything," Lorenzo continued with a chuckle, "I
told him all about our people and our history. I told him because I
wanted him to know what kind of blood flowed through him. You
preachers like to say that there is power in the blood, well, we Indians
have known that for generations upon generations. We are a circle,
reverend, we continue what our ancestors began, whether we choose to

or not. I never told Curley anything to make him angry---no, I wanted him to know that, no matter what the world threw at him, he could make it because his people had made it. I read him the Bible, in your English and in my Cherokee, so that he could see and hear and understand that, no matter what people said to him, he *never* had to choose. You see? Holy Spirit, Great Spirit---huh!! If you pray with your heart in the right place, you *will* be heard."

Lorenzo closed his eyes and sat still, peacefully for a minute, as if gathering his energy.

"I will not give up on my grandson," he said finally. "And I don't want you to, either. I see so much of myself in him. He has lost his way. That's all. You and me, we will pray hard," Lorenzo said, motioning to Michael, "and we will get that wife of his to pray hard, too. And his mother and his brothers. Too many people love Curley for him to slip away. He thinks he can, but he's wrong."

"I don't know Russell that well," Michael admitted, "but he must be something to have this many people, this many good people, so very much in love with him."

Lorenzo smiled with the pride of a grandfather. It seemed to Michael that the man had aged right there, right in front of his eyes. But the sparkle was still there, and it was still very bright.

"Yes," Michael repeated, "he must be something, indeed." Lorenzo laughed.

"Well, like I told you," he said," there's an awful lot of me in him."

"Yes," Michael agreed, "so we cannot let him slip away from us."

Lorenzo nodded.

"Pray," he instructed. "The answers never cease to amaze me, young man. Never."

CHAPTER SIXTY-TWO

The dinner was cold and the silence floated over the table, giving their romantic evening together a funereal air. Curley had tried to be funny, cracking jokes and telling amusing stories from his week, but it was useless, Minnie was not in the mood to laugh. Then she would take her turn trying to clear the air, asking him how his afternoon had gone. Curley had spent the day with Lorenzo, fishing and talking. But that only caused Curley to clam up, he didn't want to discuss his afternoon with Lorenzo, who had spent the day preaching and sounding like everybody else around Curley. All the silence added up to one inescapable conclusion: they just couldn't talk to each other anymore. So Minnie finished her meal and then cleared away her side of the table, leaving Curley to finish alone.

When he finished he took his own dishes into the kitchen, laying them beside the sink where she was cleaning. He placed his hand tenderly on her hip and leaned forward kissing the back of her neck gently. She jerked away from him and slid through his arms, moving beside of him and turning angrily to face him.

"You stop that!" she said.

"Honey pot," he said, inching closer, "what's the matter?"

"Don't call me that," she ordered, backing away from him again. "And don't get near me right now."

"What the hell's wrong with you?" he demanded. She flinched at the harshness of his tone. But she was determined not to back away, and she silently swore that she was not going to give in.

"You should know what's wrong with me," she said angrily. "This is the first night you've been home in over a week, and you're going to come walkin' up behind me with kisses and sweet talk?"

"Well, we are married and we are here alone."

"Don't you tell me that we are married you son of a bitch," she bawled, "I am not the one who needs constant reminding of that fact. I've slept alone in this house more nights than I've slept with my so-called husband, so don't you dare tell me that we're married. Not tonight, do you hear me?" Curley tried to bite back his own anger and frustration. He didn't have to stand here and take this shit, he thought, there was a hundred other places he could be.

"Look, Minnie, I was tryin' to be nice and stay here and spend a night with you. I know things have been rough between us and all, but, shit, that's the whole reason that I'm here tonight, I'm trying to spend a little time with you. Ain't that what you want me to do, for Christ's sake?"

The look on her face let him know immediately that he had made the wrong decision and, more importantly, that he had obviously made a very poor argument. In fact, he could not think of a time when he had seen her more angry.

"Is that what this is all about?" asked Minnie bitterly. "Is this your idea of charity?" Curley tried to backtrack as quickly as he knew how.

"Now, Minnie," he said, trying to show his most charming smile, "you know that ain't what I meant at all. You know better than that."

"Yeah, yeah, Russell, I do. You ain't here out of charity. You're here tonight 'cause you think you're gonna get some pussy." Curley bounced back as if he had been slapped across the face. He had never heard Minnie say anything like that, nothing even close, in fact.

"Jesus Christ, Minnie, what the hell has gotten into ya?"

"Nothin's gettin' into me tonight," she said saucily, "and don't you forget it. Do you think you can lay out drinkin' and ignore me and treat me like a piece of trash and then come home and take me to bed, Russell? Do you think that I am that cheap?"

"Look, Minnie...."

"What's the matter? All of your whores busy with other men tonight?"

"Goddamn it shut up!" Curley cried. His hand flew from his side at her. Minnie ducked away quickly, luckily, and his hand slammed through the wooden cabinet door behind her. "Owwwwwwwwww!!!! Cocksucker!!" he yelled.

"That's it," she cried, out of control, "go ahead and tear this house and me all to pieces! I don't care any more Russell. You hear? I'm tired and I ain't takin' this no more. Do you want a divorce? If that is what you want, Russell Norris, I'll give it to you free and clear. But for God's sake have the decency to come right out and ask me for it, don't keep trying to push me away, Russell, 'cause I can't take no more of livin' like this! I just can't take it." She was weeping now, her body wracked with convulsions and heartache. Curley had leaned against the sink, paying no mind to the wet spot seeping though the back side of his pants from the dish water. His hand throbbed and pounded. Still, he moved slowly, easily towards Minnie.

"I don't want no goddamn divorce," he said quietly. "That ain't what I want at all." He reached out his arms and tried to comfort her, but she lashed away from him and took several steps away again. "Goddamn it, Minnie, come here to me," he cried. "You're my wife, so stop acting so crazy. I done told you I don't want no divorce, what else do you want me to....."

"Then what do you want, Russell?" she pleaded. "What is it that you go lookin' for night after night in them bars? In the arms of those whores?"

"Look, Minnie, I ain't never...."

"Oh, God, Russell, don't make it no worse by standing there and lyin' to me. Just tell me what it is that you're lookin' for. What is it that you want? What?"

"What do I want? I want peace of mind," he said, his voice rising, "I want to lay my damn head down at night and not feel like I've thrown another day away. I want to wake up in the mornin' and feel like I have a reason to get up 'sides I have to and there's bills to be paid. That's what I want, dammit! That's exactly what I want!"

"I'm sorry," Minnie wept, "to have ruined your life. I'll be out of it as soon as I find someplace to go."

"Goddamnit, Minnie, I told you that I don't want no divorce. Stop sayin' shit like that. Just stop it!" Frustrated, Curley stormed past her and into the living room.

"I'll be back later," he said.

"No," she cried, "if you walk out that door tonight, then don't you ever come back. There won't be nothing here for you to come back to."

"Shit," he fumed, "first you don't want me no where near you and now you're gonna torch the fuckin' house if I leave? Make up your damned mind."

"I said I didn't want to be goin' to bed," Minnie said quietly, trying to calm things down, "I didn't mean that I wanted you to leave. I want to talk to you."

"About what?" Curley asked, his voice full of mockery and false concern. "I sat through that goddamn meal without a fuckin' word.

Why couldn't we talk then? Huh? What is it exactly that you think you need to tell me? What else could we have to talk about?"

"I'm havin' a baby," Minnie whispered.

"What?"

"I said I am havin' a damn baby, Russell," she screamed. "I'm havin' a baby." Curley rocked back and forth on his heels for a minute. This news, he thought, was a lot stronger than any drink he could've gotten his hands on. The entire house seemed to be swimming around him.

"Oh, Jesus, Minnie, are you sure? Maybe you just think you're...."

"I am sure, Russell," she said. Curley sat down silently on the couch, his head in his hands. Jesus, he thought, he had almost punched a pregnant woman.

"Is it mine?" he asked. Minnie said nothing, so he looked up from his palms at her. Her face was a portrait of pain and dejection. "I'm sorry," he said meekly, "I didn't mean that. I swear to God, Minnie, I didn't mean that. You know I didn't...."

"It is yours," she said without emotion, "although God knows that ain't no comfort to me, either, right now. Russell, I know what I would face if I went back home to Grandma Abernathy carrying your baby. But I will not, I cannot, let my young'un be brought into a house like this. Somebody in my family has got to put a stop to it. No child of mine is growing up in the same hell that I did. That much I am in control of."

"What are you sayin'?"

"I'm sayin' that you better make some choices. If things keep goin' like they are, I will take your baby and I will leave and I will make goddamn sure that you never see it. Do you understand me?"

Curley stood and walked to the door.

"Where are you goin?" she asked.

"Out."

"Where? When're you comin' back?"

But he was already out the door and the screen was cracking behind him.

"You bastard!!" she screamed, but if he heard her he did not turn around. She fled to the bedroom and fell across the bed. Somehow, she found more tears lurking behind her eyes, just waiting to stain her pillow.

CHAPTER SIXTY-THREE

Lorenzo had his foot pressed down with all his might. He wanted, if possible, to beat the cops to the scene. From what they had been told, it was quite a scene to behold. Curley was loose in the middle of Gastonia, and he was in rare form.

"Hurry, Daddy," Eunice pleaded. Beside of her, Minnie sat stone-faced and quiet, her eyes cast across the scenery which sped by. She had only offered a perfunctory greeting when they came to pick her up---she had know that they were coming thanks to the "kindness" of her next door neighbor, Irene Wikins. Irene had a phone and was the link for the rest of the community on all the goings on around the county. She had known about Curley's adventure probably before Lorenzo and Eunice.

"Lord, Minnie, are you holdin' up?" she had asked.

"What?" asked Minnie, in the middle of canning peaches. "Irene, what in the world are you talkin' about?"

"You mean you ain't heard about Russell?" she asked innocently. The ruse angered Minnie. After all, the old battleaxe knew that she and Russell could not afford a phone of their own. In fact, if they needed to get in touch with someone, they went to Irene's to use the phone.

"No, Irene," she said patiently. "You know good and well that I ain't heard about Russell 'cause you know good and well that I ain't got no phone." Minnie turned back to her canning. There was no need to press Irene, the woman would as good as burst in no time flat anyway. Besides, Minnie was trying harder than ever to shove Russell's antics out of her mind. She had decided that she only wanted to know if her husband was dead or dying---otherwise it just ripped up her nerves and that was not good for the baby growing inside of her. She was six months along, now, and she was beginning to feel that animalistic protection that only mother's can understand.

"Oh, I thought maybe somebody'd done come by here to get you," Irene said. She stood in the doorway, staring in through the screen, rocking back and forth, jittery with excitement and anticipation. Finally, she had waited as long as she could. "Sakes alive, girl, ain't you curious about what that husband of yorn is up to?"

"Not particularly," Minnie said quaintly but honestly, "but if it'll make you feel better to tell me...."

Irene had leapt into the story with an unconcealed lust and abandon. Curley was on one of the main streets of Gastonia, she wasn't quite sure which one, with a couple of busty blondes. They were in a car, driving back and forth on the strip. One way, Curley would accompany the back seat with Blonde Number One while the other girl drove. Then, when they had reached the end of the road, they would pull over and the girls would shift places. Minnie stopped what she was doing and, without turning, listened intently to the tale. It sounded too decadent, even for her husband. But the news that he was going to be a father had only made him worse, and lately he seemed to be courting disaster and wanting, desperately it seemed, to get caught. Minnie looked the other way at every chance. The truth was that, even after all this time, she wanted her marriage to work. She loved Curley, and she wanted to bring back the man she had married.

"Hey," Lorenzo said, "you sure you wanna do this? I mean, maybe, well......"

"I am sure," Minnie answered. Lorenzo and Eunice had shown up about half an hour after she had thrown Irene out. Lorenzo was bringing Eunice by to stay with Minnie while he went and fetched Curley one more time. But Minnie had insisted that she was going along---she wanted to be there when her husband changed shifts on the side of the road. Eunice had silently assented and gone with them.

The sound of the mobile party rolled right through the windshield and into their ears. Minnie sat up and peered through the glass. Eunice sank down into the backseat. This was more than she wanted to see of her son. Lorenzo found an embankment and pulled the car over. They would wait for the return voyage. A crowd of gawkers had gathered, watching, pointing and laughing at the terrible spectacle. Lorenzo's anger began to broil. He gripped the steering wheel with force, pretending for the moment that it was his grandson's stubborn and obnoxious neck giving way underneath. The scream of tires let them know that Curley was headed back in their direction. Lorenzo opened the door and slid his boot out onto the gravel---he was crouched and ready. Minnie opened her door, too, and waited. Her protruding stomach was not going to keep her in the front seat. Not this time.

The car, a black sedan that Lorenzo didn't recognize, came barreling down the road as if it were an ambulance making a life or death call. Eunice peeked out from underneath her hands to make sure it didn't wreck---she had images of having to sit and watch her son roll into the ditch, crashing and burning as she sat impotent. The car zipped past them a few yards and then slid to an awkward stop across the street from them. Lorenzo was out and crossing quickly, showing no signs of his age. Minnie moved slower, easing her way out of the automobile and stretching to her full height in pregnant increments.

"You're not going over there, are you?" Eunice asked from the backseat. "Russell's grandfather can handle this. He'll bring him to the car and then we can get our hands on him." Minnie sighed.

"Yes, Mrs. Norris, I am goin' over there. I didn't come here with takin' Russell home on my mind. I don't think he'll come and I don't think he'll care."

"Then what...." But Minnie was already waddling across the street, tracing Lorenzo's steps. He had already made it to the side of the idling car. The driver's door swung open and Minnie saw the woman crawl out. She was drunk as a skunk and staggered as she stood, her makeup a parody of sexuality--smeared heavily across her pouty lips and swollen face. Minnie felt her own stomach lurch within her.

"Stop right there young lady," Lorenzo ordered as the woman tried to pull open the back door. "Just you stop right there."

"Hey, Grandpa," she retorted," ain't you a little old for this party?" Lorenzo whistled through his teeth, forcing a sarcastic smile.

"Ma'am," he said, obviously using the term loosely, "I am too old, too wise, and far too sober to have anything to do with you." She cocked her head sideways, in that coy way white women do, the one that makes them look like a confused dog, and then giggled. She shook her head and pulled the backdoor open.

"What in the hell is the hold up?" came the question from the backseat. It was Curley's slurred voice, cracking and broken. Billows of cigarette smoke rolled from the open door. The woman said something, and helped her friend crawl out. As the friend slid into the front seat, she made her way into the back. She was just about to close the door when Lorenzo thrust out his hand and caught it, holding it open.

"Hey!" she protested. "What the hell are you doin', man?"

"Who the fuck...." Curley had leaned forward, ready to pounce on whomever was holding up his good time. His eyes widened in disbelief when he saw it was Lorenzo holding the door.

"Grandpa," he drawled, "what in the world are you doin' down here?"

"Come to get you," Lorenzo answered. Curley laughed.

"Well," he said, "I ain't exactly lookin' to get saved from these ladies. I think I'm good and safe. You go on back home and don't worry no more 'bout me, 'cause I am fine. Ain't nothin' for you to worry about here."

The anger surged within Lorenzo, speeding up the pace of his pulse and making his eyes bulge. His grandson was patronizing him---talking down to him. For Lorenzo, that was the intolerable sin, the one thing that no one, not even Curley, could get away with. But it was not Lorenzo's rage that carried the day. It was Minnie's. She came up from behind Lorenzo, quicker than he would ever have guessed, and before he could reach out and stop her (which he would only have done to protect *her*) she had grabbed the hair of the woman sitting beside her husband and yanked her out of the car. The woman was trying to squeal a protest and fight back at the same time, but it was no use. Her inebriated state and Minnie's own temper combined to make her little more than a punching bag, as blow after blow from Minnie met their intended target with a meaty *whump*. Curley tumbled from the backseat and tried to separate the women. That was a mistake. Minnie tossed the girl aside like an old newspaper and then began to punish him. The driver crawled out and dragged her friend to the other side of the car, presumably out of harm's way. Curley's hands were drawn like velvet curtains around his face, vainly trying to protect the only asset he had left to him. Minnie's hands pounded and pounded and Lorenzo, unsure what exactly his role should be in this little drama, stood mute and motionless as the crowd which had gathered roared their approval.

"Daddy, pull them two apart before she loses that baby." Eunice's voice snapped Lorenzo into action quickly. Several of Minnie's punches rained across his forearms, but he was able to lift her off of the ground and drop her on the other side of Eunice who made a significant border guard between the two. Minnie was weeping now, her eyes black with shadows and doubts. Eunice tried in vain to calm her. Then she turned on her son.

"How could you do this?" she demanded. "What in the hell is the matter with you, Russell?"

"Goddamn it, she started it," he protested, "throwin' punches before I could explain anything. That parts her fault. There wasn't no sense in actin' like that...."

"Fuck you," Minnie spat. "Fuck you, Russell Norris, you stupid bastard."

"You see," he hollered like a child, his finger thrust into the air towards his wife, wanting to make sure that his mother did not miss the evidence right in front of her. "You see how she does?" Lorenzo's hand shot out and slapped Curley's arm down, nearly doubling him over. Curley glanced at his grandpa, a look of shock and sadness across his face.

"It's rude to point," Lorenzo said plainly. Curley turned back to the women, then back to his wife.

"We wasn't doin' nothin' 'cept ridin' around and havin' a couple of drinks.   That's   all." Minnie's tears began to pour harder now. Curley's face was smeared with lipstick and his wrinkled shirt tail lay untucked across his middle. Only a fool could have believed that, and Minnie Norris was finished being a fool.

"It's over, Russell," she said between gulps and sobs. "It's over." She became aware that everyone was looking at her now---suddenly she was the star, not Curley. Lorenzo, Eunice, Curley, even the two strange women watched her carefully, everyone waiting for clarification.

"What?" Curley asked dumbly. "What are you talkin' about?" Minnie took a deep breath and collected herself enough to speak. She wanted to make absolutely sure that he knew this was no bluff--this was their life together and she was drawing the curtain closed on the pain and betrayal.

"Our marriage is over," she said. The look of pain and terror which dripped down Curley's face gave her a measure of satisfaction. It wasn't the glee of the bitter or the spiteful; it was the joy of knowing that, although he could never give her what she needed, at least he did still love her. She could hold onto this look on those nights in the future, those nights when she had nothing else with which to cling.

"Aw, Minnie, c'mon, you don't....."

"I will be out before you get home," she continued.

"Where you goin'?" he said petulantly. He hoped that the thought of going home to her Grandma Abernathy defeated would cause her to back off.

"Don't rightly know just yet," she said, "and I don't care. I'll sleep on the goddamn street if'n I have to," she said, her vulgarity slapping Curley and surprising him.

"Did I do this to her," he wondered, even as the booze coursed through his veins. "Did I change this woman this way?"

"But I am leavin'," she said with finality. "You can have all the little girfriends you want," she continued, "and that ain't a problem. But you can't have me. Not no more. This marriage is over." He bottom lip began to quiver. Curley could see that there was more that she wanted to say, but there was no way she could get any more out. It had been a veritable miracle that she had gotten this far, there was no point even trying for more. She nodded at Eunice and turned away. Eunice took her by the arm and began to lead her across the highway, back towards their car.

"Minnie, wait a minute," he called out. He started to go after her, but Eunice's withering glare and Lorenzo's physical presence stopped him. Curley looked his Grandpa dead in the eye, it struck him that they were now the same height. In fact, Curley may have even had a slight edge. But as Lorenzo looked at him, fire simmering beneath his eyes, Curley felt like a child again.

"Grandpa," he said, "I need to go to her. Please."

"No," Lorenzo said harshly. "You have done enough."

"But...."

"You have done enough," Lorenzo added with nasty emphasis. "Stay here and clean up this mess."

"But my marriage...."

Lorenzo had already turned and was crossing the road. Just before he stepped out over the curb he paused, his head tilting and his shoulders drooping slightly. He seemed exhausted. Then he raised his head again and turned to look at Curley. His eyes glistened with barely discernible tears.

"You are a disgrace, Curley," he said quietly. "You are a disgrace to my name." Then he turned and walked away, getting into his car and driving away. Curley watched the car's backside disappear over the hill and drop out of sight.

CHAPTER SIXTY-FOUR

The rain pelted the tin roof, coming down in buckets and drenching the earth in a wet blanket. Every now and then, Curley heard the rumbling of distant thunder. He sat in the overstuffed chair he had bought for Minnie months before, watching the lightning streak across the sky and trying to count the raindrops as they crawled forlornly down the window pane. The shotgun was loaded and ready by his side. He kept his hand resting close to the barrel, ready to grab it and fire at a moment's notice.

"An Indian minute man," he thought casually, remembering a tidbit from his days in Mr. Abernathy's schoolhouse. "Ready at a minute's notice."

Except Curley wasn't exactly expecting British regulars to come marching through his front door. He was anticipating the arrival of Mr. Cramer's movers, coming to toss him out on his ass. He hadn't shown up for work in two weeks, the same amount of time that had passed since Minnie had left him. To his shock and chagrin, she had been true to her word, and when he arrived that afternoon from Gastonia her clothes were gone and so was she. Several days later he learned that she was living with Eunice and Lorenzo and the boys. She hadn't broken ties with him completely, then, so he had reason to be at least slightly hopeful.

That hope had faded away gradually but surely as he tried to see her. Minnie wouldn't even lay her eyes upon him, sending Eunice and Lorenzo out onto the porch instead to send him away. There had been several ugly and painful confrontations before Curley finally decided to turn tail and give up. He had made no effort to see his wife at all this week. He had stayed at home instead, smoking pack upon pack of cigarettes and drinking beer. Work was something for which he just didn't have the energy or the inclination. So he stayed at home and waited for the men from the mill to come and try to remove him from the house. He would shoot them, and then he would happily go off to jail. That would show them.

The rain beat out a sleepy rhythm, teasing his mood and his eyelids. It was perfect sleeping weather, but Curley could find no rest. He would stretch his body across the bed diagonally, in an effort to make it seem less empty. He tried to take up some of the vacated space with extra pillows, but nothing worked. When he closed his eyes he saw Lorenzo's tired and exasperated face. He saw Eunice, white headed now and frail-looking, standing on their front porch, denying him entry into the one place he had known contentment, denying him access to the one woman who had given him peace. He saw Minnie, her mouth now dripping obscenities and her eyes lined with anxiety, looking at him with disappointment and mistrustful hate. He wondered when the last time was that he had heard his name spoken with anything other than contempt.

Right next to the shotgun sat a tin barrel which Curley had brought in from the yard, filled with ice and then deposited with beer. He had started the evening with twelve cold ones, and now he had eight. He had only drained away four in the last five hours. At that rate, he knew he would not be able to get drunk before the light of day. But they didn't taste right tonight. Something about the smell, along with the taste, made him feel slightly sick. Curley thought he must be coming down with something.

He stood from the chair and stretched, yawning. Sleep was around the corner now, he could feel it. He padded down the hall in his stocking feet and dropped down onto the bed, without bothering to undress. He pulled the pillow under his head up below his chin and sighed. He rubbed his legs back and forth across the sheets. They weren't exactly clean, but they felt good and cool with the breeze coming in through the open window. A slight smile creaked along the edge of his mouth as he listened to the wind and rain outside. Nights like this were spiritual. You never knew when they were coming, or if you would get to see another one. Nothing was promised, after all, so that when they did come, it was best to revel in them, to enjoy every single sound and smell that tickled the senses. Nights like these were the Great Spirit's reward for those who remained behind.

Then the unwelcome sound wafted in. Curley shot up in bed and looked around the room, as if he was expecting something dark and dreadful to be standing at the foot of the bed. He sat perfectly still---if he didn't hear that noise again then he would ascribe it to his imagination and get a good night's sleep. There it was again! The owl was calling.

"In the middle of a storm like this?" Curley thought incredulously. "What is an owl doin' out on a night like this?"

But, of course, that was a silly question. The owl was doing what Lorenzo had told Curley the owl always did---it was warning him. He crawled out of the bed and reached for his lantern and matches. He struggled but finally managed to get it lit, and then he headed back down the hall and into the living room. He sat down next to the shotgun, hoping that would give him at least a measure of security. The owl seemed to be growing louder, almost as if it were flying in a direct route through the middle of the house. Curley looked around, making sure that the animal had not managed to get in somehow, through an open window or the screen.

"Dumb ass," he ridiculed himself. There was no owl inside the house, it just sounded that way because of the wind. But the call came again, and Curley began to move even closer to himself, drawing his knees up onto the chair and holding them closely with his left hand. His right hand continued to tightly grip the shotgun. He was furious with himself for acting like such a child--it was just a fucking owl, for Christ's sake, there was just no reason for this behavior. But the owl hooted again and Curley jumped, as if waiting for the next blow to land. He stood from the chair and began to pace the floor. Several times he reached for a beer, thinking that one would help to calm his nerves, but drew his hand away. A strange, new voice within was cautioning against drinking anything. He realized that he was afraid a drink of alcohol would bring down the full wrath of the owl.

"Screw this shit," he exclaimed. Curley decided that he was going to take back control of his life right then and there. It was an owl in the night: no more, no less. He stopped walking back and forth and reached into the icy water, drawing out a bottle of beer. He popped the top off with an opener he had in his shirt pocket. "I want a goddamn beer," he said to no one and everyone all at once, "and I am going to have one."

Suddenly a vicious slam of thunder tore through the house, rocking the walls and rattling the pictures Minnie had hung with loving care. Curley screamed in terror and the bottle went flying out of his hand and crashed to the floor. Luckily, it did not shatter, but it did tilt over, spewing beer onto the floor in a sticky puddle. Curley shouted a curse and picked up the bottle with an angry rebuke, as if the inanimate object in his hands was a wayward and disobedient child.

"Jesus," he said, trying to force a laugh, "what the fuck is wrong with me tonight?" He giggled nervously and began to raise the glass to his lips when another thunder clap, followed by the screech of the owl, bellowed through the walls, causing Curley again to jump and spill beer down his chin and across his shirt.

"Shit!" he yelled. Filled with anger, frustration and confusion, Curley hurtled the bottle across the room, where it slammed into the wall and exploded, sending beer and shards of glass spraying across the room. Curley felt the sharp sting pierce his cheek and a warm trickle of blood stream down his face, just below his left eye. He dropped down into the chair, a heap of cursing and moaning.

He regained his composure after a few moments and sat still, quietly trying to wait out the messenger in the trees. When several minutes has passed without either thunder claps or owl hoots, Curley arose and went into the kitchen, where he fetched a dish rag and a broom. Cleaning the mess actually helped to calm him, and as he sank to his knees to wipe up the beer he began singing softly to himself. He told himself that was exactly what he needed to clear the air and his mind. A little music to soothe his nerves and excite him in the old way. He would turn on the radio, listen to how the Allies were doing this week, and then wait for some good ol' music to come through the waves and envelope him and his bruised psyche. Yes, he would sit back, close his eyes, and imagine that he was the one getting on the radio, that it was his voice caressing the masses through the magical medium.

He put away the rag and crossed the room, switching on the radio. He cursed to find that the batteries were dead.

"What a fuckin' night," he thought bitterly. Upon further inspection in the kitchen, he was pleased to see that Minnie had remembered to pick more up before leaving him. He went back to the radio and, after making the adjustments he needed, tried the switch again. A disc jockey with a lonely and hoarse voice was announcing some coming events in the area----several gospel singings and a letter writing campaign for local boys at the front---before he dropped the needle on the next song. Curley crossed the room and plopped himself in the chair, waiting for the music to bring the peace he so craved. He recognized the melody and the sad, choppy rhythm immediately. He thought seriously about running the short distance between them and shutting off that radio. But his legs had gone weak and he wasn't sure

that he could stand.   As the vocals began, Curley heard the owl
beginning to taunt him again.

Out in the wilderness wild and drear
sadly I've wandered for many a year
driven by hunger and filled with fear
I will arise and go.
Backward with sorrow my steps to trace,
seeking my Heavenly Father's face"

Curley's eyes filled with hot tears. He looked down at the barrel full of
beer and then at the barrel of the shotgun. Choose your poison, he
thought. It's all the same, ain't it? Outside, the wind began to pick up
and howl ghostly, along with the owl and the stranger on the radio, all
of them cursing Curley, all of them recommending him for salvation.

"Why should I perish in dark despair
Here where there's no one to help or care
When there is shelter and food to spare?
I will arise and go.
Deeply repenting the wrong I've done
Worthy no more to be called a son
I will arise and go."

Curley began to shake. His hands reached out, as if his arms could
bridge the gap and make the radio stop playing. His voice weakly
called out.
"Please," he begged, "oh, God, please stop. Please, please.....please,
stop." But there was no one there to turn down the volume or switch
off the power. Curley was weeping now. He tried to stand. He knew
that, somehow, he had to stop that goddamned singing. He just had to.

Sweet are the mem'ries that come to me
faces of loved ones again I see
Visions of home where I used to be
I will arise and go.
Others have gone who had wandered, too
they were forgiven and clothed anew."

Curley dropped helplessly to the floor, crashing painfully to his knees. His hands reached out and caught his weight, saving him from plowing face first into the hard wood floor. The tears poured harder than the rain, and his cries provided tragic punctuation to the thunder echoing all around the house. The man on the radio had stopped singing now, but there was no comfort to be found. Instead of the voice, someone began an instrumental solo. As a musician, Curley should have seen it coming. It was pretty standard practice. The sound coming from the box---what was that? His tears slowed momentarily as he attempted to unravel the mystery. That sound? What was it? He recognized it, and yet he.......

A banjo-uke? No, couldn't be. Could it? He crawled to the edge of the table upon which the radio sat and listened as carefully as he had ever listened. The solo floated out, teasing. It was! That twangy, tinny little sound, so cheap and yet so charming, that was the sound of a "banjer-uke!" Curley smiled. Then the images swept over him, ordering him to see all that had passed.

O that I had never gone astray!

He saw Rodney, standing proudly and expectantly in the doorway of his bedroom, his smile giving away the surprise. And then he saw the banjo-uke sitting on the bed, sitting there like a million dollars and just waiting for him to pick it up.

Life was all radiant with hope one day

He saw his first-ever audience---Rodney and Eunice, perched on the old couch, waiting to hear what would come out of Curley's instrument. Their smiles and their applause, Rodney leaping off the couch at the end of the song, wrapping Curley up in his embrace and lifting him up off of the floor while declaring in his loudest voice that Curley was the greatest, *the greatest*, musician he had ever heard in his whole entire life.

Now all its treasures I've thrown away

Then he saw Ray, his tear stained face aglow in agony, standing in the corner with the banjo-uke raised above his head, his voice a scream of disgust and anger. Curley watched it in slow motion, the downward track, the sound of the wood splintering into a million pieces as the instrument met its tragic demise. Then Ray's look, a look that melted Curley, a look which should have brought wisdom.

Something is saying God loves you still

Curley saw Rodney's body, skinny and limp, being carried through the house. He watched as L.D. and Houston gathered in the hallway, crying and watching the white men carry their father past them to die. He remembered the feel of Eunice's trembling hand in his own. "I love you, Russell," she had said, as if it were an immutable and unbreakable law of the universe.

Tho' you have treated his love so ill
Yet I will arise and go.

"God," Curley screamed, "please stop this. Please just leave me alone!!!" But the voices were rising now. He heard Eunice crying at night, when she thought they were all asleep. He heard the tears in Mack's voice as he ended their partnership. He heard Ray calling him a drunk. He heard Minnie, all her beauty and patience thrown on the shelf of selfishness, telling him that now he could have all the girlfriends he wanted. He heard Lucy calling him silly and childish. He heard L.D. making excuses for him to his friends from school, all of whom wondered why the great man L.D. had bragged about so much was now working in the mill just like their brothers.

"AGGGGAGAGGHHHHHHHHH!!!!!" the shrill shriek echoed through the house as Curley found his strength, hopped to his feet and sent the radio slicing through the air, smacking with a loud thud against the wall and then blowing to bits as it hit the floor. He was sobbing, his head shaking back and forth in a negative motion, his jaws working hard with nothing audible coming out. He ran to the front door and then darted out, letting the rain pelt him. He jogged the short distance across the yard and ran up the steps onto his neighbor's porch. If Larry Wilkins was home, that would take care of everything.

He pounded his fists against the screen door, hitting it hard enough to shake the glass in the windows.

"Hey!" he called out desperately. "Hey! Anybody in there? Anybody home?" He slammed his open hand against the wood now in a continuous knock, all the while screaming and yelling at the top of his lungs. Finally, he saw the flicker of light moving towards the door.

"Well, Good God in His heaven what in the good world is going on here?" asked Irene as she opened the door and peered out to see the sad figure in front of her. Curley's hair was soaked and leaping around the crown of his head like unruly soldiers and blood still trickled down his cheek. His eyes were swollen and heavy from the crying he had done. "Russell Norris what are you doing here at this hour? It is after eleven o'clock for goodness sake!"

"Look, Irene, I ain't got time to explain, I just need you to...."

"God, Russell, don't you ever learn? You're drunk, ain't you?"

"No, Irene," he said, trying to piece together some patience, "I ain't drunk. I need a favor from ya."

"A favor?" she asked spitefully. "Russell, I can't be doin' you any favors. Minnie was a friend of mine and I don't think she'd...."

"Irene," he said, plowing through the idiotic play Irene was trying to perform, "I need to use your phone. Please, that is the only thing I ask. Just please let me use your telephone to call my wife. Irene, it's the most important thing I can tell you. Please?" Irene coughed.

"My husband ain't home, Russell," she said, "and you know how people talk. I can't let you come in this house and it bein' just me and you." Curley felt the anger rising. There wasn't enough alcohol in the world to make him want to bed this woman, but he knew he would never win that argument.

"Okay," he said, "I know how important your reputation is to you." He hoped buttering her up might work. "So, will you make a call *for* me? Please, Irene?" She looked at him closely, trying to get some gage of what was going on.

"Why, Russell," she asked, narrowing her eyes and putting on her most concerned look. "Is something wrong?"

"Just please call Minnie for me Irene. She's with my Mom, and I need to see her tonight. Please tell her that I must see her right away. It's very important."

"But, Russell, if something's......"

"Just make the goddamn call, Irene!" he screamed, collecting all his reserves of energy to keep from knocking her into the house. Startled, Irene slammed the screen closed and latched it. "I'm sorry," he said, "but this is so important. Please call Minnie. Please?" She slammed the door and he watched the light slink away. He dropped his head against the frame of the door and began to cry again.

The chair seemed to have shrunk, as if it were closing in on him. He tried to find a measure of comfort, but the more he adjusted himself the worse things became. He had decided that, as soon as the sun broke through and announced the arrival of the morning, he was going to walk to his Mom's house and fetch his wife. Between Lorenzo, Eunice and Minnie, there was bound to be someone there who would know how to comfort him, how to make his terror stop. The voices came and went now, and the visions, although spaced further apart, now came with an intensity which frightened Curley almost to the point of insanity. Molly Runningwolf had been there. She had promised him that she would keep the lightning at bay, and she had been telling the truth. As she chastised him for his lack of vision and his appalling failure to appreciate his heritage, there had been not the first sound of thunder. But when she left, her petite figure fading into the wall, the storm had once again reared it's awful head and bared it's nasty teeth. Curley trembled and paced, praying for the daylight. As the fury outside grew, he became convinced that he had seen the world for the last time.

Then he had "seen" his Uncle Chiltos, yellow and broken, stumbling through the house, alone and haunting. Curley could not help but notice the resemblance between them. It was the resemblance of addiction, it was not familial. Watching his uncle move on bended knee across the room, picking up shards of glass and licking them, desperately trying to get the last residue of beer from them, Curley saw his own future. He was heading towards a dark place, where the lonely and the whipped go to die. Curley cried for mercy and for the visions to stop, and finally, after an interminably long grin from Chiltos, it had disappeared. Curley dropped his head in his hands and wept more. It seemed that he would never run out of tears. He wondered if he was revisiting every tear he had ever caused the people who loved him. It seemed a possibility in the dead of this night.

The knock on the door sent Curley cowering behind the chair. It was the owl, he thought. It was coming to get him, to take him away. Curley cried out to the door, begging for the intruder to go away and leave him be. Through the wind he heard a response, a high voice that seemed determined to fool him---the owl was making itself sound like Minnie. He thought about his wife and his mother, his Grandpa and Ray. The owl had come to take him away, and he would never get the chance to tell them what they had all meant to him. More importantly, he would never get to show them what they meant to him by living up to their expectations of him.

"Go away!" he screamed. "I ain't goin' with ya! You hear me? Now leave me alone!" Suddenly, through the muddy darkness, he saw the doorknob turning. Curley felt his heart racing and thought that it might leap right out of his chest. He struggled for breath.

"Russell?"

He saw her face, beautiful and sweet, peering around the edge of the opened door.

"Minnie!" he exclaimed, jumping from behind the door and running to her. "Oh, Minnie, thank God you came! Thank God you came to me!" He grabbed her and tugged her into the house, hugging her with all his might. He saw Eunice and Lorenzo enter the house and he loosened his grip.

"Russell," Minnie said, her voice full of confusion and tinged with reproach, "Irene called us and said that you were drinking and tearin' the place apart. She said she's scared you was gonna kill somebody if'n we didn't come to you. What's goin' on Russell?" Eunice moved past Minnie and searched her son's eyes. Lorenzo stood close behind her, and Curley saw a twinkle of light in his grandfather's eyes. He recognized something in Curley's look, something which gave the man hope for the boy.

"Curley," he said quietly, "we've come son. We're all here. What is it? What is going on?" They waited for an answer. Curley glanced at them all and then, as he tried to speak, broke down into another flood of tears.

"I'm so sorry," he wept, "I am so sorry for everything. I didn't mean it, Mom. I swear I didn't Minnie, Grandpa. I never wanted to hurt none of ya'll. I thought I could do it all, I thought.....oh, God, I am just so sorry." He dropped to his knees. Minnie fell down beside of him and out her arms around him. Lorenzo and Eunice were quickly in the floor, making a loving circle around Curley.

"Russell," Minnie said softly, "Russell talk to me. What's happened?"

"Make it stop, Minnie," he begged, "make the pain go away."

"What hurts, honey?"

"Everything," he cried, "I ain't never hurt like this, Mom," he said, turning to Eunice, "not even when Dad died. Something's happenin' to me and I don't know what it is. Please, please, please........somebody help me. Please." His body was wracked with sobs. Minnie looked at

Eunice, her face seeking guidance, but Eunice was as lost as her daughter-in-law.

"Call him," Curley said. "Please call him."

"Who?" asked Lorenzo.

"Russell," asked Minnie, "who do you want me to call."

"The preacher," he sobbed. "Call the preacher, Minnie and please tell him I gotta see him right now, tonight. Not in the mornin', not tomorrow afternoon or evenin'."

"Russell," Eunice said, "it's almost two o'clock in the morning. The preacher...."

"Minnie, please," he begged, his tear soaked eyes pleading with hers. Minnie turned to Eunice.

"Stay here with him," she ordered. Then she turned to Lorenzo. "Come with me next door, please."

They stood and trooped quickly out the door and back into the storm. Eunice pulled her son close to her breast, pressing his ear against her pounding heart.

"I'm so sorry, Mom," he cried, "I am just so sorry about it all."

"Ssssshhhhhhh," she soothed, "hush now. It's gonna be all right."

"I.......I, I.......love....you, Mom."

"I love you, too, Russell. With all of my heart."

"I let you down. I let you all down so bad."

"Don't be foolish," she admonished. "You have not let me down. You're a good son, you're just tired is all. Too much was put on you too soon, son, and I understand that better than you might think."

"I couldn't even support you," said Curley, his tears beginning again, "I couldn't even do that for Dad."

"Russell, do you know that one of the last conversations I had with your Dad in this world was about me getting a job and going to work? Son, I never expected you to keep up that entire family when even your daddy couldn't do that. Never. Besides, I went to work at the Cramer Mill because I have a hefty dose of the same disease you've got----- pride. We could've got by on the money you and Ray sent to us just fine, but I figured if I went to work those boys could have even more things, and those things could be even finer. I guess that is a problem that you and I can both blame on your Grandfather Swayney."

"I'm still sorry, Mom," he said, "I've put you through so much."

"Yes, son," she agreed, "you have. But you could never put me through so much that I wouldn't keep loving you. There's nothing that you could ever do that would make that happen. And I do love you,

Russell Norris."

"I love you, Mom."

Curley buried his head in her arms and tried to stop crying. Silently, they waited for the preacher.

&

Michael arrived before sunrise, at about four thirty in the morning. Minnie's terrified voice on the other end of his phone line had awakened him and caused him to dress faster than he would have thought humanly possible. Something was wrong with her husband, she had said, and he was asking for Michael. He had driven in the wind and rain and found the house still lit, with Eunice and Lorenzo in the living room drinking coffee. They pointed him towards the back room, the bedroom, where Minnie sat with Curley, trying to keep him calm and soothe his tattered nerves. Michael had asked for a cup of coffee, which he downed in a hurried gulp. Then he flashed an awkward and embarrassed smile at Eunice and Lorenzo and walked back into the bedroom.

"Minnie?" he asked as he walked in. "Russell?" There was no light in the room except for the occasional flash of far-off lightning. The storm was finally beginning to pass. He caught the movement out of the corner of his eye.

"Michael!" Minnie called. He saw a match flash to life and then the lantern sprang up, illuminating the room. He saw Russell, who was sitting on the bed with his legs crossed underneath him and his head in his hands. He looked quizzically at Minnie, but her glance told him that she wasn't going to able to fill him in any better than he already was.

"Russell?" he asked. Curley slowly raised his head and attempted a smile. Michael was unable to beat back the gasp which escaped him. Curley's entire appearance was haggard and pasty. He looked like he had been through hell and back.

"Hey, preacher," Curley managed, "thank you for coming."

"Russell, I....."

"Will you call me Curley," he asked in a tired voice. "That's my Indian name. You'll leave me that, won't you?"

"Russ....uh, Curley, I didn't come here to take anything from you." Michael sat down on the bed. "I came here because Minnie called me and said that you wanted me, that you were asking for me. What is it

Curley? Why did you call for me?"

"Preacher," Curley said, "I need what you're selling." Curley smiled, the first genuine smile he had felt all night. "Preacher, I want you to make this ache of mine go away. Please."

"I can't do that, Curley," Michael said, "only you can."

"But you can help?"

"I can try," Michael responded, still a little lost. "I'll try as hard as I can."

"Good. That's what I reckon I need to hear. I don't wanna stop bein' Cherokee, reverend," he said through fresh tears, "but your God has whipped me good tonight."

"You don't have to choose, Curley," came the voice from the hallway. Curley looked up quickly and saw Lorenzo standing in the door. "You'll never have to choose. Not really. And any man who says that you do is a damned liar." Curley turned and looked at Michael.

"That true, reverend?" Michael smiled.

"Well," he stated, "I might not have put it that way exactly, but yeah. That's right, Curley. I can assure you that my God, our God, is not trying to make you stop being Cherokee."

"It was God," Lorenzo added, "who made you Cherokee. It was man who made you ashamed." Michael smiled. He wondered if Lorenzo had ever considered the ministry. He thumbed through his Bible until he arrived at the passage he wanted.

"*There is neither Jew nor Greek,*" he read, "*there is neither bond nor free, there is neither male nor female: for ye are all one in Christ Jesus.*" He looked at Curley. "One in Christ Jesus," he repeated. Curley chuckled.

"I thought it was a sin to be Indian," he said. "I thought your God hated us."

"Why would you think that?" asked Michael.

"Look at me, preacher. I been askin' God to let off all night, and he ain't been listenin'. I ain't sure he still hears me. I ain't sure he heard me at all, preacher." Michael's fingers deftly worked the edges of the pages again until he found the desired passage.

"*My God, my God, why hast thou forsaken me? Why art thou so far from helping me, and from the words of my roaring? O my God, I cry in the daytime, but thou hearest me not.*" He looked at Curley. "You ever heard of King David?" he asked. Curley nodded. "Well, he wrote that. Curley, you're not the only person to feel this way."

Curley stood up from the bed and began to pace. The little room was getting hot and the walls were starting to quiver. Curley stopped as if about to say something, and then he would begin to pace again. Michael watched and waited, his fingers poised to find the next answer, his mind silently sending out pleading prayers for guidance. He had been praying for this moment for months, but now that it was here he felt powerless and unprepared. Curley's apparent agony tormented him as well, but he knew there was no easy way to end it. Suddenly Curley whirled and looked at him.

"Blessed be the poor, for their's is the kingdom of heaven. Right?"

"That's right," Michael answered. Lorenzo and Minnie nodded silently.

"Bullshit," Curley spat.

"Russell!" Minnie cried.

"That's the white man's crap," Curley continued. Michael sat and listened patiently. "You want us to follow your religion and then wait for the good stuff to come to us when we die. Well, I want mine right now, reverend." Michael took a deep breath.

"Curley," he said, "do you think of yourself as a Christian these days?"

"Uh, no," Curley said triumphantly and rebelliously.

"And look at yourself," Michael shot. "You're not following my God or my religion and I still don't think that you can say you're exactly happy. In fact, you seem miserable to me." Minnie and Lorenzo waited to see whether Curley would explode, or whether this night, which had seen Curley drop to the bottom of his soul, had actually meant something. Curley crossed the tiny space and stood over Michael, peering down on him like an angry master.

"Blessed are they that mourn," he whispered, his bottom lip quivering violently, *"for they shall be comforted."* A single tear glistened in each eye. "Well, preacher, where's my comfort? Please, tell me, where.....is.....my.......comfort?"

Michael raised himself up, becoming as tall as he could while still sitting. He gently closed his Bible. This one, this moment of such import, was going to have to come from the heart. Lorenzo held his breath.

"Peace I leave with you," Michael said, *"my peace I give unto you: not as the world giveth, give I unto you. Let not your heart be troubled, neither let it be afraid."* Michael stood. Curley was weeping silently.

"I want that," he cried quietly, "please. I want that. How?"

"For by grace are ye saved through faith; and that not of yourselves; it is the gift of God. Faith, Curley. That same faith that you have always had in yourself, put that in God. As for forgiveness of your sins, ask Christ into your heart, and that's it."

"And quit drinkin'," Minnie added quickly. Curley laughed and nodded. Lorenzo entered the room and put his hand on Curley's shoulder.

"This is about faith, Curley," Lorenzo said. "It is about being a warrior. Jesus was a warrior, like Tsali or Crazy Horse. Do not go into this if you do not mean it. This family doesn't need another disappointment. You know that."

Curley motioned for Minnie, who crossed to him. He pulled her close to him in a warm and loving embrace. She was crying now, too, but there was a bright smile on her face.

"I want this," he said to everyone in the room. He looked at Michael. "Preacher," he said, "I believe. I believe with all my heart and all my soul and I want to quit hurting these people. I want them to all be proud of me again. Hell, uh, heck, I wanna be proud of me again. I wanna be a warrior for something that matters, something that counts--like family. What does that mean, preacher?" Michael's broad smile spoke volumes.

"It means, Russell, that you are saved."

"And," came the reply, "it means that I have my son back." Curley saw Eunice standing in the door, wiping her eyes. He went to her and they nearly fell into each other's arms, laughing and crying simultaneously. They each felt Lorenzo's arms stretch around them. Minnie went to Michael and hugged him tightly.

"Thank you," she said, "for getting me my husband."

"Oh, no," Michael clarified, "that wasn't me." He saw Lorenzo looking at him and their eyes met. "That was God, that was the Great Spirit." Lorenzo smiled.

They left the bedroom and filed into the kitchen. Minnie began scrambling eggs and Eunice started a batch of frybread. Lorenzo, Michael and Curley disposed of the tin full of beer. Bottle by bottle, they emptied the contents into the muddy ground.

The night's clouds had given way to the streaming light of the coming sun. Lorenzo put his arm around Curley, and together they watched the sun rise fully into the sky.

It was a new day, and it was dawning bright and beautiful. Michael stretched and yawned and turned to his new friends.

"*He giveth power to the faint,*" he quoted happily, "*and to them that have no might he increaseth strength. Even the youths shall faint and be weary, and the young men shall utterly fall.*" He stared into Curley's eyes, sparkling with new birth and a fresh start. "*But they that wait upon the Lord shall renew their strength; they shall mount up with wings as eagles; they shall run, and not be weary; and they shall walk and not faint.*"

Curley answered Michael's grin with his own.

"Amen," he said as they turned to walk inside, "amen."

CHAPTER SIXTY-FIVE

The train rattled down the track, jerking to and fro and keeping everyone on board wide awake. Curley sat aside the newspaper he had been reading and glanced out the window. America was jetting past him now, faster than he had ever dreamed possible. He remembered what his father had once told him about the train, the car and progress in general.

"Curley," Rodney had said, "always think that the faster we can speed scenery by us, well, life goes by the same. They're connected. I don't think the white man understands that yet."

No, Dad, Curley thought, most people don't understand that yet. The car gets you places faster than your feet, and the train gets you there even faster. But what happened to all that "saved" time? You obviously couldn't store it, and it seemed that people had less and less time these days. He sighed as the trees whizzed by. Now and then, he would see someone standing by the tracks, waving a flag or holding a sign bearing well-wishes.

"Good Luck Boys!" one read.

"We're counting on You!" called another. Curley smiled and waved as he saw each one. He doubted they could see him, but the gesture made him feel better, made him feel somehow a part of them and their lives. He wanted to thank them, and if tossing his hand in the air was the only way available then that was what he would do. He reached into his shirt pocket to draw out a cigarette and felt the bulge of papers. He pulled out the package and examined it with a grin.

"To my Husband," read the top piece of paper. There were fourteen sheets there, bundled together and wrapped in a red, white and blue hair ribbon. Minnie had composed a letter for each day of the next two weeks. By then, she hoped, he would be receiving fresh letters from her. She had made him promise that he would not read them until he

reached Chicago. She did not want him reading them all at one time on the train, somewhere in West Virginia, and then not having any thoughts of her or from her for a week or more. He had promised, but the temptation was great to read what she had said. He didn't think that he could wait until Chicago. But he would try. He had promised, and Curley was once again a man who kept his promises.

He placed the letters back in his pocket and took out his pack of cigarettes, lighting one and inhaling deeply. He wondered if he would have to go without smokes in the coming days. He doubted that, given where he was going, his smoking habit would be given much consideration.

"Can I have one of them?" asked the man beside of him. Curley nodded and handed over the pack. "You nervous?" he asked. Curley couldn't help but notice how young and innocent the guy looked.

Bet he won't look so innocent when he gets back, he thought. None of them would look innocent anymore. None of them would *be* innocent anymore. Curley smiled ruefully. That wasn't much of a consideration for him---he had left his innocence behind years ago. He had fought himself and won---the Nazis would be a piece of cake.

"No," Curley answered, "I'm not." The young GI looked at him incredulously.

"I am," he whispered. "I'm 'bout scared to death." A young man sitting in the seat in front of them turned around and sat up on his knees. His ruddy cheeks and slight freckles made him look no more than twelve, and Curley suddenly found himself feeling like the old man of the group.

"You say you're scared?" he asked. Curley's seat-mate nodded. "Man, I thought it was just me," he continued, "'cause I'm a little nervous, too."

Curley closed his eyes and eased his head back against the seat as the two men, boys really, commiserated over their worries. He let the thump and grind of the train carry him away from their voices and back to the platform. They had all come out to see him off. Lorenzo had driven them all out to Kings Mountain, where the train for Chicago left. Eunice had filled a paper sack full of frybread and fresh tomatoes. Lorenzo had given him a small pouch, filled with herbs, which he instructed Curley to wear around his neck at all times.

Ray had arrived in the middle of the goodbyes. Eunice had telegraphed him to let him know that his brother was going off to war, but none of them had known whether or not he had actually received the message until they saw his gangly form crossing the platform. He and Curley had met in a powerful embrace, tears edging near the surface of their eyes. Both men, young and proud, fought back the urge, however, and covered themselves in jokes and laughter.

"I'm leaving, too," he told Curley, "I joined myself. Army."

"You?" Curley asked. "Why? What about Mack?"

Ray explained that, with so many gone already and more going everyday, there was nothing else he could do. This was a war to fight evil, and he wanted to be a part of it. He asked what had changed Curley's mind about fighting, why was he going?

"Beats the hell out of mill work," Curley cracked with a wicked wink. But Ray knew better; they all knew better. Curley had found his pride again, and his pride would not let him stand pat while the world burned. That was not the Indian way. That was not the *Norris* way. "I don't know," he said finally, his voice growing serious, "I guess 'cause it's the right thing to do." Ray nodded.

The cry of the train whistle, shrill and mournful, alerted the families gathered around that it was time to say goodbye. The faces were a mix of pride and pain. Every mother and father, every wife and child---all of them knew the terrible, unspoken truth. Someone standing in the North Carolina sun that morning wasn't coming home again. None of them could, in good conscience, hope or pray that it happened to the family beside of them or across from them, but down deep that was *exactly* what they all wanted. Just not *my* Dad. Just not *my* son. Just not *my* husband. Curley turned to Minnie.

"I gotta be goin', honey pot." She forced a smile. Curley recognized the look. It was the one she had always worn when he had thrown his guitar into Mack's trunk and headed for the road. But this was different. This time he couldn't promise her that he was ever coming back. She walked up and kissed him lightly on the cheek.

"We'll take good care of her for you," Lorenzo said.

"Put her to work learning to make frybread," Eunice joked. Her eyes dark with worry, she managed to restrain her tears. "You be careful, son."

"I will, Mom," he said, hugging her tightly.

"I love you, Russell," she whispered. The train whistle split the sky again. Men were scrambling aboard now, weeping women dragging themselves home, men with red rimmed eyes staggering off, acting tough.

"Better go if I'm gonna get a window seat," Curley joked. He thrust out his hand and shook Lorenzo's.

"I am proud," said his Grandpa. "I am proud." Curley simply nodded. He thrust out his hand again, this time towards Ray. Ray took it, but then yanked Curley into his arms with a hug and a chuckle.

"Be careful, you," he said, "and I'll see ya in Berlin?" Curley laughed.

"It's a date."

Lorenzo gathered his brood and walked them away a short distance, giving Curley and Minnie some privacy. She wasn't looking at him, her eyes were cast downward, as if not looking might make his leaving stop hurting. Or maybe she could just deny it enough and make it not be so. She was willing to try anything.

"Honey pot," he said softly, "I've gotta go. Train's gonna leave me."

"That would be okay," she said. He laughed. "I feel like I just got you back," she said, her voice beginning to shake slightly. "I almost lost you before, Russell. I don't want to lose you now, not after all we been through." He pulled her to him.

"You ain't gonna lose me, Minnie," he said. "Nobody knows better than you how stubborn I can be. And I done said I'm comin' back, so I am. I'm comin' back for you and for her." He motioned his head towards the brightly smiling child in Minnie's arms. Catherine had been born six months earlier, and she was oblivious to the fact that daddy was going to war. Curley ran a hand through the shock of black, wavy hair. "My little girl," he cooed. "My daughter." Catherine smiled at her father and gurgled something. Curley laughed, but Minnie was crying.

"I love you, Russell Norris," she said, "and if you go and get hurt I'll kill ya!" She turned her head up and their eyes met. The youth had returned to hers, and they sparkled with strength and resolve. "So come on home, okay?"

"I love you, too, honey pot," he said, holding his wife and daughter close to his heart. "I'll be fine, I swear. You have my word." And then he had kissed her. A long, deeply passionate kiss. Just thinking about that kiss.......

"Huh?" he said, startled from his nap.

"I said is that a guitar you got down there under the seat?" Curley blinked the sleep out of his eyes.

"Uh, yeah. Yeah, it is."

"Well, how 'bout playin' somethin' for us?" Several of the boys agreed.

"Yeah," one said, "anything so's we can quit talkin' 'bout where
we're headed. C'mon, play something good." Curley thought a minute,
and then decided it was a good idea. He had awakened to find that he
was miserably depressed. Dreaming about the kiss had been a bad
idea. He still wasn't scared, but he felt the teeth of homesickness
gnawing at the edges of his soul. He pulled the guitar from his case
and tuned it slightly.

"All right," he said, "whaddaya want to hear?" The men thought for
a minute.

"I know!" exclaimed Curley's seatmate. "My girlfriend's favorite
song is *The Kentucky Waltz*. How's about you play that one?"

Curley smiled and strummed the strings once, making sure that his
tuning had held.

"All right sailors," he said with a smile, "this one's for the ladies!"

And with the strains of the Kentucky Waltz drifting through the
cars, the train chugged along, darting across fields and through towns,
riding headlong into history.

Afterword

It was an unusually warm autumn day in North Carolina as my grandfather, Russell Norris and I pulled into the cemetery. The leaves had begun their change, and their colors were sprinkled across the sky. My grandfather pointed the way to our destination, until he could finally tell me to stop.

"Here it is," he said. He struggled out of the passenger side of my Ford escort and was heading up the hill when I came to his side. We walked in silence until stopping near the fence. The certainty of his steps betrayed the numerous afternoons and evenings grandpa had spent here. He placed one hand in his trousers and pointed down at his feet with the other.

"Here's Mom," he said.

I stared at the granite. Eunice Marie Swaney Norris had been laid to rest in this spot after succumbing to cancer in 1954. She died surrounded by her sons, her grandchildren, and her father and mother. Across from her resting place were two more markers—the final resting place of Lorenzo and Cora, who had followed her several years later.

"There's granddad and grandma," my grandfather stated. He pointed to an empty corner. "And that's where I'll be," he said simply.

He tried to kneel, and I took his elbow and helped him down to one knee. Quietly, he took a hand and gently stroked Eunice's stone.

"She was such a good woman," he whispered, "a very good woman."

I helped him to his feet, and we walked back to the car. We took a left at the cemetery entrance and drove several miles to Cramerton. We passed the old mill village and the house in which

Grandpa had grown up. We drove through the underpass and then made another left. Then he told me to stop. I pulled the car over to the side of the road and we got out.

This scene was different. At this makeshift cemetery there were no flowers, no fences. There were crumpled old beer cans and weeds. I followed grandpa to the only large marker in the field at the side of the road. Beneath this marble monument there was a small, fading granite slab that simply read: "RRN." This was where they had carried Rodney.

"It's a shame people don't respect this place," grandpa said as he looked at the cans. "Me and my brothers came back here and put this new marker up," he told me. "That was one of the last things Mom asked of us. We offered to move him so they could be together, but she didn't want him bothered."

If there is indeed an afterlife, then Rodney and Eunice have been reunited. But in this world, they remain apart—the mill worker still in the welfare graveyard, seemingly alone.

"You tell people about them," he told me. "*You tell them how hard they tried.*" Then he turned and headed back to the car, leaving me to ponder my legacy and my heritage.

ʬ

Russell Norris served in the Pacific theater in World War Two, aboard the USS McKinley. At the end of the war he came home to his wife. Together they raised seven children—Catherine, Wayne, Eunice (who died in infancy), Patricia (my mother), Joyce, Linda and Sandra. My grandpa and grandma have now been married nearly sixty years.

In August 2003 my grandpa was inducted into the Traditional Country Hall of Fame in the "Sidemen" category. Anyone who wants to hear him share his gift can still easily do so. Every Sunday morning he rises early, shakes of the aches and pains of his eighty five years, packs his Gibson and a bag of harmonicas, and drives across town to New Life Baptist Church where he sings and plays to and for his Creator. "New Life" is the perfect name for my grandpa's church. He has lived many lives in the time he has been given—seeker, sinner, and to a man for whom he means so much, saint.

His life has been written across the heart of his family and friends, and his influence continues to grow and spread. There are those who may ask the validity of writing a novel based on the life of a man who has never known political power or material wealth, and with those people I humbly disagree. My grandfather's life can serve to remind us all that while the story of a people and a nation may be embodied by her leaders, it is written by her people.

ABOUT THE AUTHOR

James A.Bryant, Jr. is an Assistant Professor for Secondary Education at the University of New Orleans. He lives in Slidell, Louisiana with his wife Ginger and their children Cheyenne, Autumn and James.

For more information on the author or *Curley*, please visit www.allenbryant.com.